the ENGINEER
reconditioned

OTHER BOOKS BY NEAL ASHER

Gridlinked
The Line of Polity
The Skinner
Cowl
Brass Man

NEAL ASHER

COSMOS BOOKS

THE ENGINEER RECONDITIONED

Cosmos Books
www.cosmos-books.com

Trade HB ISBN: 0-8095-5676-6

Trade PB ISBN: 0-8095-5614-6

Printed in Canada

TABLE OF CONTENTS

INTRODUCTION

_____

I am a classic overnight success i.e. that particular night was over twenty years long. It has been a struggle up the ladder, missing not a single rung, quite often stepping back down some, and every now and again having someone stand on my fingers. I spent many years in the wilderness of non-publication wondering if I'd made the right choice of vocation while I wrote the inevitable fantasy trilogy (still unpublished), then I was published in the small presses over many years, and finally . . . Macmillan.

Too often, we read of someone getting the x-thousands advance on a first book and hearing this lose sight of the fact that it doesn't normally happen that way. There is, unfortunately, a lot of truth in the image of the writer struggling away in his garret then drinking himself to death. Writing is hard, getting work published is hard, and if you want easy money, your best option is to become an estate agent.

It took me five or more years to get my first short story accepted and then that magazine folded before publication. After that slight boost (and it was a boost; someone had actually wanted my work) I managed to get more and more stories published, the occasional novella serialised, and a one-off novella published for a single cash payment. For my short stories my reward was a copy of the magazine and some complimentary letters (mostly). After another five years I was getting the occasional cheque—about enough to pay for a toner cartridge a year—then in the following five years finally gained some notoriety through the publisher, Tanjen. But then they, like so many small press publishers, went to the wall.

Unfortunately, small publishers are really up against it trying to succeed in a world dominated by huge publishing consortiums. Anthony Barker did not have sufficient spare cash to wine and dine the book buyers for the main book chains, could not afford large print runs, or divide distribution costs over many titles. Was it a shame for me, though?

Tanjen had already published my novella *The Parasite* (illustrated by Ralph Horsley), *The Engineer* was getting good reviews and apparently a thousand copies had been taken in America, and Anthony was talking about publishing a book of mine called *Gridlinked*. Ah twenty-twenty hindsight. If Tanjen had not gone to the wall when it did, I would not have sent synopsis and sample chapters of *Gridlinked* to Peter Lavery of Pan Macmillan at precisely the right time. But then again, had Tanjen not published my other books, I would not have had a full-colour *SFX* review of *The Engineer* to send along as well. Ifs buts and maybes. Maybe, in infinite parallel universes, I get run over by a bus while taking my third typescript for Tanjen to the Post Office.

Anyway, I feel *The Engineer* is a collection I have a lot to be thankful for, and one I'll always love because in size and appearance it seemed my first real book. It was a shame that people could no longer obtain it (though I heard of a guy in America gladly paying about $20 for a second-hand version). So here it is, with extra waffle from me and additional stories to tempt the completists.

the engineer

Novellas being notoriously difficult to publish, unless in collections like this, *The Engineer* has been seen nowhere but in the Tanjen edition. In this story you can find some of the roots of the runcible universe portrayed in my Macmillan books. Here you get to see one of the Jain, who made a technology that destroyed them, and other races after them . . . maybe. It was utterly natural for humans, on the archaeological evidence, to attribute the technology to the species that used it, rather than see a species used by a technology. They got it wrong, didn't they? I know some readers would like to fit this story into a chronology. Did these events occur before or after Skellor started throwing his weight around? Someone said to me that because the *Cable Hogue* is referred to in the *Gridlinked* sequence, the events here must have been just after, because had they been before, more mention would have been made of them. Well, not really. Immortal AI starships can exist for a very long time, and covering significant screw-ups is not an unusual governmental technique. Will I answer the question? Some day, in another book or short story, but not here. You see, my future history has not sprung full-grown from my forehead, but is still fermenting behind it.

PART ONE

Here dust motes are worthy of note and micro-crystals intensively studied. A fist-sized rock discovered by the deep spacer *Plumb Line* is the subject of lengthy scientific dissertations and now a marker buoy accompanies it on its quarter-completed billion-year journey. The Chasm, deep-space side of that tongue of stars called the Quarrison Drift, is empty as much of space is not . . .

"It's an egg, and as soon as we get it aboard it'll hatch out and some disgusting alien will eat us all. You mark my words."

Abaron ignored Chapra. She was an aficionado of ancient celluloid and often came out with such ridiculous statements. He continued to observe the read-outs from various scanners and frown in perplexity. Was it something others had missed, or had some joker recently dropped it here?

The sphere was three metres in diameter, completed one revolution every couple of seconds, and sped across the Chasm at approximately one-and-a-half kilometres per second. At that speed it would have taken it five million years to get here from the nearest star system in the Drift—discounting the possibility of someone having dropped it from a spaceship yesterday.

"You wait, they'll tell us to twin it with a marker buoy and study it from a distance," said Chapra, gazing at her screen. Abaron snuck a quick glance at her. She wore the appearance of a teenager: long black hair and perfect dark complexion, decorative caste mark at the centre of her forehead, and slim figure in a form-fitting bodysuit. Her cat's eyes and pointy ears were a fashionable look called partial catadapt. The new look. He shook his head, annoyed. What made her do it? She was a hundred years older than he was, and was one of the most reputable xenologists in the sector.

Chapra swung towards him. "What do you think?"

Abaron scratched at his greying beard—not for him the look of youth—then said, "I think, that in the circumstances we have detailed, they'll let us pick it up."

"Ah, the optimism of youth."

She could have been reading his mind.

"It's probably something new to the Chasm and by picking it up we won't be disturbing any . . . long-term studies."

"Stepping on any toes you mean. Ahah, here comes Judd."

Abaron glanced round. Judd was short, black-haired and Asiatic, almost Chinese in appearance had he been human, but he was Golem.

Without preamble the android told them, "You have permission to bring the sphere in."

The ship, *Schrödinger's Box*, resembled a box only in that it had an inside and an outside. Its shape was that of a grain of barley with the hair still attached and it was a kilometre long. Many scientific minds noted its resemblance to a spermatozoon, and were quick to point out the symbolic significance of this design of ship being at the forefront of human exploration and research. The AI mind that did the designing remained sensibly silent about the whole matter. Some said its reticence was due to an instruction from higher AI minds. Perhaps they were embarrassed.

Closer to and you could see that sensors and the ports for launching probes studded the ship's hull. It was a pure science vessel, on which Polity scientists had to book a place years in advance—coming to the ship, on their turn, by the onboard Skaidon gate, or runcible. The ship was run by AI and crewed by free Golem androids, most of which remained in stasis until needed. The sphere, in comparison to this ship, was a hardly noticeable speck. A drone, which in appearance was no more than a three-fingered metal claw with rocket motors attached, flew out to grab the item and bring it into an isolation chamber. In there, padded clamps clasped it, and the ship's AI discretely sampled molecules from its surface, and passively scanned its interior.

"Ninety-eight percent frozen water inside. The rest is carbon compounds and trace elements." Abaron refused to acknowledge Chapra's grin. Touch consoles, screens and holographic displays surrounded them in the central processing room. The specialised AI-linked computers that collated information, from the isolation chamber and from the ship's skin of sensors, worked silently, but there seemed a hum of power in the air.

"Should I be smug, do you think, and point out the obvious?" asked Chapra, spinning round on her swivel chair.

Abaron finally looked at her and snapped, "I wouldn't call what you said a serious scientific prediction."

Chapra pouted at him, which made him even angrier. He thumped his fingers over his touch console, calling up displays of information. He did not turn when Chapra rolled her chair up beside him.

"A hundred years time you might get just as bored," she said. Abaron paused and turned to glare at her, but she was gazing back at the holographic display above her console. "Ah, here," she said, and rolled her chair back across. He quickly followed.

Above the console now hovered a holographic representation of the sphere. Beside it information in the form of graphs, bio' equations, and Standard English scrolled up too fast for Abaron to read. Chapra picked up an interlink transmitter from her side table—the device looked like a polished ball bearing—swept back her hair to expose an interface plug behind her ear, and plugged in.

"Outer shell is a polycarbon fabric, superconductive up to seven hundred degrees Celsius." As she said this, the outer layer melted away to reveal a honeycomb structure. "The inner layer is again of polycarbon, but with interleaved calcite and calcium formations. It would appear to be structural only." She looked at Abaron. "The shell." She grinned.

Abaron ignored her. He watched as the inner shell fled, and tried to tell himself his fearful fascination was scientific curiosity.

"Water," said Chapra. "Loaded with organic impurities the most common of which is this." Using her console she projected a red circle on the sphere's surface, then expanded it to infinity, zooming in on that point to reveal a complex helical structure. It was crystalline at first, but grew to reveal individual atoms. The display spread; the structure filling the entire room and fading beyond it.

"DNA," said Abaron.

"Not quite," Chapra told him. "It's trihelical and has some very complicated protein structures wound in there as well."

Abaron was now too fascinated to be annoyed. He called up information from his console, limiting it to his screen. *This just does not happen to me*, he thought. Major events always occurred light years from where he happened to be at any one time. Great discoveries were always on the other side of the Polity, Separatist outrages a hundred worlds away.

"Damn close," he eventually said. "Bloody damned close."

"To what?" Chapra enquired kindly.

"To the theoretical models." Abaron looked at her sharply, but she had turned away. He watched her banish the large hologram and return the display to the revealed sphere of ice. She sat back, relinquishing control to the AI again.

"There's an anomaly with the water here," she said. "The nominal temperature of the sphere is fifty Kelvin, which is low enough for the water ices to have become complex ices, yet they have not changed. I would say that certain free proteins in the ice have stabilized it. We need to have a long hard look at that . . . Let's cut to the chase now shall we?"

The AI responded by excising the water ices to show the shape at the heart of the sphere. It was a creature: coiled like an embryo, reptilian. There was a tail there, finned, something like a head, strange triangular-section tentacles folded against a long ribbed body, and an arm easily recognisable as such, but ending in a hand with tens of long twiglike fingers. Chapra drew in a sharp breath. Abaron swore.

"It's an egg," he said, a species of dull dread in his voice.

"I think not," said Chapra in an abrupt reversal.

Something close to the creature, held under its long fingers, the AI picked out in bright red then projected to one side and expanded. It was a structure of folded tubes and unidentifiable components. They watched in silence as the AI took it apart, expanding sections, then further dismantling them. Equations blurred past at the bottom of the projection.

"Well?" Abaron eventually asked.

"I expected this to be an artefact, something manufactured. That would go some way to disprove the egg theory." Chapra regarded him. "But, as we are both well aware, when technology reaches a certain level its artefacts are often indistinguishable from life."

"Then it could still be an egg?" he asked, sensing a victory, if a somewhat Pyrrhic one.

"Oh no, the creature is adult. This is probably an escape pod of some kind."

"The creature—" began Abaron, hardly daring to ask.

Chapra finished for him. "—is in stasis."

Abaron licked his lips. He'd come out here to study the few micro-organic motes the *Box* trawled up. This was his ultimate wet dream: the discovery of an alien life form, possibly sentient, and wholly weird. He didn't know whether to be ecstatic or terrified.

"Do you think we'll be allowed to revive it?" he asked.

"We'll probably be instructed to do so. This is not a question of xenology but one of morality. We have rescued this creature and now we are responsible for its well-being."

"There's a lot of work to do."

"There is. We'll have to reproduce its optimum environment and sources of nourishment, and those are only the first steps. Reviving it without killing is not going to be easy. Then there's communication . . . "

"Can we be certain it's sentient?"

"At the moment nothing is certain. But what would an animal be doing in an escape pod?"

"It might just be a disgusting killer," said Abaron, making an awkward attempt at humour.

"Quite," said Chapra. She did not laugh. She waved her hand, and the AI consigned the holographic model back to its memory.

The isolation chamber was fifty metres across, circular, the ceiling and floor flat grey ceramal. There was frost on every surface. Padded clamps, like cupped hands, held the sphere at the precise centre of chamber: two metres from the floor and two metres from the ceiling. Chapra and Abaron, clad in carbon sixty coldsuits, paced around it in the usual point seven-five gees of the ship. To one side squatted a Physical Study and Research robot, telefactored from the ship's AI. The PSR was a nightmare of chrome, glass, and dull ceramal. There was something insectile about it. It bore the appearance of a giant chrome cockroach stood upright. But a cockroach never had so many arms and legs. Abaron felt nervous around the thing, even though he had been using such devices all his adult life. It was just the knowledge that in a few seconds it could strip him down to his component organs, muscles, and bones. And if that was not horror enough, it could put him back together again to complete his screaming. He shuddered.

"The cold isn't getting through your suit is it?" asked Chapra.

"No. Are we going to get on with this?"

"Not entirely up to us. This is a command decision."

Abaron felt a dull humming from the floor, then the clamps folded back and abruptly withdrew into the floor, leaving the sphere floating in place.

"Gravplate suspension," observed Chapra. "We'd best get back."

As they got out of the way the PSR moved in and embraced the sphere. It reached in with U-sound cutting appendage then, like a scarabid beetle working its ball of dung, revolved the sphere. With a high-pitched whining the cutter scribed a line around the sphere's circumference. This complete, it grasped above and below the line with its many limbs, twisted the two hemispheres in opposite directions. At first these screeched like seized bearings, but soon began to move more freely. Then in a fog of ice powder, the PSR separated them from the inner skin Abaron had earlier seen in the computer model, and put them aside. Now the machine cut again, this time following the hexagons in the honeycomb. When it finally reached into the cuts with hundreds of spatulate limbs, and levered them apart, this final outer shell opened off the central ball of ice in four parts, like the petals of a flower. Then after putting these aside the PSR really got to work.

It took the ball of water ice apart, cutting away curiously-shaped ice blocks and stacking them. Abaron wondered if the blocks needed to be such odd shapes or if that was a quirk of this particular PSR. It looked to him as if the sphere could be re-assembled from them and hold together like an interlocking Chinese puzzle. Probably there was a sensible explanation for this, though he was damned if he was going to ask Chapra.

Eventually the PSR exposed the creature, and held it up underneath its scanning heads to confirm what it must next do. Held by the huge machine like that the creature looked terribly vulnerable. Abaron jumped when the robot suddenly started to move again. It reached in with new limbs and, with that high-pitched whining, drove needles as thin as hairs into frozen flesh.

"At last count there were a hundred and fifty variations on the trihelix. We have to catalogue where the samples come from in its gut. Obviously some of them will be from its equivalent of bacteria, E coli and the like, and other parasites that live on its food." Chapra's voice was entirely analytical.

"We'll get more idea of its environment this way as well," said Abaron.

Chapra turned to regard him and he found it difficult to analyse her expression behind her visor. She pointed at the blocks of ice. "We can't even assume that it lived in water. That might have been some kind of protective amniote."

"Quite," said Abaron, then impatiently, "Why did we come down here?"

Chapra pointed at the creature. The PSR had now withdrawn.

"Permit me to lecture," she said. "I've studied alien life forms for a hundred years more than you, Abaron, and if there is one thing I've learned, it is that all our superb technologies are not enough. They can in fact be a hindrance. It is far too easy to wall yourself in with AIs and their information. It's too easy to distance yourself from your subject. That way leads to sterility and a lack of intuition. Look at it, and remember that it is alien and alive, not equations in a computer. Always remember the one unique thing humans bring to the study of alien life: imagination."

Abaron glanced up at the creature, then back at Chapra. "I haven't got time for this. I've a million tests to run." He turned and marched stiff-backed from the chamber.

Bloody woman and her touchy-feely shite, he thought.

Chapra watched Abaron go then returned her attention to the creature. As she studied it, she heard the lock behind her open, and guessed it was not him returning. She glanced round as in walked someone without a coldsuit, but then Judd had no need of such protection.

"He refuses to learn from you," said the Golem.

"He's stubborn and proud, but he does have a good mind. He'll learn eventually—we all do."

Judd folded his arms and looked up at the alien. "He is a fool and he is frightened."

"Yes, but perhaps you should remember that foolishness and fear are things you can only emulate, Judd."

"Anything I can emulate, I can understand."

"You may be Golem," she replied, "but you're young as well."

"Meaning?"

Chapra smiled. "Your knowledge grows, Judd. It would seem you have made a good start on understanding pride."

There were four tanks arrayed in the room like library shelves: each stretching from ceiling to floor, two metres wide and five metres long. Their glass walls had a very low refractivity and, because of this, it seemed as if three walls of water stood there. It would have been possible to do this with the field technology, but the contents of the tanks were very precious, and not even the ship AI wanted to risk the incredibly unlikely event of a power failure.

Each tank contained plants consisting of free-floating masses of blue spheres bound together with curling threads. Around these swam shoals of small strangely-formed pink shrimp-creatures. There were those with a tail fin, one central row of leg flippers, one hinged arm to pick and feed with. Others were tubes with the flippers and feeding parts inside. And still others were distorted hemispheres of shell with limbs and mouth parts arranged radially underneath. On the floors of these tanks their larger and more heavily-armoured brethren crawled over and occasionally dismembered each other. Abaron walked between the tanks carrying a notescreen. There were dark marks under his eyes and his movements were jerky and slightly out of control.

"It's the temperature. Perhaps it's the temperature," he said to his screen, and put his hand against the glass. Quickly he snatched it away and shook it. The water in the tanks was as near to boiling point at Earth atmospheric pressure as it was possible to get without it becoming volatile.

"Pressure," he said, staring into a tank. After a moment he looked round as the Golem Judd stepped into view from behind one of the tanks. They stared at each other for a moment then Judd nodded his head in acknowledgement. Abaron backed away a couple of steps then quickly left the room.

Chapra leant back in her swivel chair and put her feet up on her touch console. This caused a flurry of activity on the holographic display for a moment. She smiled to herself when the display settled on an alphabetical list of xenological studies of alien genetic tissue. After a moment she frowned and took her feet of the console.

"Box, how come we're not overrun with experts?" she asked.

The voice of the ship AI was omnipresent and faintly amused. "I wondered how long it would take one of you to notice. You are not overrun because I closed the runcible gate."

"Well, tell me. I don't need to be led like a child."

"Within ten minutes of your discovery being announced on the net there were over a quarter of a million priority demands for access to this vessel. Many of the demands could not have been refused at the transmission end. Had the runcible remained open this ship would have been filled to capacity. Too many cooks."

"I would have thought a few would have got through before you shut the runcible down."

"No. I shut the runcible down before your discovery was announced."

"How long before?"

"As soon as I detected the sphere."

"Ah," said Chapra, and put her feet back up on the console. "Are all our findings being relayed, all our studies?"

"Yes."

"How many official complaints so far?"

"Just over two million. You have been charged with everything from unhygienic practice to xenocide. I have put a hold on all communications."

Chapra grinned delightedly. Abaron would hate this of course. But Abaron did not see the joke of her coming aboard this ship as a partial cat-adapt. Then again, perhaps he didn't know what Schrödinger's box was.

"What about you?" she asked. "Is what you are doing legal?"

"I have unrestricted AI mandate."

That was enough. Everyone knew it was not humans who made the important decisions in the human polity: they could not be trusted. Chapra shrugged then called up a projection of the creature suspended in icy stasis in the isolation chamber. She glanced across the room when Judd entered, then returned her attention to the projection. A skating of her fingers across the touch controls brought into focus the subatomic mechanisms of life in the grip of absolute cold.

"You are studying the mechanisms of stasis," said Judd.

"That could be said," she replied. "It could also be said that I'm studying the mechanisms of . . . resurrection, awakening. They are the same."

"Can you wake this creature without killing it?"

"Yes and no. We can wake it and if there is any problem we can throw it back into stasis so fast there will be little damage done."

"There are no problems of environment?"

"None. Abaron would say there are, but he is being perfectionist. Any living creature of this complexity has a broad range of environmental tolerance. The differences he is quibbling over are the differences between Winter and Summer for a human. The only way to find the optimum is by waking the creature and studying its reactions."

"You have seniority," observed the ship AI.

"I am reluctant to hurt his feelings."

"There is pressure," said the AI. "Answers are required."

"We'll be lucky if we get anything," said Chapra. "You know the difficulties of communication with aliens—points of reference, all of that. This creature doesn't have eyes. Its primary senses seem to be related to taste and smell but on a level so complex that it might even be capable of decoding individual molecules. Add to that it living in water at a temperature that would nicely cook a human and you find a lack of common ground. We need so much more information: its technology, where it comes from . . . ah." Chapra paused for a moment then stabbed her fingers down again, deleting the projection of the creature and calling up something else. The result was a shifting, and slightly nauseating greyness. She quickly cancelled that. "I see . . . I didn't feel us drop into U-space. How long until we leave the Chasm and enter the Quarrison Drift?"

"Twenty-two hours," replied Box.

Judd added, "It will be a solstan week before we reach the system that may be the system of origin."

Chapra shifted one finger aside and pressed down.

"Abaron," she said. "You best get to the control room. We're going to do it now."

"We're up to zero now. Everything stable," said Abaron.

"That was to be expected," said Chapra. "The problems start as soon as all that body ice turns to water."

"The freezing was exceptionally efficient," Abaron allowed.

"I would say nigh perfect," said Chapra. "There's no apparent cell damage to the creature. I wonder just how much of our interference is necessary."

"The weta," said Abaron suddenly.

"Pardon."

Abaron could not help smiling; he knew something she did not know. "It's a cricket that lives in New Zealand on Earth. It has adapted itself to night-time freezing and a morning thaw without substantial damage."

"Yes, but the weta evolved to it. I doubt that is the case with this creature. What we see here is advanced cryogenics."

Annoyed Abaron said, "Or genetic manipulation."

Chapra regarded him and raised an eyebrow.

"Quite," she said, her surprise evident. "Now, let's move on to the next stage." Her hands fled over the touch keys. The holographic display showed much of the isolation chamber. It was as if they sat at their consoles just to one side of it.

"One degree above zero. Flooding chamber," said Abaron. As he said this the floor of the chamber dropped a couple of metres below the entrance lock, from below which a jetty extended. Water poured into the chamber from holes all round the wall. When it reached the nil gravity area below where the creature floated, just held in place by the tips of some of the PSR's limbs, it splashed up and floated too, in seemingly gelatinous masses.

"Deep scan is showing cell chemistry initiation. Heat generated. It is primitively warm-blooded, which is surprising considering its environment," said Chapra.

"Brief neural activity," said Abaron.

"Okay, let's shut down the null-field."

The field, created by two opposing gravplates, collapsed when Abaron shut off the plate in the ceiling. A growing column of water collapsed and the creature sagged as it gained weight.

"Enzyme activity is too fast for anterior cell chemistry. I'm taking the temperature up five degrees. Use a microwave pulse, we want all that ice thawed quickly," said Chapra, her voice urgent.

"Done," said Abaron.

"Christ! Look at that activity," said Chapra.

"It moved," said Abaron.

"The chemistry is almost too fast for scan to follow!"

"It moved," Abaron insisted.

"What?"

"I said it moved."

"Put it in the water," Chapra said.

The PSR lowered its charge into the water, which was now a metre deep. Abruptly the creature jerked away from the PSR, then feebly began paddling.

"Get the temperature up! Quick, it's going into hypothermic shock. Use the microwave pulse again if necessary."

"Ten, twenty, thirty . . . it's coming out of it."

The PSR retreated from the chamber. The creature continued to propel itself around and around. Abruptly it broke the surface with a triangular section tentacle, angled over like a periscope. The water lay two metres deep now. The creature moved to the edge of the jetty, then underneath.

"Dim the lights fifty percent," said Chapra.

"Eighty degrees," said Abaron. Wisps of steam were now blowing off the water's surface.

"Hold it at ninety and keep the pressure at one atmosphere."

"Surely it needs more."

"As I said, it'll likely have as much an adaptive range as a human. We want it tolerable enough for us to go in there."

"Why?"

Chapra glared at him. "We have to learn to communicate."

"Send a Golem in," said Abaron.

Chapra turned away. "Just do as I say."

It was the first time she had ever felt truly angry with Abaron, and was beginning to realise it might not be the last. She returned her attention to the chamber and watched as the creature slid out from under the jetty. It moved fast now. An underwater view showed that it propelled itself with a tail fin like a sharp propeller that pulsed in alternate directions. It changed direction and halted by gripping the bottom with its tentacles. It stabilized itself with two fleshy rudders jutting from its sides. The arm—it had only the one—it kept folded to its ribbed body. The head was that of a nightmare crayfish, but without eyes.

"I think you can open the way into one of your tanks now."

"That will raise the temperature," said Abaron tartly.

"Let it," said Chapra. "It'll only be for a while." She did not allow herself be drawn. *His turn to get under my skin*, she thought.

At Abaron's instruction an irised hatch slowly opened in the wall. Water poured in and the chamber filled with steam. The creature turned toward the disturbance, then backed away. Abruptly it darted to its disassembled sphere and turned one of the inner segments over on top of itself. Crustaceans and plants poured in with the water. The tank emptied and Abaron closed the hatch. Then he and Chapra watched anxiously. Eventually one of the larger crustaceans ventured over near the creature. There was a flicker of movement and the crustacean was up against the creature's mouth parts, a faint cloudiness in the water, then a cleaned shell and emptied bits of exoskeleton drifted to the bottom. The creature slowly came out of its hide.

"Yes!" yelled Abaron happily.

Chapra watched with increasing fascination as the creature took up the empty shell and used it to scrape at the bottom of the tank. When this had no effect, it carefully picked up all the shell fragments in its single hand, swam over to the jetty, then reached out of the water and deposited them on the jetty.

"I think now I can sleep," she said, and wondered if that was true. The creature's response had been perfect, disturbingly perfect.

PART TWO

Kellor took the crodorman's pawn then grinned at him across the board before picking it up. The crodorman had a look of real fear on his whorl-skinned face. It had taken a while to get that look there, since Kellor had appeared to be a perfect mark when he entered the tent. He looked young and a trifle depraved, his pouting mouth and pretty face the cosmetic choice of a certain contemptible type. His clothing, the tightly tailored white uniform of a preruncible ship captain, was also the choice of that type. The crodorman grunted in pain at the penalty shock, his eyes closed and the bigger whorls of thick skin on his face and wrists flushing red. Kellor studied him with interest. He reckoned on check in another five moves. It would be fascinating to see what level the penalty shock went up to then. The shock from checkmate killed people with a weak constitution. He wondered if the crodorman might die, and he smiled at the next expected move.

"You're Kellor," someone said.

Kellor glanced round at the man who had elbowed himself to the front of the ring of spectators. They shushed him but he ignored them. Kellor inspected the uniform and recognised the man as a General in the Separatist Confederation. Now there was a contradiction in terms. He looked up into the bearded face and saw there the harshness of rigid self-control, a mouth like a clam, and eyes a black glitter amidst frown lines.

"What can I do for you?" he asked, off-handedly making another move. He took no pieces this time, so there was no penalty shock. But Kellor was aware that his nonchalant attitude was scaring the crodorman. The General could not have come at a better time.

"I am David Conard," said the General.

How very interesting, thought Kellor. Here was the Butcher of Cheyne, the man reputedly responsible for the deaths of over two million Polity citizens. He turned from the board, a flick of a smile on his face when he saw the sweat squeezing out between the folds in the crodorman's forehead. Over ten seconds and the penalty shocks would start. You had to think quick in this game.

"You want my ship?" he asked, noting how the people who had been shushing the General had now moved back from him.

"We can't discuss this here."

Kellor nodded then glanced aside and moved his castle directly after the crodorman's move. The crodorman rapidly followed that move, a look of relief on his ugly face.

Oh silly silly crodorman.

"No problem," he said to General Conard. "I'm finished now."

The crodorman lost his look of relief and stared at the board, then he looked up at Kellor. There was no pleading in his expression, just fear and a braced expectancy. This was the bit that Kellor liked; the moment his opponent realised he had lost and that he was about to experience pain, or die. He had enjoyed this moment so often, yet it never palled; the gun pointed or the blade of a knife paused at the skin. But it could never be protracted in a real fight as it could in penalty chess. Kellor grinned at the crodorman and slowly reached out for his queen.

"This will be checkmate, I believe," he said.

The crodorman swore at him then made a sound halfway between a scream and a groan when he made the move. Kellor watched him writhe for a moment, then detached his own wrist bands and picked up his winnings. As he walked from the tent with the General the crodorman slumped across the board, either in a faint, or dead. He did not notice. By then he had lost interest.

The device was alive. Chapra defined it as a device because she was certain it was a product of technology rather than of evolution. It was also growing. Some time during their sleep period the creature had placed the thing on the bottom, at the side of the chamber furthest from where its food crustaceans congregated. It was half again the size it had been. It was now ten centimetres across: a spaghetti collection of tubes, a coral.

"You notice it's increased in size rather than complexity. It's exactly the same shape as it was," said Chapra.

Abaron grunted an acknowledgement. She knew he was deeply involved in problems with the food ecology. The crustaceans ate the artificial proteins he gave them, they could in fact ingest Terran protein and plant matter, and they seemed really healthy. But he could not get them to breed. It was possible he might never know what was lacking in their food or their environment, but opined that while he tried to find out he learned much else. Chapra reckoned it was work he preferred because it tracked him away from the alien itself.

"Where has the shell gone?" she suddenly asked. "Box, did you have it cleared from the chamber?"

"No, the creature utilized it," replied the ship AI.

"Show me."

A flicker and she was looking at an earlier view into the chamber. Another flicker and the water became totally unrefractive; it looked as if the creature, the plants, and the pseudo-shrimps were just floating through air. She watched as the creature placed the device on the bottom then began cruising in circles round the chamber. After a time it reached up on the jetty and collected all the pieces of shell. It took these to the device, and next to it, on the floor of the chamber, ground the shell to sludge and fed it into the tubes.

"What are the main constituents of those shells?" Chapra asked.

Abaron replied, "Calcium carbonate and calcium phosphate."

Chapra's hands glided for a moment then she paused in irritation and plugged in her interlink. Her hands glided again.

"The device has been increased in size structurally, using those compounds, but its other constituents are more diffuse. These are carbon and copper compounds in the main, with aluminium, microscopic amounts of tungsten carbide . . . " Chapra's voice trailed off and she sat there trancelike. After a time she turned to Abaron who was watching her carefully. "Now is our opportunity," she said.

"What do you mean?" he asked.

"I mean I'm going in there."

"You must be insane," he said. He looked slightly ill.

"Box," she said, ignoring him. "I want those compounds in the precise proportion they are in the device, only ten times the quantity, separate and held in inert containers . . . make the containers from the same material as the sphere inner shell, and in the same fashion. I leave it to you."

"What about contamination?" asked Abaron, a catch in his voice.

"None of its bacteria or viral forms have shown any pathogenic tendency in human tissue, and we are free of all harmful human viral or bacterial forms. Even the beneficent ones we do carry would not be able to survive in its environment."

"The heat?"

"I'll wear an environment suit, but I do not want to be completely cut off."

"Why?" asked Abaron, confused.

"If I completely enclose myself the creature may not be able to see me in its way. Remember, its primary senses are most like our senses of taste and smell—it has no vision."

Abaron just shook his head and returned his attention to his console and display. Chapra smiled and stood, removed her interlink. Before leaving the room she rested her hand on Abaron's shoulder.

"Xenology is not the most clever choice for a xenophobe," she said, and headed for the door.

Before she went through it he managed a reply. "It is exactly the right choice."

Once she was outside the room and beyond Abaron's hearing, Box said, "He is right, and we watch him. His fear makes him a most meticulous researcher."

"Have you followed my instructions?"

"But of course. Judd awaits you in the isolation chamber."

"Superior bastard," she muttered as she strode down the corridor.

The world of Callanasta was Diana Windermere's home world, and where the rest of the *Cable Hogue's* crew were stationed or lived on permanent call. It was also the world the *Hogue* orbited and, it had been established, that orbit was of great benefit to the Callanasta's two-centuries-old terraforming project. Diana thought it good that a breaker of worlds, just by its presence, assisted in the making of a world.

The call came while she was spear fishing for the huge adapted turbot in the estuary. She was slowly coming up on one of the great diamond shapes as it cruised along the bottom when there came a splash above her and the iron crab of a remote drone sank down toward her. The turbot shot away in a cloud of silt and Diana resisted the temptation to shoot the spear at the drone. It would only bounce off. She surfaced and the drone surfaced with her.

"This is a priority call. You are to come at once," said the drone.

Diana pulled her hemolung breather.

"Another fucking drill?" she spat.

"The crew are gating aboard at the moment. We leave the system in one hour."

The voice was different all of a sudden. Diana realised the *Hogue* AI had just spoken to her and that it sounded excited. Usually it was locked into the net and too busy in other pursuits to even talk.

Diana dropped her spear gun and opened up with her fastest crawl for the shore. She kicked off her flippers in the surf then ran down the grey strand to her beach house. She delighted in the strength of her body. To be this fit compensated for the times she had spent in hospitals being cell welded back together, just as the captaincy of the *Hogue* compensated for the years she had spent taking orders. She grinned to one side at the drone as it overtook her, carrying her flippers and spear gun.

Her beach house was made of pine shipped round from the other side of the planet and was a replica of the chalets they built in Siberia in the twenty-second century shortly after the permafrost melted. At least, that's what the catalogue said. Diana did not care so long as she had room for her weapon collection and gym—not for her the augmentations that were so popular in Security, as she considered it better to know her own strength.

Inside the chalet she stripped off her swimsuit and stepped under the shower. As she did this she heard the thump of her spear gun and flippers hitting the floor. Out of the shower she dried, pulled on her jump suit, looked around for anything she might need. There was just one thing. She took a large ceramal commando knife down from its wall display and slid it into her boot. It was unlikely that she would use it; she just took it because she felt uncomfortable without it.

In the back of the chalet stairs led down into an underground chamber that had been carved out of yellow rock of Callanasta. It always gave Diana a thrill to come down here. She rated this, her own runcible. The floor of the chamber was dark glass underneath which could be seen the shapes of machines and ducts. At the centre of the floor was a circular dais of black glass three metres in diameter. At the centre of this stood two nacreous bull's horns three metres high between which shimmered the cusp of this Skaidon gate. No living human understood the science. Iversus Skaidon had, for the brief time he survived directly interfacing with an AI. The whole science was created in a matter of minutes. Diana watched the drone shoot into the cusp and disappear. There were people who used it just as casually, but Diana could not. Always there was a moment of reflection before she stepped through. She stepped through.

No time. No space, nor pain. Just a feeling of strangeness that came not from the transference itself but from the dislocation. The air was different, as was the gravity, sounds, smells, tastes. All in an instant.

"Captain, it isn't a drill."

Weapons comp: Eric Jabro.

"I figured that," said Diana, striding away from the gate to the screens that showed Callanasta below. She needed that momentary reassurance. "Is everyone aboard?"

"I'll check."

They would be. Whatever this was, they had trained for it for the last eight years. She stared down at the planet. For eight years the planet had had tides, now it would have to do without for a while.

The suit blew cold air up under her hood. Every so often a feather of the air in the room got through. It felt as if someone had passed a red hot iron near her face.

"If the air temperature is taken lower, vision will be restricted."

Chapra stood with her back against the lock door. Judd stood a pace or two ahead of her. Was this such a good idea? She looked down at the case of hexagonal containers she held. It weighed heavy on her arm. Would the creature understand the gesture? Would it even recognise what was in these containers?

"Let's do it," she said, her words disturbing the air in front of her face and letting some of the heat in. She started to sweat.

"The creature is aware of our presence," said Judd. The Golem was linked in to Box and to the control room where Abaron sat biting his nails. Box had arbitrarily decided not to speak to them while they were in the isolation chamber as this might confuse the creature.

"There," Judd pointed to where three triangular tentacles broke the surface and zeroed in on Chapra. The fronts of these tentacles were equilateral triangles about ten centimetres on the side. Contained in these triangles was an organic complexity that had something of a lamprey's mouth, the underside of a starfish, and a computer interface plug.

"It is physically motionless now, though Abaron informs me that there is huge sensorium activity."

"Fine," said Chapra. She walked to the end of the jetty, lowered the case to the floor, then walked back to stand beside Judd. There was something strange . . . something made her shiver.

"We are being ultrasound scanned," the Golem observed.

Chapra nodded. That was what she was feeling. Her partial catadaption made her more sensitive to some things. She thought about some of the structures they had studied in the creature's head. There had been much they had been unable to fathom, but now they at least knew it used ultra-sound. Just by looking at a human's hands, eyes, and the structure of the brain it is not possible to know all of what a human is capable.

"Something like a dolphin," said Judd. "There are also complex phero-mones present in the air."

"It's talking to us," said Chapra.

"It is scanning the case," said Judd.

Before Chapra could think of any reply to that the creature propelled itself to the edge of the jetty. A tentacle poised above the case, came down, pulled the lid to one of the containers, hovered above it. Something like a butterfly's tongue flickered from the end of the tentacle. There was a pause, then the creature sampled the other cases so fast its movements were a blur. The hand came out then snatched the case into the water, gone.

"Well, thank you, too," said Chapra, but she was euphoric.

Back in the control room Abaron watched, fascinated as the creature coiled round its strange device and worked upon it in some strange manner. It opened the pots one at a time and fed tastes of the various compounds into it with its tentacles. It reached inside with its long fingers and shifted things, reached deep inside with dabs of the compounds. This was causing reactions inside the device and turning the surrounding water cloudy. Abaron could see it was growing rapidly. When it reached twenty centimetres across, the creature snared more crustaceans, feeding itself on their flesh and their shells into the device, which continued to grow. After one sleep period it lay a metre across, and was like some enormous seashell bearing the shape of a wormcast. Its outer surface was red and rough, but what he could see of the interior was iridescent white, smooth, with the tube ends turned out like lips. Movement was visible far inside, which under scan seemed the interplay of complex mechanisms, or the internal function of a living creature. The line was blurred.

"Have we any idea at all what that is?" asked Abaron.

"Could be anything. It might use it to prepare its food, make drugs, or it might even serve no purpose at all. Imagine an alien watching a human paint a picture. . . . "

"I think it serves a function."

"It's a step or two beyond complete analysis," said Box in an unusual interruption. "But there are nanomechanical structures in there and as a consequence we must limit scan."

Chapra said, her voice flat, "Then its function could be anything, and might even be everything."

"What do you mean?" asked Abaron.

"Nanomechanical—it's likely it can make whatever it wants from the molecular level up. I would guess the only constraint to be materials, environment, and the size of those tubes."

"It might make something to break out of there," said Abaron.

Chapra looked at him. "It is not a prisoner. If it wants to leave at any time and shows that capability, then we should allow it to leave."

Abaron shuddered.

"That bothers you?" Chapra enquired.

"It bothers me, but I can live with it . . . what's it doing now?"

They both turned to the projection. The creature caught one of the larger crustaceans, but rather than eat it, fed the crustacean into one of the tubes of the strange machine, then coiled round it.

"Feeding it?" wondered Abaron.

"I don't think so," said Chapra, and her fingers went reflexively to her console. After a moment she lifted her hands away. "Box, I'm not getting anything on scan."

"Scan is inadvisable at this time. The radiations of scan may damage the nanomechanical structures or interfere with whatever process is taking place."

"Ah, Schrödinger," said Chapra tightly, but she allowed a little smile at the irony.

"You're not letting us look," said Abaron in disbelief.

"Precisely," said Box.

To Abaron Chapra said, "He's right, X-rays and ultrasound could wreck things on a molecular level, and the other spectrums of scan aren't likely to do any good."

"What about underspace?"

Box said, "An underspace scan still requires a real-space medium after gating."

"Oh," said Abaron, and looked embarrassed.

"That's my lot for now," said Chapra, and she stood and left the room.

Abaron sat for an hour analysing all extraneous data, but when the creature made no further moves he decided it was time for him to sleep. After he had gone, Judd entered the room and stared at the projection. Communication between Golem and ship AI was silent but long. Eventually Judd leaned forward and turned off the display, then just stood there still as something dead.

Once in her quarters Chapra sat on her bed and stared at nothing in particular for a while.

"Box," she eventually said, still staring, "There's huge potential here."

"We have no suitable scale of measurement or comparison," the AI told her.

"I was just thinking," she went on. "The scientific community is not the only group that'll be taking an interest."

"This has been noted."

"I am glad . . . you are only a science vessel."

"I am."

"What is being done?"

"As soon as nanomechanical structures were discovered in the device Earth Central was informed and has since taken appropriate action."

Chapra lay back on her bed. "Every world that's in the net but outside of Polity control will be watching, if not doing something. Separatist organisations are almost certainly looking for ways to capitalise on this. What exactly is being done?"

"The dreadnought *Cable Hogue* has been dispatched and will arrive in two solstan weeks."

Chapra swallowed dryly. That if anything brought home the seriousness of things; dreadnoughts were not put into action for anything less than interplanetary war.

"Will we come under military control?"

"No," said Box.

Like a million scientists before her Chapra did not believe that.

Kellor watched Conard's reaction with some amusement as the vendor thanked them for their custom and floated on to the next table. Separatists were uniform in their hatred of all machine intelligences. Kellor sipped his cool-ice and waited. He reckoned on the transportation of weapons or as an outside bet a military strike, which was fine by him so long as the target was not actually within the Polity.

"We require your services," said Conard.

Kellor obliged this comment with a slight tilt of his head.

"There is a science vessel that poses a threat to the Confederation. We need to take it out."

"Polity?"

"Yes."

"Expensive."

"Ten million units of irradiated platinum."

"Behind the Line?" Kellor asked, preparing to get up and walk away.

"What do you mean?"

"Is it in Polity space?"

"No."

Kellor sipped some more of his drink and allowed a chunk of the psychedelic ice to melt on his tongue. That was a lot of irradiated platinum for destroying a science vessel outside of Polity space. There had to be a catch. There always was.

"Where is this vessel?"

"Its last reported position was at the edge of the Quarrison Drift. Entering the Drift. I have that position to within a light year. There must be no survivors; total obliteration."

"For my own sake I have to agree. I don't want the Polity taking an interest in my affairs. What complications might there be?"

"The ship could be planetside by the time we reach it." Conard gave a bleak grin before sipping his glass of mineral water. Kellor distrusted people who made a point of staying sober. It probably meant they needed a clear head to keep track of their lies.

"I don't have the equipment for a large-scale planetary action. All I have is deltawing landing craft adapted for orbital bombardment."

"We will supply soldiers and landing craft for any ground action. You have the hold space."

Kellor nodded then tilted his head as the crodorman came staggering into the vending area. The man looked drunk and angry. Kellor shook his head in mock sadness and dropped a hand down to his belt. He felt nothing but contempt for bad losers.

"How soon can you be ready?" asked Conard.

"There are a few loose ends . . . "

The crodorman approached their table, pulling something from his bulky garments.

"Trazum speck!"

Kellor knew enough crodorun to recognise the challenge and threat. He stood as the crodorman finally pulled free a cylinder of grey metal. The end of the cylinder shot away to a distance of a metre and hovered suspended, the vague shimmer of field-stiffened monofilament between it and the cylinder. Kellor drew a small flat gun and pointed it. The crodorman paused; that moment again. The gun made a sound like a plastic ruler slapped against a table. The crodorman's arm fell off. The weapon fell with it and sheared in a half a recently vacated chair. On his feet now Kellor aimed again. The crodorman had time only to look down at the blood pumping from his stump. Again that sound. A hole the size of a strawberry appeared in ridged forehead and spattered customers behind the crodorman with pieces of skull and brain. He fell back over the vending machine which whined under his weight and thanked him for his custom. As Kellor holstered his gun he noted Conard clipping a similar weapon back into a wrist holster. He filed the information away for future reference.

"That's one loose end," he said.

"It's female," said Abaron.

"I thought you had females," said Chapra. They were sitting in a small eating area. Chapra was eating prawns and Abaron occasionally gave the plateful a strange look.

"Female . . . definitions. I had two sexes and made the fundamental error of assuming that because they were so like Earth crustaceans in every respect they would be the same in meiosis . . . it's the trihelical DNA. There are three sexes, all contributing their share of the chromosomes. This is the third." He pointed at the projection. It showed a crustacean little different in outward appearance to its fellows.

"So our friend used the device to conduct a sex-change operation," said Chapra with much amusement.

"Yes," said Abaron grudgingly. He looked at the creature curled round its weird machine. "No doubt it is correcting my error with one of the other species."

"Why don't you do the rest?" asked Chapra. "Help it out."

Abaron stared at her for a moment as if trying to decide whether or not she was ridiculing him. He eventually nodded then took up his notescreen and headed out of the room.

"What has it got in there now?" Chapra asked the empty air. The projection flickered and changed, showed the creature harvesting some of the water weed and feeding it into the machine. The projection then flicked back to real time showing the creature uncurling and moving back from its machine. A cloud of small objects gusted from one white mouth.

"What is that?"

"Seeds and spores," said Box. "Initial analysis shows—" Box's voice abruptly cut off.

"Yes . . . shows what?"

The silence lasted for racked-out seconds. Chapra felt a chill. It was not often that an AI did not reply, was not there. To her knowledge this could only mean that Box's entire processing power had come on line. And that power was phenomenal.

Box said, "I am sorry to delay. There are seeds and spores for one hundred different varieties of water weed."

"But there was only one," said Chapra, and only after she had said it did she realise what Box had told her. "Jesu, it can do that?"

Box said, "From the plant material it placed in the device the creature has made seeds and spores for one hundred different varieties of water plant. The genetic coding for sixty-four percent of these plant seeds is close enough to the original plant code for it to have altered that genome. The rest fall outside that area of probability as they are bihelical DNA."

"It's an engineer, a fucking genetic engineer."

"Shall I continue?"

"Yes, sorry."

"Many of the seeds seem to have their origins in a completely different environment from what is likely the creature's native one but have been altered to survive in it. Five of the seeds are from Earth seaweeds."

"You mean Earth-type?" asked Chapra, even though she knew an AI did not make that kind of mistake.

"Earth seaweeds, specifically three types of kelp and two bladder wracks. The kelps are Furzbelows or Saccorhiza Polyschides, Sea Belt or—"

"Yes, yes, you've made your point, but what does it mean?"

"You require my answer to that?"

"I would like it. I know what mine is."

"Very well, this creature is or was a member of star-spanning race with a technology comparable if not superior to our own. At some time it or its kind visited Earth."

"Is or was?"

"We have never before encountered a creature like this yet it has obviously travelled in human space. If its point of origin does turn out to be the system for which we are heading, then the creature might post date the extinction of its own kind by as much as five million years."

"How long now until we get there?"

"Forty-eight solstan hours."

Chapra nodded to herself and returned her attention to the projection.

"Hell," she said. "What now?"

The creature had placed the sample pots on the jetty, each of which contained something.

"I'm going down there."

"Judd is on his way."

"Yes, I'm sure he is."

Diana unclipped the restraining bar from her seat as the interface helmet automatically disconnected itself from her head, from her mind. Abruptly she was human again; limited to a small and fragile bipedal form. It was to be a god to interface with the *Cable Hogue*. It was also very tiring.

"Everything nominal," said Jabro, as if he expected no answer.

"Nominal," said Diana, still seeing the shore scenes from Callanasta's surface. The tsunami had been ten metres high, but the shore baffles had absorbed most of its energy. There had been only minor flooding in some coastal areas. No deaths. But then not many people lived on that world.

"We should do a weapons test before arrival," said Jabro. Behind his back Orland grinned at Seckurg, the token Golem on the bridge.

"Why should we?" asked Diana, her face straight.

"We don't want anything to go wrong at the other end," said Jabro, just as straight-faced.

"Hogue," said Diana, addressing the ceiling as was the wont of any addressing an AI, the location of which they were unsure. "Give us a vector on something to blast."

"Asteroid field two hours away at present speed. Navigation hazard and mostly the size of Separatist dreadnoughts. Nice that," said Hogue with relish.

"How long with the Laumer engines?"

"One hour. Engines still on diagnostic."

"Take them off that and put them online. This is a priority mission."

Deep in the guts of the *Cable Hogue*, banks of crystalline cylinders phased red-violet then off the visible spectrum. The force holding the ship under the surface of underspace dragged it deeper and slammed it forward. The energy expended was such that the ship left a visible trail behind it in realspace; self-created antimatter sparkled into oblivion as it connected with stray hydrogen atoms and left black lines like stretch marks across vacuum.

One hour later the *Cable Hogue* flashed into existence in a field of asteroids with a dispersion of thousands of kilometres. Asteroids glowed and bloomed into expanding spheres of plasma. Jabro segmented an asteroid the size of Earth's moon, then hit each segment with quark bombs. The resultant flash was mistaken as a nova on a distant world, a hundred years on.

"That cost us," said the ship AI, but Jabro was laughing like a maniac and did not hear. Diana smiled to herself, knowing Hogue would not have allowed Jabro access to that particular weapons bank if the cost had been prohibitive. The cost later turned out to be a twenty minute stopover in the troposphere of a gas giant for refuelling, then the *Hogue* really opened up with its Laumer engines. The result was called The Cable, and it glowed in the skies of many a world for decades.

The heat licked at the edges of the air blast on Chapra's face as she entered the isolation chamber. It almost seemed malevolent. Judd walked out ahead of her, to the edge of the jetty, and studied the containers. The creature was floating about ten metres out and Chapra felt that faint sensation that told her she was being ultrasound scanned. After a moment she followed Judd and peered down into the containers.

"A gift?" she wondered. She squatted down and looked closely. Three of the containers held small quantities of metallic powder. There were small quantities of crystalline substances in a couple of others, and in the remaining three were minute copies of the containers themselves. Chapra reached inside and took one out. Like the originals it was transparent. There was a mere fleck of something inside it.

Judd said, "The creature showed increased scanning activity when you spoke and it is showing it again now."

Chapra stood up. "Perhaps it understands that this is how we communicate. I imagine that it communicates using ultrasound and pheromones—not an easy language to translate." She stooped and took up four of the containers. Judd took up the other four.

"I don't think these are a gift," she continued. "I think the creature is letting us know its requirements." She turned to the door then and halted in surprise. Abaron, dressed in a totally-enclosing environment suit, stood just inside the chamber.

"Abaron." She could think of nothing more to say.

"There is a communication for you," he said, his voice grating from the PA of the suit. He quickly turned back to the door, hit the control to open it, went through. Chapra and Judd followed him through the lock. In that little chamber Abaron removed his mask while Chapra flicked back her hood. His face was pouring with sweat.

"Is that suit malfunctioning?" asked Chapra sweetly, then damned herself for insensitivity—at least he was trying. She shook her head. "What do you mean 'a communication'?"

"A priority message from a place called Clavers World," he said.

"Box? I thought you weren't letting anything through."

"I merely reassigned priority. One of my subminds has been vetting all communications. This particular one may be relevant to all our actions. It is from Alexion Smith and it is on real time."

"Him. What the hell does he want?" As she said this Chapra glanced at Abaron and saw the awe on his face. "Strike that," she said. "Let's go and find out."

Junger twenty-eights, thought Kellor. He stood in the hold of his ship watching, on a nearby viewscreen, the gunships jetting across vacuum from the heavy-lifter shuttle. The General must have bribed someone in the Polity to obtain them. They were dated, and must have been scheduled for destruction at some point. Sixteen of them. Kellor licked his lips. He was not sure he liked this. The money was good and must obviously be in proportion to the risk . . . but some of the other toys the General had brought aboard bothered him. The tactical atomics weren't so bad. Kellor had used them himself on many occasions. But the CTDs were. Contra terrene devices were the kind of things to get you really noticed by Earth Central, and it was by not being overly noticeable to EC that Kellor was able to continue to operate. He really hoped the General had no intention of using them against a Polity world—that would really piss off some major minds, and a pissed-off AI was an enemy indeed.

"You have some reservations," said Conard. A few paces behind him stood his two young aides, their expressions utterly devoid of emotion and in Kellor's opinion, intelligence.

"I always have reservations when I don't know all the details," Kellor replied.

The General stood with a swagger stick tucked under one arm and managed not to look ridiculous. His uniform was neat and spotless on a diminutive frame. His face wore a mildly thoughtful expression. But Kellor had begun to understand what went on behind that expression. General David Conard hated the Polity, and most especially its AIs, with fanatical intensity. He would die to bring it down. And he would kill anyone to bring it down. Kellor considered himself a better man. As far as he was concerned people could live how they liked. He only killed for money.

"There is nothing much to add. You must first sever communications using those . . . missiles." He said the last word with contempt. It was his disgust at the thought of using smart missiles that had made Kellor finally realise the depth of Conard's hatred of AIs. "And on our subsequent arrival in the system take out the Polity ship you'll find there."

"And that's all?"

"Yes, and as I said before, 'There must be no survivors; complete obliteration.'"

"And it's only a Polity science vessel?"

"Yes."

"No colony on the world?"

"No."

"That's all right then."

Kellor turned to watch as the first of the gunships entered the hold of the *Samurai*. They had four-man crews, which meant his own crew would be outnumbered by about twenty. He would have to prepare for that eventuality. He turned back to Conard.

"Why?" he asked.

"I'm sorry?"

"Why do you want to destroy a Polity science vessel? Surely there are better military targets?"

"That does not concern you."

Kellor pretended to think about it then nod reluctant agreement. He had noted and filed the edge to Conard's voice. That edge had not been there at the beginning. Something had changed and the mission had acquired greater urgency. If the Separatists were becoming desperate to destroy that vessel then it carried something of huge potential value. With his back to the General, Keller allowed himself a cold little smile and glanced to the squat muscular bulk of his first officer. Jurens returned his look then nodded back to Conard. Kellor turned to watch.

The General strode over to a group of four of his soldiers who had come aboard the *Samurai* in the first Junger. One of these was either ill or drunk and his fellows were attempting to support him. As the General approached they quickly stepped away. Conard did not hesitate. He kicked the soldier in his testicles then kicked his feet away from under him. As the man lay on the deck groaning Conard reached down and pulled something from his neck and tossed it aside. Jurens stepped up beside Kellor.

"H-patch," he said. "Confederation soldiers like to stay stoned so's they don't have to think about what they're being ordered to do. Arseholes."

The General, just to drive the point home, began systematically kicking in the soldier's ribs. The man probably couldn't feel it. Jurens spat on the deck and turned away. Kellor followed his first officer from the hold. He too, as a young mercenary, had suffered such officers as Conard.

PART THREE

Alexion Smith looked neither old nor young. There was nothing fashionable nor particularly unfashionable about his appearance. He had short blond hair, a thin non-descript face set as a background for calm green eyes, and wore a ribbed and neatly patched environment suit. He looked . . . utilitarian. From years of association Chapra knew that this was because such things as fashion just held no interest for him. His love was for things long dead and buried: ancient ruins and ancient bones, preferably alien ruins and alien bones. He sat now at ease in a deep armchair in a projection that occupied the air over the consoles in the control room. Behind him was a window through which could be seen a barren landscape below a sky half-filled with a red-giant sun. Weird birds drifted in charcoal silhouette.

"Alex, it's nice to see you," said Chapra as she dropped into her swivel chair. Abaron took a seat in the background.

"It is nice to see you, Chapra, though I wouldn't recognise you. I take it you got fed up with the grey hair and sagging tits?"

Chapra grinned at the sound of a sharply indrawn breath behind her. "I did. I find that in this form it is easier for me to get what I want. Appearance is all even in this cosmetic age. What is it, Alex? What's given you priority over half a million other callers?"

Alexion looked out his window for a moment before returning his attention to Chapra.

"I was fascinated by your discovery out there, Chapra, and supposing that the escape pod is five million years old I considered that discovery within my remit. I've been watching and paying attention . . . picking up on every scrap of information. . . . The evidence is mostly mythological, philological . . . you know as well as I that you can excavate languages and stories as well as ruins—"

"What's your point, Alex?"

Alexion looked at her very directly, "Based on the construction of the escape pod—remains of one exactly the same were found in the Csorian time vault—and based on the machine it . . . uses—the shape of that machine was etched into the walls of the same vault and no-one knew what it was until now—and based on thousands of other fragments of information collated by AI, there is an eighty-three per cent probability that the creature you have there is . . . Jain."

Chapra shivered and heard Abaron curse. She immediately wanted to object; but the Jain died out millions of years ago, they're just dust and legends and racial memories of gods . . .

Alexion went on, "In the Sarian mythos the Jain were the great sorcerers, the transformers. Their houses were said to be black water-filled boxes built in the equatorial deserts. Their symbol was the triangle. And if that is not enough, the world to which you are heading, has been posited for over a century as likely a Jain home world."

"Okay, I'm convinced," said Chapra. "But how is this to affect what I am doing here?"

"The ship AI there, Box, is loading every Jain study, every relevant piece of information. It might help."

"Is that it?" Chapra was beginning to feel a vague disappointment.

"They moved suns, Chapra. There are those who theorise that here we are in the backwoods of a civilization that still exists. I guess my message is: for all our sakes, don't fuck up. Ciao." Alexion flickered out of existence.

Chapra turned to Abaron. "This changes nothing," she said.

Abaron nodded, but he looked scared again.

The Jain—this was how both Abaron and Chapra referred to it now, it was better than 'the creature'—took the containers from the jetty to its machine. Chapra smiled to herself. Perhaps they might never be able to speak to each other, but they understood each other. When she and Judd had collected them the containers held samples of what the Jain wanted in quantity. One of them contained a sample of only a few atoms inside a small vacuum sphere of glass. The Jain's requirements had stretched from the prosaic to the exotic. It had wanted iron, it had wanted tantalum, and it had wanted a metallic element only theorised until then. Making a few ounces of the stuff had stretched the main onboard laboratory and required five Golem to come out of stasis to assist.

"You note it only requires elements," said Chapra.

"Confirmation that it can build all the molecules it wants, so long as it has the atoms," said Abaron. He was being very correct and very logical, very in control.

"I wonder though . . . "

"What?"

"That metal, the Jainite, and the niobium . . . I've checked. There was nothing like that in the isolation chamber, nor in the tanks."

"They could have been present in the escape pod."

"No. I had Box check back on every scan. We were thorough."

"What are you saying then?"

"We missed something, or with that machine the Jain is able to synthesise atoms, even if in minute quantities."

"It's Jain," said Abaron, as if that was all the answer required.

Some hours later the Jain manufactured something else.

"The device is a scanner," said Box. "It scanned the entire ship with some kind of neutron burst."

"That's not possible," said Abaron.

"It's Jain," said Chapra, relishing the moment.

The device the Jain had built was about the size of a human head and looked like the bastard offspring of a whelk and the insides of an old valve radio. After using it the Jain saved one small component then fed the rest of it back into its bigger machine, its creation machine. Afterwards it fed in one of the large crustaceans. Then it came to the jetty and left something squatting there.

"This I have to see," said Chapra, hurrying on her way. She glimpsed Abaron licking his dry lips as he reluctantly followed her. In minutes both of them were in hotsuits and walking out on the jetty. Judd strode behind them.

"It's the crustacean. It's been altered," said Abaron, then he stepped rapidly back when the beast lifted its armoured belly up off the jetty and, walking on four armoured limbs, began to come towards them bull terrier fashion. After a moment Chapra moved back as well. The beast squatted down a couple of metres in front of them, waiting.

"Look at its back," said Abaron.

Chapra did so and there saw a triangle of ridged and pocked flesh. It was the negative of the end of the Jain's tentacles, she saw this at once.

Judd said, "This was one of the crustaceans. It has been stripped of its digestive system and now has a small organic power cell. Its sensorium has been upgraded to eighty per cent of received spectra and there are additions to its primitive brain. Its blood is heated by metallic heating elements."

"It's a probe," said Chapra. "I bet the additions to its brain are memory."

"Cannot be determined," said Judd.

"All right, I bet there are direct links between those additions and that triangle on its back."

After a pause Judd said, "There are."

Chapra turned to Abaron and tried not to notice that he had pressed himself up against the door.

"I'll bet the intention is for it to wander around the ship then come back here. Once back here the Jain probably plugs in and reads off all the information it has gathered."

"That seems likely," said Abaron, a quaver in his voice.

"Okay, let's see," said Chapra, and she hit the door control. The beast got up again, advanced to the door, and through. They followed it into the lock, opened the next door into the ship. Beyond this door awaited the Golem named Rhys, who in appearance was an Australian aborigine.

"Rhys will accompany our little guest on its tour round the ship," said Box.

The beast moved off down the corridor, clicks and buzzes coming from a sensorium that was a mass of complex spikes, facets, brushes, and dimpled plates, all shifting and swivelling.

"Is this a good idea?" said Abaron, and Chapra wondered how he had restrained himself for so long.

"I think everything is under control, and won't be allowed to get out of control . . . what is that on your belt, Rhys?"

Rhys glanced back and tapped a hand on the gun holstered at his hip. In appearance it was a Luger made out of chrome, but with a few strange additions.

"It is a singun," said Rhys, his usually happy demeanour at once very serious.

"You see?" said Chapra to Abaron.

"But . . . I didn't think such things existed."

"They do. One shot from that will have the effect of turning our friend inside out through a pin hole in space." She observed Abaron's confused expression and explained. "For about a second it generates a singularity in its target. Our friend there would be reduced to sludge."

"Wouldn't an energy weapon have been better?" asked Abaron.

Judd said, "There is a high probability that the creature can generate defences against energy weapons. We have no known defence against the singun."

Chapra decided not to point out to Abaron that use of 'we'.

"It's all rather moot," she said. "The Jain has shown no signs of hostility."

"The Jain has placed a container upon the jetty," said Box.

"Let's go see what it wants now," said Chapra, and they trooped back into the lock. Soon they were out on the jetty. The container was at the furthest end.

"What the hell is that?" wondered Chapra as she strode towards the container. Showing great fortitude, Abaron strode at her side. Inside the container was a coil of something fleshy. They halted at the container and stood over it.

"It looks like something alive," said Abaron, crushing the dread in him under the cool analytic scientist.

"It certainly—"

The coil snapped straight out of the container, cobra fast. It hit Abaron's arm, hung there for a moment as it recoiled, then snapped out into the water. Abaron yelled, staggered back, and sat down.

"Oh," he said, then looked down at his shoulder where blood was spreading between the layers of his environment suit. "It bit me." In a moment Judd lifted him up and all but carried him to the door. Chapra followed. In the lock Abaron's legs gave way and he looked more bewildered than scared.

"It's just shock," Chapra told him, but she could not put from her mind visions of an ancient celluloid film she had in her collection; of the contents of an egg shooting out and attaching to a man's face, and the consequences of that.

Box looked upon the world with all its superbly precise senses and analysed it with a mind that made the mind of any god humans had imagined appear that of an infant throwing a tantrum, and it found the world beautiful. The eye of the beholder. Box could find beauty in anything because it could look at things in so many thousands of different ways. Many philosophers in the human polity now posited that humans were not created by gods, that in fact the complete reverse applied.

At the poles of the world the temperature was the same as at Earth's equator, but at two atmospheres pressure. At its equator the environment was about as inviting to a human as the inside of a pressure cooker. The place swarmed with life much like that in the isolation chamber, but with one important exception. There were great and complex ecosystems here, but no outpost of any star-spanning civilization, and no discernible remnants, but then little might survive five million years in such hostile conditions. There were no Jain, not a trace.

Very cool and very factual Abaron said, "There are no toxins in me, there is no disgusting alien embryo waiting to burst out of my stomach in a messy spray. There is, in fact, nothing alien to my body inside me barring the two doughnuts I ate half an hour ago and the cup of coffee I washed them down with."

Chapra smiled. The attack, rather than feeding his fear, had destroyed it. Irrational fear could never long survive harsh realities.

"What happened then?"

"This." Abaron peeled back the dressing on his arm to show the wound. A perfect circle of skin a centimetre wide and few millimetres deep had been excised from his biceps.

"What do you think?"

"I think the Jain took a sample. It is as curious about us as we are about it. Only its curiosity must have a greater urgency because it is entirely dependent on us and has no idea what we might want of it."

"What do you think it might learn?"

"Everything it is possible to learn from my DNA. Being able to build and alter DNA to the extent it does it must be able to decode it down to the atomic level."

"I think you're right," said Chapra. She thought a lot else but wasn't going to spoil his moment.

"Box," said Abaron. "What happened after the . . . worm . . . bit me?"

"It swam very fast to the inside of the Jain's machine. The Jain is now wrapped round its machine. There is much nanomechanical activity."

"There," said Abaron to Chapra.

Just then the door to the medlab hissed open and in walked the Jain's probe beast, closely followed by Rhys.

Box said, "There was an ultrasound communication between this probe and the Jain six minutes after the sample was taken from your arm."

The beast squatted on the floor, facing towards Abaron, who sat on the edge of the examination couch.

"It is scanning you," said Box, then, "Your graft is ready."

"Perhaps it has come to see this," said Abaron as he lay back on the couch. The doctor, which was a close relation to the PSR but deliberately less threatening in appearance, gripped Abaron's arm above and below his biceps. What might be described as its head came down against the muscle. It quickly gobbled up the dressing. In a glare of sterilizing ultraviolet it pressed a circle of skin into place with a flattened white egg on the end of one many jointed arm. The egg had the words 'Cell Weld Inc.' printed on it. It hummed mildly. The probe beast got up, turned, and left the room.

"It's satisfied you're all right," said Chapra.

When Abaron had nothing to say to that Box said, "You may be interested to know that prior to coming here the probe beast, as you call it, was in an observation blister, looking at the stars, and seeing our arrival at system DF678.98 and the world with the name Haden. It is now returning to the isolation chamber."

"We have to see this," said Abaron. He inspected his arm as the doctor took the cell welder from his arm. There was no sign of a wound.

"The world?" asked Chapra.

"No, what the Jain does with its probe beast."

When the doctor released him Abaron headed quickly for the door. Chapra followed calmly after, faintly smiling. She let Abaron get ahead of her; out of hearing.

"Where's the xenophobe?" she asked.

"There is nothing more fearful than fear itself," said Box.

"Yet you would have thought the opposite effect."

"Human psychology. Go figure," said Box.

Rhys opened the lock doors for the probe creature. It walked out along the jetty and dropped into the water. Chapra cleared the projection of surface refractivity and they watched the beast walk across the bottom to its creator. The Jain, still clinging round its machine, turned its strange head, then after a moment let go. It coiled out a triangular-section tentacle and plugged into the probe beast's back.

"It's down-loading it, reading it," said Abaron.

Chapra was glad to hear fascination in his voice rather than the suppressed horror she had heard before. They sat watching. Chapra expected nothing more than the tentacle to detach in a few minutes, perhaps in a few hours. She did not expect what happened next. The Jain convulsed, its tentacle cracking like a whip. It broke the probe beast on the chamber floor and let it go. Leaking green blood and fizzing like sherbet the beast floated to the surface. The Jain convulsed again and coiled hedgehog fashion, all its tentacles, its head, its arm, and its tail hidden away. Nothing but a crescent of ribbed body, sinking to the bottom.

"Hell, what happened?" wondered Chapra, her hands blurring over her touch console.

Abaron just studied the projection, his hands folded in his lap. "It just discovered how long it was in stasis I reckon."

Chapra gaped at him. That had not even occurred to her.

The Jain remained coiled for twenty hours and when it finally uncoiled it swam around aimlessly for another eight hours. Chapra and Abaron used the time profitably, putting a probe down into the seas of Haden and discovering many of the same plants and creatures that now flourished in the isolation chamber.

"This certainly could be the Jain home world," said Chapra.

"Any world could be the Jain home world," said Abaron.

Chapra waited for an explanation.

"Our Jain has ably demonstrated how it can re-engineer any life form, and how it can build life forms from component atoms. How much has it re-engineered itself? Haven't we done the same? There are humans with gills and fins, humans with compound eyes and exoskeletons, humans who can live in ten gees."

"Very true," said Chapra. "We might even be Jain."

That shut Abaron up for a long time. When he finally spoke again it was to say, "We have to learn to speak to it now. We have to learn its language."

Chapra was in thorough agreement, but even she was not sure where to start. The Jain might speak using ultrasound, pheromones, molecular messages, and it might not speak at all. Its language might have billions of words, no words, ten words, or it might ignore them because it felt depressed. Scan of its wide neural structure showed a hugely complex organ in its skull, a spinal column almost as wide as that skull, and from which branched nerve channels as thick as a human arm, leading to sub-brains in the torso that were easily as complex as human brains, then leading to each of its eight tentacles, eight interfaces.

"It's back at its machine," observed Abaron. "Will it even listen when it's there?"

They watched it at work, tentacles moving here and there across the surface of its machine.

"The ends of those tentacles are interfaces and they are crammed with microscopic manipulators," said Chapra. "There must be mating plugs and microscopic controls all over the surface of that thing."

"The entire surface is perhaps one control system," said Abaron.

"The machine is expanding," Box abruptly told them. Chapra reached for her touch controls then realised she did not have to bother; they could see it now. The mouths of the tubes had been approximately forty centimetres wide and the entire structure two metres across. It was visibly growing now, in pulses.

"The machine is drawing in and circulating water," said Box. No need to confirm. They could see the movement. They watched as it drew in shrimps and water plants. Only water came out.

"It's making something quite big now," said Abaron.

"Oh really," said Chapra, her hands rattling over her console. She swore under her breath when she realised Box was still not allowing her to scan the machine, then she abruptly folded her arms and sat back.

The machine expanded until it was four metres across, the top of it out of the water, the mouths of the tubes three quarters of a metre across. In a couple of the tubes they could see flickers of light as from an undersea welder. It drew in some of the bigger crustaceans. They did not come out again.

"Looks like it's getting there," said Abaron.

The Jain reached inside one of the tubes, pulled out something bulky, a soft mollusc from its shell. It towed this object to the jetty, and with much effort heaved it up out of the water.

"Oh my God," said Abaron.

On the jetty lay a female human child of perhaps five years. At the base of her back, etched in the purples and reds of a birth mark, was the triangular interface. As they watched the child vomited water then slowly stood up. Her skin was very red.

"The heat," said Chapra.

The door to the lock opened and Judd strode into the chamber.

The Jubilan communications satellite was a confetti of bright metal wrapped round a silver ovoid half a kilometre across. Geostationary above Jubal it glittered like some huge Christmas decoration. Around it, like a swarm of silver bees, glinted shuttle craft and loaders. The dark wedge of the *Samurai* was in harsh contrast as it slid into realspace trailing streamers of red fire. From this wedge of night sped four hardly visible specks at slow relativistic speeds. Two fell on the satellite. One wavered, then was gone in a galaxy-shaped explosion. The other struck home and the bright satellite cracked open, jetting flame and human and mechanical debris. The satellite came apart in the horrible silence of vacuum. The only screams heard were over radio links, and brief.

Kellor watched the destruction with no visible sign of emotion, but he had reservations: there were always extras. He had expected no less. But this was a Polity world. The extra payment of five million was all that had swayed him. He turned his attention to the display showing the other two missiles dropping towards the planet.

"What did they use?" he asked Jurens.

Jurens glanced up from his console. "Pulsed laser. Pretty powerful. They won't have that in atmosphere and anyway, the missiles have learnt."

Kellor noted Conard's disgusted expression and dismissed it. The display showed the missiles dropping to a mountain range a hundred kilometres from their target. They'd go in ten metres above the ground. There was only one weapon that could get through their shields and armour. Kellor smiled to himself as he watched them close in like hunting wolves. Then his smile dropped away as the two missiles blinked out of existence.

One weapon . . .

"Jurens! Get us out of here! Now!"

"Wait!" shouted Conard. "The runcible!"

Jurens ignored Conard, hit the ionic boosters, then poised his hand over the controls for the U-space engines. The *Samurai* was at a quarter C but it needed just a little more. Kellor slammed his hand down on Juren's hand, and the ship dropped into U-space. It was a slow drag, the ship straining and the sounds of distorting metal reaching them on the bridge. Over one of the coms someone began screaming as they saw through an incomplete field into the infinite. Kellor felt something dragging at him, at the ship, and it was not the result of a too-quick entry into U-space. When the drag ceased, he allowed himself a grimace at the sweat he felt on his top lip and turned to face Conard's raging.

The General was severely pissed-off. He was glaring and unconsciously clenching and unclenching his hands. His two aides stood quiet in the background. A surreptitious scan had showed them both to be heavily armed. Automatics in the bridge covered them, and Jurens and Speck had weapons to hand. If the General started anything Kellor would finish it. There was no way the man could call on his other forces here. They were all sitting in their gunships which, with an order, Kellor could dump into deep space.

"They did not seem to me the smartest of missiles," hissed the General.

"Get to the point."

"You should have used a human team. AIs are not reliable."

The shear idiocy of that comment left Kellor without any reply. How could you argue with that?

Conard went on, "Humans are chosen of God and are the only ones with the right to sentience!"

Oh dear, it got worse and worse. Kellor considered killing him right then and there. It seemed the only kind thing to do. The problem was that Conard had a source of information. Kellor wanted that source before he killed the man.

"The missile did not strike home because the facility was protected by ground-based singuns. Your entire force would not have got through and if I had taken the *Samurai* in any closer, they would have gutted it."

Conard stood there still clenching and unclenching his hands. After an embarrassingly long time he seemed to get control of himself. He turned and strode out of the bridge. *That's it*, thought Kellor, *go and kick shit out of one of your subordinates.*

PART FOUR

The sifting machine had, in strips, methodically sifted a tenth of the desert's surface to a depth of one metre. At a pace of two kilometres per hour it sucked up the sand, passed it through various grids and sieves, and spat it out behind filling the trench it had made. The sand left behind the machine was level. This would last until the next earthquake or storm. One of either usually came along each day.

The process was crude and frowned upon by many archaeologists who claimed that valuable artefacts could be damaged or destroyed. Alexion Smith took the view that anything surviving five million years in that desert would not be damaged by the sifter. His robust approach to archaeology was greatly disliked. But he got results.

Smith checked the sifter every planetary day—about four solstan days—and made a find on average once every solstan year. Mostly he came to empty out strange-shaped stones and package artefacts from more recent ages for transmission to associates. On this occasion he had a find.

In the red light of the giant sun the coralline material was the colour of old blood. Under the lamps it would be pink and Smith knew where he had seen its like before. The excitement he might have felt before was lacking now. Years of research and now, out there, a real living Jain. Smith glanced up at the red sun and the psuedobirds. A shape was coming towards him and it wasn't a bird.

The crab drone landed on the cowling of the sifter with a clattering and scrabbling and once it got its balance it peered at him with stalked eyes.

"Who are you then?" asked Smith.

"I am the *Cable Hogue*," said the drone in a gravelly voice.

"Interesting name."

"I am a ship AI speaking to you through this drone. The drone is called CH143 though it sometimes calls itself Spider."

"It has an independent mind then?"

"Yes."

"Well . . . what do you want of me?"

"Your expertise."

"Go on."

"To advise on matters Jain."

Smith dropped the fragment of ancient Jain technology back into the collection box of the sifter.

"I'll come," he said.

The drone rose from the cowling.

"You have four hours to get to the runcible here. Go to the Vorstra moon for short range transference to the *Cable Hogue*."

The voice was somehow different this time.

"I take it Spider speaks now."

"Spider spoke then. Only Spider speaks now."

Smith nodded and smiled to himself, then returned his attention to what he was being told.

"By shuttle?" he asked.

"By runcible," said the drone.

"Tell me, what manner of vessel is this *Hogue*?"

"A dreadnought."

Smith felt a slight shiver of excitement. It would have to be one hell of a ship to warrant having a runcible aboard. He was about to ask what classification of dreadnought it was when the drone accelerated away with a sonic crack. After a pause he headed for his AGC, his desert boots kicking up plumes of the red sand. The sifter went on sifting.

"Initially she was your clone. That she is a she, is the least of her alterations," said Chapra. The girl lay on the examination couch in medlab, her blue eyes wide open, her body motionless. She just stared at the ceiling.

"There's the interface in her back," said Abaron. "What else?"

"A lot. She wasn't burned in there even though she was in water that is nearly at boiling point. She can withstand temperatures that would kill a normal human. Very tough. Also her brain is human, but there are sub-brains branching all down her spine. In that sense she is nearly an amalgam of Jain and human."

"Normal DNA?"

"Not trihelical, no—"

Chapra paused. The girl was sitting upright.

"Not trihelical, no—" said the girl.

"She can speak," said Abaron.

"She can speak," said the girl. Only when she heard the girl repeating Abaron's words did Chapra realise that she had used exactly his voice, as she had spoken with exactly Chapra's voice before.

"She is learning, I think," said Chapra, and listened as the girl repeated it. "We'll have to give her the meanings of words. She'll have to be taught."

The girl repeated everything she said, then smiled. Chapra did not recollect smiling. She stepped up by the couch and took the girl's hand, brushed stringy blond hair from her face.

"Come with me," she said, and gave a gentle tug. The girl got off the couch. She did not repeat the words. Chapra felt a cold shiver. The girl had recognised the instruction. That was fast. That was AI fast.

"Let's go and get you some clothes and something to eat."

"Clothes and something to eat," said the girl.

Chapra felt that shiver again. It wasn't fear. It was awe. And her awe increased when in the eating area the girl learned how to use the eating utensils in moments. All the time Chapra and Abaron kept up a running dialogue, some of which the girl repeated and some of which she ignored.

"I believe the educative process can be speeded," said Box, out of the blue.

The girl tilted her head. "Hello," she said.

The AI turned on the single screen in the eating area and ran the upper and lower case English alphabet, reciting them as they scrolled past. On the second run through the girl recited. Box did the same with the Chinese alphabet, but at twice the speed. The girl recited. The AI ran the Russian alphabet even faster. The girl recited. After that neither Chapra nor Abaron could tell what was being run as the screen was a liminal blur and Box's and the girl's voices a babble. Abruptly the screen flickered and divided and Box began to teach a word at a time: sea, seaweed, water, human, hand, eye. Chapra noted the AI presented huge amounts of information with each word. Beside seaweed, Box opened a frame to display many different kinds of seaweed, nanoscopic pictures of genetic helices, cladograms and other graphical information. She and Abaron sat back and watched in fascination. After an hour Judd came in with a touch console and ran its fibre-optic cable to a wall socket. He laid it in the girl's lap. Shortly after that the screen became a liminal blur once again and the girl's fingers were moving across the console faster than even Chapra's. At that point the two humans left. For some it is a comfort to believe there are entities far superior to themselves. For some it is a comfort to know this. For others both views are merely depressing.

"What do you think it will want?" asked Abaron, as he poured vodka into Chapra's glass.

"You mean after it has downloaded everything the girl has learnt?"

"Yeah."

They were sprawled in form-fitting loungers in Abaron's quarters. This was the first time Chapra had been in there. She noted that the only ornaments were old paper books arrayed on a shelf. A glance at one had shown it to be very old, dating from the twenty-first century before the Reliteration. The language in them was fragmented, almost impossible to understand.

"I don't know. What would we want? What would you want if you were woken five million years hence by aliens?"

Abaron thought about that for a moment then said, "I would want to find out what happened to my own kind. I'd want to get in contact with them. But then that is me. We don't know how the Jain associate. They may be rabid individualists."

"Doubtful. You don't achieve that level of technology by yourself."

"Yeah? It might be old knowledge to them."

More vodka poured into the two glasses. Chapra and Abaron were using an old human remedy for what ailed them.

By the time Chapra was washing down hangover pills with a pint of orange juice the girl was literate in eight Earth languages. She was now rifling Box's libraries of information. Human limitations slowed her and she had gone through less than one percent of the information stored.

"Any specific interests?" asked Chapra as she stepped into the shower.

"She was taking an overview of all the information; dealing in generalities. She now probably has a general idea of human history, present attainments, and socio-political structures. She was avoiding the specific until a couple of hours ago," said Box.

"What happened a couple of hours ago then?"

"She came across the first reference to the Jain and has since been concentrating on all the pertinent information. Seeing her interest I gave her access to the files recently transmitted."

"Alex's?"

"Eight per cent of them had as their source Alexion Smith."

Chapra nodded to herself then hit the shower control across to cold. She swore as the blast of icy water hit her so soon after the hot and stood it for as long as she could. She never entirely placed her reliance in hangover cures. When she finally turned off the shower and dried herself with a rough towel from the dispenser, she felt thoroughly awake. She went through into the bedroom and gazed down at Abaron lying in a tangle of sheets, still apparently asleep. Her underwear she took up in one hand and her bodysuit she slung over one shoulder, then she padded naked from his quarters to her own. If that was the way he wanted it . . .

In her own quarters Chapra slung her old clothing into the cleaner, drew another bodysuit of the next primary colour on the spectrum and dressed. Once clad she touched her caste mark with its colour stick and went through its range of colours until it matched her clothing. She then decided against eating in her quarters and headed for the communal eating area. There she halted at the door to take in the scene.

The girl sat before the screen with the touch console across her lap. To one side of her stood a hologram projector. Judd, Rhys and a third sexless and featureless Golem stood around her, slaves to her beck and call. On a table beside her was a plate of what Chapra recognised as high energy food and a beaker of vitamin drink. Here everything was secondary to the ingestion of information. Nothing could have driven that point home more thoroughly than the portable toilet beside the chair. She wondered if the girl had slept, or required sleep, then turned away and went back to eat in her quarters.

Later, in the control room, Abaron smiled at her in a surprisingly mature manner. She had expected him to be embarrassed or resentful.

"Perhaps we should have taken a tranquilizer," he quipped.

"We did," said Chapra, and he laughed. Chapra wondered if she might prefer him lacking in confidence and all screwed-up.

"Has anything interesting happened while I've been asleep?"

Chapra detailed the girl's researches and the scene that had met her when she had gone to the eating area.

"It was the toilet that did it really," she said. "She's just another probe beast, just another mechanism for obtaining information."

"I didn't go there," said Abaron, his face curiously lacking expression.

"It bothers you too?"

Abaron shrugged. "Genetically speaking she's the closest relation I've got." He looked up from his console as Box activated the projection from the isolation chamber. "Ah, we have some action." The girl had just come through the lock and was walking out on the jetty. At the end of the jetty she stripped off her clothing then dived in. It could have been a scene from anywhere on Earth had the water not been nearly at boiling point and had not the Jain immediately zeroed in on her like a hungry crocodile.

"I wonder if the Jain will smash this probe beast," said Chapra.

Abaron looked askance at her. She ignored him and cut the refractivity of the water. They watched as the Jain caught the girl with its single hand and snaked out one tentacle to plug in to her back. The actions looked almost obscene. The girl froze, arms outstretched and fingers rigid; a newt with its neutral buoyancy.

"I have received disturbing news," said Box abruptly, hardly impinging on their fascination.

"Yes, what?" said Chapra.

"There is an unidentified ship heading towards us, due to arrive in two days. On its way here it released smart missiles at the Jubilan communications satellite and the planet-based runcible. The satellite was destroyed but the missiles fired at the runcible were intercepted. Had the runcible been destroyed we would have received no warning."

"What?" said Abaron. "What was that?"

Chapra suddenly felt very cold. This had been a possibility right from the start.

"Unidentified?"

"The probability is high that it is a mercenary craft employed by the Separatist movement."

"How long until the *Cable Hogue* gets here?"

"It is translight with a new design of engine. Projected time of arrival is four days."

"*Cable Hogue*?" asked Abaron angrily.

Chapra said, "The dreadnought sent out here to protect us—"

"Oh yeah," Abaron sneered.

"My thoughts exactly, but we are not in a position to dispute the matter. I for one would prefer Earth Monitors here and an AI-directed warship than Separatists and out-Polity mercenaries."

"Why didn't you tell me?"

"Because it would have interfered with your work."

"I don't believe that."

"You don't have to. You're at the bottom of the ladder and only here because I agreed for you to come."

Abaron was still angry, but kept his mouth shut.

Chapra turned from him. "We have forty-eight Solstan hours?"

"Yes," said Box.

Abaron looked thoughtful for a moment then said, "What about the runcible?"

"It is not possible, at this time, to use it," replied Box.

"Why?"

"Since entering the Quarrison Drift we have gone beyond the range of any other runcible to which you could transmit."

Abaron swore and peered down at his touch console. He refused to look at Chapra. She repressed the sudden contempt she felt. Really, he had been right to ask . . .

"What capabilities do you have?" she asked Box.

"I do not have armament."

"Can we outrun this ship?"

"With a translight slingshot round the sun this is possible."

"What about the Jain?"

"Hang on," interrupted Abaron. "What do they want?"

"They want the Jain. Isn't that obvious?"

"No, not necessarily. What are the projections, Box?"

"Separatists are normally xenophobic in outlook. It is more likely that they are coming here to kill the Jain and destroy all its technology than to kidnap and use it," said Box.

Chapra folded her arms, nodded, and met Abaron's look of victory for a moment. He was grasping things more firmly now but Chapra had no time for such games. Things had turned deadly serious. She turned to the projection and saw that the girl was climbing out onto the jetty. The Jain's tentacle was still plugged into her back. Once she was up on the jetty the Jain began to follow her.

"Box," said the girl, looking straight from the projection at Chapra and Abaron. "It is necessary that I speak with decision makers." There was nothing of a little girl in her voice. Over the com Chapra understood the precise selection of every word. She had asked, "What about the Jain?" She realised then that it might be the Jain itself that answered the question. She stared at the projection, noticed something else. "The machine, it's shrinking again isn't it?"

"Yes," replied Box. "There is water flow and an increase in contaminants."

"I'm going down there."

"Me too," said Abaron.

Here's the test, thought Chapra. He had not been in the isolation chamber since that worm-thing had taken a chunk out of his arm. She watched him stomp out ahead of her and waited for the door to close.

"Was that true . . . about the runcible?" she asked.

"Would I lie?" asked Box.

Chapra said nothing as she followed Abaron. She was well aware that AIs sacrificed human lives for the greater good of humanity. She did not find this knowledge comforting.

As she stepped through the airlock, Chapra caught the tail end of a conversation between the girl, or rather the Jain, and Box. She understood none of it because it ran at high speed. It finished shortly after she and Abaron walked out onto the jetty. She felt suddenly superfluous. Information had already been exchanged, decisions made. The girl turned to her and Chapra saw a girl with her own character and a mind possibly superior to Chapra's own. Yet the Jain, lying there on the end of the jetty with its weird head turned towards them, was looking through the girl, who to it was just a tool, a lens to bring them into focus for it.

"I have told the Jain of the Separatist ship," said Box.

"And?" asked Chapra.

"The Jain wishes to be transported to the surface of the planet, which was its wish before I told it about the ship."

"Why does it want to go there?" asked Abaron.

Chapra glanced at him and saw that he was staring intently at the Jain. His fear was gone. There was hungry fascination in his regard.

"Why I wish to go to the surface is not relevant. Under Polity law you do not have the right to detain me, and I can also demand transport to the nearest habitable planet, which for me is Haden."

Both Chapra and Abaron stared at the girl for a long moment. It was pointless asking how she . . . it, knew so much about Polity law.

"You are aware of the threat posed to you by the Separatist ship?" she asked.

"I am aware that on this ship I am in greater danger than I would be in the sea below. None of your kind have scanners sensitive enough to detect me in that sea, and should a search be initiated I would much more easily be able to evade it or defend myself."

"Solves a couple of problems," said Abaron. "The Jain can hide from them down there and they've no reason to attack us without the Jain aboard."

Chapra glanced at him. He was naïve and in this situation that could be dangerous. "They are not coming here to kill the Jain just because they're xenocides, but to prevent Jain technology getting into Polity hands, which they'll view as just a bigger stick for ECS to beat them with. They won't risk letting us get away. Even with the Jain gone we might already have learned something vital or have acquired some super-science device. There is no doubt that they will try to destroy this ship."

"Then we have to run," said Abaron, taking the lecture well.

"After dropping our friend off," said Chapra, then, "Box, do you have a shuttle ready?"

"Yes," said Box. "Judd will pilot it. The Jain will depart when its machine is small enough to transport."

"I do not require a pilot," said the girl/Jain.

"The shuttle is Polity property and requires a Polity pilot."

Chapra wondered about that. Why did Box want Judd as a pilot? The Golem certainly would not be coming back before the Separatist ship arrived. To try and keep track of the Jain? Or was Judd's purpose more sinister? Maybe the people on that other ship had come here to kidnap and steal rather than kill and destroy. Chapra was sickened by the thought of Separatists getting hold of Jain technology. How much would Polity AIs dislike that prospect? Would they be prepared to kill the Jain to prevent it? And who was to say the Jain would not go willingly? What did it care about human politics?

The Jain, through the girl, said no more. Its tentacle detached and it slid into the water. The girl staggered then regained her balance. Her face took on a more juvenile appearance. She smiled at Chapra and Abaron, then sat down on the edge of the jetty and dangled her feet in the boiling water. The Jain wrapped itself round its machine almost as if sulking.

The Vorstra runcible sat under a clear dome in a lunarscape etched with sharp-edged shadows. Lakes of silver dust patched the surface, their source the slow crumbling of crowded rock spires. Normally this was a place of interminably slow change and stillness, but now the lakes were moving under the influence of another moon.

Alexion Smith stood before the bull's horns of the runcible, a carry sack slung over one shoulder, and his hand in the pocket of his baggy trousers. His associates often said he was as much an anachronism as the things he studied. Such criticism was far from his mind at that moment. He gazed up through the dome at a distant silver sphere, and replayed in his mind a comment made by a harried-looking runcible technician:

"Damned thing's perturbed our orbit, but they said they'd reposition us before moving off."

The *Cable Hogue* was huge. Alexion had never seen any ship this size, had thought them only the product of holofiction producers and conspiracy theory junkies. With a shake of his head he stepped up onto the black glass dais and through the shimmer of the Skaidon warp. Shortly afterwards the Vorstra moon shuddered in its orbit and the *Hogue* moved away. An hour later the burn of Laumer engines lit up the sky. In later years, Alexion was delighted to learn that Jain artefacts had been washed up on the shores of the dust lakes. Providential, somehow.

PART FIVE

Floating in an observation blister Chapra watched an aqualanding shuttle drop out of its bay towards the blue and white glare of the planet. She watched the triangle of it grow small and dark in silhouette, then glow and trail vapour as it hit atmosphere and slid into its orbital glide. Judd piloted. The Jain crouched in a cargo bay half filled with saline heated to a nice ninety-seven degrees Celsius. In its many-fingered hand it clutched its creation device shrunk down to the size of a human fist. Chapra smiled at that. How we define things: when it was large it was a machine and small it is a device. What then was the girl now the Jain had left her, now she seemed to have some character of her own? Did individuality mean anything when thought of in connection with the Jain? Could she be an individual, or would that be like calling someone with a severed corpus callosum two separate beings, two individuals? Perhaps so. It was too easy to look at her and see a human girl when she was really a mask over something wholly alien.

"Why did it leave her, Box?" she asked.

"To watch, to learn, to gather information."

As the AI said this, Chapra felt the slight surge as the ion drive ignited. She saw the flare far to her right like a sunrise and watched as the planet, with apparent slowness, slid aside.

"She could be destroyed along with us."

"The Jain can make another whenever it wants."

And that brought it home.

"Make another what?" asked Abaron, coming into the blister and catching hold of one of the frame bars as he stepped out of the ship's artificial gravity. "We're picking up G," he observed. Both of them looked to the black macula, in the reactive glass, where the sun was.

"Girl," said Chapra.

"It's not so worrying," said Abaron. "Humans make humans all the time and are they any more responsible?"

"How very mature of you," said Chapra with a grin, then a wider grin at his irritation.

"I will be starting ramscoop drive in twenty minutes. It would be better if you were inside the ship at that time," said Box.

Abaron led the way from the blister. They stepped from it into the corridor gravity of the ship and both turned toward the control room.

"How long before we go translight?" asked Chapra.

"Three hours," the ship AI told them, and as they entered the control room it went on to say, "You may be interested to know that I have received genetic maps of the five seaweeds from Earth and compared them to the samples from the planet and the ones in the isolation chamber."

"How old?" asked Chapra.

Box went on, "Cross referencing certain structures, and taking into account mutational variables, I have a extrapolation graph that peaks at four point seven three million years. This would seem to confirm that the Jain's point of origin in the escape pod was this system and that it has been in stasis for the aforementioned time."

"Damn," said Chapra.

"What's the problem with that?" asked Abaron.

"Not that . . . we just never got round to asking why it ended up in an escape pod in the first place. We know lots about what it is and what it can do, but nothing about what it was and what it did."

"I asked," said Box.

"Well?" said Chapra when Box did not go on.

"Haden is a Jain world, but not the Jain home world. Originally it was two AU from the sun. The Jain we rescued was here to Jainform it. Using its starship it towed the world to its present position and over a period I estimate to be nearly ten thousand years it seeded it with the kinds of life the Jain like. While it was seeding the world an enemy attacked and destroyed its ship. It managed to get away in the escape pod."

Chapra gave Abaron a look, then sat and tried to absorb that: a ship that could tow worlds about . . . spending ten thousand years seeding a planet . . . and an enemy that could destroy such a ship, defeat a Jain.

"Is there anything more about the enemy?" asked Abaron, putting his finger straight on a fear: more superior aliens.

"The enemy was another Jain."

And of course that was right. The Polity was huge and ever-expanding and humans had encountered many alien life forms, but the greatest enemy had remained the same: other humans. Chapra smiled. Not so damned superior after all. She flicked a couple of touch controls and summoned up views back down the length of the ship. These showed a plain of ceramal scattered with instrumentation, then the tail fading into distance. She always enjoyed watching the ramscoop engines starting: the vast orange wings of force opening out through space. At that moment she could see only the white coronal glare of the ion drive shoving the *Box* up to scoop speeds. The ramscoop would then power the fusion engines to shove it up to a speed where the translight engines could get a grip on the very fabric of space and pull the ship through into underspace. Chapra did not want to be watching the projection then. She glanced across as something at the edge of the projection caught her eye. There was a flickering there—spacial distortions.

"There has been a miscalculation," said Box.

Chapra waited. She was getting used to Box's conversational grenades. She watched, without really seeing, as a wedge of midnight entered realspace, opened ramscoop wings then stood on its tip on fusion fire, braking into the Haden system.

"The Separatist ship is here now," Box told them.

With a flash the projection disappeared and in the same moment the ship shuddered. Chapra clutched at her chair as she felt the gravity shift. Something was out. She could feel the surge as the ship changed direction. A sudden dragging force. An explosion.

"Shuttle in bay six is ready for launch," said Box.

Chapra clutched her chair. So, why did she need to know that?

"Come on!" Abaron yelled, grabbing her arm. Then it all hit home. They were being attacked. The *Schrödinger's Box* was being destroyed. She stood and ran with Abaron to bay six. The gravity kept fluctuating and the way they ran might have appeared comical at any other time, anywhere else. Great hollow booms echoed from deep in the ship, and she heard distant clangs of metal falling. Chapra felt changes in pressure. Her ears popped, which was terror for anyone who knew space. Hull breach. They reached the irised hatch to bay six. It was firmly closed and would not open on command nor at the controls.

"Box!" Abaron yelled.

Chapra shook her head. This was happening, this was real, she had to accept it. She turned. In the corridor; a shape moving very fast. It was Rhys carrying the girl under his arm. The Golem jerked to an abrupt halt by them and released the girl. She reached out and grabbed Chapra's hand.

"Step away from the door," said Rhys, and raised his singun. The weapon made no sound. A fleck of black appeared in the centre of the door and the door screamed as it folded; a sheet of paper crumpled by a fist. Then the door, now a wrinkled ovoid of metal, thumped to the floor. Rhys held out the gun to Abaron. "Here," he said. Abaron shook his head. Rhys handed it to Chapra. The butt felt slick and the gun was heavy. It was horribly real.

"Aren't you coming with us?" she asked.

The Golem grinned at her and fled away down a corridor that now seemed to be twisting, splitting. More explosions. They ran into the huge bay and gaped out through a shimmer-shield at a passing vast shape, and the burning of hellish fires. The shuttle crouched like an iron sparrow hiding from the raptor outside. Abaron opened the door. Inside, the girl refused Chapra's help and strapped herself in. Chapra dropped the gun into a wall pouch. Abaron stared at the controls, his hands clenching and unclenching. Chapra pushed him aside and sat in the pilot's chair. He took the one next to it. As they strapped in, something crashed and violet fire flared to one side of the bay. The shuttle began to slide down a tilted gravity field.

"Now!" screamed Abaron.

Chapra used override to knock out the shimmer-shield. The bay full of air exploded into vacuum, sucking the shuttle out into a Dante night. The acceleration slammed the three of them back into their seats and something went crashing down in the back of the shuttle. Chapra reached and grabbed the control column and using booster steering wrenched the shuttle in the opposite direction from that passing shape. Wreckage was spewing across space, fragments and molten metal, nebulous sheets of fire with no gravity to give them shape, then clear space. Chapra ignited the shuttle's small but powerful ionic drive. The huge wedge and the fragmenting *Box* fled behind them. She adjusted their course as now there was only one place to hide. The moons in the system were too small and the only other planet was no option at all it being a gas giant. Chapra tapped controls and one half of the screen showed a reverse view. The wedge was close to the *Box,* enfilading it with missiles. It wasn't using lasers on the big ship, nor particle weapons. Missiles were much less wasteful of energy, and much more destructive. Chapra was immediately reminded of the PSR chopping up the sphere of ice in which the Jain had slept. This looked almost surgical—what they saw of it before the screen whited-out.

"What was that?" asked Abaron.

"Laser. Burnt out all our external coms," said Chapra. She kept the acceleration on and checked a reading from the radar, which did not have enough of its delicate parts outside to be wiped out. Two shapes were accelerating after them. She only hoped they would not have the fuel to sustain that acceleration.

"Smart missiles," said Abaron, his face white and beaded with sweat.

"Yes."

They sat in silence watching the trace from the missiles grow stronger, then strong enough for them to see the shape and smooth beauty of these clever weapons. They were close. Chapra was white-knuckling the throttle for the ion drive. There was no way to get anything more out of it. Five wracked-out minutes passed before they realised the missiles were getting no closer.

"How long can we keep this up?" asked Abaron.

"Not much longer. We have to decelerate for the planet."

"If we do that they'll get us."

Chapra nodded and from the instrument readings did a high-speed calculation in her head. In twenty minutes they must begin to decelerate or they would not be able to go into orbit. Not landing was out of the question because there just was not enough fuel for them to keep on running until the *Cable Hogue* arrived. She realised she had no answers. Unless the missiles ran out of fuel they were dead.

"What do we do?" asked Abaron, obviously willing to defer to her authority. Chapra was about to tell him she did not know, but suddenly she did.

"This shuttle and the missiles are both at maximum acceleration," she said. She looked at him. "Do you think you can handle the controls. Delicately?"

"What do you want?" he asked.

"On my signal I want you to reduce our acceleration and bring the missiles in as close as you can. Fifty metres. Less if you think you can do it."

"What are you going to do?"

"Those missiles are probably the same as are being fired at the *Box*—hull piercers. Detonating them that close to us shouldn't do us any harm."

"How do you know that?" he asked dully.

"I'm old. I did other jobs before I studied xenology," she said.

"How are you going to detonate them?"

Chapra smiled at him, a little crazily, she thought, as she clamped down on that smile. "I'm going to shoot them with the singun."

Chapra got out of the pilot's chair and Abaron took over the controls. She went back into the main cabin where the girl watched her intently as she donned a spacesuit. The singun was heavy and she set its controls to the maximum. The singularity would last a full three seconds with each shot. She stepped into the airlock, attached a safety line, then over the suit com said, "I'm going out there now. Start reducing acceleration—gently—in about a minute."

Out of the artificial gravity of the shuttle Chapra felt the tug of acceleration. It felt to her as if she was leaning out the window of a tower and looking down into fire and darkness. Holding tightly to the singun she rested her arms down the hull and aimed beyond the ionic glare of the shuttle's engines. Acceleration dropped, then dropped again. Two silvery nubs rose up out of the darkness. She aimed at them and saw the range-finder on the gun going crazy as the ionic halo confused it. She fired and fired again, black bars cut through the glare. She swore, aimed carefully, fired a third time. Her visor polarised. One missile disappeared in a brief flash and the other missile tumbled away. Chapra quickly pulled herself back inside. Her arms and face were burning and she wondered just how many rads she had taken. Inside the shuttle and out of the suit, Chapra rubbed emollient cream on her face. Her arms had been heated inside the suit, but had not burned. She reckoned her face would peel, though funnily enough, the skin under her caste mark was unburned.

"You got them," said the girl. "We're safe now."

"I wish I could agree with you," said Chapra, stepping up into the control cockpit. She grinned at Abaron, but saw he did not look happy. "What is it?" she asked. He was studying the radar display.

"We're ahead of it at the moment, but there's a craft coming after us."

"Not missiles?"

"No."

Chapra sat down and began using the onboard computer. "We'll be able to get into orbit and land before it catches us. We'll be a couple of hours ahead of it."

"Will that help?"

"Of course it will."

Chapra's smile was set. She thought about infrared tracking and scanning, about the weapons that craft might have. She checked the time piece under her fingernail. They had roughly fifty hours until the *Cable Hogue* arrived. They just had to survive that long.

In high definition hologram *Schrödinger's Box* died. It drifted in space surrounded by a swarm of smart missiles and a spreading halo of dispersing air and water crystals. Occasionally a missile or two would detache from the swarm, dart in through the laser defence to pierce the hull and detonate far inside. The long tail of the ship had broken away as had many of the external sensors and probe ports. There were gaping holes in the hull rimmed with skeletal members black over red internal fires.

"There's a com laser in the nose section," said Speck, his hands moving in a caress across the weapons console. A smart missile moved in close, flashing red in coms laser fire. Another went in underneath it like a pack dog going for the underbelly. It flashed and, trailed vapour, detonated above the science vessel's skin. That area of the hologram went black for a moment, then cleared to reveal a warped and glowing area of hull. "It's down. Couple more like that to deal with and we can send one of the General's gunships across."

Kellor glanced at Conard then returned his attention to the hologram. It wasn't enough that the ship was gutted: Conard wanted no less than total annihilation, which on a ship of that size was a demolition job rather than an attack.

"There won't be anyone alive over there," Kellor said, just for the hell of it. "They're away in that shuttle."

"That will soon be remedied. I have some of my best men on it," said Conard tersely.

Kellor smiled to himself. He had met the soldier Beredec and immediately recognised a career mercenary. Conard's best men were not the usual Confederation grunts. Conard went on, "There is no-one alive over there, but there are AIs. I want them all." He turned to one of his aides. "Take four men over with you. Let Davis carry the CTD."

The aide grinned nastily and turned on his heel. Kellor looked at Jurens, who pressed a thumb against his chest then tapped the knife at his belt. Kellor gave a slight nod and Jurens grinned, exposing artificially white teeth in his bearded face. He had lost his original set to an officer just like that aide.

Atmosphere thundered against the ceramic undersides of the shuttle's stubby wings and wide body. Haden was an orange and white arc cutting the screen in two. Around the edges of the screen was a red glow from the heating hull. They had managed to dump velocity with ion engine braking but were still entering atmosphere at design limits. The shuttle gravity was sluggish to compensate for this kind of treatment and they were not completely cushioned from the violence of entry into atmosphere.

"It's going to have to be the sea," said Chapra. "We won't be able to get the speed down enough for a vertical landing. Take too long. I suggest we all get into full environment suits." She did not comment on their chances of surviving in a sea of boiling water if the shuttle broke up. Perhaps it would be better not to wear a suit at all then death would be quicker.

"Can't you use the AG units to slow us?" asked Abaron.

"A little, if I tilt them. We don't want to end up skating across the gravity field else we'll take as long to slow as if we'd stayed airborne."

Abaron nodded then went back into the passenger compartment. He was gone for a little while before he returned wearing an environment suit with the visor flipped up and carrying another suit for Chapra.

"I almost forget," he said.

"What?"

He gestured with a thumb into the passenger compartment. "She doesn't need one."

Chapra nodded, then handed the controls over to him while she pulled on her suit. In a short time the view through the screen was of the crinkles of mountains, red flat deserts and jungles of light green vegetation. The sun was bright orange, oblate, and its corona filled half the sky with concentric bands of its refracted spectrum. The rest of the sky was a red ochre that reminded of African earth.

"Are you well-strapped in back there?" Chapra asked.

"I am," replied the girl.

"Okay, be ready to be thrown about a bit. We're landing on the ocean and internal gravity is unlikely to be able to compensate quickly enough. Could be bumpy."

"I am prepared," said the girl, which was not really a little girl sort of thing to say.

The edge of the land mass came into view. An orange sea foamed against slabs of rock and wide sandy beaches. Out beyond this they lost sight of the sea as Chapra turned the shuttle to its optimum braking attitude. The constant roar increased in pitch and hot sparks of something skated across the screens.

"I'm using braking thrusters!" she shouted over the noise. The braking thrusters added to the roar and the labouring AG units, normally only used for gentle manoeuvring, made a deep thrumming sound. There was no perceptible change of velocity.

"Going in!"

The noise was terrible. They were jerked forward against their straps, flung back. Spray and volatile water foamed across the screen. Then the nose abruptly dipped and ploughed into the sea. A hand of force flung them forwards again and held them against their straps. Chapra could not get her breath. The pressure was huge, and this was with the shuttle gravity compensating, unless it was out. How was the shuttle holding together? The roar went on and on then slowly started to diminish. The pressure came off, and as it did so, Chapra turned off the AG. She looked up. Spray quickly slewed from the screen's frictionless surface. The braking thrusters were slowly bringing them to a halt. Outside was a rolling sea. A quarter kilometre ahead of them was one of a wide scattering of jungle-covered atolls. Chapra checked the radar and shivered when she saw how many of them they had missed.

"We've got a couple of leaks," said Abaron. "Automatics are dealing with them."

Chapra studied a schematic on one of the lower screens. There were more than a couple of leaks. She made some adjustments.

"I'm bringing up internal pressure to match," she said. "What's the mix out there?"

Abaron said, "We could breathe it if it was cooled down a bit."

"Funny man."

"I'm a barrel of laughs. By the way, we're sinking."

Chapra compensated with the AG; making the shuttle light as a wooden ship so it floated and bobbed on the sea. They both peered through the screen. It was Earthlike out there, yet, only the two atmospheres of pressure kept the sea from boiling. If they stepped outside the shuttle without environment suits the heat would flay them. They might survive for a few minutes while they were being boiled alive. Chapra swallowed dryly. And they must go out there.

"That's it," she said, and flicked off the braking thrusters. For a moment there was quiet then she turned on external microphones and the shuttle filled with the sound of sea. Only the sea gulls were missing.

"What have we got?" asked Abaron as he unstrapped himself.

"The edge of the continent is twenty kilometres away. We should be able to get there on AG and thrusters in about an hour." She checked the time. "Forty-five hours before the *Cable Hogue* gets here." She increased the shuttle's AG and it rose higher, came out of the water, then using the thrusters in short burst she turned it on course for the continent. "You sort out some travelling packs: medical supplies, food, spare power packs for the suits. Jesu! Will you look at that!"

Abaron leant forward and looked down at the sea. Tentacles thrashing the sea's surface and just below the waves a giant nautiloid was dragging down a huge lobster-thing with a long eel's tail and more legs than seemed probable.

"I'm glad you didn't suggest swimming," said Abaron.

Chapra glanced at him. He seemed almost happy. Perhaps he was enjoying the buzz.

Davis hurt and the painkilling patch on the side of his chest was not enough. Perhaps this was because of his previous overindulgence in such patches for recreation, though he wouldn't put it past Conard to order him under-dosed. He had a hidden supply, but dared not use it. He needed to keep his wits about him to survive the next few days. It would take very little provocation for Conard to set one of his trained dogs on him, and maybe it was the General's intention for Davis to die up this particular shit creek. His ribs were broken and not only was he likely under-dosed, he had been denied access to the bone welder. That he might come back to the ship with a punctured lung was the least of his worries. He wondered if he would be coming back at all.

"This is not a good day," said Artris, fingering the settings on his pulse gun. He too was one of Conard's least favourite soldiers.

"Surprise me," said Davis.

"There'll be Golem over there," Artris told them.

Davis moved all his weapon's energy settings up to their highest. His ribs started to ache even more.

"Golem?" said Jan, the youngster.

"Cut the chat back there!" yelled Conard's pet, Talist.

"Guess who'll be directing operations from the Junger," mumbled Artris.

Talist glanced round from the flight controls but said no more when the bay doors opened. The clang of docking clamps releasing shook the hull and the Junger moved slowly forward on its track. The soldiers closed down their masks limiting all talk to com.

"Out and away," said Talist. "ETA five minutes maximum."

Once the Junger was out past the doors and sliding into the light of the burning ship it accelerated and corrected. The wrecked science vessel came into view and rapidly grew in the screen. When Davis saw the size of it he once again wondered about the futility of the Separatist cause. This was just a science vessel and it was the size of a city. Polity battle ships were bigger, a lot bigger.

"God be with us," said Sheena, the other member of the troop. This elicited no reply.

"Weapons check," said Talist, then, "Davis, you take the CTD in."

It figured. Davis checked over his weapon then took up the chrome cylinder from its clamps on the floor and fixed it to his suit straps. There was no AG in the shuttle but the device seemed heavy. No one said anything more for the long five minutes.

Talist matched the ponderous spin of the *Box* then carefully manoeuvred the Junger to a cavity in the wall of wreckage.

"You all know what is expected of you. We want the CTD as near to the ship AI as you can get it. Just get in there and get the job done. Any trouble and I want to know about it right away."

Trouble started when they were halfway into the ship on their suit jets.

"What's that? Something moving above you, Artris," said Sheena.

Artris's weapon strobed and slagged wreckage, blew it into vacuum. The sound over the radio was like a diesel engine starting. Nearby something silver and spidery darted aside. Davis opened up, a line of flashes down a structural member, a blur of movement, and a silver leg spiralling through vacuum. Golem; without the hindrance of artificial skin, metal skeletons. One landed on Artris and he managed to yell before his breath gusted out through his smashed visor. He hung in vacuum struggling for breath he would not find as the Golem efficiently completed its task by opening up his suit from neck to crotch. Davis got it when it used Artris as a launch platform to come at him. Spewing molten metal it fell past him.

"What's going on in there!? What's happening!?"

"Golem. Got Artris. Shit! Over there! Move!"

The static from weapons fire drowned out anything else. They opened up their suit jets and traversed the corridor of wreckage at lethal speed. More Golem appeared out of the tangled metal. Subliminally Davis saw Sheena impaled on a stanchion, her blood a candy floss cloud all around her. He fired in bursts. Metal splashed like solder. Ceramal ship's skeleton retained white heat, sometimes warped. The CTD was a heavy pain against his ribs. Jan screamed as a skeletal silver hand slammed him to a halt. Even over the suit radio Davis heard breaking bone. Spinning in mid flight he hit that Golem once and it released Jan. Out of control the boy slammed into a metal wall.

"I've got a leak! I've got a leak!" he had time to yell before a Golem came running past on magnetic feet and kicked the helmet from his head. Davis tumbled through the air, his suit warning bleeping as a laser flashed across his legs. He was in a chamber near the centre. As he got himself under control he saw a ship's runcible below his feet. It was operating when it should have nowhere to open to. Perhaps that was where the dark-skinned Golem was going with the silver ovoid of the ship AI: nowhere. Davis aimed at them but did not fire. The Golem stared at him, perhaps expecting to die. Davis glanced at the CTD display as it told him in glowing letters that it was armed and how so very little time he had left to live. Talist was probably halfway back to the *Samurai* even now. Davis released the straps and kicked the device away. So the runcible might be open on nothing and no one ever came back from that. But who was to say no one ever survived? To the best of his knowledge no one survived a CTD blast at this range. He slammed on his suit jets and followed the Golem and the AI through the cusp. He entered blackness on the edge of white-hot light.

"You know, we really should think of a name for you," said Abaron as he released the girl's safety straps. She smiled at him and sat on the edge of her seat.

"How about Jane?" she suggested.

"Hah!" Abaron surprised himself with that bark of laughter. But then in the last few hours he had been surprising himself a lot. He had never before felt so alive.

"Chapra, what do you think?"

"Think about what?"

"A name for our friend here. She suggests 'Jane'."

"Sounds fine to me. Have you got those packs ready yet, Tarzan?"

"Sorry?"

"Never mind."

Abaron looked down at the two packs. He had tried to cover every conceivable bet, but there was so much they could not take. He put the packs next to the airlock then turned back to the girl. "I think it might be an idea to put you in a suit anyway, Jane. What do you think?"

"It will offer some protection, though obviously I do not need it for the same purpose as yourselves."

Abaron winced, realising he was patronising her. She might look like a little girl, but in that body was an alien mind probably far superior to his own. He pulled a small suit from a locker and handed it to her. Without assistance she put it on and reduced it at all the expansion points. Shortly after he felt the thrusters cut out and the AG go off. Chapra came through from the cockpit.

"Let's move it," she said. "We've only half an hour to get clear of the shuttle. That other craft is nearly here."

Abaron pulled his visor down and popped the inner door. He took up both packs and handed one to Chapra. He noted the singun hung on her utility belt. He went first into the lock, and remembering those monsters they had seen in the sea, pulled a short range cutting laser from his pack and held it ready as he opened the outer door.

Nothing immediately attacked. The shuttle was up on a beach of red sand scattered with nautiloid shells up to a metre across, into the cover of which scurried thumb-sized lobster things as soon as he stepped out. Two steps from the lock he looked out to sea at the swarm of atolls and saw the heave and glistening backs of great beasts swimming between them. Inland towered trees the size of redwoods, but with globular blue objects on their branches rather than needles. Jammed between these giants was a tangle of life that on Earth would have consisted of smaller trees, bushes, and vines. The only resemblance these growths bore to such was that they filled the same niche. It seemed a frightening place to negotiate and a perfect place to hide. Abaron wondered what creatures were making the racket of groans and shrieks issuing from there. Soon Jane and Chapra joined him. Chapra led the way into the hot shadows under the trees. There she drew the singun and aimed it at something on the ground. Abaron stepped forward in time to see a giant leech heaving itself out of her way.

Half an hour into the tangle Abaron was thoroughly grateful for his suit's impenetrable fabric and the hard chainglass visor. There were insectile horrors here: blood-suckers and flesh eaters with all their cutlery in their mouths. Beetles as big as hiking boots landed on him and immediately tried to bite him. His chest ached where a wingless mosquito-thing the size of a cat leapt up and tried to ram into him probosces like the barrels of a shotgun. That thing he cut away with the laser before it broke his ribs. Chapra twice used the singun on things charging out at them with intent that did not seem joyous greeting. They bore appearance of Rottweilers crossed with hornets, before the singularity converted them to sludge. The expected danger revealed itself to them when they had been travelling for an our.

The explosion was loud and brief, and it silenced the jungle racket for a few minutes.

"The shuttle," said Chapra.

"Will they come after us?" asked Abaron, then he fell silent at the sound of boosters overhead. The three of them stood waiting. They could see nothing through the foliage. Nearby an actinic flash then blast was followed by the monolithic fall of a great tree.

"Can they detect us?" asked Abaron.

"Only if our suits leak, and then it won't matter to us."

"Suits?"

"They could use infrared and maybe pick up cold spots, even then . . . " Chapra gestured up at the thick foliage.

The next explosion was close. A lightning flash, and a hand of force knocked Abaron stumbling. It hurled Jane to the ground and knocked Chapra against a tree.

"Oh shit! Run!" shouted Chapra, and she led the way to the right.

"I thought you said they can't detect us!" yelled Abaron.

"The gun!" Chapra yelled back. "Both those explosions were where I shot those things! It uses an underspace tech to open the singularity! That's what they're picking up!"

Another explosion behind, this time in a straight line from the last two. Gasping, they eventually stumbled to a halt, and rested at the base of one of the forest giants. When they moved on again it was to the distant and repeated sound of explosions and a loud sawing sound that Chapra identified as a particle beam fired in atmosphere. Shortly after that, sparks and smoke boiled out of the jungle, driving out swarms of creatures. The three had to flee as well—back towards the shore. One look at the white fire consuming the trees was enough to tell them their suits would never survive it. Near the beach, attacking hornet-dogs forced Chapra to use the singun again. Immediately lasers droned in the air and turned the dog-things into exploding ash.

"Stay exactly where you are! You have been targeted!"

The ship slid above them. It was an old-style AG gunship but no less effective for that. Chapra stood with the singun at her side. Abaron waited for her to raise it and for the three of them to die.

"Throw the weapon to your right!"

The ground suddenly boiled in front of Chapra. She threw the singun to her right. The gunship came down on the beach, its gun turrets locked on them every moment. Abruptly Jane screamed. Abaron turned, thinking she had been fired on, saw she had pulled off her visor and hood and ripped open the front of her suit. She was staggering away. Her face and chest were bright red. She screamed again and fell to the ground. Abaron and Chapra exchanged a look, then looked back at the gunship as its hatch popped and four people came out carrying pulsed-energy assault rifles.

"Move forward," one of them said, then, "You, drop the laser cutter!"

Abaron let go of the thing as if it was hot. He had forgotten he was holding it. He and Chapra moved forward as instructed.

"Right, lay face down with your arms and legs spread."

They did as instructed. Abaron heard one of them move over to Jane.

"She's dead, sir. No pulse."

"What the hell did she do that for? She's just a girl."

Dead, thought Abaron, no, she had probably just turned her heart off for a moment.

"What'll we do with her, sir?"

"Just leave her. Find the weapon, it was an EC singun."

Abaron heard the greed in that voice. Of course the Separatists would be very glad to get their hands on that kind of weapons technology. He lay there staring at one of the thumb-lobsters as it checked out his visor with its feelers. He wondered if they would be killed here on the beach or if they were to be questioned first.

"I can't find it, sir."

"Then try harder you—what the fuck is that!"

There was a brief yell cut off by a sucking explosion. Abaron heard the sound of something moving in the sea and thought about monsters. There were two more screams and they carried on; dreadful panicked screaming. Abaron pushed himself to his feet shortly before Chapra. The beach was alive with movement. Worms coiled in the sand and leapt serpent fast. One their captors staggered past, blood pouring from holes in his environment suit, other worms flicking away from him, others attaching. Abaron well knew what kind of worms could penetrate an environment suit. Another sucking explosion and a man disappeared and reappeared as a rain of organic slurry. Stuttering white fire from an assault rifle. Abaron turned and saw Jane cut in half at the waist. She fell away from her hips and legs, face-down in the sand, then calmly propped herself up with one arm and fired twice more. Of the four Separatists little remained but spreading stains on the sand; organic slurry that excited the thumb lobsters. Abaron grabbed up the laser cutter and ran for the craft, expecting to be cut down at any moment. Some of the worms hit him but did not bite. Inside the craft were two more Separatists. Shock and blood loss from hundreds of coin-sized holes the worms had punched into their bodies, had very quickly killed them. What remained of them hardly looked human.

Outside the gunship Abaron leant against the hull and tried very hard not to be sick in his suit. After a moment he looked to the sea and saw the Jain resting in the shallows, worm-things swarming in the water all around it. Beyond it, partially concealed by the reflection off the surface, Abaron could see a shell-mouth a couple of metres wide, at the end of a tube disappearing into the depths. He could not really grasp what that meant; couldn't make any sense of it.

"I thank you," he said, and nodded to it. The weird head dipped in reply, it seemed. Abaron went to Chapra who was by Jane.

"Get her legs," said Chapra, holding the girl upright.

Jane seemed quite calm about the fact that she had been cut in half. Get her legs? Abaron glanced aside to where the other half of her lay. Then he looked back to her.

"I can be repaired," she said.

Abaron picked up the legs, surprised at their weight. Chapra carried the top half. They took Jane to the Jain, who took her in its tentacles, pulled her under the sea, and into the mouth of its machine grown huge there. The worms went with it.

PART SIX

"Tell me about the Jain," said Diane.

"There is little provable fact. From the few artefacts discovered and from some cultural archaeology it is evident that their technology was . . . is far in advance of ours," said Alexion. He did not look away from the information scrolling up on the screen before him. It was just too fascinating: some things proven beyond doubt, others now possible, and so many more questions to ask. Alexion normally did not hold much of an opinion about the current political situation, but would gladly see the Separatists hung who might halt this lovely flow of information.

"Their nanotech is fantastic. It might easily be called picotech . . . "

"Are they warlike?"

Alexion looked round. "There's so much space. Why?"

"We are."

"We're stupid."

Diane shrugged.

"I suppose it is possible. God help anyone they declared war upon."

"Meaning?"

"As I said to Chapra, 'the Jain moved suns' and we're fairly sure of that. I have to wonder if a race capable of that kind of thing would have any enemies left at all."

Alexion returned to his work and Diane grimaced at the back of his head. They would be there soon, ahead of schedule because of the Laumer engines and ready to deal with an enemy they knew. Smith was with them on the off-chance they found an enemy they did not know. She wondered if he was aware of how closely his ideas and summations were being inspected by the *Hogue* AI. Thus thought of, that AI spoke to them in its gravelly voice.

"*Schrödinger's Box* destroyed. Am receiving extreme range runcible transmission."

"Seal containment sphere. Maximum security."

"Done."

Alexion looked round and Diane shrugged once again.

"Best guess as to what is coming through?" she asked him.

The AI answered her. "They are through. I have a Golem android, Box, and an armed Confederation soldier. . . . Disarmed."

Diane grinned. She turned to go.

"May I come with you? I think my studies have ended for now," asked Alexion.

Without stopping, Diane nodded. Side by side, they entered a drop shaft.

"In time that soldier may come to think of himself as very lucky," she said.

Dropping through the irised gravity field Alexion looked at her questioningly.

"In ship warfare there's little room for mercy and less room for prisoners. He may be the only one we leave alive."

Alexion shivered. Shortly after, in the containment sphere, he observed the Golem Rhys holding a pulse-rifle on the Confederation soldier. But the man was not up to much. He was flat on a four-gee gravplate, groaning weakly as blood ran from his flattened nose. Smith surmised that though the man might be glad to be alive, he was not particularly enjoying the experience just then.

The night sky of Haden was black and starless but light was provided by strange luminescence under the sea, igniting and going out, lighting large glassy shapes. The two human bodies lay on the sand, swarmed over by finger lobsters and flat black cruciform creatures moving as slowly as starfish. Abaron and Chapra sat inside the back of the gunship with the coolers on and their visors open. They had intended to eat here, but the mess in the cockpit and the smell circulated by the coolers scotched that idea.

"What other jobs did you do before you studied xenology then?" asked Abaron.

Chapra grinned. "I was an Earth Central Enforcer for twenty years, then a Monitor for another six."

Abaron tapped the controls before them with the metal spoon he had intended to use. "So you should be able to fly this."

"Yes, I can fly this. . . . You don't seem surprised."

"I'm beyond surprise."

The communicator beeped and a voice spoke out of it in gibberish.

"That's Faculan. He's asking someone called Beredec to respond."

"I wonder which one he was."

"Who knows? Anyway, there'll be more gunships down here before long."

"What next?"

"Back into the jungle. We—"

"What is it?"

Chapra wordlessly pointed out the screen at the naked figure striding from the sea.

"That didn't take long, not long at all," said Abaron.

Jane grinned up at them then disappeared from sight as she went to the airlock. They turned in their seats as she entered the ship.

"You've grown," said Chapra.

Her hair was longer. She was bigger. She had the body of a pubescent girl, only there was a hardness to her musculature that did not look quite right.

"Whole body growth accelerated the repair process," she said, then, "The artificial human, Judd, will be coming here in his shuttle to lead you to a place of safety."

"Lead?" asked Chapra.

"It might be prudent to bring this gunship."

"How long before he gets here?" said Abaron, climbing to his feet.

"Judd will be here in ten minutes."

Chapra stared at Jane. She looked so different. She was beautiful, and she would make a beautiful adult. "Do you want clothing?" she asked, then wondered at her impulses.

"That won't be necessary."

Abaron grinned at Chapra, who ignored him.

"Let's get out of here for a while," she said, looking round at the blood-bespattered cockpit.

"Don't you need to familiarise yourself?" Abaron asked.

"No need."

They filed back outside after Jane. The sand was now swarming with the thumb-lobsters and cruciform fish, and watching these scrape up the gory sand they did not attend to their surroundings closely enough. One of the giant wingless mosquitoes attacked Jane. She caught it, almost negligently, then tore it in half without a word before pointed out the shuttle as it glided toward them just a few metres above the sea.

"Strong," said Abaron.

Chapra only nodded.

The shuttle beached with a deep grinding crunching as the AG cut and allowed the full weight down on the sand. Judd came out through the airlock.

"I am here to lead you to a place of potential safety," he said.

Chapra thought that a strange way of wording it. The Golem also seemed twitchy to her. There was something wrong with it. Had the Jain damaged it?

"We only need to hide for a day or so." She checked her timepiece. "ECS are punctual if nothing else and I can't see that ship standing up to a dreadnought."

Judd stood there blinking at her.

"What's the problem, Judd?" she asked.

Judd said, "I do not have Box to advise me so I do not know if facts should be concealed from you. I have very little practical or theoretical human psychology."

Chapra absorbed that but Abaron looked shocked. Chapra remembered how she had felt on first discovering that AIs could lie, cheat, and kill just like humans. The only difference was that AIs did it with firm purpose, and were better at it.

"If it concerns our survival then facts should not be concealed. Trust me, I'm a scientist," said Chapra, then felt a sinking sensation when Judd did not acknowledge humour. It was bad.

"The situation is not amenable to survival," said the Golem.

"Clarify."

"The *Cable Hogue* arrived forty hours ahead of schedule and now stands within striking distance of the Separatist ship. It will not strike because the Separatist ship is carrying CTDs and is threatening to use them on the planet."

"Sounds like a stand-off to me."

"The Separatist in charge is General David Conard. His gunships are even now entering atmosphere. I project that he intends to destroy us and the Jain. If he does not succeed with the gunships he will use atomics. If he does not succeed with atomics he will use the CTDs. If the *Cable Hogue* intervenes he will use the CTDs anyway."

"But that's crazy!" said Abaron. "If they do that they won't get away from here."

"Who ever accused Separatists of sanity?" said Chapra, and turned to walk to the gunship. Jane went with Judd. Abaron followed Chapra. We humans should stick together, she thought, we get on so well.

Kellor stared at the read-outs. Nothing.

"Any reply yet?" he asked communications officer Speck.

"Nothing for us, and I can't pick up anything else through those scramble fields."

"Any idea of what class we're up against?"

"Not a clue. It could be a shuttle behind that chaff or an Alpha dreadnought. At least they're holding off."

"Yeah, but for how long?"

"They'll hold off," said Conard. "This is a classic terrorist hostage situation."

Yes, thought Kellor, *and we all know the usual messy denouement of such situations: no win for anyone but the fanatics.* And this situation was getting messier every moment. First the four soldiers taken out in the CTD blast just, as far as Kellor could see, because they were at the top of Conard's shit list. Then the loss of contact with the shuttle planetside. Now this. It was time to resolve a thing or two. Before he could turn his attention to that Speck said, "Wait a minute. We've got a communication coming through."

"Put it through on holo," said Kellor, and turned his chair to a flickering cylinder appearing in the middle of the floor. In it resolved a woman's face. Kellor thought the captain of the ECS ship very attractive, in an Amazonian way.

"Who am I speaking to?" she asked.

Kellor glanced at Conard. Conard nodded.

"Speck, let the General talk to her," said Kellor.

Speck operated the controls to the ceiling holocamera. The woman's image turned toward Conard. In the bridge of the ECS ship Conard would now be projected.

"Conard," she said, and Kellor immediately noted a hardness to her face.

"Sergeant Windermere, you have risen through the ranks."

"No doubt they still call you The General."

"They do. What can I do for you, Windermere? You know the situation and you can do nothing. If you bring your ship any closer or intervene in any way, the three CTDs, which were stolen from the Droon complex on Titan, will be fired at this planet."

"I had hoped to appeal to some source of common sense there. You realise, Conard, that you won't get away from this one unless I allow you to go."

"What do you mean by that curious statement?"

"I've been authorised to allow you to pull away and leave unmolested so long as you do it now. So long as you call back those gunships."

"That would be so fine for you," spat Conard. "Then ECS can just drift on in and pick up a science to subjugate us all."

Ah, thought Kellor, *now this conversation is getting interesting.*

"What science? You destroyed the Jain and its machine when you destroyed the *Schrödinger's Box*."

"I cannot believe that your scientists learned nothing in that time."

"They learned a great deal and it was instantly transmitted into the net. By now the things they learned are common knowledge to thousands of researchers."

"I am supposed to believe that? ECS would not allow such technology into the public domain. No. I will make certain."

Conard signalled for communications to be cut.

The cave was huge. The sea flowed into it and the roof was fifty metres above. Chapra followed the shuttle inside and before it was necessary for her to turn on the gunship's lights, Judd put the shuttle down on a stony shore.

"I'm not sure I want to go out there," said Chapra.

Abaron nodded in agreement. On the shore stood two lobster creatures, each about three metres long.

"I bet they've got triangles on their backs," he said Chapra.

They both remained seated as Judd and Jane came over from the shuttle and boarded.

"The other gunships are very close. Why have you remained in here?" asked Jane.

"We were a little worried about them," said Abaron, pointing.

"They are the equivalent of your PSRs. They are here to demount the guns from this ship and set them for defence."

"Okay," said Abaron, and stood.

Chapra noted he had acquired a handgun from somewhere and tucked it in his utility belt.

"Come with me," said Judd once they were outside the ship, and he led them to the dark mouths of caves worn into the stone at the head of the dark beach. From behind them came a ripping crash. They turned to see that one of the lobster-things had ripped a gun turret out of the gunship. They turned back when Judd took up a veined sphere and shook it to produce a chemical light. As they entered the cave, Jane passed them on her way out. There must have been another entrance. When two Janes came walking toward them carrying objects like living rifles, they began to understand.

The Junger twenty-eight was a square-sectioned stubby cross with a spherical cockpit at one end. On the arms either side of the cockpit were sideways projecting gun turrets each containing one rapid-fire ten millimetre cannon and one pulsed laser. The cannon's rate of fire was adjustable from one to five thousand shells a second. Each spherical shell contained enough explosive to vaporise a human being. The lasers could cut a human being in half. Slung underneath were missiles that could not be used in the close confines of the cave for fear of collapsing it on the ship. The opposition had no such fears.

With a low droning the first Junger entered the cave as fast as its pilot dared in the confines. A burst of fire from its right turret gun jerked the shuttle fifty metres into the air and slammed it against the back of the cave. At that point a missile from a demounted launcher hit the Junger. The flash was brief and bright enough to blind. Molten metal and fragments of white hot ceramoplastics hit the walls of the cave. The next Junger went the same way and perhaps because it managed to take out the beached gunship two more followed it in. Rapid fire hit these. Bits of them hit the walls of the cave. When no more gunships followed, the two lobster-things with turret guns mounted on their backs, retreated into the smaller caves at the back of the beach. They were well clear by the time the incendiary missiles swarmed in and converted the main cavern into a furnace. They only came out of hiding when the bombardment had finished. A hot glow from molten spots on the walls lit the way for the soldiers who flew in using AG harnesses. The lobster things made a rain of human wreckage in the steam until there were no more bullets for their guns. They kept on aiming and firing, like the mechanisms they were. Pulsed energy fire cooked them on the beach.

The first soldier to encounter the enemy in the smaller caves hesitated too long. He just found it too difficult to open fire on a naked pubescent girl. The girl raised something like a metre-long razor fish and it repeatedly spat at him. The soldier hung in the air screaming as worms bored through his environment suit and into his flesh. The next soldier shot the girl, hurling her back with her chest burst open and jetting smoke. Then it was his turn to scream when the worms leaped from his comrade and started on him.

The General's aides were both young men, and probably very inexperienced. Kellor had noticed that people who did not feel secure in positions of power tended to gather other people around them who were not too much of a threat. He, on the other hand, felt completely secure and had as his first officer and com officer, Jurens and Speck, who were both hardened mercenaries with years of experience. Kellor glanced at Jurens and gave a slight nod when Talist, the aide Jurens had chosen, went to puke in the toilet just off the bridge, then returned his attention to Conard. There would be no sound from the toilet, but there might be a bit of a mess. Jurens' preference was a knife for close work.

The young man in the hologram was trying not to cry. Blood was pouring from two circular holes in his cheek and in the background other soldiers were screaming.

"Little girls!" yelled Conard. "Fucking worms!"

The whole incredible fiasco brought home to Kellor that there could be only one result now. There seemed no chance of him thieving some of this Jain technology, and he still had no idea who Conard's contact was. If he judged Conard right, the man would go tactical next, and if that didn't bring the ECS ship in, Christ knows what would. He glanced aside as Jurens came out of the toilet looking annoyed. Kellor attributed this to the patch of blood on his first officer's trousers—Jurens made a mess but was normally very good on not getting it on himself.

"We'll have to use the tacticals," said Conard.

It gave Kellor no satisfaction to be right. He gave the nod to Speck, who had moved close to the other aide. Speck preferred the garrotte for close work. He was so completely casual as he opened out the shining wire and looped it over the aide's head. One quick jerk and a ballet twist and step away. The aide staggered, making horrible gobbling sounds and spewing blood everywhere. His head still remained on his shoulders by dint of the garrotte stopping at his vertebrae. Conard spun round and saw the man stumble and fall: the spastic movements, the bubbling tube of an oesophagus sticking out where it should not. He turned back and froze, staring into the hollow-mirrored cube that was the hole-making end of Kellor's favourite little plasma gun. Kellor smiled. That moment again.

"No tacticals," he said. "Tell him."

Conard glanced at the hologram. The young soldier could only see Conard, and was too far gone in shock to know something was wrong.

Conard said, "Fire all the tactical nuclear weapons into that cave."

You've killed me, thought Kellor, then lowered his weapon and incinerated Conard's groin and thighs so the man dropped screaming to the deck. Speck quickly transferred the holocamera to Kellor.

"Obey that order and you won't get out of there alive," said Kellor to the soldier. "And if you return now there'll be a good bonus in it for you." He knew he'd made a mistake right from the first word. The soldier stared at him for a moment then cut com. Kellor looked down at Conard who had stopped screaming and was now groaning. There would have been no pain at first anyway, thought Kellor, though there was pain now. He deliberately stood on Conard's thigh so the cooked skin tore away from muscle. Conard started screaming again and scrabbled at his wrist holster. Kellor stamped on his hand then removed Conard's little gun. He'd almost forgotten about that.

The sounds of battle died though the screaming lasted for some time after. The Janes did not scream. They fought even with the most hideous wounds. Abaron had seen one of them stooping over a struggling soldier, choking the man with something. It was only when Abaron stepped in close and shot the man in the head that he realised the Jane had the stump of her wrist jammed in the man's mouth. That Jane had nodded her thanks and run back into the fray. Abaron retreated behind the slabs he and Chapra had chosen as their last place of defence.

"What's happening now?" he asked. "Have we won?"

"You heard what Judd said," said Chapra. She lay with the singun propped before her, staring out to where the cave was lit by luminescents spattered on the walls and floor. Suddenly she tensed, then relaxed. Judd and two Janes came quickly to join them.

"We must go deeper," said Judd.

"Oh my God," said Chapra, perhaps guessing.

The ground shifted and rock began to rain down. Abaron had time to see a wall of fire hurtling towards them before a Jane pushed him down and pressed herself over his head—protecting his precious brain. Without that protection his death might have been less protracted and painful.

"Have you got them on com yet!" yelled Kellor. He knew he was losing it. "For Chrissake try again!"

Speck kept sending, kept trying to get something.

"Shut up!" yelled Kellor and fired once, silencing Conard's crying. He turned back to the com consoles and screens. Tactical nukes, a hundred square kilometres incinerated. Thank Christ the CTDs remained aboard under ship control. He peered at the readouts on another screen. Nothing but chaff and fuzz. Well, if the ECS ship attacked he'd make a fight of it, maybe get away . . . Then the *Cable Hogue* shut down its screens and jamming. There was an energy surge. Some kind of particle weapon. All the screens went out for a moment. When they re-established Kellor saw that the remaining gunships were now just metallic fog.

"Get us out of here!" he screamed at Jurens as he reached for the controls to the CTD launcher. Perhaps it would delay . . . perhaps . . .

"Oh Christ," said Speck, dull horror in his voice.

The sheer hopelessness of the situation made Kellor hesitate for a moment, a second. In that second he knew how they had felt, all those opponents, in their moment of defeat. And in that second the dreadnought wrenched the *Samurai* from orbit, killing most of its crew with the massive acceleration. The flattened and distorted ship left a trail of fire across space, then rode a light-speed gravity wave towards the sun, where the antimatter in the CTDs would make not a wit of difference. The nine minutes of that journey were the longest of Kellor's life as his shattered body lay hard against the deck. With the ship inside the gravity wave he did not feel any more acceleration. What held him down was a fluke of broken computers and distorted conduits that had re-established artificial gravity at six gees.

He couldn't even scream.

Diana was still boiling. Vacillation and bloody incompetence and when there came the inevitable enquiry she knew they'd manage to make the shit stick to her. If she'd had her own way she'd have gone straight in and they wouldn't have had a chance to use nukes. She looked at the screen showing the blasted ground the shuttle overflew.

"How far?" she asked.

"Ten kilometres. We should be there in a few minutes, Captain," said the pilot, obviously a little nervous.

Diana snorted. Well perhaps they could salvage something from this mess. She glanced at Alexion, who had remained curiously reticent after witnessing the destruction of the mercenary ship. People took their first taste of war in different ways. His reaction to the ground blast had been a look of extreme pain. His precious Jain, gone.

The shore soon came into view and the pilot brought the shuttle down by the ATV parked there. Troops were standing by the ATV dressed in full environment and radiation suits. Diana pulled down the visor on her gear and headed for the lock. Alexion meekly followed.

"Where is it?" she asked the commander, before he had a chance to salute. The man pointed down the beach. "Okay, let's have a look." Diana walked down the ash-covered sand to the figure sat upon a rock.

"Which one are you?" she asked.

Its soft outer covering had been burned away and what remained was a seared metal skeleton containing the sealed mechanisms of its existence. It regarded her with brown lidless eyes set in its blackened skull. Its white teeth were stained, and because its lips were gone it seemed to be grinning.

"I am Judd," it rasped at her, black flakes shooting from its mouth.

"What happened to them, Judd? The other Golem, Chapra and Abaron?"

"Died. All died."

"Chapra and Abaron are dead?"

"No."

"You said they died."

"Yes."

Obviously screwed, thought Diana. They might get something from its memory.

"What about the Jain? We know it wasn't killed in the ship." As she said this Diana surveyed the devastation and focused on the bloated creatures floating in the shallows. The neutron bursts had almost certainly done for the alien. It was now as much part of history as the rest of its kind. Perhaps Smith could excavate it. She returned her attention to Judd as the Golem raised a hand missing three fingers and pointed with the remaining one out to sea.

"Here. Soon."

Diana stared down at the sea. Abruptly she stood. Movement out there. She glanced at her soldiers as they nervously fingered their weapons. Something was coming out of the sea.

"Let's not have any more incidents," she said loudly.

It was red, whatever it was, and huge. It broke the surface like the back of a whale and ploughed in to the shore. A giant red worm, thought Diana, then remembered the description of the Jain machine.

"No shooting!" She turned on Alexion. "What the hell is that?"

It heaved up onto the beach, sending a wave of sea water that washed to Diana's boots. The mouth was three metres wide, speckled at the lips and iridescent white inside. The mouth of a long and impossible shell. The water drained away and Diana could see nothing deep inside but a gradual thickening of shadow.

"Christ knows," said Alexion.

Movement. Two shapes walking out—human shapes. Chapra and Abaron strode out of the Jain machine, the remains of their environment suits hanging on them in tatters, visors discarded, hoods pulled back. But were they Chapra and Abaron? How could they be alive? They were standing in temperatures that should take off their skins.

"You'd best come to the shuttle," said Diana, watching them intently.

Chapra stood before Diana. "We are human. He repaired us, rebuilt us."

Abaron said, "I guess he found it easier to alter us to survive here than to repair our suits."

Chapra turned to Alexion. "Alex, it's good to see you." She smiled and Diana saw Smith's strange look of yearning.

"It's good to see you. New body?"

A weak joke.

"I'm me," she said, that smile still there. "The Jain is very good at what it does. If anything I've been improved. So much is clear now. And this body . . . "

"What have you learnt?"

"A fraction. Some figure after the point. There's so much . . . I cannot explain . . . "

"Try."

"It will take time. Have you a century or so free?"

Alexion stepped forward, impulsively Diana thought. She caught his shoulder and halted him. He turned to her. "I have to do this. In my research the questions always outnumber the answers. Always. You can't stop me. I'm not security."

"Come along," said Diana. "I should think you want to get home."

"No."

She released her hold. His choice. Alexion went to stand with Chapra and Abaron. Chapra grinned at him then returned her attention to Diana.

"We're staying here. There's so much to learn. You understand?"

Diana felt she might.

"Here, a gift." Chapra held out her fist to Diana.

With reluctance Diana held out the flat of her gloved hand. Chapra dropped something into it then turned back to the tunnel. Alexion followed, eagerly. As the three of them walked into the Jain machine, Diana saw through a tear in Abaron's suit a triangle at the base of his spine. She shuddered, and just stood there until they were gone. Eventually the tube filled with sea water and drew back into the sea. She opened her hand to look at the small red shell Chapra had given her. It was shaped like a worm cast; a small coral of convolute tubes. She'd seen recordings; she knew what it was—knew it was the future. There was not much Diana feared. She feared this.

snairls

This story was first published in issue 10 (1995) of *Grotesque*, a wonderful magazine produced in Ireland by David Logan, and yet another of those small press magazines not to survive. Those who have read *The Skinner* will immediately recognise Janer and the hornets he carries around with him, though his location will not be so familiar. The word *Snairls* is a combination of snails and air, air-snails if you like, and bloody difficult to say out loud as I discovered when rehearsing this story for a reading in a Midlands bookshop. It goes to show how mistakes can be picked up by reading stuff out loud, just like the 'how to' books tell you. In fact I didn't bother reading this one. I read a later story about sharks to the book shop staff and other writers there—they being the only audience—then scuttled off to a nearby pub to bullshit with Rhys Hughes and Mark Chadbourne, meagrely sip beer, and wish I didn't have to drive home.

The other passengers went to their cabins and cowered there like the limp city dwellers they were. The cabins were shell-walled dead stuff, braced by shock-absorbing muscle, and internally free of slime. Janer was no city man and there was so much more he wanted to see and experience. He had yet to walk Upper Shell and look from the Spire, and it was not in his nature to give up so easily. Besides, now might be his only chance before his freedom of movement was once again curtailed.

"It means a storm is coming or we are coming to a storm," the CG told him before casually stripping off his uniform and sealing it in a plastic bag. Embarrassed by the man's nakedness Janer looked around the CG's cabin. The walls glistened. When he glanced back, the CG was watching him analytically. Janer tried to keep his eyes level with the man's. Crew were different, he had known that, but seeing one naked was . . . disconcerting. On the front of the CG's body was a diamond of white flesh extending from his white genitalia to the base of his throat. It was segmented like the body of some worm, each segment a couple of inches wide, and there were other differences he tried not to observe too closely.

"You'd best do the same," said the CG, wryly noting his discomfiture. "Clothing becomes crusted and stiff if it dries, or takes on a heavy build up. Only skin sheds it well."

"As you say."

Janer left the Chief Geneticist in his cabin—a cyst in the body of the Graaf—and headed down the glistening artery of a corridor, half-lit by bioluminescent globes clinging to the fleshy walls and sucking their juice. Everywhere these things. Janer had not realised they were alive until he saw one detach its tick mouth and scuttle along the wall to a new feeding spot. For a day after that the skin on his back crawled whenever he walked underneath one. But in the end one must get used to the presence of life: it was everything around him.

Soon he saw that many of the crew of the Graaf had dispensed with their clothes. Eller, naked on a hyaline strut bone, rested her chin on her knee and grinned at him. She slowly and deliberately parted her other leg to one side as he slowed to make some passing greeting or wry comment. He found he had no words and quickened his pace, aware of the flush rising in his face. The diamond of white wormflesh on the front of her body included her hairless genitalia and ended at a narrow point by her anus. There was something incredibly erotic about it. Behind him he heard her chuckle. Damn. He would have to do something about her. There were stories about what went on inside a snairl when the walls slimed. The creators of holofiction became quite sweaty-palmed about the subject. Janer wanted to find out. He wanted to find out a lot of things—for himself for a change.

In his dry and civilized cabin Janer stripped off his clothing and pulled on the rubber trunks of his surfsuit. He didn't want to wander about the Graaf with a permanent erection waving about in front of him. That kind of thing delimited serious conversation. Admittedly, he did intend to screw Eller at the first opportunity. Finally into his trunks and considering what else he might take out with him he turned to the sudden buzz from beside his compscreen. Jumpy today—very jumpy.

The hornet rose into the air above the antique plastic keyboard—a blur of wings suspending a severed-thumb body and dangly mosquito legs. Faceted eyes glittering. All over its body the hornet was painted with intricate designs in red and yellow-green fluorescent paint.

"I thought you were exploring," said Janer. The hivelink behind his ear buzzed for a moment before the mind replied.

"The slime could kill this unit and I only have five on the Graaf."

"Where are the others?"

"They are in Upper Shell, but even there the conditions are inimical."

"How come? There's no slime there."

"No, but there are rooks."

"How inconvenient."

"They require instruction."

"Are they intelligent enough to learn?"

"You were."

Janer sighed. The 'you' in this case was the human race. It wasn't having another dig at him, for a change.

It had come as one shock in many when arrogant humanity had discovered it wasn't the only sentient race on Earth. It was just the loudest and most destructive. Dolphins and whales had always been candidates because of their aesthetic appeal and stories of rescued swimmers. Research in that area had soon cleared things up. Dolphins couldn't tell the difference between a human swimmer and a sick fellow, and were substantially more stupid than the animal humans had been turning into pork on a regular basis. Whales had the intelligence of the average cow. When a hornet built its nest in a VR suit and lodged its protests on the Internet it had taken a long time for anyone to believe. They were stinging things, creepy crawlies, how could they possibly be intelligent? At ten thousand years of age the youngest hivemind showed them. People believed.

"You want to come out in the box, I take it?"

The buzzing of the hivemind seemed contemplative. Thoughts that once took the time of a hornet's flight between nests flicked at the speed of light between hivelinks. Janer held out his hand and the hornet settled on it, vibrating, its legs pressing into his skin like blunt pins. His flesh rebelled but he controlled the urge to shudder and fling the insect away from him. He was getting better at it now: his payment, his service to this mind, for killing a hornet that had tried to settle on his shoulder in a crowded ringball stadium. It had been tired that hornet; searching for somewhere to land and rest, tempted by the beaker of coke Janer had been drinking. His reaction had been instinctive; the phobic horror of insects had risen up inside him and he had knocked the hornet to the ground and stamped on it. The police had come for him the next day. Killing a hornet was not precisely murder, as each creature was just one very small part of the mind. There were stiff penalties, though.

"It would be interesting to observe the interior during the storm. Yes, the box," the mind eventually told him. The hornet launched itself from his hand and hovered above his bed. The box was there: a shaped perspex container with one skinstick surface. It landed by this and crawled inside. Janer picked the box up and pressed it against his shoulder where it stuck.

"There are no phobes on this ship," the mind observed, as if picking up on what Janer had been thinking. He wasn't the only one who had trouble with the idea of allowing huge stinging insects to fly around them unmolested. There were others whose service to a mind had to be without contact with its hornets, who became hysterical in their presence, some who just paid over a large amount of money, and some who required . . . adjustments.

"Not surprising," Janer replied casually. "Spend your life inside a floating mollusc and you're sure to lose some of your aversions."

The mind replied to this with something like a snort as its hornet rattled around in the box and settled itself down in the shaped pedestal provided for it. Like this was better for Janer. Now the hornet was no more to him than a camera for the remote and disperse mind, and the voice a disembodied thing. If he didn't look at it he could convince himself that there was only a machine perched on his shoulder. That anus-clenching shudder left him and he could concentrate on other matters. He stooped and picked up a pair of grip shoes, then discarded them. The crew did not wear them so he would try to do without as well. He stepped out of his cabin into a slime-coated artery.

"Why does it produce it?" he wondered loudly.

"A defensive measure for molluscs. It senses the storm and prepares itself."

"How does the slime help?"

"Retroactive reaction. It would have helped if it was being attacked by a predator."

"So the Geneticists didn't straighten every kink in the helix."

"Never say that here," the link hornet warned.

"Would I be so foolish," said Janer dryly.

There was no reply but Janer seemed to get the impression of a feeling something akin to a raised eyebrow. Yes, so I stepped on a hornet in a moment of panic. It won't happen again. In ten years when my service contract is finished I should be well inured to them. Cunning bastards those minds.

Under his bare feet the floor was rough and sticky, not at all slippery as he had expected. When he lifted his foot it was still attached by a thousand hair-thin strands.

"They got part of the way there . . . the Geneticists," he said.

"What do you mean?"

Janer bowed his shoulder down so the link hornet could see his feet and the tacky mess on the scaled floor.

The hornet said, "Partial adaptation. Unable to get rid of the slime they convert it into a more acceptable form."

"On the floors anyway," said Janer. "Elsewhere it's just as thick and slippery as your usual mucous.

"Of course, they may have made the floors the slime absorption points and what you are encountering here is the residue. The moisture would go first."

"Yes," said Janer, without much interest. Ten paces from his door and he turned to study what was revealed of his cabin between the ceiling and floor of flesh. It was an oblate bone-yellow sphere from which extended organic-looking struts to pierce the flesh, these in turn held by ropes of grey muscle. How like parasites were humans in the uterine living spaces of the Graaf snairl—squirming endoparasites, gall wasps. A little way further along he could see some of the next cabin and a face at a plastiglass portal. That would be Asharn the merchant. Somewhere in this snairl was stored his cargo of exotic organics—synaptic chips, non-specific human augmentations like eyes to see in the dark, guaranteed multiple orgasm vaginas, cetacean capacity lungs, and other things the merchant had hinted at with nods and winks and meaningful looks at the hornet. Crime, if it was to be committed successfully, had to be done so away from prying eyes, especially if they were faceted. Janer had displayed his lack of interest in anything the merchant might have, well aware of a feeling of huge amusement coming through the hivelink.

"The storm closes," the link hornet told him. "I see it now, an anvil of cloud walking on legs of lightning."

Janer closed his eyes. He really wanted to go there, where the other hornets and the rooks were. Would the mind let him, as its eyes were already there? He asked.

"Later," the mind told him. "First I want to see the inside of this snairl during storm."

Janer wondered exactly what it was the mind wanted to see. Did it want to observe the orgy purported to take place? What possible interest could it have in human sex? Or was he just missing something? Had he not been told something? He walked aimlessly then in the body of the snairl and thought about his first sight of it. It had drifted through the sky, a faerie castle in the clouds, only the flicker of rotors on the Lower Shell betraying its motive force. Sunlight refracted through the spiral of nacre helium chambers revealing them like the internals of some diatom. The living body of the snairl clung chancrous below, its tail thrashing the air as angry as a cat, grey and silver tendrils treeing up into the shell and fading. One creature: ugliness clinging to beauty, tenaciously.

Crew ceased working at their tasks, as Janer walked by, and watched him with evident surprise. The slime on the walls thickened and some arteries were hung with glistening ropes of it. In one such place he saw two crew members coupling ferociously and stopped to watch. They were oblivious to him; tightly wrapped in an embrace and foaming the slime with their frenetic movements. Damn the mind, he thought. He was going to find Eller. Ever since he had come onboard she had been dropping broad hints. The last hint had been too broad to ignore. He headed in the direction of the cyst-cabins of the crew, hoping to find her there.

"The storm is round us," said the mind, "and now the snairl holds its position. It will not move on now."

"What do you mean?"

He was definitely not being told something. There was no reply and he was about to ask again when Eller stepped out into the artery before him and beckoned. He hurried towards her and stood in front of her. There was a thin layer of slime on her body and her black hair was slick against her head. Nictitating membranes blinked over her eyes and when she opened her mouth he noted her tongue was pure white, like the lips of her vagina. She reached down and inserted her fingers in the top of his trunks.

"Why these?"

"I'm not used to nakedness," he told her.

"You'll get used to it."

She tugged him through the cervix in a fleshy wall and into her cabin.

Once within the narrow confines Janer looked around. Slime coated the floor and walls and no personal objects were visible. The floor was soft under his feet. He sensed the curiosity of the mind and it voiced no objections when he removed the box from his shoulder and placed it on ridge of hard flesh protruding from the wall. Eller stood at the middle of the cyst for a moment inspecting him from head to foot.

"I was to be with Ableman," she said.

"Why not?"

"I like the exotic."

This was hardly how Janer classified himself, but at that moment he was almost without thought. She stepped forward, took hold of his trunks, and pulled them down to his ankles.

"Ah," she said, rubbing her cheek against his penis, then scraped her nails down his thighs. He grabbed for her and she slid away. He grabbed again and she allowed it, then tripped him to the floor. The slime was warm.

She sat astride his chest, slid back, then reached between her legs and slid his penis inside herself. Janer did not last very long and was immediately aware that something else was operating here. He had never reacted like this before. That he had come did not seem to affect her as she rode him, her eyes rolled up in her head. He was hard again in a moment, but not inside her. She didn't stop. He got hold of her and threw her down on the floor, mounted her, her legs locking behind him and her ankle spurs scraping his skin. His mind was a white blur of pleasure into which the hivemind spoke a few unheeded words.

"Aphrodisiac in the slime. How interesting."

The hornet scuttled back into its box and fastidiously cleaned itself. The substance had no effect on a creature without gender.

They rested in an oozing tangle, foamed slime all about them. At last able to think Janer reacted to the hornet's words.

"Why? Why is it in the slime?"

Eller sat upright, glanced from him to the box, then lay back with a squelch, a dreamy smile on her face.

"It is not normally there," the mind replied. "Rumours of increased sexual activity during storms are greatly exaggerated. This activity does come during a time of slime production, this production being for other reasons."

"And what are they?"

The mind was silent. Janer looked to Eller for an explanation, but she was looking at him in a particular way and he quickly lost interest in the subject. He reached for her but she caught his wrists in her rough palms.

"Slowly now," she said.

Janer nodded mutely then glanced around as he felt the cabin shift. The storm; it was buffeting the snairl. He hoped it wasn't just a squall as Eller took hold of his head and pressed it down between her legs. The slime didn't matter. But for a faint peppery taste he hardly noticed it. He hardly noticed anything but what he was doing. Eller moaned and dug her nails in his head, hooked her leg over his shoulder and dug her spur in his back. Abruptly she pushed him away and it was her turn to sink down and take his penis in her mouth. She worked on him with her lips and white tongue, brought him near to coming then stopped and backed away. They were both panting harshly. She slid away from him and lay back with her legs widely parted, rubbing at herself with both hands, her moans louder. Janer saw that slime was actually being generated by the segmented flesh on the front of her torso. It didn't matter. He pulled himself over her, entered her yet again, his fists against the floor either side of her hips. As he started to move he lifted one hand from the floor and ran it over that ribbed flesh. She went wild, writhing and yelling underneath him. Hardly in control himself he used both hands, pressing and caressing, and something gave. She yelled with ecstacy. Janer came unendingly. He felt as if she were draining him, as if his head would burst, as if his guts were spurting out of his penis.

As the wave subsided Janer looked down and saw with growing horror that his hands had sunk between the segments of her torso. He felt a sudden panicky revulsion and pulled away. She lay limp on the floor, her eyes glazed. Was she dead? Oh no, no . . . He glanced to the hornet on its fleshy shelf, unmoving in its box, an ornate piece of jewellery, all-seeing.

"It's all right," said Eller, and he stared at her with relief. The segments of her torso were open, exposing organs under glassy slime. Janer swallowed bile and had just enough presence of mind to grab up the hornet box before fleeing through the fleshy door. In his cabin he used the small shower unit then viciously dried himself with a towel. Once clean and dry he felt suddenly exhausted and collapsed on his bed.

"The geneticists did more than create the snairls, they created the crews as well," the hivelink told him.

"I didn't realise how much . . . so much."

"They are like us—all one," it told him.

He heard it and slept, but he didn't understand.

"We will go to Upper Shell now," said the hivelink.

Still feeling bleary Janer glanced from the shirt he was holding to the hornet on the bedside stand. It was drinking from the dispenser Janer had placed there. The device contained a sickly sweet protein-laced syrup that was all the hornet needed to sustain it. Janer stared at it blankly for a moment then returned his attention to his clothes. He couldn't put two thoughts together. Should he dress or shouldn't he? He dropped the clothing he had been putting on then selected a monofilament overall from his wardrobe. It was guaranteed impervious to anything and its outer surface was frictionless—the slime wouldn't stick to it. He found gloves and slip-on shoes of a similar material. In the neck pocket there was a hood and mask. He possessed no goggles and no respirator so would have to do without. Was he overreacting? He thought not. Suitably attired he made coffee and checked through his food supplies. The hyperclam he ignored, as it was supposed to have aphrodisiac qualities, and instead chose a meatfruit, which somewhere in its ancestry had a pig and a peach tree. Real pigs were a protected species now.

There were two of them outside his cabin. A young man was vigorously buggering another young man while a young girl lay on the floor to one side playing with herself and looking annoyed. As soon as she spotted Janer she became hopeful, but he shook his head and moved quickly away. He would have to watch that in case anyone grabbed him. The hornet box had not stuck to the monofilament overall, and the hornet was in his top pocket peeking out at everything. He could feel it moving against his chest occasionally, but was too drained in every way to find any reaction to that. Quickly he strode along the artery, then along another that spiralled up through snairl flesh. Whenever he saw crew he saw sexual activity or its aftermath. Most of them were oblivious to him. With almost clinical detachment now he observed bodies opened at the front and oozing, men thrusting into women or other men in any position from genitals upward. It was as if the white wormflesh was an extension of their sexual organs. He saw and he moved on, not unaffected, aware that the substance in the slime was also in the moist air taken into his lungs. At one point, when a woman slid across a floor to him, he had to grit his teeth and stride on. He really wanted to stay with her.

At length Janer came to drier areas where shell material stabbed the walls and ran in reefs along the floors. He peered through doors half organic and half manufactured, into cargo areas and beyond them saw translucent shell thrashed by rain and lit by flashes of lightning. Only seeing this did he realise how he had grown used to the halflight in the snairl—the muted blue glow of the bioluminescent globes pinned to every wall.

"The shafts are ahead," the hivelink told him needlessly. He had studied a plan of the internal layout of the snairl before boarding. In a moment he came to open mouths of metal that curved up into darkness. He stepped into one, groped until he found a rung, climbed.

He was in the dark for only a short time before he reached a hatch that irised open as he reached the rung below it. The sudden light made his eyes ache momentarily as he climbed up into it. This is what he wanted to see. The floor was smooth and iridescent. To his right the curving wall of near transparent shell showed him the vastness of sky, welcoming after the confines of the snairl body. From a floor space three metres wide, he gazed out at thick strobelit cloud and down at the snairl body below, its huge glistening head swaying from side to side, horns probing the storm. To his left bulged the huge helium bags veined with snairlflesh. The floor sloped up following the spiral of the shell. He climbed, breathing easily air that gradually cleared of the taint of the living body below. Cold breezes gusted in at him from occasional splits in the ancient shell. He tasted rain and cloud, and thunder made the floor vibrate. The moisture here gathered in small droplets and ran away. He climbed spiral after spiral, each one tighter than the last. Higher up he noted the bird droppings on the floor, some kind of nest between helium bags, two dead rooks on the floor.

"Instruction?" he asked.

"They lack the intelligence to learn. It has been the same with their kind since the time they ruled the Earth."

Birds—the direct descendants of the dinosaurs. There were hiveminds old enough to remember, but they were strange and did not communicate much with the younger minds, and not at all with the human race.

Eventually Janer reached the glassy cone of the spire and its level circular floor. He saw the other hornets clinging to the transparent wall, flaws in glass. He walked over to the opposite side of the chamber and gazed out.

"You are content now?" asked the hivemind.

"I feel an easing of certain tensions," he replied.

"That's good, because we'll be spending the rest of the journey here." Janer paused. "Why?"

"Look it the direction my companions are looking."

Abruptly the hornet launched from his pocket and was buzzing in the air. He gazed across the chamber, past the hornets, stared intently through the wall at the tumble of cloud. Then he saw it, wreathed in lightning: another faerie castle, another snairl approaching.

"It is not the storm that causes the activity below, but the anticipation of this snairl. Every five hundred years they mate."

"Esua!"

"Yes, this is why we are here. This is why we are interested."

Janer noted the royal we. The hivemind was completely at the link.

"Why such great interest?"

"This snairl is male," the mind told him.

"I don't understand."

"Like their mollusc brethren, male snairls manufacture in their bodies a harpoon of calcite they use to spear the female and hold it close. Normal snails then mate and part. For a male snairl, the making of this harpoon is a killing effort. Such mate only once."

"It will die?"

"Yes."

"There is danger then. What of the crew, the passengers?"

"Look down."

Janer peered down past the body of the snairl and saw egg-shaped objects being spewed out into the air, opening gliding wings, falling through the sky.

"They are safe."

"The passengers, yes. For the crew there is never any escape."

Janer whirled round and faced the hovering hornet. "What! No warning! Just let them die!"

He turned and ran back. Eller. He found that he did care what happened to her.

"Fool," the link told him. "The geneticists made both: snairl and crew."

Again, Janer did not hear.

Janer was halfway down Upper Shell when the snairls met. The impact threw him back against the helium bags, and the shells clashed and rang. He saw fragments of shell fly glittering through the air. There was a giant sound: a bubbling groan, the sighing of caves. As the shells rocked and scraped he staggered to the wall and looked down in time to see the male snairl extrude a barbed spear of cloudy glass and thrust into the body of the female, and the bodies ooze together. Foamed slime spiralled up on the wind like spindrift. The towered shells closed throwing Janer back against the helium bags then parted high, ground at the base. Janer went head-first into the glassy wall, lost it all in a flash of black.

Janer's immediate reaction to consciousness was to vomit on the floor and clutch at his head. There was a weird buzzing from his hivelink, something he had never heard before. Perhaps he had broken it. He staggered upright and tried to blink the double images from his eyes. Unsteady on his feet, it was a moment before he realised the snairl was back on an even keel. At the wall he peered down. The sky was clearing and he could see everything in detail. The female was gone. The male snairl hung in an arc under its shell, flaccid, its connections to the shell stretched taut. The crew. Eller. Supporting himself against the wall Janer made his way down, wondering as he went, how long he had been out. Minutes? Hours? As soon as he reached the down-tube into the snairl body he realised it must have been some time.

The floor was drying, tacky, as he stepped out of the tube, and he wondered about that until he heard the rustling of air pumps—something previously disguised by the living sounds of the snairl. They were not biotech and would run until clogged with decaying flesh. A biolight lay nearby, its legs waving weakly in the air, and its tick-mouth gaping and clicking hungrily. The air smelt of death. Janer carefully stepped round the biolight, but he need not have worried; it was too weak to get at him and would never have got through his monofilament clothing. He peered down the corridor artery at the other biolights there and one fell while he watched. They would all be hungry. He pulled the hood and mask from the neck-pocket of his overall, and put on the gloves. They would go for exposed bodyhis eyes and mouth. He would just have to be very careful.

Janer found the first of the crew shortly after crushing under his foot the third biolight to drop on him. As he crushed it, its juices spread in a glowing pool and Janer left bright foot-prints behind him. He noticed then a change in the quantity and spectrum of the lighting.

The man had crawled away from his partner with five biolights attached to his back. Their glow was reddish, their energy drawn from near to human blood. The man had left a thick slime trail that was now skinned over. The woman was curled in a corner with a biolight attached to the side of her head. As he turned to her the biolight fell away, leaving a bloody hole, and tried to drag itself towards him. He stood on it and it burst with a wet pop. The woman turned her head, opened her mouth with a dry click and tried to open her crusted eyes. He stooped down by her and caught hold of her.

"Dead," she rasped, her last breath hissing out foul in his face. He let her go and ran, something of what the hivemind had said coming back to him—the geneticists made *both*. He remembered then that he had never seen crew eating, never seen much in the way of personal effects . . . *They are like us—all one.* They were dying now their host was dead, like the bio-lights.

The door ripped like wet paper as he pulled it aside. Eller blinked at him from her place on the floor in the ropes of slime. A pot of water rested to one side of her. She had cleaned her face and her eyes, but her eyes were dull, drying out.

"Eller . . . this . . . "

"Janer," she said and smiled, shifted. Her body had grown long, gaps as wide as his arm between the segments, there her heart, beating slowly, there her intestine, drawn taut. He knelt beside her and she managed to get a hand up to his shoulder. She shifted again.

"Kiss me . . . just once more," she said.

Janer was leaning forward when he heard the low buzzing. Distorted speech came through his link, but he could not make it out. He turned his head slightly as the hornet darted in. Eller made a horrible sound, some-where between a groan and a hiss, jerked her hand away, her mouth opening wide at the pain as the hornet launched itself from her arm. It had stung her. Janer wanted to crush it at once, then he saw her mouth; her white tongue open at the end like a flower, rasping teeth wet inside it. More buzzing, more glittery shapes in the room. Five hornets hovered between him and Eller, darted at him, and because he could no longer hear their speech his fear returned and he stumbled back. Eller tried to crawl towards him and he realised, *like the biolights*, and shuddered in horror. The hornets drove him out into the corridor. The walls were cracking and liquefying now. The death stink had turned to something else, now. Stumbling ahead of the in-sects he was numb to thought. They drove him to the Upper Shell.

The floor was cool against his cheek. The hornet, standing on the side of his neck and working with the cellular structure behind his ear, finished its task and flew from him.

"We were unaware of the danger," the mind told him.

"It's wrong, that they should die like that."

"They all lived for as long as the snairl. Though they could feed on other things after its death they would not long survive it. The chemistry is too complex. They are one being, like ourselves."

"Is all this what you came to learn?"

"No."

"What then?"

"The shell does not decay. The body below will drop soon and the shell will need to be counterweighted. We came for the salvage. Here we can be safe."

Janer, his shoulder against the crystal wall of the spire, could see them. The cloud was vast and grey, and moved with purpose. He could feel the presence of many minds—a million hives. The hornets were coming to their new home.

spatterjay

Spatterjay is the planet where all the action takes place in *The Skinner*, and all the characters and events here will be familiar to readers of that book. This story is in fact a precursor, whereas from *Snairls* I only snatched Janer and his hornets. Again it was a story published in *Grotesque* (issue 8 '95) and suitably so, though not enough so to justify changing the title to 'Splatterjay'. It is a story whose genesis was in a nightmare of long blue and bony hands reaching out of dense jungle to grab someone, and of trout in a stream, which weren't. It spent a number of years in a folder, in the form of a few scribbled lines, then grew out of some free-association writing I was doing to limber up my brain one day. Acorns and all that.

Sweating green blood, a lung bird wheezed from the tree tops, its flaccid wings groping for the clouds. Ambel tucked his trumpet-mouthed blunderbuss under his arm and despondently watched its limping progress.

"Suitable protein," suggested Jane.

"There isn't any. Would you eat that?" asked Peck.

"Depends on how hungry I got."

"I guess we could make a stew."

Ambel made no comment on this, but he closed up his blunderbuss and aimed. The weapon flashed and banged, sparkles of still-burning powder gouting through the air. A cloud of acrid smoke obscured view for a moment, then they saw the bird falling into the trees, bits breaking away from its ill-made body.

"Let's go," said Peck.

They trotted through the knee-high putrephallus weeds, their masks pulled up over their mouths and noses. The pear-trunk trees shivered as they passed. By the time they reached the area where the bird had fallen it was gone. They caught a glimpse of something huge and glistening dragging the squawking and flapping mess into the deep dingle.

"Bastard," said Peck, turning to Ambel. Ambel shook his head as he squatted down and thumped another paper cartridge down into the barrel of his buss.

Jane lifted her mask, winced at the smell wafting off the weeds then said, "Leech. A big one. Best leave it alone."

"Can you eat leeches?" asked Peck. He always got a bit weird when he hadn't had enough to eat.

Ambel shook his head.

"Too acid," he said. "Makes you fart like a wind machine and burns your ring when you crap. Know a guy died of it once. Terminal wind. Blew his arse hole across the room."

Peck snorted disbelievingly. "Well, we gotta get something to take back." He looked towards the dingle.

"Not there," said Jane. "We'll go back to the beach and circle round. Might get a rhinoworm coming in."

The three moved back through the weeds onto the green sand of the beach. Ambel gazed out at the ship and noticed that the masts were still bare. They needed a sail something bad. They needed food, yes, but whatever they got from the island would only keep them going for a little while, as they were. They had to get back to port and get some real Earth-food inside them; some dome-grown grain and meat.

"They say there are people out here who survive on wild food. They say the Skinner lives out here on one of the islands," said Jane.

"You gotta be kidding, all alive, and Hoop?" said Peck.

Ambel nodded morosely to himself. "They all survive, but they ain't people no more, Hoop included."

That killed the conversation until they reached the first stream winding out from the deep dingle. Ambel looked into the water and thinking about the dome he thought; salmon, then, seeing how they were grouped he thought; eels. But of course some of them broke from the water, their glistening ribbed backs rolling in the glitter, round thread-cutting mouths probing the air.

"Leeches again," said Peck. "There anything edible on this island?"

"Yes," said Jane avidly as she pointed out to sea.

The rhinoworm was as long as a man and its sinuous body as thick. It was aptly named. It had the head of a rhino, little different from those pictured in the old zoology books, and it had the body of a thick eel. It was pink and red-speckled. They watched it approach the mouth of the stream and rear its head out of the water with a leech writhing and flicking in its narrow mouth. Ambel's blunderbuss boomed, part of its head disappeared, and it sank back down into the water, clouding it blue.

"Quick! Quick!" shouted Jane, leaping up and down. Peck waded out, hooked his grapple into its flesh and waded back in, trailing the line out behind him. He was nearly ashore when he yelled and splashed in very quickly.

"Gerrit off! Gerrit off!"

A four-foot long leech had attached itself to his hip. He fell in the sand and grabbed hold of the horrible thing in both hands to try and prevent it boring in even further. Jane grabbed up the line and began hauling in the rhinoworm while Ambel tended to Peck. He did the only thing that was possible in the circumstances; he grabbed hold of the leech in both hands, put his foot against Peck's leg, and hauled with all his might. Peck let out a scream as the leech pulled away with a fist-sized plug of his flesh in its circular mouth. Ambel bashed the creature against a rock until the lump came free, then after trampling the creature to slurry he handed the piece of flesh back to Peck. Peck screwed it back into his leg, then wrapped a bandage from his pack round it to hold it in place.

"Help me with this," said Jane. She had got the rhinoworm to the edge of the water, but could not haul it up onto the sand by herself. A mass of leeches was building up round it, each of them after its plug of flesh. Ambel rushed over and helped her haul it in, then the both of them stomped as many of the creatures as they could. As they stomped the last of them Peck was able to join them and relished splattering the last few.

"Right, let's chop it and head back to the ship," said Ambel. They proceeded to slice the rhinoworm into huge lumps, which they packed into their waterproof packs, and staggering under their loads, headed back up the beach. Before they set out Peck was able to take his bandage off. The plug of flesh had healed back into place and his muscle was working again. When they reached the rowing boat and were dumping the packs into it Jane grinned at Peck.

"The Earther'll want to see your leg. Probably want blood samples and a few pots of piss outa you as well," she said.

"Bollocks," said Peck, and gave the boat a shove. "Don't know what she's all worked up about. We ain't that different."

Ambel, who was, so the Earther had said, built like a tank, rowed the boat, being careful not to put too much pressure on the oars and go snapping them again. Jane, as skinny and small as a starveling child, had undone her shirt to her waist and sat plaiting her hair and looking at Ambel meaningfully. She was always horny after a meat hunt, and when all her attempts to get Ambel into her bunk failed, as they always did, she turned to the next available crewman. During the next few hours the crewmen would be falling over each other as they tried to stay close to her. Peck had opened one of the packs and was cutting slices of rhinoworm meat to stuff into his mouth. He had injury hunger; another phenomenon the Earther woman was eager to study. Shortly they arrived at the wooden cliff of the side of the ship and the meat was hauled aboard. The three followed, after passing up the oars, then Ambel hauled the rowing boat up the side and held it in place while others strapped it just below the gunnels. The Earther woman came out of her cabin to watch this and when it was done she returned shaking her head in amazement.

"How long before you were mobile again?" asked Erlin as she inspected the circular scar. They all had these scars, every member of the crew; white and neat circular scars on their bluish skin.

"Eh?" said Peck, brilliantly.

"How long after this injury were you able to stand again, to walk again?"

"Couple of minutes after I screwed the plug back."

"Let me get this right. Ambel thumped the leech against a rock until it released the piece of your leg it had excised. You then took that piece of flesh and screwed it back into your leg."

"Yeah, so what?"

"Doesn't that strike you as a little odd?"

"Who you callin odd? At least I ain't the colour of burnt sugar. Bleedin Earthers always callin us odd."

It was the strangest piece of racism Erlin had ever encountered. Her first doctorate had been in history because she had been fascinated by her genetic heritage. Not that she was a true Negro, there had been none for more than a five hundred years, nor any other definite racial types, but her skin was very dark. She was almost a throwback, but for her white hair and blue eyes. The people here though, on this strange little world, were very different from the usual run of humanity. She handed Peck a couple of bottles.

"Here. I want your next urine samples. Now I'll take some blood." This she did, quickly and efficiently. You could not take too much time over such things with hoopers as they healed so fast a needle would block in less than thirty seconds. When Peck grumbled his way back out onto deck she got the blood under her nanoscope and found the fibrous structures she had expected to find. It was all coming together now. She had a damned good idea of what was going on and reckoned that when she made her report, Spatterjay would be descended on by just about every science team in the Polity.

Ambel grinned to himself as Jane dragged Peck below decks and the rest of the group broke up in disappointment. He carved himself a slice of rhinoworm and chewed on it contemplatively. They really did need a sail. He did not like to hang around the islands for too long as he was well aware that the Skinner was still active. One day he intended to come here alone and catch the mad bastard. One day. He turned as Erlin came out on deck and stood next to him gazing with distaste at the worm steak.

"Want a bit?" he asked her. Her food ran out a couple of days ago and he knew she must be hungry.

"I wouldn't mind if it was cooked," she said.

He shook his head. "Destroys the flavour."

"No, the stuff tastes awful—what it destroys is all the nutritional value for humans."

Ambel nodded and carved another slice. He held it out to her, blue blood dripping down his fingers. "Go on, it'll do you good."

Erlin took the slice and nibbled a bit off the edge. A sudden look of astonishment transformed her features. She ate the whole slice.

"It tastes good," she said. "When I first had some it tasted like copper and curry powder."

He carved her another slice, and as he did this she studied his hugely broad back. His bluish skin was mottled, looked almost patterned. It was only then that she realised the effect was caused by leech scars layered upon each other in their thousands.

"Did you fall in the sea or something?" she asked.

"Once or twice," he said, turning and handing her some more meat.

"You have a lot of leech scars. I didn't realise it until just now. You're covered with them. Could I have a blood sample from you?"

"Sometime," he said, not meeting her eyes.

She was about to say more when there was a shout from the cabin roof.

"Sail! Sail coming in!"

Erlin peered up at the sky. She had heard about this but never seen it. When the hover car had dropped her at the ship it had been as it was now: bare masted and moored by this island.

The sail undulated in on the east wind; a great veined sheet turning the flesh-filtered light underneath it a strange orangy pink. It caught hold of the top of the mainmast with one long bony hand, swung round and replaced that grip with a coil of its tail before moving that hand along with many others down onto the spars. Its lizard head on a long whiplike neck came questing down to the deck. Ambel pulled the worm steak off its spike and walked up to the creature's head. The sail licked its lips with a dark-blue forked tongue and eyed the steak hungrily.

"How are you called?" asked Ambel, as was only proper.

"I am Windcatcher," replied the sail, as replied all sails, never having mastered the idea that names could be an individual thing. Ambel gave it the steak, which it chomped down hungrily. Erlin watched the lumps of meat travelling up its translucent neck to where its stomach could be seen bubbling between the first two spars. When it had finished the meat it yawned loudly, shrugged the vast sheet of its body, then wrapped its neck round the mast and closed its eyes.

"Amazing," said Erlin, but by that time Ambel had moved away and was giving orders. Erlin walked up to the triangular head resting on the deck and wondered if she might be able to get a sample without waking it. She stepped a little closer and removed a hand microtome from her overall pocket. The sail opened one demonic red eye and looked at her.

"Bugger off," it said, then closed its eye.

The anchor socketed with a crash and crewman Boris ran yelling down the deck, swiping at a frog-whelk that had come up clinging to the chain, leapt onboard, and bitten a lump out of his calf before running away making a sound suspiciously like a titter. Boris cornered it by the forecabin and threatened it with a hammer. The whelk considered its options, looking from side to side with its stalked eyes, then spat out its prize before sidling towards the rail. Boris snatched his missing part and shoved it back into place before limping back to his station. Erlin looked on with her mouth hanging open, then quickly ducked into her cabin when she saw the whelk eyeing her estimatingly from the rail. There was a thump against her door just as she got it closed. Outside she heard yelling and cursing, then a squeal of surprise and a wet crunch. When she edged her cabin door open she saw Ambel toss something over the side then reach down and scrape something off his boot with his knife. He grinned at her.

"All clear," he said.

Erlin closed her door, leant her back against it, then slid down until she was sitting on the floor. Culture shock? She would just have to get used to it. She bit down hard on a giggle.

On the third day of sail Erlin finally got Ambel into her cabin for a blood sample, but, when she pushed the syringe into him she could get nothing into it, and after a moment it popped out of his arm. Thoroughly determined now, Erlin tried a chainglass scalpel on his skin with a pad held ready to soak some blood up. The scalpel went in all right, but when she pulled it out again the wound sealed instantly. She tried again with two scalpels, side by side, to hold the wound open between. The gap she opened abruptly filled with flesh and skinned over. When she removed the scalpels those wounds closed as quickly as the first.

"Doctor at the port tried once. Don't reckon I got any blood any more."

Erlin thought about the fibrous structures she had seen down the nanoscope. Peck, who claimed to be a hundred and eighty years old, had the most in his blood she had ever seen. The rest of the crew she had taken samples from; Jane, Boris, Pland, and Mede, who were comparative infants at ages ranging from fifty to a hundred and ten, had proportionally less.

"How old are you, Ambel?"

"Oh, a bit."

Ambel rolled down his shirt sleeve and looked shifty.

"Come on. This is really important."

"Don't rightly know. Been on the ships for a while."

Erlin wasn't having that. "You do know. Don't fob me off!"

Ambel looked uncomfortable. "No one believes me," he complained.

"I will."

Ambel got up and headed for the door, as he opened it he mumbled, "Spatterjay Hoop was a crazy git." He went out onto the deck.

Erlin sat down on the chair and shook her head. They were all crazy gits, and Ambel was no better. If he thought she was going to believe he knew Spatterjay Hoop, the man after whom this strange little world was named more than five centuries ago, then he was probably worse. Ridiculous idea. Wasn't it?

"Sail's awake! Sail's awake!" bellowed Boris from his favourite vantage on the roof of the forecabin. The head was questing around the deck, its eyes blinking sleepily. As Erlin came out of her cabin to see what new madness might occur, the sail looked at her, yawned, then sneezed. Ambel ran for the hatch cover, opened it and jumped down inside, then climbed out with a worm steak on his shoulder. He held it out for the sail, which took it in its mouth, hesitated a moment, then spat it out on the deck.

"Wormy," it said with disgust.

Ambel shrugged. The sail watched him for a moment then unwound itself from the mast, released its holds and undulated away through the air. The ship slowed as Erlin walked over to the steak and inspected it. A long thin worm poked its head out of the meat, grinned at her with a mouth full of small triangular teeth, then dived back in. Ambel picked the meat up and threw it over the side before Erlin could object. He eyed her carefully.

"I've had worms," he said, then said to Boris, "see anything?"

Boris pointed off to one side. "Island over there."

"Better get some more meat," said Ambel.

Erlin wondered how it was they ever got anywhere if this was the rate they always travelled. And was it her imagination, or were they all looking a lot more blue than they had before? She sat against a rail and watched as they unhooked the rowing boat and Ambel lowered it into the water. The island was a distant speck and she wondered about going with them this time. When Ambel rowed the boat out still attached to the ship with a thick hawser, she realised what he intended to do. She stared with her mouth falling open as he began to really dig in with the steel oars. Slowly he pulled the ship round and began towing god knows how many tons of timber and metal towards the island.

It took most of the day and the sun was going into fade-out by the time Boris dropped the anchor and peered with deep suspicion down the length of its chain. Ambel turned the rowing boat back to the ship and leaving it on the water he hauled himself up the hawser onto the deck.

"I want to come with you this time," said Erlin.

Ambel shrugged. "Morning," he said then turned and bellowed down the deck, "Pland, boxies here, get a line out."

Pland, a squat little man who spent most of his time at the helm muttering to himself and chewing bits of purple seaweed that squeaked when he bit them, glared at Ambel then slouched off to one of the rail lockers. He removed a line coiled round a wooden frame. It had a weight at the end of it and two small side lines bearing hooks.

"What about bait?" he asked.

Ambel went below deck and came up with their last steak held away from his body on his knife.

"Aw, come on," Pland wailed.

"Just do it," said Ambel.

Erlin watched while Pland tapped at the steak until a worm poked its head out. He reached out to it and it quickly sank its teeth in his hand. Grimacing and swearing he drew his hand away, pulling the worm from the meat. Once it flopped free he pulled it from his hand, a small squirt of blood hitting the deck, then he impaled the worm on a hook. The worm squawked and writhed about, but Pland tied it in place with another piece of line. He did the same again for the other hook then dropped the line over the side. His hand had healed by the time Erlin approached him.

"Do you often get the bait like that?" she asked.

"Better than some ways. Least we ain't the only meat on board."

Erlin was contemplating that when Pland stepped on a worm, which was trying to sneak away from the meat, and grinned with satisfaction. The worm writhed about and bit at his boot.

"You next you little bastard," he said.

Erlin walked to her cabin, suddenly feeling the need to lie down for a little while. When she returned to the lamplit deck Pland had quite a catch. Boxies were another aptly named Spatterjay life form. They were simply cube-shaped fish with eyes on one face of the cube and a tail sticking out of the other. Pland had stacked a number of them next to him like building blocks. Ambel was standing behind him biting chunks out of one like an apple. As he ate it the boxy blinked at him mournfully. Between bites Ambel was giving Pland his considered advice.

"Gently now, don't tug so hard or it'll be off again."

He did and it did. Pland swore as the line slid through his hands until he was unwinding it from the frame again. Erlin walked up and stood beside Ambel, trying not to meet the boxy eye to eye.

"Reckon he's got a turble on," said Ambel. He picked up a boxy and held it out to her. "Want one?" Erlin tried to refuse, but she was really hungry. She held her hand over its eyes and bit into it. It was like eating curried squid with pieces of banana in it. Rather palatable really, if only all those other boxies wouldn't look at her so.

"Wouldn't it be kinder to kill them first?" she asked.

He stared at her shocked. "Kill boxies?"

She noticed he had eaten his one down to its spine. All that remained was the tail at one end and a little face at the other. He tossed this back into the sea and she watched in amazement as it swam away. For a moment she thought she was going to vomit. When she did not, and in fact took another bite out of her boxy before she could think about it, she was almost startled. Is this what they called going native?

Come sunrise Erlin, Ambel, Peck and Boris were in the boat heading for the shore. Erlin had a pack of equipment and in her pocket a surgical laser the case of which she had managed to open, to remove its safety governor. It was completely illegal, but she felt a damned sight safer with a weapon that could cut through anything within two metres of her on this crazy world. Anyway, Polity law was supposed to apply here, but it seemed to go no further than the security fence round the gating facility. Hoopers seemed to find the ideas of law and justice nearly as amusing as politics. They just got on with things. She often wondered about Ambel. Was he the captain of the ship, or was he deferred to because he could settle an argument by ripping people's arms out of their sockets?

Ambel rowed the boat into the green sand beach, then with two more strokes of the oars brought it up onto the sand. He did it effortlessly, as if it made no difference to him what substance was supporting the boat. They climbed out and Ambel hoisted out his blunderbuss and rested it across his shoulder. There it was again. The thing probably weighed about a hundred kilograms. Ambel ambled up the beach.

"See if we can get another rhinoworm. Boxies ain't that filling, and we need the meat for a sail," he said.

They walked along the green strand ignoring the rustlings and gruntings from the dingle. Erlin was jumpy. Every time anything moved in the tangled undergrowth she had the nib of her laser pointing in that direction. The life forms of Spatterjay seemed to have a propensity for taking chunks out of one, and she would not heal as quickly as crew. Abruptly they all drew to a halt around Ambel, who had stopped and was peering at something in the sand. Erlin took a look and wondered what the problem was. All that lay there was a piece of screening from an old re-entry vehicle. Ambel raised his gaze from the yellowing glassite and stared down to the shoreline. There was quite a distance between.

"Oh shit, I thought it was further west," said Boris, with feeling.

"Are we . . . is this . . . you know?" said Peck.

"Yes," said Ambel. "Back to the boat."

At that moment the dingle parted and an arm came out. It was six metres long, thin, and seemed as hard as bone. The long long hand stretched two metres from wrist to fingertip. It was a blue that was almost black. It plucked Peck from the sand and pulled him into the dingle. Erlin stared at what was on the other end of the arm and wasn't sure she believed what she was seeing. Peck was shrieking as loud as he could. The noise he was making was joined by a loud maniacal laughing and giggling as the dingle closed, then both sounds receded.

"Damn and buggeration!" said Ambel.

Erlin thought that an understatement.

"Back to the boat now, yes?" said Boris eagerly.

"You go," said Ambel. "Take the Earther back with you." With that Ambel entered the dingle.

"What was that?"

Boris forced a grin. "Oh, the Skinner. Let's go now shall we?"

"No," said Erlin, and quickly followed Ambel. By the time she caught him up she wondered if she had gone insane. The Skinner? The names on Spatterjay were usually quite apt, so what did the Skinner do?

"You should've gone back to the ship," said Ambel, then glanced over her shoulder. "You too."

Erlin looked behind to see Boris approaching, his grin turned rictus on his face.

"Just couldn't miss the fun," he said.

They moved on into the dingle, pear-trunk trees ashiver, and suspicious looking vines draped in the branches of something like an inverted pine tree. In all direction the undergrowth tangled all into darkness, yet it was easy to follow the Skinner's path of crushed vegetation.

"Big one," said Boris, and they all crouched down at Ambel's signal and kept very quiet. A giant leech oozed past nearby, waving its wad-cutter at them for a moment.

"They normally don't bother," said Ambel. "But if they do you don't get it back. One got Pland a year or two back. Been a bit cranky ever since."

Erlin tried to make sense of that. Surely not? The leech's mouth had been half a metre across.

"Keep away from the pear-trunk trees," Ambel told her as they moved off again.

Pear-trunk trees? She looked up into the branches and saw things hanging there, but they did not look like pears. Of course, the trunk. It was squat and pear-shaped. The bark was real strange though. She wondered about its structure . . .

"I said keep away—"

The pear-trunk tree shivered and Erlin screamed.

"All right, I got it!" yelled Boris. He tugged on the leech attached to her back and she screamed some more. It took Ambel's help to pull the leech off. She lay face down in the mould sobbing. She could feel the hole in her back.

"Don't worry," said Ambel. "I got it." He beat the leech on the ground until it released the lump of flesh it had unscrewed. Erlin regarded him with tears streaming from her eyes. God it hurt. Until now the whole process had seemed so unreal.

"That won't work," she said as Ambel approached with part of her back between his forefinger and thumb.

"Course it will," he said.

He screwed it into her back and the pain immediately started to fade. Slowly she got to her feet and tried to reach round to the wound. There was blood, but she couldn't quite reach . . .

"You're one of us now," said Boris.

Erlin stared at him. Of course, the leeches. It all made sense now. She had to get her blood under the nanoscope as soon as she could.

"Come on," said Ambel, shouldering his blunderbuss.

When they reached the putrephallus stand at the edge of the dingle, Erlin refused the mask Boris offered her until the smell hit her, then she snatched it from him and quickly placed it over her face. The weeds were green and, again, well named. There was an Earth fungus that looked similar, but that did not throb quite so disconcertingly.

"See the hill. He lives up there," said Ambel.

Boris eyed him suspiciously. "You've been here before."

"Couple of times. Chopped him up last time and spread him all over the island. Reckon it took him a century or two to pull himself together."

"Someone tried burning once," said Boris. "Wouldn't burn."

The conversation went completely over Erlin's head.

Beyond the putrephallus the hill rose up into a gentle pimple in the centre of the island. Ambel unshouldered his buss and began walking up the slope, his head darting from side to side. Definitely bluer, thought Erlin. Then she looked upslope just as the nightmare loomed into view and came screaming and giggling down towards them, something flaccid, and which she had no wish to identify, held in its long fingers. It was like a man who had been put on a rack for a hundred years, every joint and muscle stretched out impossibly. It was huge blue and spidery and came capering down the hill as if to welcome them. Ambel's blunderbuss boomed and a great cloud of smoke wafted away. The Skinner went, "Oh!" and fell on its back.

"Quick!" shouted Ambel, drawing his knife. Boris did likewise and followed him. They reached the Skinner just as it sat upright, reached round behind itself, and threadled its long hand through the hole Ambel had made in its chest. Ambel and Boris skidded to a halt.

"Shit!"

"Bugger!"

Erlin ran past them and swiped with her laser scalpel. The Skinner's long head thudded on the ground and looked at her accusingly. She laughed a little crazily and proceeded to cut the rest of the monster into pieces.

"That's the ticket!" bellowed Ambel, and proceeded to pick up bits and hurl them in every direction. Boris joined him and soon the Skinner was scattered all over the hillside and in the jungle below, barring the head that Ambel held onto, and the flaccid thing it had been carrying. Erlin saw it direct for the first time and immediately threw up.

"Oh God! Peck!"

It was Peck, outwardly.

Ambel looked at Boris and nodded towards the skin. Boris picked it up and shook it, then turned it round and peered at the split from the circle cut round the anus to the one cut round the mouth.

"He's gonna be a bit cranky for a while," said Boris.

Ambel nodded in agreement. Erlin turned away. They had both gone mad, she had to get help for them. When she turned back they were walking back up the hill. She quickly followed.

She had nothing left to throw up when she followed them into the basin in the top of the hill. She just retched a little. The rest of Peck was jammed between two rocks, writhing about and making horrible noises. Erlin followed them down and watched in horror as they dragged him down and dropped him on the ground. All his muscles she could see, all his veins. His lidless eye-balls glared up at the sky. She advanced with her laser switched on. It was the only merciful thing to do.

"No!" Ambel knocked the laser from her hand. "Don't you think he's got enough problems? Find his clothes."

Erlin dropped to her knees, not sure if she wanted to cry or laugh. No, this was not happening . . . but it was. When she looked up, Ambel and Boris were putting Peck's skin back on him, tugging the wrinkles up his legs and pressing the air bubbles out . . . and Peck was helping them.

As she watched Peck climb unsteadily into the boat she said to Ambel, "What are you going to do with the head?"

Ambel held the Skinner's head up in one hand.

"I'll put it in a box, then he'll never be able to pull himself together properly."

Erlin had lost all her doubt. Of course, why not? She wondered about the report she must make. A nice scientific dissertation about how the leech fibre kept everything alive so that the leeches would have more prey to feed on, that was fine, but what about the Skinner? How would she tell them what the fibre had turned Spatterjay Hoop into, and what happened to humans too-long deprived of the Earth proteins that kept the fibres in abeyance? No, she would move her research in another direction—something about the leech symbiosis with the pear-trunk trees. She was relieved, as they came to the ship, to see a couple of sails circling above it. Both Boris and Ambel were now a much darker shade of blue, and Ambel seemed to be getting taller. Her own blueness was hidden by the natural colour of her skin, though Ambel had told her she had a pretty blue-white circle in the middle of her back.

jable sharks

Here's the story I did read in that book shop, and with grim relish over the gory bits. It was first published in *Storycellar* (issue 5 '95), and continues the nautical theme of the previous story but ventures to that place I like to visit, and will be visiting some more in this collection, the regressed colony. This is an alien world, the creatures tell you that, and the reference to 'ship metal' should tell you something else. Here you will also find a monster that had its inception in the fantasy trilogy gathering dust in my attic. One day I must pull that all down, blow off the dust, and write again about the fage . . .

The ship: three masts stitched across the horizon, black against the lemon sky. The hull is a cliff of wood topped with rails supported by tallow urns. Carvings everywhere. Wood and bone knitted together, interlaced, cunningly crafted. Along its sides are longboats braced like a beetle's wing cases. It seems deformed—top heavy. In the rigging are five crew, two hanging idle and one in the crow's nest, the twins reefing a sail. Below the deck are five more: three sleeping, the Barrelman, and Cook. On the deck to make things even are five others, for the moment.

Bosun Hinks handlines for green mackerel and the Captain sits in drugged stupor. Hinks pays him no mind. It is a fear the Captain has never named that drives him to the smoke, but he is not as bad as some, better than most, and only gives orders when the sharks are in. The rest of the time Hinks has charge. From his handline he now glances to Cheyne and Pallister who are sharpening the great knives ready for the next jable run. These harpoons are made of manbone and laminated shark skin. One of them is tipped with rare hull-metal, but it is never used during a run, being too valuable to lose.

"Ketra! Ketra!"

Hinks ties his handline to the rail and stares to where Chaff lies with arm stumps leaking into his bedding and the smell of his dying sickening the air. Tiredly Hinks climbs to his feet and walks over to the dying man. Cheyne is quickly with him.

"Chaff . . . Chaff, it's Hinks." He squats down beside the man and touches a palm to sweat-soaked hair. "Chaff."

Behind him Cheyne pulls a long bronze-edged stiletto from his sash and waits.

"Chaff, speak to me, please."

"He would choose death."

It is Pallister who speaks, Second Knife now that Chaff is dying.

"I would choose death and I would expect my friends and shipmates to release me, even had I no tongue to ask it."

He looks with especial concern to Cheyne. Cheyne has no tongue.

"Ketra! Ketra!"

Hinks glances to the Captain. "The Captain says no knife until he asks for it. By the Book. By the book."

All three of them regard the large black book resting next to the Captain's hooka. The book he always has with him but never seems to read.

They are aware of its presence, its weight, that it is the source of the fear that drives the Captain to his choice of oblivion. They listen to the creak of his chair as he rocks slowly back and forth puffing the smoke into the air.

"He will not see now," says Pallister.

They observe the reddened eyes fixing on the horizon as the rocking of the chair gradually comes to counter that of the ship. The glow of the gauze-wrapped wad of dreamfish waxes and wanes like the beating of a sick heart. Hinks turns from the Captain to the two knifemen.

"He asked us then. You will back me on this."

Pallister nods and glances at Cheyne who nods also. Cheyne tests the point of his stiletto with a callused thumb. A bead of blood falls to the waxed deck. Above; stillness. The one in the crow's nest watches. The four who are closer pretend concerns elsewhere. It is a hot and sultry day with not a breath of wind. There is little need for them to be up, but there the air is fresher in the rigging and the responsibility is nil.

"I cannot order you, Cheyne."

Cheyne nods, then steps past to stoop down next to Chaff. Pallister and Hinks stand between him and the Captain. There is a crunch as of a vegetable being segmented. There is the spastic kicking of legs, then stillness. Chaff no longer suffers.

"Man born of Earth who strives upon this sea . . . "

The prayers are sincere and the sermon long and boring for the crew. The Captain assuages the guilt he feels at missing Chaff's death by reading the man's last rights. What remains of Chaff has been stitched into an old sailcloth and weighted with lumps of salt. Hinks watches it slide into the sea, a small splash, nothing really. Below decks the Barrelman cuts ligaments and drops Chaff's bones into the maggot barrel. As is the way, his bones will be fashioned into a great knife along with the skin of the jable shark his other remains will summon. The shark is not long in coming.

"Fin. Fin. Fin."

Pallister thumps the haft of his great knife against the deck. The chant is taken up by the rest of the crew as a fin a yard high slices their slow wake and takes the cloth-wrapped bloody morsel before the salt can take it right down. It is bad luck, but they are used to that.

"Fin. Fin. Fin."

"Second Boat!" yells the Captain, and the windlasses are manned. With a clatter of bone ratchets the boat folds out level. The twins leap aboard to stow the coils of rope and floats. They are not allowed to touch Pallister's barbs for he believes it is bad luck for them to be handled by women. Cheyne is not so superstitious and hands his down. As the boat is loaded the Barrelman comes out on deck and the chant becomes quieter in deference to him. He has the black skin that marked him for his position from birth, for only by the hands of those born of the dark may the dead be handled before their last passage into it. His face and shaven skull are dyed white and his eyes are blue. All the crew fear and love him.

Six crew board the longboat: the twins, Pallister and Cheyne, Hinks and the Captain. The Barrelman has charge of the ship, but then, he always has had charge.

"Lower away!"

The ratchets clatter again and the boat drops to the sea. As it hits the surface the fin turns and moves in. Who is hunting whom? Hinks wonders as four scapula oars dig into the water and shoot the boat forward.

"It comes!" The Captain clutches a wax-proofed copy of the book to his chest as he shouts. "First knife!"

Cheyne stands with a great knife ready. Behind the blade he has mounted one of the detachable barbs from which a rope coils to a sea-cork float. The sunlight glints on the waves and the jable shark approaches in a tide of golden bands. They can all see its dead button eyes.

"Steady." The Captain is firm. Cheyne is firm. The shark's expression is all tooth-bone and flesh-ripping horror.

"Now!" The Captain, a second after Cheyne has made his cut.

The boat is rocked at the edge of a strike. The fin clips an oar as it is raised. The rope thrums as it goes out and the float hits the water with a dull flat smack. Cheyne stands with his knife emptied of its barb and the shark paints a red line from behind its right eye, a curving line, as it turns.

"Second knife!"

Pallister has his place and is ready. Soon two lines of blood flee the boat, turn, return, three lines then four, until at last the shark has had enough and tries to dive.

"Row, boys, row!"

They pursue the bobbing and jerking floats that reflect the shark's struggles. Down below; a cloud of blood at the nexus of four taut ropes. Then out of the cloud the toothed horror comes again, slowed and tangled. Cheyne's unbarbed cut is true and the great knife goes in behind the shark's head and severs its cartilaginous spine. The shark is held on the surface in the tangle of ropes and floats, and the blood spreads.

"Heave, boys, heave!"

The Captain holds the Book in his hand, the proper book, the ship's book. One of the twins mutters something filthy about his continual use of 'boys'. There was no proof to the rumour, though.

By slow increments and ratchetting clicks they hoist the jable shark from the sea using the same windlasses used to lower the boat. The weight heels the ship over and bloody water rains down its side. No fins are in sight, but there is time yet. Hinks hauls with the crew. Two sharks snapping at a dead one on the side of a ship is enough to pull that ship over. He knows. He has seen. In the long boat Cheyne and Pallister keep ready to drive sharks away, but only adapted squid swarm around the ship. Even so, they will not be washing their bloody hands in the water as Chaff did.

The white water of an approaching fin is seen as they lower the corpse onto the deck and open the blood drains. Cheyne and Pallister soon attach lines to the boat and the new shark only manages to nudge it once before it is hauled up the side of the ship.

"Open her up, boys. Let the shark soul free."

It is Cheyne's honour under the sight of the Barrelman. He uses the hull metal great knife in one flamboyant slice. Steaming guts avalanche across the deck at the unzipping. The opening of the stomach at the last spills a hundred weight of turtle crabs, an almond-shaped shell the size of a barrel, the remains of Chaff and, what appears to be the corpse of a small boy until it convulses and spews salt water from its lungs.

"Shark soul," hisses Pallister as the Captain hauls the boy to his feet. Hinks glares at the Knifeman, then turns to one of the twins as she speaks.

"Sea people?" she wonders.

Hinks stares at her. Is she Jan or Char? He has never known as they deliberately confuse. He turns back as the Captain pushes away damp fair hair to inspect the boy's neck for gill slits.

"Not of the sea people," he tells the crew. "Where are you from, boy? How is it you come live from the belly of this shark?"

The boy stares at him with blue and innocent eyes and Hinks does not like the expression that twists the Captain's mouth.

"Deal with this shark. I shall question him in my cabin."

He pulls the naked boy away and the twins nod an affirmative to each other.

"That is not a boy. That is the soul of this shark come to avenge. We must cast it back in the sea."

"Pallister, why so sure of this?"

"Always 'release the soul' and we see nothing. This time, something. A reason for the words. We always throw the innards and their contents back though they could be used."

"'Tis no soul of a shark." They turn as the Barrelman comes upon the deck. "Yet it seems not likely it is a boy."

"What should we do?"

"As the Captain instructs. As always: by the Book of the Sea."

With great knives and small knives they cut the shark. The innards go back into the sea after, with cursory ceremony, the remains of Chaff. The hull thumps with movement below the waves: squid and the butting of sharks. Barnacles never grow on the hull of a jable hunter, but weed often grows on the teeth left jammed into the wood.

They skin the shark and the Barrelman takes its skin to preserve and prepare for lamination—one of the many uses of a skin with a colour and a texture called jable. The salted meat they store in the barrels he marks, the fat is rendered for oil, and the cartilage stored in brine for later use in the manufacture of glue. When all is done, they wash the deck clean and replace the blood drains. All around the sea foams and great dark bodies surface and dive. All around, fins.

Night seems to drive the last of the sharks away or perhaps another jable hunter has cast a bucket of blood into the sea. Hinks knows there are those who prefer to hunt by the light of the moons, those who make it a mystic thing of ceremony and sacrifice, and toast each kill with shark's blood drunk from whelk-shell cups. As he pulls in nacreous glitters of green mackerel and snaps their necks with his forefinger and thumb he wonders what questions the Captain might be asking now. It has been some time since he took the boy to his cabin. No matter, no concern. Hinks casts his line of lures back into the sea as the two yellow moons the twins have their names from break over the horizon like glaring eyes.

"He buggers an innocent while Pallister talks of shark souls, Cheyne sharpens all his knives, and you catch mackerel we don't need."

Hinks stares the pile of mackerel next to him then looks up at one of the twins. "Are you Jan?"

She ignores the question. "In Piezel they would crush his testicles and throw him to the jable. We sit idle while he gratifies lust."

"Many would, given opportunity."

She steps more into the moonlight and stands with her hands on her hips. "I might give you opportunity, Hinks. It is for me to say yes or no and for you to accept or not. This boy has been given no such choices."

Hinks reels his handline back onto its frame then climbs tiredly to his feet. It is his responsibility, just like with Chaff. They all know what the Captain is doing and they all know it is wrong, but only he can do anything, by the Book.

"Back me up then. Where is your sister?"

"She is testing the point of Cheyne's most important knife."

Hinks is surprised. In all the time the twins had been on board he had never known either of them to bed another member of the crew. The rumour was that they preferred their own sex, but then that was always the rumour when men's egos are bruised.

"A strange night, and I wonder why you told me . . . Is she recruiting to your cause?"

"No and yes. She has been with Cheyne since the season began and he is in agreement about the Captain."

"I heard nothing."

"Cheyne does not gossip."

Hinks shakes his head. Of course Cheyne does not gossip. Cheyne does not speak at all and has not spoken since the excision and cautery of the fungal infection in his mouth and throat.

Through the double moon shadows they walk to the forward hatch and the single stair that goes down to the Captain's cabin. As they slip below decks, Hinks shakes a biolight to luminescence and carries it before him. Soon they are before the door of shark skin stretched on its frame of man-bone. They listen. Nothing. Hinks reaches to scratch on the door, but it opens, unlatched. They enter.

"It is murder. Murder has been done here."

Hinks nods agreement, the rich smell of slaughter in his nostrils. What else could this be? The Captain lies sprawled across his bunk in a tangle of bloody sheets. Driven up through his groin and into his guts is a spike made of solid glass, like an icicle. But maybe this was not the first cause of his death, since neat as a cylinder his right eye-socket has been reamed out to the back of his skull. Hinks knows the horrible fear of the supernatural. They heard nothing, perhaps a shark soul was loose on this ship.

"Man overboard!"

The yell is from above and breaks into their nightmare reverie. Hinks gains some command over himself and pushes the unnamed twin back to the door. What now? Another murder, or a murderer seeking to escape? Past the twin he rushes up on deck. The Barrelman is there leaning over the rail and Pallister is beside him.

"Who is it?" Hinks asks.

"I do not know. I do not know." The Barrelman's voice is strange, as if surprised at itself.

"Pallister?"

"I don't know, but he is done." Pallister points to the floating body and to the fin slicing moonlit water just beyond it. Hinks watches the inevitable: the fin disappearing, the body snatched from below.

"Dead or unconscious when he went in, like as not," says Pallister, then after glancing to the twin, "or she."

"Get the crew on deck, all of them you can find, find that boy if you can, bring them all, bring them all here. Murder has been done. The Captain is dead in his cabin and who knows who the shark took."

It takes little time for them all to be roused and assembled as many of them were coming onto the deck as Hinks made his speech. He counts and he appraises. Cheyne and the other twin look flushed. Cook has certainly been sampling the sea apple wine again and the others seem no different from normal. All are here but the boy and the Captain. Hinks wants to be sure, though.

"I want the ship searched forward to aft, every unsealed barrel checked and every sail locker. Check the crow's nest as well." He turns to the Barrelman. "What say you, Barrelman?" The Barrelman shakes his head and goes below to his own kingdom. Cook follows him.

No boy is found, just as Hinks expected. He speaks with Pallister and Cheyne as allies always and knows a loneliness when he realises he cannot trust even them. In the end he must ask those questions.

"Pallister, did you throw the boy back into the sea?"

"As the Book is my witness, Hinks, I did not."

Hinks inspects the rest of the crew who stand nervously around. Which one of them? Which of them committed murder? It could be any, even the twin who had him go to the Captain's cabin might have come from there earlier.

"Somebody cast the boy into the sea, dead or alive, no difference. Somebody has murdered our Captain."

"The boy," says Pallister. "The shark soul. It killed him and returned to its element."

"You talk like a Reader," spat one of the twins.

Hinks stares at her. "Which one are you? Tell me now."

"I am Jan."

The rest of the crew study her carefully. So, Hinks decides, Jan is the one with her hair tied back and Char the one who was bedding Cheyne, this night, anyway.

"She may be right, Pallister. What matter? If what you say is true then there is no blame or guilt to attach anywhere and I will be glad. But I must be sure."

"What are your thoughts?" asks Pallister.

"I think one of you killed the Captain, and the boy, in disgust," he gazes at all the crew, "or fear," he now looks particularly at Pallister. "And the boy was thrown into the sea to bring belief in your story."

"It could have been you," says Jan.

"Yes, but I know it was not," says Hinks. "Now you and Pallister will come with me and we will once again view the body before it is passed on to the Barrelman. The rest of you prepare sail for the morning wind. We head directly for Piezel."

"What weapon is this?" Pallister braces his foot against the Captain's groin and tries to pull the spike from him. His hands slip along the glassy surface. "Too deeply imbedded, perhaps in his spine. It was put there with some force." Hinks, suspicious of every action now, tries to remove the spike himself. He cannot.

"And what weapon caused this?" asks Jan, pointing at the neatly reamed hole in the Captain's head. Hinks has no answer for her.

"Hinks." Pallister has moved back by the door and is pointing at the floor. "This is not the work of a man." Hinks looks down and sees a trail of slime leading to the door. He turns to the table beside the Captain's bed and picks up the Book of the Sea. As he opens it to the first page there is a scream of horror, turned rapidly to one of agony.

Crew, and he lies in a pool of blood upon the deck. Hinks turns him over gently. Holes have been bored into his neck. Another scream from below just as four more of the crew come onto the deck, amongst them are Cheyne and Char. Cheyne snatches up the metalled great knife and stares at the hatch to the crew quarters.

"What is it? What is happening?"

"Something . . . Something killing them," Char replies to her sister.

"What does it look like? Tell me, tell me now," demands Hinks.

"It is a man sometimes, and it crawls. There is slime and a tube like a wood bore . . . I cannot . . . "

Hinks curses and in the moonlight he opens the book. He searches down the first tissue-thin page and finds the sea-life section: Dangers of the Sea. There are more sharks than he realised, giant squid and flatworms capable of ingesting a man. It is there. He finds it only a few pages in under 'Sea Fages and Related Mullusca'. There is a picture of the glass dart; a love dart used during mating. It is barbed hence the reason Pallister could not remove it. Another scream just as Hinks reads the section which tells him of the shell they found in the stomach of the shark. Just then the hatch crashes open and out come the Barrelman and two others. All now watch the hatch and wait for what might come next. Pallister has armed himself, and the remaining great knives are shared. Only Barrelman, Hinks, and Jan are without weapons.

"What is it Hinks? Tell us?" asks Pallister, terror barely suppressed in his voice.

"It is a Fage. A kind of mollusc. That was its shell we saw inside the shark," Hinks tells them all, and some of the terror departs. It is named. It is in the Book. Hinks continues to read, moving his finger from word to word, some of them unfamiliar, metamorph and shifter, syphon and ovipositor. He begins to feel a greater dread. The boy . . . He turns the page and sees the picture of a man, and something next to it that is half a man.

"Dear God . . . "

He looks up directly at the Barrelman standing behind the shoulder-to-shoulder crew. Out of the corner of his eye the Barrelman returns his regard, but does not turn his head. His head is deforming, pushing forward and taking on a goatish shape, lips peeling back from something that glistens. The Barrelman is not. It is the Fage.

"Look out!"

The man directly in front of the Fage turns, screams, falls to the deck with half of his face ripped away. His screams take on a liquid quality. Back into the glistening head part the glassy tube of the syphon retracts. All of its skin now glistens. Arms merge with sides, legs merge, now a standing slug shape it falls on Char, who is locked in place in her terror. It slides over her fast. There is a brief struggle. It leaves her slime coated and spurting blood from the hole bored through her ribs into her heart. There is a scream, fear, rage. A great knife pins the Fage, goes right in. The reaction is horrifyingly quick. A slime coated tentacle exudes then cracks like a whip. A man smashes through a rail and goes bonelessly over the side. The great knife falls out, leaving only a white mark on the grey skin. That cry again. It is Cheyne. He comes in with the steel great knife, ducks the tentacle then lops it off. He cuts again and the Fage falls in half. He cuts again and again in his rage. In moments the deck is spread with writhing pieces of slimy flesh no larger than a man's head. Cheyne drops his great knife, kneels down by Char. He cries silence.

"Oh God . . . Is it dead at last? Is it dead? I would have preferred the soul of a shark. Yes . . . I would have preferred that." Pallister is babbling. Hinks stands. He had not even time to get to his feet. That fast, it happened that fast. He looks at the remains of the crew. Jan, standing with her mouth open in shock, Pallister, babbling to himself now that no one else is listening, Cheyne, silent, three other crew, one on the deck with his face hanging off, but still alive, one squatting by the mast gazing about him in bewilderment, one mechanically stabbing pieces of the Fage with a great knife and flicking them over the side.

"You, Tanis."

The man by the mast stands and looks to Hinks with a kind of hope. Hinks keeps the Book firmly tucked under his arm as he gives his orders.

"Help him . . . in whatever way he requires."

Tanis gazes with compassion to his companion on the deck and draws a knife from his belt sheath. Cheyne is still grieving but now Jan is with him and they hold each other. Hinks does not want to go below decks just yet. He does not want to see what is there.

"Hinks . . . sir," the other crewman calls to him.

"What is it . . . Lal?"

Hinks walks over and stands beside him.

"Watch," says Lal.

The man skewers a piece of the Fage and throws it into the sea—as it hits the water it changes into a turtle crab, the next piece turns into a green mackerel, and the next into a small shark. Hinks understands now why the Captain was always frightened. The Book is heavy under his arm and he has only seen a few of its many thin pages. He wonders what the Captain read that frightened him so badly, and if he ever read any more.

the thrake

Now here's another story from the runcible universe. It first appeared in *Fiction Furnace* 3 (summer '93) along with a line drawing I'd done of the orbonnai, Paul. In this you can see some more of the outfall I got from reading a veterinary book on helminthology (the study of parasitic worms), which was lent to me by the vet who proof-read *The Parasite* for me many years before it was actually published. Similar outfall is the parasitic ecology of *The Skinner*. Anyway, I like this story, for its parasites, for its pop at fundamentalism, and for the way it all tied together so neatly. Since its publication in the old *The Engineer* it has also appeared in Dave Summer's *Hadrosaur Tales* 16 (2003).

To Mark, the runcible was the altar to some cybernetic god of technology, and he felt like an acolyte come before it for the first time. He considered it the nearest thing to an icon in this Godless society, and consequently looked upon it as an enemy of his faith.

Skaidon technology.

The religion.

The room containing the runcible was a fifty metre sphere of mirrored metal—the containment sphere beyond which the buffers operated. It was floored with black glass, and mounted on a central stepped pedestal or the same substance, were the ten metre incurving bull's horns of the runcible itself. Between these shimmered the cusp of the Skaidon warp, or the spoon. Mark could remember someone trying to explain five-dimensional singularity mechanics to him, but the subject did not interest him.

They dined on mince and slices of quince.

He was to be quince: he was to be a mitter traveller.

He advanced into the room, across the black glass to the steps, mounted them. Before the cusp he paused for a moment and tapped the cross, tattooed on his wrist, for luck.

Our Father who art in Heaven—

He stepped through.

STOPSTART.

Hallowed be thy name.

He had travelled by runcible many times before, and on every occasion found it a deeply disturbing experience. He could not grasp that the step he had just taken had been light-years long. The universe should not be so big. He refused to believe there were things the unaugmented human mind could not understand.

"Mark Christian?"

He turned his attention to the woman waiting on the black glass of this second runcible chamber. She was short, with the muscular body of one raised on a plus G planet. Her hair was cropped and dyed with rainbow spirals and she wore skin-tight monofilament overalls. Her eyes were the eyes of a cat. In terms of Earth fashion she was about two years out of date.

Mark allowed himself a smug little smile as he walked down the steps to meet her. "Yes, I am. Pleased to meet you."

He pumped her hand and gazed beyond her to the door of the chamber. Where was the Director? Who was this woman? He would have to have words. Didn't they realise who he was?

"I am Carmen Smith. Welcome to Station Seventeen."

"Oh, really?"

Mark released her hand with a touch of distaste. She had calluses!

"If you will come with me I will show you to your quarters. Sorry not to have a welcoming committee here, but we are very busy and don't spend much time on the social niceties."

He only realised his gaffe when he was following her out.

Carmen Smith. . . . Oh God!

He had just met the Director.

Xenoethnologist my ass. I don't need this.

"I take it you received all your immuno treatments?"

It was a stupid question to ask, she was well aware, but she did not think she would be having a sensible conversation with this idiot.

"Yes," said Christian.

Carmen noticed he was a little pale. "You do know this is an open runcible?"

Mark nodded. Carmen studied him for a moment, wondering what his problem might be. Perhaps he knew of her objections to him coming here. She shook her head and turned to the door. It slid open and they stepped outside.

The sky was alien. No other word applied. He could have said it was the colour of blackberry cordial shone through with a sun lamp or that the clouds were like the froth on fermenting red wine. But those were descriptions taking as their basis things from Earth—things familiar. The sky was not familiar. It was something seen in Technicolor nightmares and the strangest of dreams. He stood under a sky an unimaginable distance from Earth. Another world. Another place. An element in the dreams of another species. Abruptly he realised Carmen was speaking to him.

"—it's fatal to anthropomorphise."

"Sorry . . . ?"

"The Orbonnai are very like us physiologically."

"Oh, yes . . . I am trained in these matters."

"I thought it best to warn you. There have been members of Station Seventeen who had formed too close an attachment to the likes of Paul."

"Paul?"

Carmen gazed at him speculatively. Abruptly he felt foolish, but the sky and the weird contorted landscape below it had denuded him of words. He shrugged as if making himself more comfortable in his fashionable jacket.

"That is anthropomorphising in itself," he said. "I myself adhere to Gordon's dictum; 'If it is alien, give it an alien name.' 'Paul' is far too prosaic."

He glanced at her again and took in the angular beauty of her tanned features. She'd had alterations other than her eyes, yet, because she was out of date she seemed more . . . plausible.

She said, "The runcible technicians named him Paul. Edron, the co-ordinator of the planetary biostudy team, then tried to have his name changed to Xanthos or some such. Never caught on."

Mark nodded to himself like someone with access to privileged information. "I would be most interested to view any studies made of him."

Carmen glanced at him. "I'll have the recordings sent to your quarters directly."

After leaving the shower and donning his silk Faberge lounging suit, Mark dropped in the chair before his viewing screen and caressed a touchplate with his finger. The screen flickered on to show him a scene of dense jungle on the edge of a stream with banks of blue sand. He fast-forwarded it until there were signs of movement from the jungle. A narrative began as he watched. He jumped with surprise then glanced around guiltily before returning his attention to the screen.

The orboni edged out of the jungle, wire-taut as it surveyed its surroundings, then squatted down in the sand at the edge of the river. It was difficult not to ascribe human characteristics to it, with its bilateral symmetry, arms and legs, and its upright stance. Yet, it was bone-white and with a head like the bare skull of a bird. Half listening to the narrative, Mark watched it intently.

"—and the immediate and invalid assumption being that Paul was a tool user. Note the three fingered hands and opposable thumb. As we now know, Daneson was in error. It is far too easy to anthropomorphise when faced with creatures which bear such a close physiological resemblance to humanity. Here we see the true use of that opposable thumb, and more importantly, the long mid-finger with its hooked point. It is relevant at this point to add, that the Orbonnai do not have nails. As Gordon once had the temerity to conjecture; 'If they don't have nails they don't use tools. Imagine bashing your finger with a hammer.' A most dubious—"

Mark turned the sound down as he observed Paul. He did not need the distraction of this babble. He knew what he was searching for, and he knew he would find it. According to the highest Church authorities the Orbonnai were pre-ascension.

The orboni reached into the stream and fumbled around for a while. Eventually it withdrew its hand, holding a snail the size of an ash-tray. Mark watched it intently as it inspected its prize, and felt a momentary flush of excitement. Could it be that all the evidence he needed would be on these memory crystals? He noted a number of rocks laying nearby. Would Paul make the connection? The way he was inspecting the snail looked very much as if he was satisfying his curiosity. Mark willed Paul to pick up a stone. If there was no evidence here then he would have to go outside. He shuddered at the thought and turned the sound up again.

"—Again he was in error. This 'turning' of the nautiloid is not due to aesthetic appreciation. It is an instinctive behaviour that mimics the tumbling of the mollusc in the current of the stream when it has been dislodged from its hold on the bottom. Shortly we will see the reason for this."

Abruptly Paul darted his 'long' finger inside the snail, twisted it, and pulled out the white squidlike body it contained. With relish he pecked this up, tipped his head back and shook it to get the morsel down. He discarded the shell.

"There. A study of nautiloid behaviour shows they open the clypeus of their shells to reattach themselves to the bed of stream after about thirty seconds 'tumbling'. This is what Paul was after. Other studies have shown that the Orbonnai still follow this instinctive behaviour even with empty nautiloid shells taken from the beds of the streams. Empty or otherwise, these shells are always discarded after thirty seconds. It is well to note that the blue nautiloid, which has a tumbling response time of fifty seconds, has displaced the green nautiloids in the Graffus island chain, as it is slowly doing here, and that there are no Orbonnai there."

"Stupid woman," said Mark, and ran the recording forward.

"—the miracidia of the so-called 'brain fluke' parasite are caused to break secondary encystment by the heating of the faeces. Their vector here is—"

"—once in nautiloid waters they begin their cyclic swimming patterns. This greatly increases their chances of finding a host—"

"—a matter of conjecture. If green nautiloids are the infested form of blue nautiloids then—"

Mark swore and jerked the memory crystal from the machine. He looked at the label in disbelief.

A BRIEF ANALYSIS OF HELMINTH PARASITE VECTORS IN NAUTILOID—ORBONNAI-THRAKE POPULATIONS BY CARMEN SMITH.

He closed his eyes and tapped his cross for luck, then re-inserted the crystal and ran it to near its end. When he turned it on the scene presented to him froze him in his seat.

"—but of course the thrake has no need to be this mobile. It is my opinion that this is a throw-back to the tumbling delay, and a time prior to such widespread infestation. This is, of course, based on tenuous evidence. There may be a cyclic—"

Mark was not listening. He was staring in horror at the creature on the screen. It bore the appearance of a giant metallic wood-louse bent into an L. It had four short insectile legs on the ground, and six of what could only be described as arms. They were long, had two joints. The pair nearest its head ended in crablike pincers, and the pair below ended in clubs. The final pair Mark could not see because they were the ones holding down the orboni, while the thrake dismembered it with its pincers, and conveyed it piece by piece to its nightmare, machine-like mandibles and grinding mouth.

"My God!"

He had never been more sincere in that exclamation. He felt sick. He jerked the crystal from the viewer and tossed it to one side as if it were infectious. He then took up the next crystal.

SOME XENOETHNOLOGICAL ASPECTS OF THRAKE . . .

"Barbarians!"

He tossed the crystal aside and took up the next.

"Let me get this right. You wish to go out alone to study the Orbonnai. I do hope you are aware of the . . . difficulties," said Carmen.

"I saw that obscene recording of the thrake creature," said Mark.

Carmen looked askance at him then shook her head.

"They're no problem—"

"I beg to differ."

"You can beg all you like, but no amount of begging is going to get you near the Orbonnai. They move very fast when they want to . . . well, in most cases. Most of the recordings we've managed to make have been by remote chameleon drone. Paul was the exception. He came close to the station to feed because he was old and had been driven away from his group by a younger male."

"Then perhaps he is the one I should seek. In that other," Mark pursed his lips in distaste, "recording, I noted that Paul had been radio tagged."

"Which crystal was that?"

"You are well aware of the one I am referring to."

"Oh yes, 'Sexual Dynamics In Orbonnai Family Groups'. I remember it—a most definitive study."

"I still wish to make my own observations."

Carmen stared at him in annoyance for a moment. "I will do everything I can to prevent you. You were foisted on us here at Seventeen by the New Christian Church at Carth. It is unfortunate that Earth Central have not seen fit to keep the likes of you off our backs."

"I resent your inferences, Madam."

"And I resent your beliefs. I find the practising of your particular brand of pseudoscience here, where real science is being carried out, most distasteful, and quite possibly damaging. I know why you are here. Your Church knows there are creatures of near-human appearance and all of a sudden they've got the missionary bug. When are you going to learn—"

"I do not have to tolerate this. Creation Science has its basis in the most sublime of works. The New Carth Bible is—Where are you going! Come back here!"

Carmen ignored him.

Once back in his room Mark picked up a memory crystal at random and smashed it against the wall. Then he dropped to his knees. "Oh Lord, give me the strength to go on. Give me the will to bear this ignorance of your plan and your presence." He bowed his head and clasped his hands below his chin.

Didn't they understand? What worth had their universe of facts without a binding deity? How could they believe the magnificent complexity and pattern of the universe was not created by God? He hated so-called 'true' scientists. Where would the human race be without God to guide it? He unclasped his hands and stood up. As a Christian in the face of adversity, he would do what he had to do. It had always been so. *Their* science was irrelevant. He opened his case and removed some things he would need.

Carmen slammed the door to her office. She was angry because she had allowed him to get to her. But what other reaction was there in the face of such pig-headed stupidity? She sat down at her desk and stared blindly at the papers before her.

He had not studied the crystals fully, else he would have realised the futility of his mission. But then that was always the way with people like him. They based their 'science' on a false premise and discarded anything that did not fit. They rambled on about watchmakers and complex construction and gave simplistic explanations: a human being is complex therefore it was made, because conventional science does not have all the answers, the ones it does have are wrong. For his kind facts were twisted to match theories, rather than theories proven or disproven by facts.

Carmen repressed the urge to smash something and reached across and pressed the button on her intercom. "Davidson?"

"Here, lab twelve."

"If you're not on anything important can you come up to my office."

"Just running some computer models. The AI can handle it. I'll be up in about a quarter of an hour. What's up?"

"What do you think?"

"No word from Earth Central yet?"

"There was a vague promise of a monitor being sent, but you know how it is with them. They think that causing a furore is free advertising for the Churches. Best to let them die a natural death. Interference is frowned on. Freedom of choice and all that."

"I preferred the pre-runcible attitude: belief in superior 'It'll be all right in the end' deities equated with dangerous irresponsibility."

"Yeah, see you shortly anyway. We've got to sort out how to deal with the arsehole. He wants to 'make his own observations.'"

There was a silence before Davidson replied. "Freeman told me he saw him down at the stores kitting himself out. You mean you haven't given him permission?"

Carmen closed her eyes and rubbed at her forehead. She was getting a headache. She suspected it would get worse. "We didn't actually get to that. Got side-tracked. Go to the stores yourself will you and see if he's taken a radio tracker. Also get Freeman to charge up that last chameleon drone."

"I'm on it."

Carmen leant back in her chair and stared at the map up on her wall. She had been going to warn him. Him with expensive clothes, city ways and archaic beliefs. Outside Station Seventeen was a wilderness that thus far had claimed three lives, and they had been professionals. Did he think his God would help him once he was lost and starving? That would be a first. All the proteins and sugars out there were inverted. You could eat your fill of fruit and meat every day and still starve to death, if you were not poisoned beforehand. No matter. The water would get him first. It was so contaminated with mercury salts it was a standing joke that the streams grew longer in warm weather.

Carmen shook her head. The ache was growing worse.

"Ugh! Filthy creature!"

Mark stamped the leaf-shaped worm into the ground and winced as his boot rubbed on the raw spot on the back of his ankle. Then he inspected the red ring on the back of his hand where the worm had clung for a moment before convulsing and falling off. This was just too much. He looked around at the nigh impenetrable jungle then continued on down the track he hoped had been made by Orbonnai. He would show them that a creation scientist was as capable of doing fieldwork as the best of them.

The sky was growing darker by the time he reached the stream and he offered up a silent prayer of thanks before stooping down at its edge to fill his water bottle. Once that was done and he had drunk his fill, he unhitched his pack and took out the tracker. The direction finder pointed roughly up the course of the stream. There should be no problem. His God was with him. He sat down on the blue sand to rest for a moment. He was tired, but well-satisfied with himself. He had made a stand, as all good Christians should.

The nautiloid was bumbling along below the surface directly in front of him when he saw it. With great daring he reached into the water and took it out. With a click it retracted into its shell. He held it in his hand, checked his watch, then began turning it as he had seen Paul do. After thirty seconds nothing had happened. He tossed it to the ground and stood up.

"Rubbish," he said, and went on his way.

The blue nautiloid, with its fifty-second response time, crawled back into the stream once he was gone.

Carmen studied the man seated opposite her and felt bewilderment. He represented Earth Central, yet, he looked so . . . mediocre. It was obvious he had no alterations. The face he wore had not seen cosmetic surgery since his birth. His eyes were muddy green and there was a scar on his chin. His clothing had nothing to recommend it either, other than functionality. He wore a green monofilament coverall and cheap plastimesh hiking boots.

He steepled his fingers before his face before commenting on what she had told him. "The orboni he showed greatest interest in is this Paul. What would you say are his chances of reaching this creature without getting himself killed?"

"Quite good. Paul is dying and cannot move about very much. He has already started to venture into the less complex environment of the savannah."

"And you have a chameleon drone following Paul."

"Yes . . . we couldn't think of much else to do really. An air search . . . I mean . . . the jungle . . . "

"I take your point. But you do have more than one chameleon drone."
Carmen nodded.

"Then I would suggest you send them into the jungle to search the area between here and Paul's present location. Mark Christian did take a radio tracker so it is likely he is heading directly toward this orboni."

"I suppose we could."

"There is some problem?"

"The remaining drones are being used in an intensive study of the Thrakai. The study has prime status."

The man pressed his finger against his temple. It was a gesture Carmen had seen before. Visible alterations were not the only ones. He was direct-linked to the runcible AI.

"I see," he said, and looked at her with a raised eyebrow. "A class three sentience?"

Carmen nodded again. It was not polite to interrupt someone when they were in the midst of a conversation with an AI as those intelligences tended not to repeat themselves. Eventually he shook his head and showed signs of annoyance.

"And this fool is trailing after the Orbonnai?"

"We passed all the recordings on to him. He did not see fit to study them."

The monitor bowed his head for a moment before going on. "It would appear this is an intervention situation rather than a monitoring one. He must be stopped. The policy of Earth Central is one of 'observation only' during encounters with any sentience above class eight. We cannot have theocratic interference with class three sentiences." The monitor looked thoughtful, finishing with, "Recall your drones and send them into the jungle. This man must be stopped."

Mark was stillness itself as he watched the orboni, even though the pains in his stomach had increased.

It was Paul. He knew it was Paul.

And he is praying!

This was what he had come for. Here was purpose.

Paul knelt at the edge of the stream with his head down on the blue sand. He had remained so for some time. Mark maintained his position and slowly lowered his holocorder. His arm was beginning to hurt, but he believed he had enough evidence for the Bishop. He continued to watch, gradually becoming more uncomfortable, and wondering when Paul was going to move. Some time passed before the orboni jerked upright and shuffled to the edge of the stream. Mark raised the holocorder again.

Paul was poised at the edge of the stream for some time before he dipped his hand in and pulled out a nautiloid. He held it up before himself for a long time.

He's not turning it!

Abruptly his arm jerked to one side and the nautiloid was smashed on a rock.

Yes! Yes!

In a moment he had the nautiloid in his beak, but then he seemed to lose interest, and the fleshy body, crusted with sand and broken shell, dropped to the sand. Mark lowered the holocorder. That was not relevant and could be deleted from the crystal. He followed the orboni as it stood and began to make its unsteady way along the bank of the stream.

It seemed almost as if there was no transition at all when they came from the jungle out into the open. Twice Paul fell to his knees in an attitude of prayer. On the second occasion Mark only got to film part of it, because he was suddenly and violently sick.

Backwoods worlds!

He felt hot and shivery and the light seemed too bright.

Oh Father, give thy servant the strength to go on.

It was only as the glare seemed to clear, that he saw the pyramid of skulls—Orbonnai skulls, stacked so their beaks were all pointing to the east. The stack was higher than his head.

"Thank you, Lord," he said, and filmed the pyramid before continuing to follow Paul. This was proof that the Orbonnai respected their dead. Better than tool using, as good as the act of worship. Mark walked on with the light in his eyes.

The third time the orboni went down the light seemed to turn to a heavenly glare. Mark nearly fell over the creature, but instead fell to his knees at its side. He clasped his hands before his chest just as the creature was pulling itself upright. He gazed at it, searching for some sign of fellow feeling, of an understanding of the mystery of worship. The orboni made a squealing sound and he felt something rake his face.

"No, wait! I understand!"

Paul was staggering away. Mark stood to go after it when a silvery sphere materialised in the air above him. He glanced up at it then ignored it, for he had more important things to do. It was a chameleon drone with its emulation field off. He wiped blood from his face and went after the orboni.

Paul stumbled along ahead of him. But for some reason he could not catch up. He felt slightly drunk. His legs did not seem to be obeying him.

"Wait! Come back . . . please."

He stopped and took a breather. Liquid bubbled in his chest and his stomach heaved again, but he was retching dry.

"Wait . . . "

When he finally got the retching under control he looked for Paul again. And saw horror.

Paul was bowed to the ground again, and rearing above him was a thrake. Mark froze, his brain working sluggishly. He had not realised they were so big. The thrake towered over Paul—it must have been over ten feet tall.

No, not that, that is not The One.

Mark unhitched his pack and removed from it a small glassy pistol. He fired once, but his hand was shaking too much, and scrub began to smoke beside the thrake.

"Get back! Get away from him!.. Paul, that creature is no god. It is . . . an icon . . . God is . . . "

The thrake turned its nightmare mouth and convolute sensorium towards him. He swallowed bile and fired again. This time his shot hit and it emitted a bubbling scream as part of its hide gusted smoke, then turned and ran.

"God is . . . "

A dark shadow blotted out the sky above. He looked up and saw someone looking down at him.

"God?" he said, and fainted.

"Feeling better?"

Paul nodded to the kind-faced man and took another drink from the pure water in the flask. He tried not to look at Carmen Smith, who was standing beside the raft with her arms folded and a look of disgust on her face.

The man said, "We would have taken you back, but your condition is not too bad. Those injections will keep you going until they can give you a transfusion at Seventeen. The cut on your face should cause no problems. Anyway, I believe Professor Smith has something to show to you."

Mark nodded and got unsteadily to his feet. He was feeling better. He may have been delirious, but he had seen what he had seen. He looked to Carmen.

"Please, come with me," she said, all politeness.

When he saw where she was leading him he said, "Paul . . . " Paul, still frozen in an attitude of prayer.

"Yes, Paul. He is quite dead, though you did not make his dying any easier."

"The thrake . . . "

"The thrakai feed on the Orbonnai. They always have done."

With more certainty he said, "That does not make it right."

Carmen smiled with nasty relish. "You know, we picked up on you by the stream when you first saw this orboni. What did you think you saw there?"

Mark straightened up. "I saw a reasoning creature taking the first steps toward tool using."

"And this attitude? An attitude of worship?"

Mark nodded, less sure. He glanced round at the man and noticed for the first time that he was clothed in the workmanlike gear of an agent from Earth Central. He was not sure if the man's expression was one of sympathy or contempt. He turned back to Carmen and saw she now held a small surgical shear.

"I suppose you saw that this orboni's God was the thrake—a monster. I wonder what it saw?"

She stooped to the orboni and sliced off the top of its skull. A writhing ball of flatworms spilled out. "In the end it saw nothing at all. It was blind." She prodded at the worms with the toe of her boot. "You know what I saw at the stream? I saw an animal with a brain so badly damaged it had lost the use of its normal instinctive abilities. When it fell to its knees, it did so, not to worship, but because its inner ear was full of parasites and it kept losing its sense of balance. Look at them. Look at them, Mark Christian."

Mark stared at the writhing mass of worms as they broke apart and began to die on the bluish dirt.

Carmen continued, relentlessly. "Tell me, did your God that made the lion and the lamb make the worms that eat them from the inside out?"

"I have faith."

At that point the monitor stepped between them and stared down with clinical detachment at the opened skull of the orboni.

"I presume," he said, "that the thrake has its place in this parasite's life cycle."

Carmen looked to him. "Yes, the thrake shits their eggs. The parasite goes from there to the water and into the nautiloids. The Orbonnai ingest them and become so riddled they're easy prey."

As she finished the anger drained out of her.

"Are the thrakai damaged in any way by these parasites?" asked the monitor.

Carmen shook her head. "It's difficult to tell. The life-cycle is so interlinked that you cannot make—"

They are ignoring me.

"—an easy assessment based on—"

Suddenly angry, Mark interrupted. "Do you think you've won? Do you think that somehow you have proven to me that the Orbonnai are not pre-ascension! I will return to Carth and report my findings. Those skulls . . . On the basis of them, a mission will be sent here for the . . . "

He trailed off when he noticed they were not listening to him. They were looking past him into the scrub. He turned and saw the thrake he had shot at, standing no more than ten yards away.

"My God! Shoot it! Drive it away!"

He turned and saw the monitor and Carmen looking at each other.

Carmen said, "We can't have that . . . a mission here."

The monitor nodded. "It won't happen." He turned to Mark. "You will not be returning to Carth. You will be coming with me to Earth Central to answer to the charge of attempted unlawful killing."

"What? . . . Who?"

The monitor pointed at the thrake. "You attempted to kill a grade three sentience. That is a serious offence."

Carmen said, "The Thrakai were the ones you should have been studying for your spurious proofs. They're the ones that build those mounds of skulls. Perhaps they worship the Orbonnai. Members of the prehistoric societies of Earth used to worship the animals they ate."

They turned from him then to watch the thrake. It started to move in, slowly, like an animal stalking its prey. Mark could see it had its many joined arms opened out ready to grab any of them that tried to escape. He started to back away, but the monitor's hand came down on his shoulder with the finality of a guillotine.

"There's no need for panic," the monitor said to him, then to Carmen, "What should we do now?"

"Back away slowly, towards the raft. It only wants the orboni. They've tried human flesh before, and found it distasteful."

Mark wanted to shout out how wrong she was as they moved away from the body of Paul. He wanted to run, but the hand on his shoulder seemed to suck the will out of him. It was all he could do to keep his legs moving. Soon, the three of them were backed up against the raft and the thrake had reached the corpse. Mark watched in horror as it severed Paul's head, then continued to advance on them, with the head held in its lower appendages.

"My God . . . do something!"

Suddenly Carmen was walking forwards, her arms spread wide, like the thrake's. Soon she was standing before it, below it. It paused over her like a wall of scrap-iron about to fall, then slowly it stooped, placed the head at her feet, then turned and moved away. In a moment it had picked up the rest of the corpse and was loping for the horizon. Carmen stooped down and picked up the head.

"Souvenir?" she asked Mark.

He stared at her, feeling sick. She tossed the head back on the ground.

"Let's get out of here," she said, tiredly.

The monitor's hand did not leave Mark's shoulder as they boarded the raft.

proctors

Recently, Lavie Tidhar, a reviewer on Dusksite, managed to obtain a copy of *The Engineer* (Tanjen), and at the launch party for Tor UK said to me he really liked the 'Owner' stories and felt them to contain material for plenty of books. He is absolutely right, and if I can just drag over a few more versions of myself from parallel universes I can get on and write that stuff, and rewrite the four fantasy books and the contemporary novel, produce large collections of *Mason's Rats* stories, write the next Heliothane/Umbrathane book, produce many more short stories, start pushing the TV scripts, and write more of them . . . Of course, what I really need is the capability of a ten-thousand-year-old immortal with godlike powers and vast intelligence and wisdom. I wouldn't mind the spaceship too.

Mr Coti pulled his rain cape closer about his shoulders and looked nervously out from under his barley-bowl hat. Cloud occluded the light of the moons. The rain was coming down in sheets and, having turned the street into a quagmire, was now turning it into a stream. This was good for Coti's work, since as a board-cutter in the wilderness, he was much in demand at this time of the year, but the cutting of boards was the last thing on his mind at that moment. It was imperative he got to Chief Scientist Lumi before they found him. This was his only insurance of survival: once he had imparted his news, Cromwell would leave him alone. Cromwell would not dare to go up against C S Lumi.

Coti halted at the corner of Blue Street, the boards creaky and slippery underneath him, and for a moment thought he might be able to reach his destination without mishap—Lumi's house was only a street away—then he saw the caped figures lurking in a side alley and darted back for cover. Few options now remained to him. He could either make a run for Lumi's house while making as much noise as possible and attracting all the attention he could, but the probable result of this would be a dart in the back, or he could sneak there, using what cover he could, but he reckoned every access would be covered. He decided his best option was neither of these. He would hide until morning and try to get to Lumi when he came out. Cromwell's people always preferred the cover of darkness for their nefarious doings. Hugging a wall Coti stepped off the boardwalk and crept back down the alley he had been about to leave. Back that way he had spotted a suitable woodpile he could hide in, but before he reached it, a girl stepped out of a shadowed doorway.

The girl was young and innocent looking and Coti thought she might just live here and have nothing to do with Cromwell. When she grinned and said, "Mr Coti," he knew otherwise. Two bulky figures followed her out of the doorway and stepped past her to grab him. Coti pulled his board cutter and switched it on. It hummed in the rain, inset lights flickering from red to green and back again. He swung it at his nearest assailant, who screamed and fell back as a board-thick slice of flesh and bone peeled from his shoulder. The second man dropkicked Coti in the chest. The cutter flew from his grip and landed sizzling in the mud. In a moment, the man had Coti on his knees with his arm wrenched up around his back. The girl stepped forward, pulling something from under her rain cape while the first man staggered to the wall to lean against it moaning while he clutched his half-severed arm.

"Hurt the fucker! Hurt him!" said that one.

She knocked away Coti's hat, grabbed his hair, and pulled his head back. Coti awaited the cut that would open his throat, but it never came.

"You know what a blade beetle is?" she asked him.

Coti managed to scream just before the blade went into his guts. He retched and choked at the feel of it cutting into him, the feel of it still there. The girl held up an empty handle before his face and when the man released him, Coti fell face down in the mud, clutching at the full wound in his belly. Why did they have to do it like that? They didn't have to do it like that. The pain and horror of the knife wound in his guts were redoubled with a blade that remained inside, and began to make a nest there.

C S Lumi had been working in his laboratory since dawn when his doorbell chimed. It was not that he was by nature an early riser, but that the privilege he had been granted brought with it a deep feeling of responsibility. He saved the information he had been collating, from his notescreen to his house computer, took a long contemplative look at the nautiloids feeding in their tank, then took off his lab coat and headed for the door. The Chief Constable stood waiting for him.

"Sorry to bother you so early, sir, but there has been a killing."

Lumi studied the constable's leather uniform and thought how closely it made him resemble a Proctor. He thought how one day he might write a paper on the psychological effects of this.

"No bother, Brown, come in."

Chief Constable Brown removed his leather helmet, wiped his feet on the door mat, and stepped into the hall to stand almost at attention. Lumi had no authority over the police, nor any position in local politics, but having been granted privilege by the Owner, he was looked upon with respect and deferred to by all.

"Was it anyone I know?" he asked.

"Unfortunately, yes, it was Coti, the board cutter."

Lumi looked round in surprise as he pulled on his jacket. "Why would anyone want to kill him? Where did this happen, and how?"

"It happened very close to here, in the alley leading to the wood yard." Brown paused, obviously uncomfortable. "We think he was killed with a blade-beetle."

"Cromwell," said Lumi, his expression grim.

"There is, of course, no proof of this. We are questioning his people, but they will all alibi each other."

Lumi snorted and picked up the bag containing his study kit. "Let's go and have a look then."

Out on the boardwalk he gazed up at the clear sky, then down at the pools in the street. What a night for dying, and to die in such a way . . . Brown headed down the boardwalk to the street bridge, beyond which Lumi could see a crowd round a taped-off area. In the centre of this area lay a muddy shape. It had been done in the alley. Coti must have managed to crawl that far before the beetle reached a vital organ or he had collapsed from blood loss.

The crowd parted before Lumi then closed behind him as he ducked under the tape and squatted by the corpse. Coti was on his back, his face in death relaxed into a kind of idiocy that belied the agony he must have suffered. Lumi opened his kit, pulled on a pair of surgical gloves, then removed a long set of tongs and a reinforced plastic bag. He parted the wound with his fingers and pushed the tongs up the path of lacerated organs into the chest cavity. There was movement there and he closed the tongs on something hard and slick, and withdrew it from the body.

"Oh my god," said someone in the crowd, turning and rapidly staggering away.

The blade beetle was the length of a hand and shaped like an almond. Its legs were flat paddles and the edges of these and its wing cases, as Lumi well knew, were sharper than broken glass. It was an adult, he saw; there would be eggs in the body.

"We won't learn much from this," he said, inserting the feebly moving beetle into the bag and sealing it in. "Check his clothing and so-forth then bring him over for autopsy. He'll have to be burnt right after." He glanced round at the Chief Constable, who was looking on white-faced, then he stood. "Let's see where he was killed."

Brown led Lumi down the alley, following the trail Coti had left, dragging himself through the mud. Grooves with red puddles in them.

"Stop."

Brown looked round at Lumi in surprise.

Lumi tilted his head. "Do you hear it?"

The Chief Constable listened as well. "Something humming?"

"There," said Lumi, pointing down into the mud. He stooped down and removed his tongs again, delved into the mud for a moment, then came up with a metal cylinder with flashing lights on it. He clicked a switch and the lights went out.

"That's a board cutter," the constable told him.

"I am aware of that. What it would be nice to know is if it has cut something."

Brown smiled.

"Evidence, hard physical evidence," he said, then, as he hurried back out of the alley, "I'll get my men." When he returned, Lumi was scraping mortar from between the bricks of one wall and placing it in a bag.

"They tried to wash it off, but it soaked into the mortar. One of them was badly injured. Probably had something cut right off—there's a fragment of bone here. Find someone badly injured and I'll do a genetic cross-match, then you'll likely have your killer, or be very close to him."

"Sir!"

The shout came from the constable probing the mud at the end of the alley. Lumi looked down there and saw the crowd hurriedly dispersing.

"What is it, Walker?" asked Brown.

Walker did not reply. He hurriedly stepped back to the wall of the alley and stared out into the street. Suddenly a huge figure loomed there; eight feet tall and leathery skinned, long robes, a staff, a face visored with leathery skin, no eyes apparent, a grim slit of a mouth. A Proctor.

"Oh shit," said Brown.

The Proctor strode down the alley, its staff punching holes in the mud. It halted when it was looming over them, regarding them with the featureless thrust of its head.

"Death," it said, its voice flat and barren of anything human.

Lumi stood up and sealed the plastic bag he had been filling.

"We are investigating it," he said.

"Lumi," said the Proctor, then abruptly turned away and strode out of the alley.

"What the hell?" said Brown.

"I don't know."

"But they never take an interest in local law."

"I said I don't know."

Lumi gazed after the retreating Proctor. They enforced the laws of the Owner: No one to enter the restricted zones, no building in or corruption of the wilder zones, no more taken from them by a human than a human can carry without mechanical aid, and of course, the population stricture. It was this last that inspired terror of the Proctors. The population was set at two billion and must never go above that number. Whenever it did the Proctors turned killer. It did not matter who died just so long as the population number was brought down again. This was why it was law that every man and woman must be sterilized after engendering only two children. To flout this law was punishable by death. In Lumi's opinion this was the right way of going about things. On Earth no such laws had been in existence, and the horror of what had resulted was still remembered.

Cromwell tapped a cigarette against its box and inserted it in his mouth. A quick pull on it had it burning and he blew a stream of smoke from his nostrils. The guard watched him warily out of the corner of his eye, his rifle braced before him and his stance rigid. Cromwell stood looking thoughtfully at the door. He flicked ash on the ground and took another drag. This was difficult. People not co-operating with him was one matter, but this one . . . she hardly seemed to be aware of his presence. It was as if she considered him of no importance whatsoever. She would have to be made aware. He nodded to the guard.

"Open the door," he said.

The guard removed a key from his pocket and did as instructed. Cromwell entered the cell and stood inspecting his prisoner as the guard closed the door behind him. She was an attractive blond-haired woman in a single skin-tight coverall. She sat in a lotus position in the centre of the cold concrete floor.

"You have had time to consider my proposal," said Cromwell.

The woman glanced up at him and nodded absently.

"Will you give me access to your ship?"

She shook her head.

"Perhaps I am not making myself clear. Perhaps you actually think you have choices in this matter. Well, in a way you do . . . you see, there are drugs I can use, some nasty little insects that are local to this area, pain, endless amounts of pain."

The woman met his stare directly. Her expression showed an analytical curiosity now. "What do you want from my ship?"

Cromwell stared at her for a moment, took another drag on his cigarette.

"High tech weaponry," he said at last.

"There is none," she told him.

"Unfortunately I do not believe you. You can of course prove me wrong by allowing me access."

"I think not," said the woman.

Cromwell grinned nastily. She was not a very good liar. There were weapons aboard her ship, weapons probably powerful enough to deal with Proctors. Cromwell's grin turned to a sneer when he thought about that. Damned Proctors. The Owner was a myth kept alive by idiots like the Chief Scientist. Only the Proctors with their stupid arbitrary restrictions were real. He winced when he thought about the money he had outlaid on the sluice from his paper mill. The sluice had led into a river in the wilder and there had been no interference until the day of the first outflow. A Proctor had walked out of the wilder and methodically smashed the sluice to pieces. Cromwell ordered his men to fire on it, but only two dared to do so. They had been brave men. He was generous in compensating their families. These thoughts in mind he stepped forward and grabbed hold of the woman's hair.

"You'll let me in your ship or I'll skin you from the feet up," he hissed. The next moment he found himself on his back on the floor, the woman standing over him.

"I do not understand you," she said, and it sounded as if she really did not. "If you had such weaponry the Owner would never allow you to use it."

"There is no Owner," Cromwell spat. "I would use the weapons on the Proctors to free us from them!"

The woman sat down on the floor again, staring at him all the while.

"I come from Earth," she said. "I am here to see the Owner to tell him we are ready for his guidance now. He exists."

Cromwell stood up, stared at her in disgust, then banged on the door of the cell. He stomped down the corridor pulling another cigarette from his packet and lighting it. At the end of the corridor he mounted a stairway that led up to his office. There he paced for a while before eventually throwing himself into his chair and flicking on the communicator.

"Owner my ass," he said as he punched up a coded number.

The screen flicked on and the face of a young woman gazed out at him.

"Is it done?" he asked.

"Yes."

"Any problems?"

"Yes."

Cromwell had not expected that.

"Go on," he said carefully.

"Your son was injured."

Cromwell sat back in his chair and stared at the woman coldly.

"How badly?"

"The board cutter had his cutting tool with him. He took a lump off your son's arm before we killed him. We took him to Doctor Grable. He's in a room in the nursing home."

"Evidence?"

"We cleared as much as we could find, but it was dark . . . the residents were showing an interest, sir."

"Keep him concealed. No one is to know where he is. The board cutter . . . he had no time to speak to anyone?"

"We got him before he reached Lumi's house."

"That, is not what I asked."

"He spoke to no one."

"Very well." Cromwell stubbed out his cigarette as he considered his options. "If they start genetic testing we'll have to move fast. Has there been any Proctor activity?"

"I'm told one was seen at the scene of the killing while Lumi was there."

Cromwell swallowed dryly. They should not be interested. It was not in their remit.

"Okay, keep your eyes and ears open. Anything unusual and I want to know. If they start testing I want Jamie moved to Cosburgh. Keep me informed." He cut her off then quickly punched in another number. After a pause a bald-headed man with a walrus mustache looked out of him.

"Doctor Grable," he said.

Lumi studied the two patterns on the screen then turned to Brown.

"It wasn't Cromwell, but there is a close match. I would say it was a relative, perhaps his son or his brother. I suggest you check them both out. No general testing, that will alert him."

"We'll check all the nursing homes. If he's badly injured Cromwell will have him in one of them," he said.

"How about Grable's place?"

"My men are moving in now."

Jamie Cromwell lay on the surgical table feeling slightly sick. There was no pain with the nerve-blocker in place, but he could feel the pullings and cuttings at his shoulder as Grable installed the plastic joint. This was not the kind of adventure he liked. It had always been fun going out to 'sort things out' with Keela. He loved the feeling of power, loved being able to say the words, "Kill him". There was nothing else that gave the same buzz.

"How long will I be laid-up?" he asked.

"Oh you'll be up and about after this. But you won't be able to use this arm for three weeks, and I would suggest plenty of rest," said Grable.

Jamie considered telling him that he should save his suggestions for his other patients. He was working on Jamie Cromwell, there was a difference, but when he looked at the doctor's bloodied surgical gloves and close work eye visor, he desisted. There was no telling what the doctor could do to harm him. Jamie did not like pain when it was his own.

"What's that?!"

"Be still!" Grable held him down on the table as he tried to rise. The sound of gunfire had come from outside, and there was shouting now. Grable stood up and walked to the window.

"Constables," he said, after a moment. "A large force of them."

"I must get out of here," said Jamie. He sat up, supporting his arm and trying not to look at the bloody mess of his shoulder. One glance had been enough: the plastic joint was in place in raw flesh and tied-off arteries, all sealed under a layer of translucent jelly. He carefully lowered his legs over the side of the table. Grable was looking at him strangely.

"I have to go," he repeated.

"No," said Grable. "You must not. They will catch you and question you."

"What else is there to do then?" aske Jamie.

Grable turned from the window and went to his medical cabinet. He opened a drawer and removed an old-fashioned syringe. While Jamie watched he squeezed out the air. How would this help him to escape? Grable approached.

"Here, sit down again," he said.

Jamie had a sudden horrible suspicion. "What is that for?"

"It will calm you, relax you."

Jamie did not want to be calm and he did not believe Grable. He lashed out and kicked the doctor between the legs. The doctor swore and bowed over. Jamie swore at the pain of a broken toe and a sudden foretaste of pain from his shoulder. In the surgical gown he staggered for the door. There he turned back in time to see the doctor reaching for the syringe where it had stuck point-down in the wooden floor. Jamie opened to the door and fled.

"Come back!" the doctor bellowed, and Jamie heard him coming after as he stumbled towards the stairs. He reached the landing just as the doctor caught up with him. He tried to yell at the constables he could see coming into the reception area. The doctor's hard hand slammed over his mouth, and he was shoved back against the wall. The doctor lifted the syringe to plunge it in Jamie's neck. Jamie kneed him in an already tender spot. He had learnt a lot from Keela. As the doctor gasped again Jamie grabbed the syringe hand with his free hand, and pulled it down in an arc to stab it into the doctor's thigh.

"Oh! Oh, you bastard!"

Grable staggered back and gaped down in horror at the syringe. He pulled it out of his leg and saw it was empty.

"I must—" he managed, turning back towards his surgery, then he fell on the floor. By the time his screams and convulsions had finished the constables had reached that floor. As they led Jamie away he looked back and noted how the doctor had ripped off his fingernails while clawing at the floor, and how the convulsions had displaced one eye from its socket and broken his teeth.

"Why was he killed?" asked Lumi, his eyes not straying from the nautiloids in their tank.

"He saw something he was not supposed to see," said Brown as he looked round the laboratory.

"And what was that?"

The Chief Constable returned his attention to Lumi to see what reaction his words might elicit. "He saw a spacecraft that had landed in the wilder."

Lumi turned from his nautiloids. "Spacecraft?"

"Yes."

"The Owner?"

"No."

"Please explain."

"A spacecraft of unknown origin landed in a wilder zone ten days ago. Apparently Cromwell's people found out about it first and sealed off the area. Coti saw the ship before they did that. He avoided Cromwell's people there, but they caught up with him in Blue Street. He was killed to silence him."

"Cromwell must see great advantage in this craft. If it is not something to do with the Owner then it's likely from Earth or the colonies. Perhaps he thinks the war is reaching out to us again, the fool. Has Jamie given any indication that his father thinks this?"

"He says that this is his father's belief."

"What of the crew?"

"One pilot, a woman, whom Cromwell has captured."

"This is fascinating," said Lumi. "Have you closed in on Cromwell yet?"

"All his residences have been raided. He left this morning with a large group of his people and headed into the wilder."

"Then he's gone to this ship and taken the pilot with him. He must not get his hands on any high tech weapons. He will bring disaster on us. We must go after him immediately."

"I agree," said Brown. He was staring at the tank again.

"We need a tracker," said Lumi.

Brown turned to look at him. "In this we are lucky. Bradebus is in town. My people have gone to hire him."

Lumi looked at him. "You've been ahead of me all the way," he said. "Why do you come here?"

Brown smiled bleakly. He pointed at the tank. "Are they the ones? These creatures?"

"Yes, they are the nautiloids the Owner allowed me into the restricted zone to study," said Lumi.

"What was he like . . . if you don't mind me asking?"

Lumi thought back to that time when he was twenty-five years old and hiking along the Choom beaches of the wilder, on the edge of the restricted zone, in search of fossil nautiloids to back up his theory that they were not Earth-import life forms. He remembered his frustration when he stood at the marker line: silver posts spaced fifty metres apart. To step through that line was instant death for a human. Human bones in fact lay on the beach there. So wrapped up in his frustration had he been that he thought this the reason he had not heard the man approach. This was not the reason. He turned to see a big man in a black suit of strange design: a suit piped and padded and linked to half-seen machines floating in the air about him. His hair had been white, cropped, his eyes as red as a devil's. Lumi had known in an instant he faced the Owner. The half-seen mechanisms were the subspace machinery of the Great Ship Vardelex, and part of the Owner himself—extensions of his mind and senses, grown and added to over ten thousand years.

"You are Lumi," he had said, and in that moment the machines had faded away around him and his eyes had turned from red to a quite normal hazel.

"I am," Lumi managed.

The Owner pointed to mountains in the restricted zone. "Up there are the fossils you seek. You will not find them anywhere else on this planet."

Was he being taunted, Lumi wondered.

"You may study them at your leisure." The Owner stared at him very directly. "I place no restrictions on you in this matter because I know you to be responsible."

Lumi felt sick with excitement and fear. He gestured at the fence. "I cannot . . ."

"It will not harm you. I have instructed the fence here not to harm you. You may pass through."

Lumi could not do it. All his upbringing, all the social conditioning, the hundreds of years of tradition . . . He was terrified. The Owner saw this in an instant, took hold of his arm with a hand as cold as ice, and marched him between the silver posts. On the other side of the fence Lumi had fallen to his knees and been sick on the sand.

"You may pass through this section of fence for the rest of your natural life. You may study the fossils and nautiloids and whatever else you may find here of interest to you."

Lumi had gazed up into eyes returned to red, the weird machinery back.

"Why . . . have you allowed me this?" he managed.

"Because I can," the Owner had said, a strange smile on his face.

"What was he like?" Lumi said in reply to Brown's question. "My meeting with him has been detailed time and time again, much has been spouted about how human the Owner is when he disconnects himself from his machines. I think that is exactly the case. He isn't human. He probably ceased to be human thousands of years ago. You know what I felt most strongly about that meeting? It was that only a fragment of him communicated with me, the largest fragment permissable."

"What do you mean?"

Lumi shook his head. "A man does not discuss philosophy with a microbe."

"You think the gap that wide."

Lumi pointed at the nautiloids. "He let me study those. Only in the last few years have I come to a conclusion about them, that conclusion recently backed up by evidence from the fossil beds. They are native to this planet, as are creatures like the blade beetles, but they were extinct before the Owner got here. This was a dead world. He populated it with life forms from Earth and then resurrected some of the old life forms. He must have got the information from their fossils somehow. I also think he created the Proctors, and that they are not machines as is often thought, but highly sophisticated living creatures. I think that in these things we see only a hint of his power."

"Do you think he is a god?"

"As near as makes no difference to us. Think of the war. Our ancestors came here in an escape craft from a ship capable of destroying planets and which itself had been destroyed. The Owner allowed them to settle . . . it's an old story . . . but think about some other facts: This world was in the war zone yet nothing touched it, nothing came into the system unless the Owner allowed it. The two warring factions of the human race had no power here whatsoever."

"Then, what power does Cromwell have?"

"He could get us all killed. With high tech weapons he is sure to try to destroy Proctors. It might be that he could become just enough of an irritant to get himself flattened."

"A good thing, surely?"

"One microbe or the whole Petri dish. The laws are for a reason. We are here on sufferance. The population stricture should have told you enough. The people killed when the population tops two billion are not the idiots who can't control their gonads and there is no enforced birth-control or sterilisation unless we do it. The Owner's message in this should be evident: We keep our own house in order. I have a horrible feeling, no, I am certain, that if Cromwell starts killing Proctors then the Proctors will start killing back, and they won't stop."

Bradebus the tracker was the most irascible old man Lumi had ever known. He was also reputedly the best tracker known and had often helped the Constabulary find criminals who had fled into the wilder.

"Who you after then?" the old man asked, scratching at a ragged mess of a beard.

Brown looked to Lumi then said, "Cromwell."

"Ah! Got something on the bastard then?"

"You could say that. He's gone into the wilder with many of his people. We want to catch up with them as soon as possible."

"Who's going?"

"Myself, Chief Scientist Lumi here, and fifteen constables."

"When did he go?"

"This morning."

Bradebus stared at Lumi calculatingly then gulped down the rest of his glass of whisky. The barman waddled forward and immediately refilled the glass.

"We want to leave as soon as possible," said Lumi.

Bradebus took a gulp from his glass and grinned. "Oh, we'll catch up all right. Can't say we'll take him by surprise though, not with fifteen clod-hoppers along."

"The men are ready now," said Brown to Lumi.

Bradebus said, "You know more or less what direction he took?"

"Yes," said Brown.

"You go along then. I'll catch you directly."

"This is important, Bradebus," said Brown.

"It always is," said the tracker, turning his back on them.

The edge of the wilder was marked by a line of black metal posts. On one side of this line were arable fields and lands for livestock, on the other side the deep woodland that was the wilder itself. The bus drew to a halt in a circular parking area, in which the road terminated, and Lumi and the constables disembarked. The men and women were all in field kit and carried an assortment of weapons. Lumi was in his hiking gear and carried no weapons. Brown was quick to remark on this.

"Sir, I would feel better if you carried this," he said, and handed over a pistol belt. Lumi drew the weapon and inspected it. It was a ten-bore revolver with eight chambers. A weapon you only needed to hit a man with once. Lumi considered rejecting it then changed his mind. Such an act might have been admirable in some circles, but here and now it would have been foolish. He strapped the weapon on and observed the constables unloading more powerful armament.

"What's that?"

"Missile launcher," said Brown. "If he gets to the ship and takes it up . . . " Brown did not need to elaborate. "Okay, let's go," he said to his men. And they walked between the black posts into the wood.

This close to the perimeter there were many well-trodden paths. They moved at a slow pace following the main track Cromwell's group had reportedly followed. By evening they had not left that track, and stopped at a well-used camp site.

"We'll wait here for him," said Lumi, and went to set up his tent. Before retiring he ate a meal with the ten men and five women under Brown's command, drank tea, and listened to Brown briefing them. They had known nothing of their mission prior to entering the wilder.

The night sounds kept Lumi awake for some time and in the full dark he heard the arrival of Bradebus announced by the guards. He slid out of his sleeping bag and after pulling on some clothing went out to see the man. The night was lit by the second and third moons; one a pitted and dented thing that was called the Old Man, the other a mirror-bright sphere that had acquired no name. It was simply called the Third Moon.

The tracker was dressed in clothing made from animal skins and wore a long coat of bear fur. He carried a short hunting carbine, a knife nearer the size of a machete, and two pistols holstered at his belt. He was squatted by the remains of the fire when Lumi saw him.

"We didn't expect you until the morning," commented Lumi by way of something to say.

Bradebus nodded. "Morning we go off the track to the north. Should catch up with them a bit. Loop in the track." He poked at the fire with a stick.

"Is that a good idea? They might turn off."

Bradebus studied him estimatingly. "They're out here after something. If it was close I'd have known about it by now. Must be in the deep wilder. They'll stay on the main track." He continued staring at Lumi, waiting.

Lumi nodded and returned to his tent. He was not yet ready to tell the tracker what this was all about.

Morning was yet to make its presence felt when Brown called outside Lumi's tent then went on to rouse his constables. Lumi swore, stuck his head out into the darkness, then checked the luminous dial of his watch. An hour until sunrise. When they set out the foliage above had become distinguishable from the sky, and it was just possible not to walk into the trees when Bradebus led them off the track. They had travelled for an hour more before the birds started singing, and travelled for three more hours before stopping to remove rations from their packs to eat while they walked. Lumi noticed that Bradebus watched this with amusement, then wandered on chewing at a piece of jerky that smelt suspect, and washing this down with gulps from his hip flask. At midday Lumi went up to walk beside him.

"Ready to tell me what it's all about?" asked the tracker, his words only slightly slurred.

"A spaceship has landed in the wilder. Cromwell has the pilot. We think he is after weapons."

Bradebus nodded. "Lot of Proctor activity round here lately."

Lumi did not know what to make of that.

Shortly after this they rejoined the the main track and the tracker pointed at the signs of a large groups passing that way. "Gained about two hours on them," he said.

Lumi wondered if it would be enough. Another day's march and they would be getting into the deep wilder. They camped part way into the night, when they were all too tired to make good time, and when blade beetles started to be attracted to the lamps they carried. One man required stitches in his upper arm before he could go to his tent.

Lumi woke and did not know why. Had there been a sound? With utmost caution he pulled the revolver from its holster and slid out of his tent into the night.

"Everything all right?" he asked the guard.

The woman glanced at him then looked back out into the darkness. "The tracker went out there a moment ago. Don't know what he's up to," she said.

"Which direction?"

The woman pointed.

"I'll just go and take a look."

Lumi walked out into the wood as the woman muttered something about 'shitting in the trees'. Yes, that could be the reason the old man had gone out, but Lumi found he entertained suspicions about the old man. Might he be in the employ of Cromwell? Might he be leading them astray? Ahead of him he heard the rustle of leaves. He moved towards it, saw a flicker of blue light, moved towards that. As he drew closer the light grew brighter. There was an area of blue light, a huge shape moving about in it. A hand caught him by the shoulder and a hand closed over his mouth.

"Shush now," said Bradebus, and took his hand away.

"Proctor," said Lumi as the huge shape became recogniseable.

"Oh yes, lots of them here. Lots of them."

There was something strange in his voice. Lumi watched Bradebus in confusion as the old man turned away and headed back towards the camp.

Then the scientist glanced back at the light as it faded, before following the old man in. Had Bradebus come out here because he had heard a Proctor? Or had there been a more sinister reason? Lumi shivered in the night.

The next day of travel was marked only by the advent of their seeing a Proctor striding through the woodland far to one side. Otherwise it was exhausting and uneventful. Lumi quickly ate the food prepared for him and drank his tea before crawling into his tent and the comfort of his sleeping bag. In the dark before dawn they set out into more rugged country where deciduous trees gave way to conifers and patches of stone revealed sky above and a glimpse of distant mountains. There was a track of sorts that Bradebus led them from without a word of explanation. Lumi felt too tired to question, or to reassure Brown, but did have the energy to follow when Brown hurried to catch up with the tracker and demand an explanation.

"You'll see," said Bradebus, and hurried them on. Soon he brought them to the edge of the pines and a flat area of stone. Beyond the stone was nothing but purpled by distance mountains and sky. He waved them forward and walked to the edge. Lumi stood at his shoulder and looked down into the forest a thousand metres below. It was an awesome sight. Bradebus pointed.

"There," he said.

There it was, lying on the shores of a lake, a silver cylinder amongst trees that only reached up to half its diameter.

"One would think a vantage point like this would be watched," said Brown, glancing around.

"It is," said Bradebus. "Cromwell's people have been watching us for some time now." He turned to Brown. "I said we would come as no surprise to him."

Brown snorted in annoyance and walked away.

"How many people does Cromwell have with him would you say?" asked Lumi.

"Ten came with him, including the one from the ship—she has strange shoes—and about here I would reckon another ten."

"We will have to be very careful then."

"They won't be as well armed, nor very well trained."

They came across the first of them an hour later.

Keela squatted down in front of the woman and handed her a bowl of soup. It was accepted graciously and the woman sipped at it while Keela tested the chain attaching her to the tree.

"He'll torture you," said Keela.

"Yes, I imagine he will."

"Why don't you just let him in? If there are no weapons as you say . . . "

"I am not amenable to coercion."

"I don't understand," said Keela, settling down on the pine needles. "Why are you here?"

The woman looked up from her soup and observed Keela with disconcerting eyes. "It is strange, is it not, that you ask me this now?"

"Well?"

"I am an ambassador from the human federation. I have come here to seek the wisdom if not the assistance of the Owner."

"Why?"

"He is ten thousand years old. From who else would I seek wisdom?"

"He doesn't exist," said Keela.

The woman smiled and continued to sip her soup. Chagrined, Keela rose to her feet and stomped away.

"Anything?" Cromwell asked her.

"She just doesn't make sense."

"Then we'll have to force her to make sense."

Cromwell gazed speculatively at the glowing point of his cigarette.

They heard the crack of the shot simultaneous with the smack of the bullet against flesh. A constable staggered to one side, fell from the narrow path, and tumbled down the heather-tufted slope. Lumi had a glimpse of jetting blood, a raw exposure of flesh the size of a cooking apple.

"Down!" came the belated cry. Constables ran for cover behind the boulders at the base of the cliff as another shot range out and smashed splinters from rock. Lumi found himself behind a boulder with Bradebus and watched him take aim with his hunting carbine. He looked into the woodland below and could see nothing. The carbine went off with a satisfying explosion.

"Got the bugger."

Immediately Bradebus was up and running down the slope. It all happened too quickly for Lumi. He followed after with the dazed constables and swearing Brown.

The man lay dead behind a splintered pine tree. Bradebus had shot him through the tree. The mangled bullet and wood splinters had made quite a mess. Lumi looked at the tracker questioningly. The man held out a handful of bullets. Lumi picked one up and inspected it: pointed steel tip, large caseless charge, enough to shoot a man through a tree, but of no use otherwise. There were no animals large enough to justify such bullets. How was it that they had come into this lowly tracker's possession?

"Spread out now, and move with caution. Lambert, you stay back," said Brown. Lambert was the one who carried the missile launcher. Before they moved off Brown went to confirm the fallen man was dead. Lumi went with him. Half his head was gone, somewhere on the slope above.

They moved cautiously. Shots soon rang out again. The sound of bullets cracking through tree branches. A curtailed scream. Lumi saw the tracker running, his knife drawn and bloody. He was grinning. He looked like he was having fun. Two constables stayed back after that exchange, one to tend to the leg wound of the other. Nearby lay the corpses of two anonymous men and a woman, their blood draining into the pine needles. The second exchange was more intense, then abruptly ceased when Cromwell's people withdrew.

"What the fuck!" said Brown.

Lumi saw he was looking to one side. Two Proctors were striding through the trees towards the ship. There was another out to the other side of them.

"How many, I wonder?" said Bradebus in a whimsical voice.

This is very important, thought Lumi. As far as he knew the Proctors only enforced those few of the Owner's laws. There were two thousand of them, one for every million human beings on this, the Owner's world. Seeing them together was an event rare enough to be recorded. The last time Proctors had been seen together had been forty-three years before, just two of them, and the observer of this rare occurance had said they seemed almost embarrassed about the matter and had quickly parted. Three Proctors here, in this small area of trees, how many more were there in the vicinity?

The ship and the lake became visible through the trees. Brown scanned the area through compact binoculars.

"They're dug in round the ship behind log barricades. The camp is clear. Can't tell how many of them there are. There's a woman chained to a tree between us and them." He scanned to one side, then with his expression dumb-founded he handed the binoculars to Lumi and pointed. Lumi brought the lenses to his eyes.

Proctors.

They were on the lake shore, moving through the trees. As he watched, one walked up out of the water of the lake as if it had just walked across the bottom, which might well have been the case. What were they here for? They seemed to be doing little more than waiting and watching; leaning on their staffs and gazing into the distance like old-Earth Masai. The parallel was perhaps not the best. Are we their cattle? Lumi wondered. Just then Cromwell's people opened fire and Brown slammed him down to eat pine needles. The constables fired back with their automatic weapons until Brown yelled at them to stop.

"The woman! You'll hit the woman!"

Lumi looked out to her. She was sat in a position of meditation, not trying to bury herself as would be expected. All the firing ceased.

"Surrender and we won't kill her!" came Cromwell's shout.

"He doesn't want to kill her anyway, she hasn't let him in her ship," said Bradebus.

How do you know that? Lumi had no time to ask the question. The tracker fired twice. There was a yell of surprise. He turned to Brown.

"You don't have to shoot low to get them. That Cromwell isn't the best tactician. Just shoot at the hull of the ship above them and the ricochets will do the rest."

Brown looked where indicated and grinned, then his grin faded.

"The woman," he said.

"I would say that problem is about to be solved," said the tracker.

The Proctor came striding in from the side and positioned itself between the woman and Cromwell's people. It drove its staff into the ground then reached down to take hold of the chain. It was a thick chain. The Proctor snapped it like a cord of plasticene. Cromwell stood up then. He was yelling something as he depressed the trigger of his weapon and emptied its clip. The Proctor's field flared blue about it and no shots reached the woman as it led her away with a huge leathery hand on her shoulder. It kept itself between her and Cromwell all the time. Cromwell should have remembered the outfall from his factory. It seemed he was not thinking straight, because after he had emptied one clip he remained standing while he fumbled for another. The woman was out of the way. The constables remembered many crimes, many slights, dead friends. How many bullets hit him at once is moot. It would have been difficult to count the holes in what remained.

"Cease firing!" Brown shouted, once Cromwell had disappeared out of sight. From Cromwell's people entrenched below the ship there was no more firing once the constables lowered their weapons. The sounds of argument could be heard, then a weapon was tossed out in front of the stacked logs and a man rose slowly to his feet with his hands in the air. Someone was yelling at him and he was ignoring that yelling. He stepped out from cover with his hands up.

"Brave fellow," said Bradebus as he watched the man walk across the no-man's land between. Twenty feet from the constables the man halted.

"I surrender myself," said the man. He looked scared but determined.

"Come behind here and lay face down on the ground," said Brown. When the man had done this Brown searched him and cuffed him. "How many of the others will give themselves up?" he asked.

"Most of them," the man replied. "Cromwell was all that kept us."

"Loyalty?" asked Brown.

"Fear, for ourselves and our families."

Brown raised a sardonic eyebrow at that but did not refute it. "What about the rest?"

"A few who have reason to hate Proctors, only them."

Shortly after this more weapons were tossed out and another five men and two women approached to give themselves up.

"How many more?" asked Brown.

"Keela is there, her and two of Cromwell's closest."

Brown flicked on the com unit on his belt and turned it to public address.

"Will you die?" he asked the hold-outs. He signalled to his constables to be ready. "Where you are we can bounce bullets off that ship until you are all dead. Is this the end you want?"

A silence drew as taut as as a garrote. Eventually three weapons were tossed out and three people stood: Keela and the two men. They walked over to be cuffed with the rest.

The night sky was black and moonless, unusually, in that three moons orbited the Owner's planet. The forest was lit by campfires and weird blue glows like the flash of glow worms from where the Proctors waited. Brown, Bradebus, and Lumi shared the glow of a fire, steaming mugs of tea, and bread rolls filled with steaks from a deer Bradebus had shot and wild onions he had collected.

"We must find out why she came here, and what interest the Proctors have in her," said Lumi.

"And how do you suggest we go about that?" asked Brown, a hint of sarcasm in his voice.

"Why not go and ask?" said Bradebus, and the other two looked at him as if he had suggested eating blade beetles. "Well, why not?"

Lumi and Brown looked at each other. It was Lumi who replied. "For one, they would not answer, for two, we might end up dead."

"She would answer, and what rules have you broken that might bring their anger down on you?" Bradebus stood up. "Come on, let's go see them."

Lumi and Brown stood up staring in amazement at each other as Bradebus strode off towards the Proctors. Lumi hesitated for a moment, then quickly followed.

"I have the prisoners, my men . . . " said Brown, not inclined to follow.

Lumi waved him back and continued on. Brown sat back down and poured himself more tea. He did not want to say anything about all the leaders being killed.

The Proctors were seated around under the trees all facing in one direction. Lumi and Bradebus walked between them and soon came in sight of a campfire, and Proctors beyond that facing inward. The woman was by the fire eating something that had been cooking over it. The rise and fall of speech could be heard. Three Proctors sat around the fire with her, their staffs driven into the ground behind them.

" . . . fourteen star systems and the new gates are opening more all the time," they heard, followed by the grating voice of one of the Proctors.

"So much to learn, to see. This must be the time."

By then Lumi and Bradebus had reached the fire. The woman looked up at them cautiously. The Proctor that had been speaking turned its head in their direction and watched them approach. Lumi was the first to speak.

"Are you uninjured?" he asked the woman.

She nodded. He continued. "I am Chief Scientist Lumi and my companion is the tracker Bradebus . . . by what name should we address you?"

The woman smiled. "At last someone with a civilised attitude. No one has yet asked me my name. The man Cromwell considered me a means to an end, though it turned out it was his own. These Proctors speak beyond names." She stood up. "I am Manx Evitel, ambassador from Earth." She held out a greasy hand, which Lumi took.

"Names have importance to us," said the Proctor, and Lumi looked at it in startlement. "All of us have names. We are one but we name ourselves singly, but what purpose identification to us?"

"What is your name, then?" asked Lumi, as he moved in and squatted by the fire. Bradebus came with him, his mouth closed and his expression alert.

"I am called David," said the Proctor.

"Why . . . why are you here, David?" asked Lumi.

"Here is opportunity," said the Proctor.

Lumi left it, it sounded cryptic enough to be an avoidance, and he had no wish to push Proctors. He turned back to the woman, who had seated herself again.

"Why are you here then?"

She smiled again. "I am here as an ambassador. The wars have been over for many centuries now and the human federation grows faster than some of us can cope with. I have come here to seek the Owner, we need his wisdom, his great knowledge. He travelled the galaxy millennia ago in his great ship. There are things he will know."

"It's more than that," said Bradebus.

She looked at him. "Yes, it is more. Our expansion has brought us to the edge of an alien civilisation. It is vast and they are . . . difficult to understand, yet, from what we have learnt in our few encounters, they know about the Owner. He has been there. There will be things he knows . . . There is so much he knows."

"Some believe the Owner is dead," said Lumi.

"This . . . is possible," said the Proctor, David.

"How?"

"We have been one with the mind of the Owner for millennia. In the last fifty years the contact has been broken and we have gained independent existence. This is why we are here. We want to see and know more than this world. We want to do more than enforce the Owner's law."

"You have what you seek," said Bradebus to Manx Evitel. She looked abruptly surprised at this, then regarded the Proctor calculatingly.

"You have not been in contact with the Owner for some time then?" The Proctor shook its head.

"Has anyone seen the Owner since?" She glanced at Lumi and Bradebus. Lumi realised he must be the last to have seen him.

"Twenty years ago I saw him," he said.

Evitel nodded and turned back to the Proctor. "What use might you be to us should we transport you from this place?"

The Proctor said, "The Owner called them the Snark-kind in reference to a poem by one Lewis Carrol. He traded with them and observed their civilisation for two hundred years. Every one of us knows what he learnt about them. We were one with the Owner's mind."

Evitel abruptly got up and faced her ship. "Ship, open," she said.

In the side of the great cylinder a slot of light appeared, and with eerie silence a segment of metal folded down, straightened out, became a ramp. Lumi stood and glanced back towards the camp where he could hear shouting. Suddenly there was gunfire. Lumi and Bradebus began running in that direction. More gunfire. A figure ahead, crouching, something across its shoulder. A spear of light.

"Shit!" said Bradebus, both he and Lumi hitting the ground. There was an explosion behind them. In the light of the flame Lumi saw the girl Keela with the missile launcher across her shoulder. He drew his pistol, fired twice. She staggered and fell.

The Proctor David lay on the ground, flickers of blue light on his skin. His side was open to expose something like organs and something like electronics. Evitel stood to one side. A shimmer winked out around her. All along, a personal force shield, Cromwell could not have harmed her.

The Proctors began standing, something like a growl of anger coming from them.

"How the hell did she get hold of that?!" Lumi shouted at Brown as he reached Keela and turned her over onto her back, his pistol in her face.

"She knocked out Lambert. We didn't think she . . . she is a third child . . . "

Enough, thought Lumi, there was never any getting away from the stigma.

Brown stared in terror at the Proctors, they were moving now, all their fields flicking on. Lumi watched them too, not knowing how to stop what he felt sure was to come. A Proctor had been killed, the first ever.

"Tell them to stop," he said to Evitel.

"Wait!" she shouted. The Proctors ignored her.

"Hold," said Bradebus. He was crouched down by the corpse of David. All the Proctors froze then turned in his direction. Lumi saw the man's rough clothing fade, become a black body suit, piped and padded and linked to half-seen machines, saw his appearance change. The Owner. He touched David. He and the Proctor flickered out of existence. There was a crack as air rushed to fill the space. The remaining Proctors turned towards the ship and slowly began to mount the ramp. More of them came out of the woods.

Twilight, birds beginning to sing, immediate warmth in the forest. The Proctors were all aboard, but for one called Mark. He and Evitel sat by a fire with Lumi and Brown. The other constables were taking the prisoners, the wounded, and the dead, back to the town.

"We are one with his mind again," said Mark.

"What is he doing?" asked Lumi.

"He has repaired David."

"What are his intentions?" asked Evitel.

"You may ask him."

The Owner came out of the forest with David walking behind him. He said, "It was my intention that the Proctors go with you. They have my knowledge and they have wisdom." He squatted by the fire, the machines gone, his eyes normal. He grinned at Lumi. "I had intended not to show myself, but, six thousand years of wisdom and knowledge is too much to lose." He looked towards David and nodded. Mark rose, the two Proctors walked towards Evitel's ship.

"Why the subterfuge?" asked Lumi.

"Because I wanted it," was the reply.

"I would have preferred you to come," said Evitel.

"For that there will be no need. My Proctors will be sufficient to the Snark-kind." He looked at Lumi and Brown, then pointed out beyond the lake. In the sky they saw falling lights like a meteor shower. "This place has remained closed for too long. Here my constructors will build a spaceport and this world will join with the human Polity. All my laws will no longer apply. There is much room in space. I leave this place in trust." He stood.

"Where will you be?" asked Evitel.

"Around," said the Owner.

The ash of the fire gusted as air replaced him. The third moon, like a polished metal ball, rose in the twilight sky, made a right angled turn far above them, receded into dark. Lumi felt the tug of the huge mass moving away, heard waves breaking on the lake shore, squinted at the sudden flare of a star drive igniting.

the owner

There's not much to add about this story. It's another 'Owner' one in its distinct future history, but has no history itself (i.e. wasn't published anywhere but in *The Engineer* collection). I reckon I've got about four or five future histories going now, and probably will start more of them. Looking at the ongoing creation of the 'runcible universe' I wonder how many writers love or feel trapped by their speculative creations, or both.

There is a place where stands an ancient pillar. It is taller than a man, just, and wider. It is a plain cylinder without plinth or capital and is made of grey corrosion-free metal. Its surface is intagliated with strange runes, or circuit diagrams, and it stands upon sand in a bleak place where few have heard of Ozymandias. It is real, absolutely and solidly real, as if its location has formed round it—an accretion of reality. Standing on the sand by this pillar is a swordsman. He is just in its shadow; all dark fabric and iron, and seemingly part of that shadow. Such fancy he would perhaps allow a smile, knowing a permanence greater than that of the grey metal.

They were tired of running, tired of forever being on guard, and tired of the fear, but there was only one alternative. Cheydar knew this and it churned him up inside. Sometimes he felt a hopelessness so strong he just wanted to stop, to sit down and wait for the end, but he hadn't, not yet. The Code would not allow him suicide without permission.

When he saw him, the man seated on a boulder out on the flats, watching them, Cheydar thought, *Here is another killer come for the Cariphe's reward.* And, as he waved his two sons to his side and moved out from the campfire he wondered if he might die this day. The boys spaced themselves and pumped full the gas cylinders of their air guns. Cheydar was weary, loath to kill yet again, frightened he might not be able to. Behind him Suen held her daughter close and looked on. Suen, wife of Tarrin, to whom he and his family were sworn service of life. All this for her and the girl now. He knew that sometimes she damned the loyalty that kept him and his kin with her, only sometimes, without it there was only that one alternative.

The man was motionless. It seemed as if he might have sat there all night watching their camp. When he finally moved, when he finally came down from his rock, it was at the precise moment the sun gnawed a red-hot lump out of the horizon. Cheydar felt his throat clench: The Daybreak Warrior. Then he damned himself for a fool and the bitterness inside threatened to overwhelm him. He was too old for such fairy tales. If only Tarrin had been as wise.

"He looks a handy one this," he said.

It was the way the man had come down from the boulder: lithe, strong. That had been a four metre drop and he had taken it as if it was nothing and was strolling towards them with the loose-limbed gait of a trained fighter . . . killer.

"Not handy enough to outrun an iron dart," said Eric, Cheydar's eldest.

If only that were so, but the three would not fire at this man unless he attacked. Honour would not permit murder. They must wait until he had come close and offered challenge, and gained the opportunity to kill them one at a time. Cheydar had taken on two challengers and killed them both. Would he be able to kill this one? A bitter part of himself observed that dying first he would at least not get to see his sons die. He observed the approaching killer and shivered. The killer was a hard-faced man with cropped blond hair. His age was indeterminate. His stature short but heavily muscled. His clothing was dramatically black and leaning towards leather. Over his leather tunic he wore chain mail. Sticking up above his shoulders were the pommels of two swords. There were knives at his belt, in his boot, probably elsewhere. Three metres from the Cheydar and his sons he halted and squatted.

"Who are you and what do you want?" Cheydar demanded.

The man looked past Cheydar and directly at Suen. "They burned your husband on the frame," he stated matter-of-factly.

"Have a care," said Cheydar, and glanced round at Suen. Would she ever get over it? Would she ever look as if she wanted to live? She had bribed the Jack-o-the-frame to use green wood so Tarrin would have a quick and relatively pain-free death from smoke inhalation. He had taken her money and still used coke and dry wood. Tarrin had screamed for a very long time. Now Suen was outlawed for attempting to bribe an official of the Cariphe. She winced and turned her face away, hugged her daughter to her. Her daughter flicked a long suffering look at Cheydar's son David, and carefully tried to extricate herself. The stranger turned his attention from Suen to Cheydar.

"He nearly got you, didn't he? You're getting too tired."

Cheydar suddenly felt cold. This was the thought that had been occupying him for days. The last killer had nearly got through his guard, nearly gutted him. This man must have seen, must have been watching.

"Who are you?" Cheydar asked yet again.

"Call me Dagon. I have come to join you."

Cheydar felt that tightness in his throat yet again. Dagon. The name of the Daybreak Warrior. He did not need this kind of thing, not now, not when he was weak enough to hope, weak enough to believe.

"Why should we allow you into our company? Why should we trust you?"

The stranger stood abruptly. There was a look on his face. Cheydar could not identify it, but it made his skin creep.

"Where is your hospitality? I am thirsty and I am hungry," said Dagon.

Cheydar felt a flush of shame, felt his face burning. Such was the way of things: the most basic tenets of the Code lost in only five days and strangers greeted at the campfire with hostility.

"You will forgive me," he said tightly, and glanced aside at each of his sons. They lowered their air guns as Dagon came forward. "Please, eat at my fire, and drink." Even as he spoke the ritual words Cheydar was aware they could ill afford the food; straight porridge gruel and not much of that. He backed off as Dagon stepped past him, his hand on his sword. It could be a ploy. There could be one quick draw and swipe when Cheydar might least be aware. Perhaps Eric might get him, he was much faster than David, but even that was doubtful. Cheydar knew the measure of men and this one looked as if he would not die easy.

The man squatted by the fire, smiled at Sheda and bowed his head to Suen, then with a deliberately long look at Cheydar he folded his legs and sat, not a position he could quickly gain his feet from. Cheydar nodded and moved to the fire, sat opposite him. The boys stood well back, air guns still ready, holsters for spare cylinders clipped open. Sheda, with a businesslike expression, pulled away from her mother and spooned gruel into a bowl, which she handed to Dagon. He thanked her, placed the bowl in his lap and carefully removed the pack from his back, exposing the sheaths of the swords. Well made, Cheydar observed from the glance he got. Dagon removed jerked meat from his pack.

"Let me offer this in return. It is little enough."

Ritual. He knew it verbatim. Cheydar felt his mouth watering as he looked at the meat. They had eaten nothing but gruel for four days. He took three pieces and tossed two of them to Eric and David, chewed on his own piece, found it tasted wonderful, better than he had ever had before. Suen and Sheda ravenously chewed into their meat.

"I have this also. Little enough."

Apples and cheese. How was it he had such fresh food so far from civilization? Cheydar did not want to ask. He asked other questions instead.

"It is a burdensome name you carry," he said.

Dagon nodded. "I sometimes think that if I had been named differently I would have been a farmer, or an inn keeper."

"What are you now?" Cheydar shot back.

"Many things. For your purposes I can be a killer of men. What do you say?"

"I say tell me how you know so much."

"I have followed you since the burning."

"Why?" asked Suen, taking part at last. It was not right for her bondsman to deal in this matter. She must take on her mantle of power. Her time was now.

Dagon said, "Because the Owner brought you people here in the Greatship Vardelex so you could build a new life. Because soon the Owner will return for an accounting, to see that his strictures have been obeyed, that the contract you people have with him has been held to. Because before the end of this demicycle the Owner and his Proctors will once again walk the world."

Suen gaped at the stranger and tried to take in his words: all that her husband believed and had understood, and they burnt Tarrin for those words in the Square of Heros before the Cariphe's palace in Ompotec. Stupid stupid words had lost Suen her husband, a son, a home, and would soon lose her her life. She could only run so far before the Cariphe's people caught up with her. She looked at Cheydar: grey, old. How long could she depend on his strength? For how long had she that right? Soon the priest soldiers would be upon them, for their sport, and they would die. At least out here it might be a cleaner death. She studied this young man who called himself Dagon, out of nursery rhymes and bedtime tales, and thought about what he had said. The Heresy of Ompotec. Ironically the name of the only place where it was called heresy and where the Cariphe and all his sick minions dwelt. Verbatim, but for one tiny alteration. She glanced at Cheydar and wondered if he had noticed. This man had said you people rather than we. She felt cold and she did not want to ask the obvious question.

"If you come with us it may well be the death of you," she said. She would give him every chance to go, every warning. This she told herself to assuage her guilt. "We have no hearth nor home—" Abruptly she stopped.

No, it was wrong. "You cannot stay with us. You must go . . . " She gazed at him, straight into grey-green eyes that seemed too wise. That was it, she realised. Look away from him and he is a young warrior. Look into his eyes you know he makes only his own choices.

He nodded, then lifted a strong sun-tanned hand and pointed off to their left. "It is too late for me to walk away now. They will not allow it. Guilt by association you could say, not that they observe any code."

Cheydar leapt to his feet his hand slamming down on the butt of his sword. Eight men were coming towards them at a steady trot. Eight fully-armoured and armed priest soldiers of the Cariphe. Too late now for anything but survival.

"Into the rocks!"

Suen went to take her daughter by the hand, but her daughter stayed close to David and avoided this mothering. Instead Suen took up a weapons belt from which hung a dagger and a short crossbow. Cheydar took up his own air gun and trotted behind her, his sons following. Dagon stood by the fire watching the soldiers approach, then after a moment he followed the others.

"We need a vantage, a place to defend."

Dagon pointed up into the rocks and scrub. "Up there."

They took him at his word and scrambled that way.

"I will stay."

As he helped Suen up the slope Cheydar watched him suspiciously. Dagon returned the look then grinned and disappeared into the scrub of bushes and cycads. Cheydar had no time for him now. The priest soldiers had broken into a run and were spreading out.

"Check your targets," he told his sons. "Our friend is down there, if friend he be."

"Of course he is, father," said David. "He is the daybreak warrior."

Cheydar ignored that, cracked down the barrel of his gun, inserted an iron dart, then worked the hand pump on the charge cylinder. The leading soldier was close enough now. He brought the intricately carved butt of his gun up against his shoulder, flipped up the sight, then aimed and fired in one. The crack of the air gun was vicious and immediately followed by the horrible crunch of impact. A priest soldier staggered back with his hands coming up to a suddenly bloody face. There were two more cracks and a dart hit the rocks just in front of him and went whining over his head. He ducked down.

"Yes!" shouted Eric. Crouched down Cheydar saw that his son had hit one of them in the thigh. That one was struggling for cover. Another lay with a bloody throat. There had been no exclamation from David. The rest were now in cover provided by the bushes round their camp, and no doubt would be drawing close. Cheydar recharged the cylinder on his gun and put in another dart. Only in close fighting would he resort to the spare cylinders on his belt. His sons, he saw, were doing the same. He watched, allowed himself a little smile when he saw Eric aiming at a swiftly moving figure in black, then lowering his gun. Let us see what you are worth, Dagon. A scream was swift to answer him, followed only moments after by the gagging gurgle Cheydar recognised as the sound issuing from a cut throat. One or two? He wondered.

"Who is he?" Suen asked.

"Just a killer, out to make a name for himself," whispered Cheydar, but it did not sound right. There was a yell. Two soldiers running, a figure standing. Eric aimed again and David knocked his gun aside with the barrel of his own. Cheydar felt a fist closing in his stomach. Now. It was beautiful, if death can be called that. The two swords; crescents of morning sunlight. One man down on his knees his forehead against the ground, the other man standing for a moment until his head toppled from his shoulders. Cheydar had only seen the second blow.

"Fast," Eric breathed.

"Perfect," said David, his observation analytical.

Cheydar had no words. His mouth was dry. He looked from the scene to see one priest soldier running away just as fast as he could. He levelled his air gun, adjusted the sight for the extra distance, fired. The man sprawled then crawled on for a little while, his back rapidly soaking with blood. He tried to haul himself up by the hard dark green leaves of a cycad, then he fell again. Cheydar turned to his sons.

"Go down, see that they are all dead. Get their supplies, weapons, all we might need."

There was nothing in the Code against looting the dead.

Steeleye was the name of the third moon, or the Still Moon, for since the time of its cataclysmic arrival it had remained stationary in the sky above, day and night. In appearance it was a polished ball of metal, and there was something ominous about it, something attentive. It had appeared in the time when Cheydar had trained for service, causing floods and earth quakes. It stood vigil in the sky when he learned bladework, unarmed combat, and the maintenance of dart guns. That time was exciting; change was imminent, things would happen. . . . But the years passed, the tides settled and the ground ceased to shake. And the only change had been the growth in the power and oppressiveness of the Cariphate. It seemed like a betrayal to Cheydar. The moon just became ordinary. He turned his attention back from it to the conversation.

"He would not have allowed it. He would not allow the Cariphe to do the things he does. His Proctors would stop the killing. His Proctors would enforce His law."

He could see Suen regretted the outburst the moment she finished. She shouldn't have said that, but wasn't it true? All that her husband had believed: a better time, a golden age that would come again. Suen closed her eyes and shook her head. Her anger was always greatest when she missed him most, but in Cheydar's experience railing against injustice only brought it down on you.

"Why did the Proctors go away?" he asked, embarrassed and clumsily trying to move away from the subject of Tarrin's execution as he poked at the fire with a stick. He wasn't really interested in why the Proctors had gone away. He wondered if anything about those indestructible monsters of the past and their ten-thousand year old demigod master could have anything to do with him and his life.

"They did not go away. They are sleeping," said Sheda with that certainty only a teenager can have. "Daddy said they sleep in the Forbidden Zone and that they can be woken." As she finished speaking she looked at David and flushed at her own boldness.

Now wouldn't that be something, thought Cheydar, and shivered. He stared through the flames at Dagon. The man had been very quiet and still. Eventually he spoke.

"Why should you want to wake them?" he asked.

"Justice!" spat Suen, but she sounded suddenly unsure.

"The only justice they bring is the Owner's," Dagon replied. "They enforce only his laws and his laws say nothing about you people killing each other."

"'You people.' You do not consider yourself one of us?" Suen asked.

Dagon looked briefly annoyed. "A manner of speech, nothing more. But I tell you this, I have read the Agreement."

Suen snorted her disbelief.

Cheydar said, "It is etched into a metal pillar around which the Ompotec temple is built. Only select members of the priesthood are allowed to see it."

Dagon smiled mildly and shook his head. "Wrong, there are in all fifty-eight of the message pillars and every death post round the forbidden zones has the Agreement etched in its surface. Anyone prepared to take a bit of a walk can read it. I've seen it many times." Suen and Cheydar stared at him. They did not know how to refute that. He continued, "Understand that the priesthood uses any and all methods to gather power to itself. Like all religious organizations its greatest power stems from the claim to forbidden knowledge, the ability to intercede with the divine, all of that, though the Owner is hardly divine."

"What does it say?" asked David, speaking for the first time that evening, uncomfortably aware of Sheda's attention firmly fixed upon him.

Dagon glanced at him. "It is quite simple: No one to enter the forbidden zones, no building in or corruption of the Wilder zones, no more taken from them by a human than a human can carry without mechanical aid. There is also a population stricture, but that is hardly necessary as the population here is in decline."

"There has to be more than that," said Suen.

"There is not. The Owner is a great believer in personal responsibility. Beyond preventing damage to his property he doesn't have much more interest in planetary populations."

"You are an Owner expert all at once," said Suen.

"I've studied him all my life."

"Like my husband."

Dagon regarded her very directly, "No, not like your husband. My research was into original materials, not the wishful thinking and distortion that came after."

"What do you mean?"

"The Owner has fascinated scholars for centuries and a great deal has been written about him, and a lot of what has been written is simply not true."

"How do you know what is true?" asked Cheydar.

Dagon showed annoyance again, quickly repressed it. "Simple research. Consider the entire mythology that's arisen about the Proctors. To some they are saviours, and their enforcing of law will bring about Utopia. To others they are demons and this is perhaps closest. They enforced the Wilder laws. If someone used a cart to haul wood out of the Wilder a Proctor would turn up and smash the cart. They simply prevented the law being broken. But it was the population stricture that inspired terror of the Proctors. The populaton here is set at two billion and must never go above that number. When it did, about two centuries ago, the Proctors turned killer. For every child born at that two billion limit a human was killed. It was completely random. It might have been a baby that died or an octogenerian on his death bed."

"I do not believe this," said Suen, but her voice was not firm. She turned to Cheydar. "I want to go into the Wilder. I want to read what is written on a death post."

Cheydar was watching Dagon thinking, *simply a killer?* He nodded, feeling his stomach clench. To actually go to the edge of a Forbidden Zone . . . He turned to Suen and saw something else there in her expression: a kind of set stubborness, a determination to carry something through. He had seen that look before and it brought to him a feeling of hopeless dread She nodded once as if by his look he had guessed her intention and she was confirming it. She reached into her pack and took out a leather-bound book. She held it up.

"In the morning we head for the Forbidden Zone beyond North Forest, by the coast," she said. Cheydar knew the book. It was one of Tarrin's.

"We will be caught and killed before we get there," he said. "Any route will take us through the Cariphe's lands. If we go South we can take the road to Elmarch and the Forbidden Zone there nearly touches on the road."

"We go to North Forest, by the coast."

There would be no arguing with her. She turned to Dagon, who had taken out one of his swords and was running a stone up and down the blade.

"Will you be with us?"

"Of course," he said. He looked around at them. "Sleep now, I will watch."

Cheydar returned the look.

"Wake me in two hours," he said.

Dagon took out a pocket watch, checked it, then nodded and moved off into the darkness.

The sky was lightening, but the sun had yet to break over the horizon. Like a corroded coin the sulphurous moon Linx traversed the sky, one edge gilded by the approaching sun. Steeleye was a misty orb all but lost behind thin cirrus. There was frost on the boulders, layers of mist out in the scrub.

"Father will be very annoyed," said Eric.

"Ah, but he will be well rested," said Dagon. He stood next to a boulder, an air gun cradled before him. Eric did not recognise the design. He walked up and stood beside this warrior.

"Your weapon," he said.

Dagon flipped the gun round, handed it across.

Eric said, "Valved gas cylinder . . . how many shots?"

"Five. The darts are in that revolving barrel and are automatically presented."

"I've never seen its like before."

"They're made in Elmarch and are standard issue to the army there. They're the reason the Cariphe keeps to his borders."

"I'd like to go there. So would David. They say it is always sunny and the King's navy is always looking for volunteers." Eric handed the weapon back.

"They're normally volunteered with a club on the back of the head. Try the Border Legion, you'll have better luck there."

Dagon turned and started walking back to the camp. Eric followed.

"That's where you're from then?"

"Yes."

Eric glanced back. He's from Elmarch, he thought, staring at the ground. Something . . . He shook his head and halted. Yes. Where Dagon had stood there were two prints in the frosted ground ivy. No prints other than those

Eric had just made coming out here and the both of them were now making as they walked back. There had to be a reasonable explanation. No man could stand as still as a statue all night, or fly, or just appear out of thin air.

"I would say that if we skulked all the way to North Forest we'd more likely be caught than if we just travelled there openly. Head into Giltown, rent a carriage and take it right to the edge of the Wilder. Much less chance of getting caught," said Cheydar. He felt that if they must make this insane journey it would be best to do it quickly.

"I leave that decision in your hands. You are the soldier," said Suen.

Cheydar grimaced. Subterfuge was hardly soldier's work. He turned to Dagon. "What do you think?"

"I think you're right," answered the warrior. "The priesthood is geared that way: they'll be looking for people who look guilty, who are trying to hide, they'll always be looking for that kind. Best to go boldly, pretend to Lord Right, even priestliness." The last word came out with a touch of contempt.

"You don't have much liking of priests do you," said Suen.

"I just don't like the ignorance of faith," he shot back at her.

The coach house at Giltown was a sprawling affair with many attached stables and low buildings for the coaches and, because it was on the main trade route from Elmarch, the carts of traders. Even from a distance the bellowing of the titanotheres could be heard, and in the fields all around grew tree ferns; fodder for the great beasts.

Beyond the coach house the rest of the town consisted of red brick houses with many storeys leaning precariously over a street leading down to a dock crowded with low black barges. It was on these that goods were brought up from the richer southern country and traded for metal ores mined around Ompotec.

"The priesthood keeps to the agreement," said Cheydar as he walked at Dagon's side to the reception building of the coach house. "There is never mining in the Wilder, nothing like that."

"There has never been the need," replied Dagon. "The established mines supply all the demand there is." He looked at Cheydar. "If they did mine in the Wilder that would bring the Proctors back and believe me, that's the last thing the priesthood wants. They have no wish to appear in any way powerless."

The main building of the coachhouse was ringed with a low veranda on which priest soldiers lolled and inspected passers by. Dagon and Cheydar ignored them as they mounted the steps and went in through the main door. Within, a fat bald official sat at a desk sorting through sheaves of paper. He glanced at them over half-moon glasses and continued with his work until Dagon, as agreed, walked up and addressed him.

"The Lady Vemeer requires a coach to take her North," he said, and dropped a bag of metal money on the table. Cheydar contained his surprise; that hadn't been in the game plan.

The official delicately pulled at the strings of the bag and opened it. His eyes widened at what he saw inside and with a glance to the door he quickly slid it across his desk and dropped it in his lap.

"We are in a hurry, a Metrarch awaits her presence."

"The gold phaeton would be best. I will take you to it." He slid the money into a pocket, picked up some forms from a stack beside him and led the way to the door. Once outside he turned away from the priest soldiers and led the way round the side of the building. The soldiers inspected the trio with expected suspicion, but did nothing.

"Will you be requiring a driver?"

"No."

"Ah."

They shortly came to a man who sat on the edge of a water trough while watching some girls work at cleaning out the huge stables. The man looked bored. He held a short whip in one hand and was methodically slapping it against his leg. To one side, in a compound with fences five feet tall and made of tree trunks, a male titanothere ate from a huge basket fixed to the stable wall. The grey hide behind its head was goad-scarred and there were calluses on its sloping back and sagging belly, from the cart straps. A couple of the fist-shaped horns on its head had been broken off, probably in mating fights, and its small piggy eyes regarded the world with seeming indifference. It flicked warble flies away from its huge rump with an inadequate tail, twitched its mussel-shell ears. When it leaned its many tons against the fence the tree trunks bowed and looked as if they might break.

"Feruth, the gold phaeton, how quickly can you have it ready?"

The man pushed himself upright and gave Cheydar and Dagon a probing look. "What's the hurry?"

"A lady visiting a Metrarch," said the official.

"Ah." The man made no move until the official tapped his pocket and the clink of money could be heard. He grinned, nodded. "I'll have it ready in a couple of hours." He moved off.

The official turned away from him to Cheydar and Dagon. He met Cheydar's look. "Yes, I know; shocking isn't it?"

Dagon said, "You'll send for us when the coach is ready?"

"Yes. Where will you be?"

"The tavern. The lady waits there now. We shall have a meal there and hope to hear from you soon after?"

"So it will be."

The official gave a little bow to them and they moved off.

"They have no honour, these people," said Cheydar, after a moment.

"Money and power command respect. There are few people who can even be true to themselves. You should have realised that long ago."

"You are cynical, Dagon."

"I see things as they are."

"You believe so?"

"Unfortunately, I know so."

Cheydar allowed that to sink in for a moment then said, "The money, did Suen give it to you?"

"It was my own."

"You shall be re-imbursed."

Cheydar just caught the quickly repressed smile.

The tavern was similar in construction to the coach house; red brick and sagging, ringed with wooden verandas. The areas around the buildings were dry, as was the slabbed road. The verandas round most buildings were an indication that later in the year the combination of rain and traffic would turn the bald ground to a quagmire. Dagon stepped up onto the veranda first, and while waiting behind him, Cheydar glanced back the way they had come. That the priest soldiers from the coach house had followed them he gave no indication until he was inside the building.

"We have company, five of them," he said.

"I know."

"What would you suggest? You seem more able at subterfuge than myself."

"I feel that should they seek identification from us subterfuge will be wasted."

"Even if we kill them all here, others will come after us riding titanotheres and catch us on the road."

"I will think of something," said Dagon.

The room beyond the door was like a thousand other rooms of taverns. Suen and the rest sat at a long table, sipping at goblets of orange wine while a young man laid out food for them. Cheydar noted with approval that his sons, though staring at the food wide-eyed, were waiting for Suen to break bread and offer them a piece. Ritual; the lady feeding her bondsmen.

"Go and join them. I will go to the bar."

Cheydar made to obey then stopped himself. "You give commands very easily," he said, his face grim.

"Now is not the time, Cheydar. I can get us out of this."

"You are isolating yourself."

"Yes."

"Why?"

At that moment the five priest soldiers came in through the door. Cheydar met Dagon's look only for a moment then went and sat with Suen. From there he watched Dagon walk to the bar, a sudden arrogance in his walk, contempt in the glance he threw at the soldiers. The soldiers gazed around the tavern then followed him.

"What is happening?" asked Suen.

"I don't . . . " Cheydar stared, then realised. Of course. He cursed then turned to Suen. "I think he's going to force a duel. Even priest soldiers stick to some of the Code."

"What do you mean?"

"Win or lose the rest of them will not harass us, not immediately. One night must pass between blood lettings else duel will degenerate into open brawl or battle."

"Can we be sure of that?"

"With them, no, Lady. It is the best chance we have, though."

At the bar there was a sudden altercation. Dagon shoved one of the soldiers back.

"Be prepared to stand by your words!" he shouted, as if angry and very offended. Cheydar noted that he had picked on the officer. He aimed to behead, perhaps literally. The officer regained his balance and said something more. Dagon struck him back handed across the face then stepped to one side as another of the men made a grab for him. His sword was an arc of light between. One of the men stumbled back holding his forearm. The others kept out of the way. Cheydar was on his feet, with his air gun in his hand, and coming up beside Dagon in a moment. His sons were behind him. Dagon glanced at him.

"This scum offers insult to our Lady," he said with vehemence. Cheydar thought he acted the part well. He looked to the officer, whose eyes never wavered from the tip of Dagon's sword. Though his hand was at the short sword in his belt, he made no move to draw it.

"This scum should be made to pay, then," said Cheydar.

The officer watched. He was thin-faced and had the wiry toughness of a trained fighter. He did not draw. He knew his chances. Dagon stepped forward a little way and ritualistically spat on his boots.

"My choice, then," said the officer. This was what he was waiting for, Cheydar realised. "The time I chose is one hour from now, the place I chose is the street outside, and I chose air guns as the weapons of combat."

Cheydar nodded to himself; a sensible choice. Dagon had demonstrated his speed with the sword.

"So be it," said Dagon, and sheathed his sword in one smooth motion. As he did this hands strayed to the hilts of short swords. Cheydar smiled and raised the barrel of his gun. Hands drew back. Dagon nodded and stepped past him. They moved to the table where Dagon dispensed with his swords and took up his gun. The priest soldiers tramped from the tavern. Cheydar saw that Eric was grinning.

"What amuses you, boy?" he asked.

"Dagon's weapon—it has five shots. It is a repeater."

Cheydar nodded in confirmation when he saw the weapon, then he felt misgivings.

"You and David, keep your weapons gassed and cover the others. There may be some objection." Cheydar knew that in air gun duels it was often not the first shot that counted and that the winner was he who could reload the fastest and have more time to aim for the second shot. Dagon would not have to reload and could probably fire off all four of his remaining shots while the officer reloaded. The officer's men might consider this an infraction of the rules.

The sun was poised above the coach house and Linx was making its second daily journey across the sky, but this time was partially in silhouette and looked like a hole punched there. Dagon walked out across the worn ground and stood midway between the coach house and a titanothere fence. The fat official from the coach house stood a few yards to one side of him and fidgetted nervously; adjudicators were often shot by accident and he had not wanted the task. From where he stood Cheydar directed Eric and David to move away from him to the far ends of the veranda and be ready. He noted that over by the other end of the coach house a three-wheeled phaeton was being hitched to the backs of two patient cud-chewing titanotheres. Perhaps they could get this over with and be quickly on their way. He turned his attention to the right as the officer stepped out of a building just beyond the coach house and began walking towards Dagon. Six other priest soldiers walked out behind him and moved off in different directions. That could be taken two ways, either they were setting themselves for attack, or they were just covering their officer's back. The officer walked, his air gun held one-handed at his side, until he came face to face with Dagon. The fat official approached.

"Standard procedure," he said distastefully. "Stand back to back with your weapons held as you wish, then start walking at my count. I will count to ten then shout 'now'. You turn and fire at that shout, not before." He backed away quickly as Dagon and the officer turned their backs to each other. "One, two, three . . . " The count seemed to take no time at all. He reached ten and the officer turned and fired. Dagon staggered forward. "Bastard," said Cheydar. There had been no 'now' and the official was unlikely to object. There was a silence as Dagon regained his balance. The officer dropped his expended cylinder and was putting in a new dart when Dagon turned, and holding his gun one-handed up to his shoulder, took careful aim, and fired. The dart cracked against the officer's gun and ricochetted up into his jaw. He stepped back making a keening sound, his cheek hanging off in a flap and his side teeth exposed in a bloody grin. He put another cylinder in his gun. Dagon fired again and there was the hollow fleshy thump indicative of a chest hit. The officer keeled over and lay coughing blood. Dagon walked up to him, watched him for a moment, then walked towards Cheydar. Cheydar watched the soldiers, then glanced aside as the official stepped up to him.

"Your phaeton is ready," he said, his face deliberately clear of expression. "I suggest you get in it now and leave." Cheydar nodded agreement and turned his attention to Dagon.

"Are you hit?"

"Yes."

Cheydar looked at his left arm. Blood was trickling from his fingertips. "How bad?"

"The bone is broken. The dart is still in me."

Cheydar nodded to the interior of the tavern. "We will deal with it now."

"It would be better if we left," said Dagon.

"Don't be foolish. If there is to be a fight later on today or tomorrow I do not want you weak from blood loss. We deal with it now."

Dagon looked at him with evident surprise then smiled. "You are right. You are absolutely right," he said.

Cheydar wondered why he took such delight in being wrong, but dispelled the thought when Dagon staggered as they entered the tavern and he stepped to support him. Suen rushed to help once they were inside.

"Sheda, get my things," she said. They sat Dagon in a chair and Eric stood guard at the door. "Sheda! Damn, where is that girl?" Cheydar looked around then continued to cut away Dagon's shirt. He took a look at the wound then went to his own pack and removed a field-surgery kit. Suen walked to a back door and looked out. "Sheda!" Cheydar put a tourniquet around the top of Dagon's arm then tossed powder on the split below.

"That should deaden it some," he said. "I have to get the dart out." He cleaned a pair of surgical pliers in alcohol and a pair of spatulas that he handed to Suen. "When I say, hold open the wound with these." They waited a short time until the powder did its work, then at Cheydar's instruction Suen pushed the spatualas into the split and opened it wide. The dart was imbedded in broken bone. Cheydar got the pliers on it, but had to shove his fingers in the wound so one end of the break did not get pulled out as he tugged at the dart. Dagon turned to look at him with a sickly grin on his face, then he fainted. Cheydar stitched his wound and splinted his arm while he lay unconscious on the floor.

"Now we have to get him to the phaeton. Where is David?" Cheydar turned to Eric, who looked momentarily guilty before removing a fold of paper from his tunic and handing it over. Cheydar unfolded the note and read it. He was angry for a moment then guilty to feel relieved. He handed the note to Suen. She read the note then suddenly looked very angry. Cheydar waited for the explosion, as Dagon regained consciousness and struggled to sit upright. Cheydar squatted to help him.

"What's going on?" Dagon asked Suen.

"David and Sheda have gone. They've taken or are taking a barge to Elmarch."

"We have time to stop them," said Suen, screwing up the note.

"Why?" asked Dagon.

"Why!" Suen all but screeched. "She is my daughter. She is just a little girl!"

Dagon gave her such a look of contempt it was almost a blow. She stepped back. "That little girl has been lying with David since I joined you, and probably long before. She's found love, or infatuation if you will, and you want her at your side to go and die with you below a death post."

"I am not going to die," said Suen, quietly, almost whispering.

"Then you can find them in Elmarch sometime after. They will be safer there." Dagon staggered to his feet. Suen stared at him, probably knowing him to be right but loath to agree. She turned away as Cheydar and Eric began to collect up their things.

"I blame you for this," she snarled at Cheydar. He nodded acquiescence and continued with what he was doing. Suen abruptly sat down and began crying into her hands. Cheydar reached out to touch her shoulder and she knocked his hand away. As they loaded the phaeton she made no objection. She boarded without a word.

It took four days to reach the last coach house before North wood and during the four stops on the way for the feeding of the titanothere they mostly stayed inside the capacious phaeton and ate cold food. For a day Dagon ran a fever, but this was quickly dealt with by drugs bought at their first stop. No one followed. Perhaps the soldiers were embarrassed by the cowardly duelling tactics of their officer, or frightened by the way he was dispatched. At the last coach house they bought supplies and set out afoot along one of the many paths into the Wilder.

"Perhaps we should have hired a guide," said Cheydar as the trees closed around them. He preferred to be out in the open. Too much that was unexpected could come upon them in this place. There were dangerous creatures in the Wilder and dangerous men. He unhooked his airgun, dart pack and blades, and handed them to Eric to free himself of iron before checking their course. He laid the compass on the map, turned the map, grunted his satisfaction then put map and compass away. His son returned to him his weapons. They continued.

"We'll be at the coast by the evening," said Cheydar. No-one felt inclined to reply to him. The forest brought its own silence that it seemed should not be disturbed by rude human chatter. Suen had had very little to say since her daughter had run away. Perhaps, Cheydar thought, she was beginning to realise what was most important. He had. He was glad David had gone and only sad that Eric had not gone with him. The two of them had not yet sworm any oath to Tarrin's family and it was not necessary for them to serve to the limit; death.

They walked all morning and most of the afternoon through thick deciduous woodland. Great oaks, chestnuts, nettle elms, and the like, towering all around them. The nettle elms were bare, but the oaks still held onto the Autumn leaves other trees were in the process of shedding. The ground was swamped with leaves in shades of red and gold, and every breeze brought more of them kiting down. Through this colourful layer pushed fungi in bright poisonous colours and colours the same as the leaves. Dagon collected some of the latter in a cloth bag he hung at his belt. Eric and Cheydar, not knowing which fungi might be edible confined themselves to picking up sweet chestnuts, and walnuts. Suen just tramped along.

"Let us take a break now," said Cheydar, in the afternoon. "The last four days have been wearing. Here at least we can relax some. Here." He gestured to an area clear of briers below an ancient walnut tree. Suen nodded to him and slumped down on a pile of leaves by the trunk. "Take yourself off," said Cheydar to Eric, while looking at his mistress. "Bring us some fresh meat. I'll light the fire." Dagon and Cheydar cleared a space in the leaves and collected together a pile of the ample fallen wood. Cheydar waved Dagon away as he built a fire. Dagon went to sit by Suen.

"You have to let them go some time," the warrior said.

Cheydar glanced over, seeing Suen looking up at the tree from where she lay with her cropped golden hair on the leaves, blending with them. He felt something twist in his stomach; concentrated on the conversation.

"I don't need your comfort," she told Dagon.

"But you do, and I think it would comfort you to know that David carries with him enough money for them both to live in comfort in Elmarch for a year or even more." He looked at her with mild eyes.

She sat upright. "You?"

"I gave him the money."

"You knew then," she said, angry now.

"Yes."

"You could have said something."

"I could have, but I did not see their choice as foolish." Suen just glared at him. He continued, "I think Sheda hoped you would follow, that you would abandon this meaningless quest."

Smoke wafted into Cheydar's face as his fire caught; made his eyes water.

"It is not meaningless," said Suen.

"What meaning then does it have?"

Cheydar left the fire to its own devices and joined them, squatting down on his heels. Suen reached into her pack and removed her husband's book. She shook it at them as she spoke.

"My husband recorded here that there is a breach in the fence two miles in from the coast. Only a few miles North East of this there is a building in the forest. In that building are the Proctors."

Dagon looked thoughtful for a moment. "What makes you think the breach is still there?"

"Why should it not be?"

Dagon grimaced. "What would you intend should you reach this building?"

"I will wake the Proctors and lead them back through the breach."

"Why should they go with you? Why should they even wake for you?"

"They will. I'm not interested in argument, Dagon. I did not ask you to join us. You said when you first joined us that you believed the Owner to be returning for an accounting and that his Proctors would once again walk the world, yet you show no signs of this belief. I am going there. Cheydar will follow me because I know he would not obey me if I ordered him not to. Eric should perhaps return . . . " She looked at Cheydar, then returned her attention to Dagon. "You do not have to come, yet you are, that's your choice. Kindly stop trying to dissuade me from the choices I have made."

Dagon bowed his head, "I apologise. You are correct. I do not have the right to make other people's choices for them, even should those choices kill."

Suen turned her face from him. "Here is Eric."

Eric came back to the fire with four squirrels, skinned and gutted, hanging on a stick. He was grinning like a maniac. He had been enjoying himself. Cheydar thought it unlikely he would be able to send this son away. He took a pan out of his pack and tipped in a little water. They dined on squirrels broiled with mushrooms and sweet chestnuts. They ate walnuts while they waited for the squirrels to cook, as there were plenty on the ground, then they sat around the fire talking of anything but Proctors and the Owner. It was pointless moving on, as darkness was gathering the forest close about them. Dagon took first watch.

Waking to take his watch, Eric saw that Dagon had apparently not moved all night. *So that is it,* he thought, remembering footprints in frost. He wondered how any man could be possessed of such a stillness.

"You have not moved all your watch," Eric said to him.

"That is true," said Dagon. "The leaves create too much noise."

"How can you be so still?"

"It comes from inside."

Eric did not understand, but was not prepared to admit this. He saw that Dagon had his arm out of its sling.

"You can move your arm?"

"It is healing quickly. This is a good body."

Eric watched him walking back to the embers of the campfire. *He is deliberately mysterious,* he thought, *to make us think he is more than we reckon . . . or is he deliberately mysterious to cover that there is something strange about him?* Eric blinked in the darkness. It was all too complicated.

Morning brought a thick fog into the trees that coated everything with well-defined ice crystals and brought leaves tumbling down ungently. The fire was roaring up well with the extra wood Cheydar had thrown on it and he kept it within sight as he patrolled, his air gun charged and ready to come up against his shoulder. It would be too easy to get lost in this, and he definitely did not want to be lost now. The chuckling bark came again, to his left this time. Whatever it was it could be circling round to get at the others. He hurried back to the fire. When he got there he saw the other three were awake.

"What is it?" Eric asked.

"Hyeanadon," Dagon supplied. He tossed his air gun to Eric then drew his sword. Eric looked at him with surprise. "Our darts will not stop it if it decides it is hungry enough to attack us." He glanced at Suen who was staring at him white faced. "You take Eric's gun." He turned to Cheydar. "I know, I'm sorry, but I know about these creatures and I doubt you've encountered one."

"Your other sword," said Cheydar, holding out his hand. His own blade was a short stabbing blade used in combat with an armoured opponent. He would use that as well as the sword Dagon handed over. It was light. Just holding it gave Cheydar a surge of confidence. It was so very very sharp.

"Let's move," he said, taking up his pack. "We cannot stay here all day." He led the way back onto the path, sliced a leaf in half as it fell in front of him. Confidence died as the two halves reached the ground and Eric fired one shot. The huge creature made a yipping growling sound, its teeth clashing over where the dart had struck it, then it disappeared into the fog. That sound was answered by chuckling barks from two different directions.

"They hunt in packs," said Dagon.

"Really," said Cheydar, studying the sword he held and wishing he was somewhere else. Eric loaded another dart. He looked no less scared than the rest of them. Of course Cheydar had heard of such creatures. It made him cringe to think of how he let his son go hunting squirrels.

"Remember, they are only animals," said Dagon.

"That's a comfort," said Cheydar. How long had those teeth been? Two inches, three inches? And how high at the shoulder had the creature been? Higher than his own head at least.

"Shoot for the eyes, cut for the legs," said Dagon.

"Yes, of course."

The fog seemed to grow thicker as the morning progressed, and frost formed on loose clothing. Cheydar was thankful for Autumn leaves as the hyaenadons could not attack in silence. Any other time of the year and they would have been dead long since. One hyaenodon would make a noisy growling feint while another tried to sneak up on them. Every time it was the noise of the leaves that gave it away. The leaves also told them that the creatures were still with them all the time between attacks. Two attacks were driven off, steel darts smacking against rock-hard skulls. On the third attack the hyaenodon kept coming.

Cheydar dropped his air gun and braced himself with the sword held two-handed before him. The hyaenodon came in a snarling charge, its shoulders and head thick with the blood of its dart wounds. Eric pumped darts into it and it was half blinded by the time it reached them. Dagon strode to meet it, stepped neatly to one side and cut across with full force, his whole body in the cut. A ton of hyaenodon went past him nose down in the leaves, its left forelimb clinging by a sliver of flesh and skin. Cheydar struck down with his blade and it carved meat from the creature's face but did not penetrate bone. Its huge jaws clashed at him as it struggled to right itself. Dagon's sword went in through its side, twisted, came out on a fountain of blood. Cheydar stepped round, hacked down on its neck. Three hacks it took to reach a spine he could not sever. The stink of the creature's vomit and excrement thickened the air. Cheydar drew his short sword to drive between vertebrae, then turned as Dagon bounded past him. Another of the creatures was coming from the other side and only Eric faced it. Cheydar felt his stomach clench. Eric had perhaps one shot to fire. He was dead.

"Get out of the way!" Cheydar bellowed, running after Dagon.

Eric took careful aim, pressed the trigger. The hyaenodon stumbled, shook its head. Eric shouldered the air gun, reached up, and hauled himself up onto the oak limb above his head. Dagon met the second hyaenodon like the first, brought it down, heart stabbed. It died vomitting up its last meal in which Cheydar was sure he saw the chewed remains of a human hand. Eric grinned like a maniac from the oak tree. Suen just kept saying, "Oh my God. Oh my God." But she shrugged away Cheydar's hand when he rested it on her shoulder. A third hyaenodon retreated into the fog.

In the middle of the afternoon the fog cleared as far back as they could see through the trees, and the hyaenodon that had been trailing them disappeared. Then they saw a herd of chalicotheres that were the hyaenodon's usual prey. Perhaps it went after them or returned to the ready source of meat its fellows had become.

The trail began to cut across the face of a steep slope, and after consulting his map and compass, Cheydar led them down the slope to a fast-moving river, with gravel beds between half submerged slabs of rock. Armour-headed salmon swam in the deeper pools hunting trilobites the size of a human hand. They followed this river downstream and as evening encroached they heard the cadence of waves on a shingle beach and came out of forest by the sea, gleaming in yellow moonlight.

"Not a place to swim," said Cheydar, pointing out at a huge fin.

"It's only a basking shark," said Dagon.

Cheydar looked at him with annoyance.

"Is there anything you don't know?" he asked sarcastically.

Dagon looked at him, didn't reply.

They walked on for some while longer until the setting sun illuminated a silver post in the trees above the beach. They climbed above the beach and came upon the post, no closer than five metres. The post was higher than a man and as wide. It was a plain silver cylinder with what could have been runes, or could have been circuit diagrams, etched into its surface.

Cheydar stared at it and felt a crawling superstitious dread. He had been raised on stories about these things, about the power, the death. So many people had died trying to cross fence lines, or by just crossing accidentally. He glanced to his left, into the forest. No trees grew in line to the next post. There was just short grass and lichen on the ground. It was like this all the way along; trees never grew close enough to a fence where their falling might damage a post. No creepers or vines grew, nothing grew that might obscure posts from view. A human, crossing the line between posts would die, dramatically. Animals crossed the line without ill effect. It was just the way it was.

"Where are these words?" Suen asked Dagon. He pointed to a framed area on the post and looked at her. Her lips pulled back from her teeth in sudden anger. "And how are we supposed to understand that?"

"Your husband would have understood it. The language is old-Earth English; the language of scholars, the language that was yours when you came here."

"Ours," said Suen pointedly. She led the way into forest then, keeping to the edge of the trees, away from the death posts.

Eventually they came to an area where trees had fallen on ground turned boggy, their roots clawing at the sky. Beyond this was a break in the ground risen to head hieght; a recently risen wall of mud. Just before the break, spring water bubbled and new streams were cutting their way into the forest. They moved away from the fence line and got past this by climbing the trunk of a fallen elm. Above the break only a couple of trees had come down. The ground was dry here, but there were deep cracks in it where it had moved.

"Underground river," said Dagon. "Changed its course; undermined everything." And one of the things it had undermined was a death post. The post was tilted at an angle and glassy underground cables exposed.

"Here," said Suen, "if we cross on the side the post is tilted from we will not be harmed."

"It is good to be so certain," said Dagon.

"You do not have to try," snapped Suen.

Cheydar gazed across the line and wondered if he dared cross, even to follow Suen. There was too much dread caught up in the idea. Never before had he so feared death. Perhaps it was because there was nothing here he could fight. He turned to say something to Dagon; anything to ease the tension in him. The snarling bark came just behind him and he was jerked off his feet by his back pack, shaken, then hurled to one side as the straps of his pack broke. He struck a tree and fell to the ground half-stunned and staggeringly tried to right himself as the hyaenodon went for Suen. Air guns cracked and the creature turned, its teeth clashing at the air. Cheydar ran at it, drawing the sword Dagon had given him. He saw Dagon in front of it, sword drawn, ready for the cut, but the creature turned at the last moment and its jaws snapped on the sword and broke it in half. Then it had Dagon in its jaws, shaking him, still running, into fence line. The air filled with lightnings. Clamped in the creature's jaws, Dagon was sheathed head to foot in fire. The hyaenodon went down, releasing him; a burning thing on the ground that after a moment rose into the air again as if impaled on the lightnings. Cheydar saw this, smelt burning fur and burning flesh, black after-images flickering across his vision. Then the lightnings went out. Dagon's blackened corpse dropped to the ground beyond the fence, extremities breaking and falling away in charcoal shells. The hyaenodon was not burnt, but it did not move again. Cheydar gritted his teeth over sickness and horrified surprise. Not him, not Dagon, he shouldn't have died.

"Why did it kill the hyaenodon?" asked Eric, his voice flat.

"The power was there to kill a man. The hyaenodon just got in the way because it was holding him in its mouth," replied Cheydar. They were both standing back by the trees looking at Suen who stood close to the fence and stared at the blackened corpse. What could she possibly say or do now? It was time to turn back and follow David and Sheda to Elmarch. Time to end this pointless quest. Perhaps, thought Cheydar in the most secret part of his mind, for an ending to oaths. Suen had ceased to have a right to his loyalty when she no longer supplied his food, a roof over his head, and a means to decent interment after his death. Only plain stubborness had kept him with her.

"What will we do now?" asked Eric.

Cheydar paused a moment over his reply and saw Suen take a step towards the fence. He did not believe she would go further. She feared death as much as any and a working fence was certain death. In some stories it had even been described as the fence separating the living world from the land of the dead.

"We will go to Elmarch, perhaps down the coast so we avoid all the Cariphe's lands. We'll take service there. Perhaps the army . . . No!"

Suen was striding towards the blackened corpse of the Daybreak Warrior. Cheydar ran after her with Eric close behind him. They did not reach her in time. She crossed the line of the fence, came to stand over the corpse. Cheydar hesitated only a moment at the line, Eric not at all. As they reached her she was breathing heavily and had an insane look to her face. Cheydar realised she had meant to die. The fence had not killed her, perhaps something had gone wrong, burnt out. Cheydar realised he was shaking. He reached out to rest a hand on her shoulder, but at that moment she dropped to her knees and bowed down, sobbing. Cheydar felt sick with fear after the fact. He glanced at Eric whose face was now white with shock at the realisation of what they had done. They had crossed the fence. They were in the Forbidden Zone.

Digging with Dagon's broken sword and the pan Cheydar carried, they buried what remained of the warrior and stabbed the broken sword in the ground to mark the spot. By the time this was done they had all regained a certain grim composure. They would go on and find this building that contained Proctors, and then . . . Cheydar had no idea what would happen then. Perhaps the Proctors would kill them for being in the Forbidden Zone. Perhaps Suen would lead them to Ompotec and there exterminate the Cariphe and his priest soldiers. Whatever, Cheydar preferred to walk forwards. He doubted he would have the nerve left to turn round and walk back through the fence.

In the long shadows of evening, after covering perhaps two miles, they built a fire and roasted a wild pig Eric had shot only a short distance from the fence. It was one of the normal kind; similar to the domesticated ones, not one of the forest giants Cheydar had heard tell of. They really did not need another encounter like the one with the hyaenadons.

"I thought there was something special about him," said Eric. "He stood watch all night without moving."

"There was something special about him," said Cheydar. "He was a great warrior, fearless and strong. It took death posts to stop him. Nothing else could." He looked at Suen who was staring out into the darkness. "What did you think, my lady?"

"He knew things, and he was not one of us," she said. "He wasn't meant to die."

"None of us are," said Cheydar, then he stood to take the first watch. As he stepped away from the light of the fire to stand in darkness, he felt bitter. Her final comment had been right, he felt, yet he dared not admit to himself why he thought this was so. He walked a circuit in the darkness then slowly made his way back to the fire where he sat warming his back and watching. A chill breeze shifted the fire behind him when he had been watching for an hour. This slowly increased in strength and in only a few minutes the others had woken.

"Winter is upon us," said Suen, sitting up with a blanket wrapped round her shoulders. Cheydar wondered why he thought this comment so futile and why he felt that this wind had nothing to do with Winter. It grew in strength, at first a muted roar through the trees blowing leaves before it. Then its strength increased. Soon the roar was no longer muted and a blizzard of leaves was blasting across their campsite. The flames from the fire came out below the stack of wood and flat along the ground. Out in the darkness a tree went down with an abrupt crash, then another. They huddled against the wind. Cheydar tossed a log on the fire and this prevented it being blasted away. The wind fed it leaves and it spat out sprays of embers.

"This is not right!" he shouted over the roar. Suen and Eric just stared at him. They were in the Forbidden Zone Who knew what was right? Cheydar looked up, why, he did not know. "God save us," he said, and they heard his words clear and gazed up as well.

Steeleye, the third moon, now filled a quarter of the sky, gigantic, impossibly close. It wasn't a moon like the others. Cheydar realised he had always known that. It was one of those things never spoken of in the Cariphate; it was a moon put there by god to light our nights. Heretical to believe otherwise. Cheydar saw the constructions on its surface; the angular shapes and the towers, the glint of power, vast cities of machines, giant ramscoop engines, and the flare plates of fusion drives . . . here, no moon fallen in place by the luck of natural forces brought to balance, but a ship, a ship so vast it stunned the mind, a Great Ship. Here then was the Vardalex; the Owner's ship. And as Cheydar stared, wondering when he might be crushed, red fire flashed and swirled between constructs the size of mountains and flashed down, here, there, again and again.

"That was over Ompotec!" Eric shouted.

Cheydar wanted to crawl under his blanket and hide, or he wanted to get up and shout at the sky. He sat, unable to move. There could be no doubt; this was the stuff of ancient stories, of the wars they had fled, of vast ships and planet-destroying powers. What of Ompotec? Granted the place was a sack of scorpions, but there were good people there as well.

"The wind is easing," he said, because it was, and there seemed little else to say. He lowered his gaze, returned his attention to the forest, to things he could deal with. "Suen, Eric." They turned to him, then turned to see what he saw, said nothing, again, what was there to say?

The Proctor stood five paces from the fire, leaning on a thick metal staff intagliated like a death post. It was eight feet tall, robed and hooded, but the hood not enough to hide the eyeless leathery head and grim slit of a mouth. It gestured with one huge six-fingered hand. It wanted them to follow, this was clear. Cheydar stood up. At least it had not killed them, perhaps it intended to throw them out of the Forbidden Zone. Eric and Suen stood also. They grabbed up their belongings and followed the Proctor into the darkness and the leaves, and the cold blast of the wind. It was leading them away from the fence, Cheydar realised.

As they walked bowed through the darkness the wind began to abate, and a stinging hail rattled on the leaves. Every few hundred paces Cheydar had to look up at the sky to remind himself what was happening. He tried to recapture the excitement he had felt as a youth when Steeleye had first appeared in the sky. There was awe, but with it the wisdom of age had brought fear. He saw that after the first time Suen did not look up again. She stared resolutely ahead and was the first to see the grey loom of the building in the darkness, and the dark mouth of a doorway. The Proctor led them into that darkness.

"This must be the place," said Suen. There was something avid in her voice. Cheydar surveyed the dusty gloom and wondered at it. He had not been able to see much beyond the grey bulk of this place in the concealing trees, but it had not seemed to him to be of any great extent. The Proctor had gone to one side. He could hear it moving about. Suddenly there was light. Suen gasped. Eric swore.

"Nothing here," said Cheydar. He turned to the Proctor for answers and saw that it just stood with its back to the wall, waiting, patient as a stone. Something stirred then. Air feathered his face. He turned, felt Eric's fingers digging into his biceps, heard Suen moan with fright, felt his legs go weak and his stomach turn over.

"No Proctors here but Galeb," said the apparition. "He stayed for whatever reasons Proctors have. His fellows went to other worlds, other civilizations, a long time ago. There is nothing here for you."

Cheydar could see Dagon in there; in the shape of the face, somewhat in the tone of the voice, but otherwise this could not be mistaken for anything less than the Owner himself. His eyes were pupilless red, and he was pale like an albino, half-seen machines hung about him, were connected to him, plugged down into sockets in his head, neck and spine; his link with the ship and with the rest of a mind that had outgrown its human skull, his mind. He seemed solid, the machines less so. There was a feeling of power in the air, of forces bearing down on this point like mountains turned on their tips.

"You . . . the Owner," said Suen.

Dagon, the Owner, looked at her and she flinched back.

"Didn't you know that?" he asked.

"I thought . . . but you died."

"Dagon is just an aspect of me, a part of me, the oldest part and a part not yet reintegrated else Ompotec would still be standing and the Cariphe's garrison still living."

The red fire, thought Cheydar, and felt a deep vicious satisfaction.

"What do you mean?" asked Suen.

"I do not interfere in human affairs," said the Owner. "The Cariphe would not have lasted. The King of Elmarch was preparing to bring him down even as your husband burned . . . All part of the ebb and flow in the tide of human affairs." There was a shimmer. Something changed. The machines became distant and Cheydar saw that the eyes were no longer red.

"But I do interfere in human affairs." And it was Dagon speaking now; the man they had travelled with. He looked directly at Suen. "Proctors would have done no good, but this has, for you. When I died on the fence all that I was returned here to this." He gestured behind him at the half-seen machines. "I held my integrity long enough to open the fence, to destroy the Cariphate. That I speak to you like this, now, is a boon my whole self grants. There will be more killing, Suen, when the army of Elmarch hunts down the last of the priest soldiers. But once the King has access to the mines around Ompotec, a new age will be born. You'll see the start of that." He turned to Eric. "Join the the Border Legion, like I said. You'll do well there." Finally he regarded Cheydar. "And you . . . do what you must. You are a good man, Cheydar." There was pain then in Dagon's face. The last he managed was, "I've been before, perhaps . . . sometime . . . "

"Wait," said Cheydar, and knew his request to be futile. The Owner was back, the eyes like a fire seen through rubies. The machines showing a solid face turned out from that other place where they were, somewhere above.

The Owner said, "That is all. Galeb will lead you to the fence. The death posts will be reactivated in the morning."

"But you can't—" began Suen, a note of righteousness in her voice that had Cheydar cringing.

The Owner interrupted, "Suen, you are on my property. You have until morning not to be. Galeb will lead you and if you will not go he will kill you. That is all."

Air dragged at them as it rushed to fill the space the Owner had occupied. Dagon had been there even at the end, but buried under layers of something ancient and frighteningly complex. Cheydar took Suen by the arm and led her out. Eric followed, trying not to grin at such adventure.

"We'll go by the coast to Elmarch, find David and Sheda," said Cheydar, wondering if Suen would ever be able to live.

"Yes," she said, and leant against him. He shrugged her off and followed the grey shape of the Proctor into the dark.

the torbeast's
prison

Now onto the additions to this collection. *The Torbeast's Prison* was first published in Graeme Hurry's excellent *Kimota* (issue 13, 2000), is an off-shoot of *Cowl*, but not the novel, the novella that came before it. I guess I have always liked time travel ever since hiding behind the settee when Dr Who was running away from those mobile dustbins. In a story-telling context, I love the self-referencing logic of it all and how very often the story arc can be tied into a loop. And now, proving that truth is sometimes stranger than fiction: I wrote *Cowl* (the novella) with its tors and its torbeast, before any publisher called Tor had even impinged on my consciousness. Strange how I am now being published in America by Tor and in Britain by Macmillan's Tor UK imprint. A bit loopy really.

I was in a park, it was spring and the birds were singing. The Earth was beneath my feet as was the black sphere; poised at the edge of the real. In two hours there would be another shift and then for the ensuing fifty hours and forty-three minutes I would be confined to that black surface below its metallic sky. I had two hours in which to feed myself, two hours of sunlight and human contact, two hours to acquire some luxuries. The money in my pocket would be of no use here unless I could get to a coin dealer. The last shift had put me down at the inception of the second Roman invasion of Britain, and I had taken the coins from the pouch of a legionary who had crawled into a briar patch to die, out of sight of the Iceni warrior who had split his gut. The head of the Emperor Claudius was impressed on them.

A jogger came sweating and wheezing past me with a Walkman plugged into his ears. From his dress, and from that single electrical device, I guessed this time to be the late twentieth or early twenty-first century. This man was no use to me, for people did not often go jogging with money in their pockets. I scanned around and spotted a smartly-dressed man sitting on a park bench with a briefcase beside him. He was opening a sandwich box. I sauntered over and sat beside him.

"Morning," I said.

He looked askance at me and I wondered if it was morning. I checked my surroundings. The jogger was fast disappearing and the only other people in view were a couple of teenagers near the park gates. Quickly then. I chopped him hard across the windpipe and felt cartilage give under the edge of my hand. Choking and clutching at his throat the man tried to rise. I knelt on the bench next to him and snapped his neck. As he shivered and convulsed into stillness I picked up his sandwich box and ate the contents. When I'd finished them, and the packet of crisps and apple, I searched him. His clothing yielded a fat wallet, cigarettes and a lighter, a pen knife, some change, and key ring from which depended a pencil torch. I lit a cigarette, following the same impulse that had made me eat the sandwiches—a hope that the other hunger would be staved off. The items I placed in the briefcase with the paperwork, pens, and scientific calculator, and then hurried from the park with it.

I try to remember when it started, but there is a haziness to my memory and a deal of inconsistency. I think I was born in the twenty-eighth century, but how is it I know things about later centuries? How is it I also know things BC that have never been written in history books? The frightening thought is that I have been to these times, experienced these things, and have been shifting for so long that I've simply forgotten. I would ask the sphere, but our communication is not a verbal thing.

As I reached the shops, my watch, a complicated affair that has more functions than seem feasible, displayed the hour and ten minutes remaining to me. There I purchased a sleeping bag and a camp stove, dried food and coffee, whisky and bottled water, and other items to sustain me. I acquired some warm clothing—hiking gear and a body warmer—a rucksack which I packed full of anything of conceivable use. The nylon climbing rope I packed in last was for a very particular purpose. The only weapons available for purchase were a crossbow and a large sheath knife. I spent until the wallet was empty then, heavily burdened, headed back for the park. Whilst walking I smoked more cigarettes as the craving in me grew. By then it was getting dark and I realised how wrong I had been with my greeting to the man who still lay dead on the park bench. The teenagers were waiting for me inside the entrance to the park. Call it fate.

It had to be further into the twenty-first century than I had at first thought. Any earlier and the boy would not have been armed as he was. This was Britain and projectile weapons had been banned for some time. In America any self-respecting mugger would have come at me with an automatic pistol. Here, at this time, muggers had taken to using juiced-up tasers; devices that threw out a wire-connected dart and zapped the recipient. I felt the sharp pain as it entered my chest and the flash threw everything into the negative for me. I didn't go over. The jolt merely burnt away any vestige of my remaining self-control. I dropped the pack and the other items, and took two swift paces forwards. AD humans; so weak and slow. I swatted him on the side of his head and he fell. The one to my right was only just opening his mouth to yell a warning when I caught him by the throat, my thumb on his windpipe. Pressing with my thumb and opening myself, I became a well down which the energy field generated by complex molecular chains flowed. I drank of what is the very structure of time; the field of life which encompasses where we may travel, and delimits it. The consequence of this was a disintegration of molecular bonds. The boy became a steaming slurry held up by rapidly dissolving skin and clothing. I released what remained of him and shook slime from my hand before turning to his companion. Soon finished, I took up my acquisitions and headed for my arrival point, feeling fuller and more potent than I had a few minutes before, and less human.

"Have you fed well then, Marten?"

The voice that issued out of the night possessed a jarring familiarity. I turned and saw someone standing off to my right. He was unidentifiable in the darkness.

"Is that my name?" I asked.

"It is," said the figure.

"Then what is your name?"

"Call me Hallack, if it suits you, or not. But listen first. You only have a few minutes left here and there are things you should remember," he said.

"I feel there are many things I should remember," I replied.

The man squatted down in the darkness. I moved to go towards him but he held up his hand.

"No closer to me, Marten. I would hold onto the force of my life."

"What do you have to tell me then?"

"A brief story: In the year two hundred," he gestured about himself with his hand "the twenty-eighth century to these people, a creature was born that resembled humankind only in a rough approximation of form. It was called Cowl and it was brilliant, insane, and horrifyingly dangerous. It built an organic time machine that took it to the Nodus—the beginning of things—and there it tried to destroy the human race, or rather supplant it with a race of copies of itself. In the process it shoved itself off mainline time and we survived."

"Is that all?" I asked contemptuously, but the surge of feeling this brief story had elicited was strong indeed.

"That is all for the moment," said the man. "Your time to depart is upon you, and I don't want to be here when it comes."

I glanced at my watch; about a minute remained. When I looked up I felt that tugging at the inner core of me which I identified with travel in time. The mysterious man was gone. I moved away from him to my point of entry to this Earth. When the time on my watch reached precisely two hours, the Earth shifted away from me.

My new boots possessed a grip. I wouldn't have slipped over unless during an interspace shift. Anyway, no footwear knowable would have kept me upright in such a situation. The sphere would not let me go and its attraction slammed me flat every time. If only it had done the same for my belongings.

The sphere's surface is matt and without indentation or hole. I had acquired many items of comfort during Earthward shifts only to lose them in interspace during some unknowable violent manoeuvre. Often I was pinned to the surface like a man crucified, only to see food and water, blankets and stoves go hurtling into grey space. I tried suction pads, epoxy glues, welding. But the sphere goes frictionless on these occasions. Nothing remained bar myself and, of course, the tor. I knew the name, but not what it was.

I didn't know how many shifts ago it appeared. Long enough for the human forearm that had appeared with it, ripped off at the elbow, to rot away, and for the bones to be flung away during a shift. Its appearance was that of a large coiled holly leaf fashioned of glass and bright metal and seemed a perilous thing for someone to wear on their arm. It stuck to the surface of the sphere like a burr picked up on the fur of a huge animal. I didn't know why. This time I decided to use it as an anchor point for my belongings.

After securing my belongings to the tor with the nylon climbing rope, I spread out the sleeping bag and set up the stove. It seems too prosaic to mention that I enjoyed my first cup of tea in . . . an age. I felt low of course. The huge potency and euphoria I had felt at draining the two boys was gone as it always went as soon as my feet touched the black surface. I felt guilty as well and tried to buck myself with the only consolation I had, that is, should I kill a direct ancestor to myself in this manner I'll shove myself off the main line and straight down the probability slope. This would confine me to the past of a line where I was never born and where time travel would be impossible. I would end up at some point in an alternate history and the sphere would be unable to draw me back . . . I think.

Twelve hours. The manoeuvres were coming earlier and earlier. Luckily I was on my back with the sleeping bag underneath me when the cold wind hit. I felt it only momentarily before I was seemingly encased in invisible steel. For a second I felt victorious as I had managed to clasp the neck of the whisky bottle at the last moment. Unfortunately the rest of the bottle was out of the field and it smashed as I was slammed back. I couldn't see the rest of my acquisitions. As I lay there all I could see was the grey sky swirling in mind-numbing patterns and the occasional flicker of a black shape. One of those black shapes became distinct as a human form before being swept away. This was the first time I had seen this and it opened a world of speculation. Was I being pursued? If so, why? And: do my pursuers know who I am? As the sphere shifted I felt its rage and its jealous protectiveness of me. I also heard the whispering murmur that is the nearest it comes to speech and, understanding none of it, was affected at a visceral level by it.

The manoeuvres lasted a further twelve hours. After that time I was delighted to discover my rucksack still secured to the tor. The stove was gone, all but one of the water bottles burst, and the crossbow smashed, but I had enough left to bring some comfort to my remaining hours before the next Earthward shift. On the button, twenty-six hours later, that occurred.

I stood on the black surface and waited while the grey faded to cloud-scudded blue and that black surface softened under me and became the wet sand of a beach. The gentle slap of waves encroached on my hearing and the call of a gull complemented my loneliness. Behind me were mud cliffs gradually being eroded by the sea. The presence of fossil belemnites and ammonites in the nearby rocks informed me that I had not gone too far back. When I walked to the head of the beach and inspected the flotsam and jetsam, a spherical coke can with its hologram surface providing the illusion of a fish swimming inside, showed me I must be somewhere and when in the late twenty-first century. I began to walk along the beach, feeling no inclination to go anywhere for supplies and definitely disinclined to encounter any people. The hunger was growing in me with alarming rapidity even then. I did not think I would be able to control it in even the limited fashion I had before. I had gone only a matter of paces when the woman called to me from the cliff top.

"Marten!" she shouted, and I assumed she was calling to some child. "Marten! Wait, I'll come down to you!"

She was calling to me—I could not deny this. Was that my name then? I'd heard it recently hadn't I? I waited for her, one part of me wanting to shout a warning to her, the other part of me avid for her presence. Some distance up the beach she found a path down to me and then came jogging along the beach to me. Her black hair was cropped short around a face as sharp-featured and white as my own. Her clothing had the look of an acceleration suit. She was not of this century. I held up my hand when she was twenty paces from me.

"Stay there. You are not safe," I said, both glad and disappointed when she slowed to a walk. She was puzzled and angry.

"None of us are safe. What happened? Did you use it?"

I could not fathom her question.

"Don't come any closer. If you come closer I might kill you."

"Hallack said you had it under control now," she told me, and continued walking towards me.

"Who are you?" I asked.

"Bellan, you know that . . . oh my god!"

She turned at the last moment, perhaps suddenly realising her danger, at least that is what I thought then. Her turning to flee set me moving. Suddenly I was just a hunting animal. I brought her face down in the sand and closed my hand on the back of her neck.

"The beast, Marten! It's not you! Try to remember!"

These cryptic words were curtailed by her screams. She was definitely from a later century—stronger and more complex, her force was a rich and varied thing. She took a long time to start coming apart, but I was sure I was done when I finally got off her and stepped back, for her flesh was slewing from a collapsing skeleton. However, she managed to crawl for a couple of yards making liquid gasps before she finally deliquesced. I couldn't figure her words as I walked on, and when I finally returned to the sphere its muttering was louder and I found it difficult to remember.

There was a time, I know, when there was no communication. I stood on that black surface below the iron sky and shifted and travelled. I fed often. I know this. Could it be that I am deluding myself? Perhaps I am not human. Perhaps humanity is a superficial sheen I have acquired throughout my feedings? Why then this attachment to the twenty-eighth century? This one question convinces me that I am human and perhaps only lost that humanity for a little while.

Seventeen shifts passed. The manoeuvres came sooner and sooner so that it seemed my feet only had to touch the black surface and I would be slammed on my back for periods of ten to the full fifty hours. Every Earth-shift I came through exhausted and hungry and I killed and fed. On the seventeenth shift the sphere nearly lost me. For a time I was hurtling alone through limbo before it picked me up again and dragged me on. After this shift I felt the hunger but possessed the will not to feed. Upon the sphere again I saw that my belongings were gone. The tor had been ripped away and lost during the same manoeuvres that had nearly lost me my place. Of a sudden I remembered the woman, shapes I had seen in the greyness, people calling to me and trying to tell me something. Returning to me with almost the force of faith was that I was a prisoner and that once the opposite had applied. It was in the dunes of a desert in an age when craft like uprooted buildings tumbled through the sky that I re-encountered the truth.

"Marten, here at last."

I turned and saw a man and a woman seated side by side on the dune-face nearby. He wore the robes of a Turag and his eyes were piercing green. I knew him, and in that moment of knowing him I remembered an all too brief conversation. She . . . she wore something like an acceleration suit and dark cropped hair framing a familiar thin face. Seventeen shifts ago I had killed her: Bellan. I looked to the man.

"You spoke of Cowl," I said.

He gestured me closer. It seemed he was not afraid of me now. I moved closer trying to plumb that familiarity of his features. He gestured to the sand at his feet. Before sitting I glanced at Bellan. She smiled at me and I felt a hand grasp my insides and squeeze. I needed no explanations of what had happened. I have been travelling randomly in time long enough. In her existence she had yet to have that fatal encounter.

"As we speak you will remember," she said.

He said, "Without the tor there it does not have so close a link outside and will not have as much control over you."

"What . . . what are you talking about?"

"First another little story. We told each other such, quite often," he said.

"Who are you?" I asked.

"You know my name."

"It is Hallack, but that means I only know your name." I glanced at the woman. I dared not say that I already knew her's.

"I am Bellan," she told me. I could not meet her eyes when she smiled again.

Hallack said, "You will remember . . . now, I shall continue where I left off. It has only been moments for me. . . . Cowl's organic time machine, or complex time machine, took him way back to the Nodus at such a rate that he managed to overshoot it and thus remain partially inaccessible to his enemies, ie the rest of humanity. Back there he took the young beast he had fashioned; a creature for which time was like the air to a bird, a creature that hunted in time, a creature that fished in time for prey. How to describe this monster?" He looked to Bellan and she took up his narrative.

"Originally it was a distinct and describable creature, but it grew into something vast: landscapes of beast, a whole alternate occupied, Mandlebrotian endless feeding mouths and tendrils. On its back grow scales like holly leaves of glassy metal that curl when they fall away into perilous bracelets. Who put these bracelets on can travel in time, usually directly into the creature's mouths. Cowl sent these items uptime to collect samplings of future humanity to see if his efforts were succeeding. These items were called tors; complex organic time machines in themselves; scales from the back of the torbeast."

I visualised this description and knew that I had indeed seen this creature somewhere, somewhen. I thought of the tor that had lain on the surface of the sphere.

"Why do you tell me this?" I said, gazing at each of them. "What connection do I have with this Cowl, or with this torbeast?"

He replied, "How do you kill a creature that travels in and manipulates time by instinct? You cannot. Cowl is gone. He sits in an alternate from which he cannot travel, forever gnawing on his own rage. The beast was a danger to us all so we laid our plans and we sacrificed a million lives to imprison it."

"You still have not told me."

"For fifty hours out of every fifty-two you are trapped on the surface of its prison. At one time you were its warder, until it drew one of its own scales to the surface, and until it began to speak to you," said Bellan.

"I would be free of it," I said, quickly.

"It is why we are here," said Hallack.

"We've been following you for a long time. The beast feeds through you," she nodded at my sudden guilty expression. "Meagre fare for it, but enough to empower its leaps through time and keep it ahead of us, and enough, should you feed it enough, for it eventually to break from its prison."

How could I tell her the true source of the sick guilt I felt?

Hallack pulled a cloth package from behind himself and unwrapped it. He revealed a tor.

"You must place this upon your arm. It is all we have. Our own machines are too slow and too crude. It is ironic that only with what it used to entrap you may you escape."

The sphere was below me; poised on the edge of the real. I could hear a muttering. Perhaps I fooled myself. Perhaps it was really a distant snarling. He rolled the tor down the dune-face to me.

"Put it on and shift to another time. Escape it, Marten," said Hallack.

It was thorned glass and silver; a perilous thing to slip onto my forearm. I took it up. It was heavy and it cut my hands. The pain seemed distant. I gazed up at Hallack and Bellan. They were backing away up the dune face. Behind them flowing irises were opening in the air as they returned to their machines. I slid the tor over my right forearm. Skin peeled and flesh parted like earth before the plough. I groaned at the sudden increase in pain as blood jetted from slitted arteries. The pain was intense, but it seemed to promise something else. Very quickly the blood ceased to flow. I studied the thing. It was bonding to my flesh, and the bones beneath, just as I knew it would. Then the tor, parasitic form that it was, cleaned my blood for me, scrubbed my mind, made me a more wholesome beast on which it could feed. And memory returned like falling wall.

Oh Hallack my brother. Dear friend Bellan. Below me the muttering from the sphere became a raging scream. I shifted as it shifted Earthward and tried to snatch me up. Suddenly I was falling into the grey abyss, through a tunnel of bones. Someone fell past me screaming my name, then the sphere was falling upon me. I shifted sideways and saw the Earth as through a distorting lens; its continents on fire. I felt something groping for me, unable to find me, but well able to find the tor. I shifted again and hurled myself for the world. All my will was concentrated on this act. All its will was exerted to hold me back. Something had to give and what gave was my arm. I felt it snap and tear, and I felt the tendon rip away from somewhere inside my shoulder. There was no pain at first. I felt and heard its muttering and raging as it receded from me, lost me, and I lay my head upon a flat rock while my arm stump bled into the matted grass all around.

"Marten!"

Hallack, my brother. I regained a delirious consciousness, watched him shooting some sort of weapon into the air to scare-off a hunting smilodon. He bound my arm and talked all the while. He said how we must move quickly to find Bellan, before her field loci went beyond the detection of his own.

"The late twenty-first," I managed and he stared at me in a puzzled way. "That's where she is."

"How do you know, Marten?" he asked.

"Because that's where I killed her."

Perhaps we can get there . . . in time.

tiger tiger

Honest, I didn't know of the Alfred Bester one of the same name until long after I'd written this (which is surprising with the amount of SF I've read), but then probably Mr Bester was not the first to snitch those two words as a title, and I certainly won't be the last. In this story the tigers came first, then the title, and it being an 'Owner' story it seemed almost inevitable that I had to put in that line from the poem at the start. The Owner is like the Old Testament God, who is, I suppose, everyone's expression of the ultimate power fantasy. And that's his appeal. No matter how liberal or well-meaning any of us is, we want that power, though many of us would never admit that.

> *'What immortal hand or eye*
> *Could frame thy fearful symmetry?'*

A tiger had taken the orphan Jeleel Welder down by the Wishpool. Her blood speckled the Rhode's dark green leaves and they found her soul, on its unbreakable silver chain, depending from its roots. Sapher found tracks near the pool and told their story to the villagers.

"It took her here while she washed Baum's shirts. She fought it here and it dragged her to here and this blood is where it bit her. It is arterial blood and there is much of it. She probably died before it took her deep into the Rhode and ate her," he said.

He was very matter of fact about it all and Tamsin felt sorrow for his brother. He knew how much Sapher had loved Jeleel. How intensely he had courted her. The villagers peered to the Rhode. The dendrons were in flower and deep in them was all perfumed shadow.

"This cannot be," said Baum, the Elder, pointing the grey spade of his beard at Sapher. "The Agreement. He does not allow this."

"The Agreement," spat Sapher. He stabbed his spear into the earth to demonstrate how he felt about the Agreement.

Baum continued, "I know your thoughts on this, but there has to be some other explanation. 'Man must not kill tiger and tiger will not kill man.' The Owner was very specific." As he mentioned the Owner, he touched his pendant with his forefinger then made the sign: his hand held out flat, parallel with the ground.

"The Agreement is just that. It does not bind. What about Temron Drivetech? He killed a tiger. Who is to say that tigers may not break the Agreement as did he? Perhaps this is their vengeance," said Sapher.

"Vengeance was done upon Temron," said Baum.

They all nodded and remembered. After his sister had died of the ague Temron had denied the Agreement and vehemently claimed that there could be no Owner. He had then, in the madness of his grief, told the village that his sister would be buried in a tiger-skin burial robe. He had killed a tiger and done this thing; his sister wrapped in skin that was still bloody. The following night Temron had disappeared.

"You say vengeance was done upon him. I saw no evidence of it. I saw only his footprints leading into the Rhode. I saw only that he left us," said Sapher.

"What Temron's fate may have been is irrelevant. What do we do now?" said Tamsin. He watched his brother. He needed to hear this, though he did not want to.

"We go after the tiger and we kill it," said Sapher.

"I cannot allow that," said Baum.

Sapher ignored him and turned to the villagers. "Who will come with me? This must be done. Too long we have been bound by superstition and fear. We are stronger and more cunning than the tigers. We should rule here, as is right!"

Some stepped forwards, but others shook their heads and turned away—returned to the village. Ephis came up and stood beside Tamsin.

"You will go with him?" she asked, frightened that she might lose this newly found love.

"I must," said Tamsin, placing his hand against the side of her face. "He is my brother."

"This is madness," she said. "The Owner will punish us."

"Your father has faith so you must have faith," he said.

She pushed his hand away. "Can you doubt the truth of the Agreement?"

He smiled at her. She was like so many of the villagers; she never questioned the old teachings, never wondered what might or might not be true. He loved her but sometimes her beliefs caused painful argument. If only her father had not been Baum. This, he decided, was not the time for argument—his brother needed him.

"I have to go," he said.

She regarded him for a long moment.

"Then I will go with you," she said.

Though half the village agreed to go with him, Sapher was livid at the rest.

"Yes, crawl back to your huts and sleep untroubled. When the tigers come in the night to eat you I will laugh and climb a tree to watch," he sneered at those who departed.

Amongst those who remained were Tamsin, Sapher and Ephis, Torril and Chand—husband and wife who had always been closest to Sapher, and who hunted with him all the time. The surprise members were Baum and Ghort.

"My daughter is all I have now. I will come with you. I will interfere in no way. I will not stop you killing the tiger, nor will I help you," said Baum.

"I will come," said Ghort.

They all looked round. The huge man was sitting on a boulder with his elbow on his knee and his chin resting on the palm of his hand. He blinked blue eyes at them and said no more. That was the thing about Ghort: no one noticed he was there until he let them know. When they did know they were again awakened to the fact that this was the man who had lifted a fallen coral ash from his hunting partner Dorlis, and who had, at a run, carried Dorlis the ten kilometres back to the village. A vain rescue though, for Dorlis had taken poison rather than spend the rest of his life a cripple.

"Why should you come?" asked Sapher, bitterness still in his voice. Tamsin glared at his brother, hoping he would say no more. Ghort would be a valued member of such an expedition and must not be put off.

"I come because I wish to," said Ghort.

"You believe in the Owner," said Sapher.

Ghort just regarded him with those blue eyes. Sapher turned away in frustration.

"Very well," he said after a moment. "Be back here in the hour. You know what supplies to bring, and if any of you have access to family weapons you may bring them."

"Family weapons?" said Baum, outraged.

Sapher glared at him and he desisted.

They wore the canvas trousers and jackets that were necessary for travelling deep into the Rhode. The only family weapon brought to the hunt was the one Sapher carried: the Logisticson's gun. Tamsin allowed this even though the gun had been his assigned responsibility from his fifteenth year. Since its last firing, in Tamsin's grandfather's time, it took a month of bright sunlight to get it up to eighty per cent of a charge. It would take no more. That charge also tended to bleed away during the hours of darkness. It was all something to do with the flickering red lights on the side of the weapon, but Tamsin could not decipher them—the manual had been lost four generations ago.

Torril and Chand brought their hunting bows and long knives, plus all the usual supplies for a hunt when the prey were deer and swamp elk, not tigers. Tamsin was not skilled in the use of a bow, so he brought his father's two spears—serviceable weapons with wide blades fashioned of ship metal; blades that took ages to lose their edge and ages to sharpen again.

Ghort came with only one spear, but what a spear it was. The blade was two hands wide and as long as a normal man's forearm. The Smith had taken months to cut the metal for it, from the old hull, and months to sharpen it. It was Ghort's reward for his rescue of Dorlis, who killed himself the day after the presentation.

Ephis brought her crossbow with its quarrels fashioned of Rhode wood. Her father, Baum, brought no weapons at all. He brought the Agreement. Sapher looked set to explode when he saw this, instead, he climbed a rock to address them all.

"We have two hours left until darkness," he said, then waited a moment until sure of all their attention before continuing. "The tiger went east to the Ship. We will camp there for the night then use it as our base while we hunt the beast down. The Plain of Landing is probably its main hunting ground." He glared at them all belligerently, daring them to dispute his words.

"He can tell an awful lot from a few tracks," Ephis whispered to Tamsin. Tamsin glared at her, then moved away from her to be closer to his brother.

"If we work together on this we should have the beast's skin within days. We will kill this tiger for Jeleel!"

As he said this he punched the air with the family gun. There came a grumbling response from the crowd that could have meant anything.

Then a voice spoke up from the back. "Does Jeleel want you to kill a tiger?"

For a moment there was absolute silence, then heads turned to seek the source of that voice. Abruptly the crowd parted and a raggedy scarecrow of a man walked through.

"Owner save us!" exclaimed Baum, clutching the Agreement to his chest.

"That option he left to you," said the man, then he held out his hand to Baum. "Now give me Jeleel's soul pendant."

"Who are you to make demands?" yelled Sapher, jumping down off his rock.

Tamsin moved up beside him and grabbed his arm. "That's Temron: the tiger killer," he said, and this news stilled even Sapher.

They watched while Baum groped about in his pouch and eventually came up with a tangle of chains and pendents.

"That's old Nigella, and that's Dolic. Ah, here." He separated out a pendant "I see you've lost yours," he said as he handed Jeleel's pendant across to Temron.

Temron smiled and closed his fist around the object.

"I have been dead for eight years and now I am back," he said.

At this there came a concerted muttering and most people moved back from him. All except one, Tamsin noted. Ghort moved closer, his expression strangely intense.

Temron continued, "I died out in the Rhode because I broke the Agreement. I died alone and in pain, but at least my pain was my own."

Temron raised his fist and a voice spoke out that all recognised. It was Jeleel's voice:

"Now, with what I know, I wonder if I should forgive him. I find that I cannot. Life was sweet and seemed likely to become sweeter. I was innocent," said the voice.

A woman wailed and fell to her knees. The voice went on:

"Do not weep, mother. You will be with me again some day."

"Who has done this?" the woman shouted.

"Sapher did this to me. He raped me, then he beat me and cut me with his knives, then he tied rocks in my dress and threw me into the Wishpool. Despite his beatings and his cuttings, I drowned in the end."

"You murderer!" Baum bellowed.

Tamsin was turning to his brother when Sapher yelled.

"Nooo!"

An actinic flash burnt the air and a sound like a rock hitting a tree trunk, opened it. Tamsin staggered back with the smell of burning flesh in his nostrils. He saw Baum falling with smoke pouring from the embered cavity of his chest. His brother had fired the gun.

"Sapher!"

Sapher turned the weapon on Tamsin. Tamsin saw the look in his eyes and dived to one side. Behind him he heard a scream. He rolled and ran into the Rhode. Fire behind him. Screams and chaos. His brother had raped and murdered Jeleel. Tamsin ran in semidark until a root tripped him and brought him to his knees. He pulled himself to a tangle of trunks and tried to bite down on the tears that threatened. Had he known this already? He dared not entertain the thought. Distantly he heard shouting and the sounds of people running. Then close to he heard something and moved as quietly as he could to observe.

It was Temron walking up a path through the Rhode. He seemed almost to be gliding, moving faster forward than his pace should actually have taken him. He also seemed somehow blurred. Behind him Ghort was running to catch up. Temron turned when the big man was close.

Ghort staggered to a halt and rested his weight on his spear. Temron seemed to be fading into the background, or perhaps it was that another background was reaching out from somewhere to grab him back. Abruptly he came back into focus and was no longer Temron. Dark hair turned white over a thin face. Dark eyes turned red, demonic. Canvas clothing transformed into something more like the inside of a machine than attire for a human being. Around him, undefineable engines lurked at the limit of perception; gathered and poised like a planetoid only moments before impact. Ghort sank down onto his hocks and placed his spear on the path next to him. He kept his eyes down while he regained his breath. The entity before him did not move. It just nailed him with its viper eyes. Eventually Ghort looked up.

"Owner," he said. "Take me with you."

The Owner's reply came after a suitable pause. Tamsin felt that this pause was not for reflection. This was a god after all.

"Are you wise, Ghort?" the Owner asked, and the voice had nuances of power. Hearing it, Tamsin realised it might be possible to kill with a word.

"I am wise," said Ghort.

"Ah," said the Owner. "Yet patience is integral to wisdom."

The Owner turned and things distorted somehow, as if he was attached to everything around him by invisible threads. For a moment Tamsin saw something vast—the inside of an iron cathedral. Then the Owner was gone and Ghort was bowed down with his forehead in the dirt. Tamsin thought he might be crying.

Tamsin waited a moment or two then moved over to the big man and stood next to him. Ghort abruptly pulled himself upright and brushed dirt from his forehead. He sighed, then abruptly turned and studied Tamsin.

"You saw?" he asked.

"I saw, but I'm not sure what I saw," said Tamsin.

"What you saw," said Ghort contemplatively. He went on, "What you saw was the Owner. Surely you realise that?"

"I don't believe in gods or supernatural beings. Everything has a reason," said Tamsin.

"Yes, you're sure of that," said Ghort, observing him. "You are very unusual in your attitude to life. Practically unique. It's probably why he let you see him."

"Let me?"

"Don't believe for one moment that he wasn't aware of your presence," said Ghort.

Tamsin closed his eyes and tried to straighten things out in the storm that was raging between his ears. "I do not believe in gods or supernatural beings," he said stubbornly. He opened his eyes when Ghort's hand clamped on his shoulder.

"He is not a god nor a supernatural being, Tamsin. What he is is a ten thousand year old man with the power of a god and command of a technology that seems almost supernatural."

Tamsin suddenly felt very calm as things began to click into place.

"We . . . we knew more," he said.

"Yes, you did," replied Ghort.

"Who then, are you?" Tamsin asked.

Ghort slipped his hand from Tamsin's shoulder and cupped Tamsin's soul pendant in his palm. His expression was almost wistful.

"These are your blessing, for you will never die. For the very same reasons they are my curse. You have believed that your souls are kept safe in your pendant after you die until the time that they transmigrate to heaven. How much truth can you stand, Tamsin?"

"All of it. Only truth is important."

"Very well. You are recorded to your pendant and when you die that recording is transmitted to the Owner's database. You essentially become part of him; a very small part of an immensely powerful mind. With me that does not happen. I am my pendant and there is no transmission. I have died and woken in a crib more times than I care to remember."

Tamsin was silent for a long moment.

"I do not understand all your words," he said, "but I will. Now we must return to the Wishpool to find out what has happened. Then I think we must pursue my brother." He paused then pulled his pendant from Ghort's hand. Ghort dropped his hand to his side. Tamsin went on, "Would the Owner accept the soul of a murderer?"

Ghort said, "Oh yes, he accepts all information."

Baum, Torril, and three others lay dead. By the time Ghort and Tamsin had reached the pool the corpses had been laid out side by side and their pendents removed. Chand wept over the body of her husband and Ephis sat by her father. Tamsin wondered what comfort the truth would be to them. Most love, he realised, is selfish, and all they knew was that who they loved was gone. Tamsin walked over to Chester, who was now village elder.

"What of my brother?" he asked.

Chester glanced up, a mass of pendents clutched in his hand.

"Your brother? Your brother ran into the Rhode when no more charge remained in the weapon. A weapon that was your responsibility, Tamsin Logisticson."

"I will get it back," said Tamsin.

"Best you do that, boy, but before you do, go take a look at the corpse on the end there. Perhaps sight of it will stiffen your sinews."

It was Jeleel. Tamsin could only feel horror and bewilderment at what Sapher had done to her. A fast anger and faster knife he could understand. What had been done to Jeleel had taken time. He stepped back and gazed round at the villagers. Many of them were walking around with stunned expressions, and leaden movement. He turned to Ghort.

"My brother must be found. Will you come with me?"

Ghort nodded as he surveyed the scene. "I'll come, but Tamsin, what will you do when you find your brother?"

"I don't know yet. But he must never come back."

They set out just as it was becoming dark, into the perfumed under-shadows of the Rhode.

"We could wait until morning, but daylight is my brother's friend."

The steel eye of the moon provided enough silvery light to make travelling a possibility. In an hour they had reached the edge of the Rhode and were gazing out across the Plain of Landing.

"You sure this is right?" asked Ghort.

Tamsin said, "I am not the tracker my brother is, but I would guess he has headed for the Ship. The place has always held an attraction for him. Tell me, were you on that ship?"

"I was not. You people had been here some time when I arrived."

"Where did you come from?"

"Another world, originally. The Great Ship at the last." Ghort pointed to the moon as he said this and Tamsin wondered what he might mean. He knew about other worlds. The teaching was that they had come from another world to this one—a world that was owned. The Owner had agreed to let them stay under certain terms. Thus the Agreement had been made. But the Great Ship? What was that? It seemed now that everything Ghort said raised another question.

"Was the Great Ship like ours? Tell me about it," he said, and while they travelled, Ghort did that thing.

The long grasses of the plain rustled all around them in the night breezes. They heard the coughing growl of a tiger in the night, but it was not a sound that held any fear for them. Tigers will not attack men. It was written. An hour's travelling brought the Ship within sight; a broken shell of metal lying at the end of the gulley it had cut many centuries ago. They stopped and crouched down.

"Let us move quietly now," said Tamsin. He had heard enough for a while. His head felt bloated with words, with confirmations and denials. He understood that what was religion to his fellows was just historical fact. He understood that the Agreement was real, but that worship was inappropriate. Much more he had yet to sort out in his mind. He glanced at Ghort, but the big man was looking away from him. He was staring back the way they had come. Tamsin followed the direction of his gaze.

The tiger sat on its haunches with its tail flicking. Its eyes were silver stars and moonlight glinted on the moisture on its fur. It was magnificent; a full grown adult in its prime, easily capable of snapping a man's spine with one swipe of its paw.

"Would Sapher have gone up against him," said Tamsin, surprised at his own bitterness.

"Perhaps—he is sick enough," said Ghort, and as if his words were an acknowledgement and a dismissal. The tiger growled then slid into the shadows. They listened to its hissing progress as it passed them and went deeper into the grasses. The silence that followed was broken only when Tamsin signalled that they should move in. This they quickly did.

The Ship was grey metal upon a lattice of white metal struts. It lay like a scattering of the broken eggs of some titanic bird. Monoliths of hull metal rose out of the ground. Skeletal lattice glinted in the moonlight where hull metal had been stripped away. This was all that remained. The contents of the ship had either been taken out over the centuries or decayed to dust. Grasses grew inside the shell and vines crept up the slick metal. With geologic slowness nature reclaimed what had been taken from it.

Tamsin held his spear in readinesss but did not know how he would react should he encounter his brother. They moved into the shadows cast by the ancient hull then split to search the length of the ship. Soon they returned to the centre.

"I felt sure he would come here," said Tamsin. "It's where he always ran when we were children. It's where he hid when he did something wrong."

"It is where he came to do wrong as well," said Ghort.

"What do you mean?" asked Tamsin.

Ghort gestured for him to follow and led him to the part of the ship he had searched.

"There," he said, pointing to a shape lying below mounded vines creeping up a section of hull. Tamsin stepped closer and saw that a tiger lay there. It was dead. Half its head burnt away.

"Is that the . . . " Tamsin trailed off as Ghort shook his head.

"It's not the one we saw. This one is younger, and a female. It seems your brother did not empty the charge of the gun back there."

"But why kill it?" asked Tamsin. "He killed Jeleel, not this tiger."

Ghort nodded then pointed. Tamsin turned to see the tiger they had first seen, standing close by and watching them. It shook its head and let go a short coughing growl. It turned away, paused, and then looked back at them.

"I think we should follow it, don't you," said Ghort.

"Why should we do that?" Tamsin asked.

Ghort pointed to the horizon, which was now made distinct by an orange glow. The steel moon was now at its zenith and the same glow etched one side of it. Sunrise was imminent.

"In very little time Sapher will again be armed. We must find him quickly. We must end this."

"You still have not explained why we should follow this tiger," said Tamsin.

"Because it will lead us to Sapher," said Ghort.

"Why should it do that?" asked Tamsin.

"Tigers don't behave like this. I think the Owner still has an interest here," Ghort replied.

Tamsin felt his stomach lurch: the things he had seen this night, the things he had been told.

"You would know. You've had plenty of time to observe them," he said.

"That I have," replied Ghort. "That I have."

The tiger led them away from the ship and along trails beaten through the grass. The sun broke the horizon and leached colour back into the world. The tiger's coat was gold and snow and its eyes pure topaz each time it looked back at them. As the sun cleared the horizon they heard movement in the grasses all around them. The tiger brought them to a clearing beaten down in the grass. In this clearing tigers patrolled. Tamsin had never seen so many together. In the centre of the clearing lay a boulder of grey metal laced with golden pipes and strange cooling veins.

"Piece of a jump engine," said Ghort.

Only because of what he had been told in the last hour did Tamsin understand what Ghort meant. He acknowledged this additional information, but could not relate it to any reality he knew. His attention focused on the tigers, and then on the figure crouching on top of the artefact.

Sapher was naked and there was blood all over him. Keeping a wary eye on the tigers, which in turn completely ignored him, Tamsin walked towards his brother. He saw that Sapher had the gun next to him catching the rays of the early sun. He raised his spear to his shoulder, not sure what he would do next.

"Have you come to kill me, Tamsin?" said Sapher. "Please try."

Tamsin halted and lowered his spear.

"Why, Sapher? Why did you do it?" he asked.

"Because I did not know right from wrong. Because I had no empathy. Because I was insane, brother," said Sapher, and as he said it he looked at the gun next to him.

"I don't understand," said Tamsin.

Sapher looked up.

"You saw the tiger?" he asked, then after Tamsin nodded he continued, "We can kill each other with impunity and it is for us to decide if it's a crime or not. The tigers are his, though, and if we kill them we will be punished."

"What is your punishment to be?" asked Ghort, from beside Tamsin.

Sapher glanced at the big man and Tamsin saw that there were tears in his brother's eyes.

"Be?" said Sapher. "I've already been punished."

"A whipping, is that enough?" asked Tamsin, his anger growing.

Sapher stared at him.

"No, brother, I stripped myself and ran through the grass naked so it would cut and flail me. I wanted the pain, brother, but it was not enough. The Owner's punishments are more subtle and more powerful than that."

"What was your punishment?" Tamsin asked.

"Sanity," Sapher replied, and picked up the gun.

Tamsin threw his spear. There was a flash of light and that spear turned to ash. Its blade fell red hot out of the air to clang against the base of the artefact and there set a small fire. For a moment Tamsin thought Sapher had shot his spear out of the air. He had not. The gun was pointed off to one side.

"Too easy," said Sapher, then he put the gun up against his own face and pulled the trigger.

Tamsin ran to his brother as he fell to the ground. Sapher lay in the grass gasping in agony. His face was burned down to the bone. He had not waited long enough and there had not been sufficient charge in the gun. Tamsin halted then turned to Ghort.

"Please," was all he said.

Ghort drove his wide-bladed spear into Sapher's chest, and ended it.

All but one of the tigers slid off into the grasses the moment Sapher died. The tiger that remained was the one that had led them to the clearing. How could it have been any other? It watched them while they dug a hole with Ghort's spear and placed Sapher in it. It watched them while they filled it in, then it moved towards them when they were ready to return to the village.

"Is that it now?" said Ghort. "Have you finished?"

The air distorted and emitted a low plangent groan. In place of the tiger now stood the shape of Temron.

"I'm never finished," said the Owner.

Tamsin stepped forward. He held the gun at his side.

"Why are we less than animals to you?" he asked.

The Owner regarded him, eyes changing to red now, face slewing and blurring and changing.

"We have an agreement," he said.

Tamsin fought his anger. He'd just asked the question one might ask of a god. The Owner was not a god. He had to remember that. He glanced aside as Ghort stepped forward.

"I'm ready now," said the big man.

The Owner nodded and gestured for him to come forward. Ghort did so. The Owner reached out and took hold of his pendant, pulling and snapping the chain. Ghort sagged, sank to his knees, then with a sigh he fell over onto his side. Tamsin moved closer. His brother had killed himself because of this . . . man. He knew that the Ghort he knew was now dead. He had the gun. It was charged. . . . But he knew that was wrong. He knew that he didn't understand anywhere near enough.

"He was Ghort—quiet and dependable and distant . . . yet he told me he has lived many lives. Who was he?"

With Ghort's pendant clutched in his right hand the Owner carefully studied Tamsin.

"He was a foolish man who served me badly. Now he is a wise man who will serve me well," he said.

Tamsin closed his eyes. Quite deliberately he raised the gun then shoved it into his belt pouch. He said, "You are real and now everything has changed. How can I be at peace? How can I just live the life I have always lived?"

"My answer should be that it is not for me to answer you. But you are somewhat unique, Tamsin. I can give you more if you wish it. Most people don't. Most people lack the imagination to see beyond the simple act of living. Would you serve me, Tamsin?"

"Yes, I would."

"Then first, Tamsin, you must learn wisdom and the patience that is integral to it."

Tamsin felt his soul pendant grow hot against his chest, then slowly begin to cool. He pressed the palm of his hand against it and tried not to be frightened of what he knew it meant. As the air around him distorted and the immensity behind reached out to pull him back the Owner spoke again.

"Raise your people up, Tamsin," he said.

Tamsin knew that he would, and that he had more than one lifetime in which to do so.

the gurnard

I have to say this is one of my favorite stories and surprise surprise
here I am again having a go at religion, getting wrapped up in a
weird planetary ecology involving a nasty parasite, and liberally
sprinkling it all with some gratuitous violence. This story was another casualty of Tanjen folding, for Anthony had started his own
magazine called *Night Dreams* in which he published the first half of
this in '96. The mag did not last long enough for anyone to see the
second half. However, in '98 Graeme Hurry came to the rescue and
published the complete story in *Kimota*.

Either side of the door to this church of the Fish, two iron-scaled creations gaze down from posts of heather wood. They are representational of Gurnards only in that they are readily identifiable as fish. Church artisans, like the Clergy, have never allowed anything so irrelevant as fact to get in the way of their calling.

On the iron scaling of the door itself, Sirus Beck knocked with the butt of his gun, then holstered the weapon. Whilst waiting impatiently, he gazed out at hills like pregnant seals below the falling box of the moon. Beyond the hills, snow-clad mountains faded into green sky and could be mistaken for cloud. There flowed the Changing Waters. He knew this just as he knew so much else about the Church, for his teachers had driven it into him with a leather strap. It was his conceit that he would have fled this place even without the feel of the strap across his back. At an early age, he had learnt to read, and absorbed much from the church library that the other acolytes had missed. It was his conceit that he had left because he had not been stupid enough to believe, and he had not expected to come back. Returning his attention to the nearby hills, he noted a flock of sheep flowing across the land, and dropped a hand to the butt of his gun before turning at the sound of the view-hatch grating open.

"Yes?" asked the belligerent face beyond the grid of thick wires.

Beck recalled that someone had ordered the grid fixed there after a sheep had knocked on the door then ripped off the face of the acolyte who had opened the hatch. This sort of thing often happened.

"I am summoned," said Beck, not trying too hard to hide his irritation.

"Hah!" came the informed reply.

When there was no further reaction, Beck felt the impetus build. It frightened him. If this fool did not let him in on request, he would have to attempt bribery, or scale the lichenous wall, or pick the lock. The only other option would have him throwing himself against the door and clawing at the iron.

"Will you let me in or will you explain to the Wife of Ovens why you turned away a Baptiser?"

That brought a frown to the bristly visage and Beck then saw, by the broken teeth and scars, that this man had already run contrary to Church law.

"You know what'll happen if you're lying?"

Beck nodded. Of course he knew. He did not want them to seal him in a drowning jar, but he *had* been summoned. Choice did not come into it, for the voice of the Gurnard had spoken to him on a cellular level and he did not have the knowledge to resist it. Bolts and latches clacked and rattled inside before the door was quickly drawn open. Scarface stood there in stiffened hide armour, a crossbow across his arm, cocked and loaded with a barbed quarrel. With a glance over his shoulder, Beck quickly stepped inside.

The inside of the church was all dank stone across which biolights crept in search of the bladders of blood that were hung to feed them, and as a consequence of that nourishment, the glow of the genfactored creatures was red. The algal life coating the floor in patterns as of frost on a window, was scuffed by the passage of many feet, but still regrowing in places it all but concealed the mosaics. On the ceiling these mosaics were clear behind translucent stone. They depicted strange hoofed animals with woolly pelts, the like of which Beck had never before seen—though their heads were similar to those of sheep. Other just as unlikely herd beasts crowded the ceiling along with birds and fishes, plants, insects. The doctrine of the Church had it that these were creatures of Earth. *And as real*, thought Beck.

"Come with me," said Scarface, and led Beck down corridors he remembered from what he considered the most grey and miserable time of his life. As an orphan he had not been given any choices. As one of the Trindar Becks he had fled before they broke his will. Scarface led him into an area to one side of the entrance hall. He wanted to go straight ahead and down as he was impelled to do, but the pressure wasn't so bad now he was inside the church and he could handle a detour or two. He immediately recognised the door he was brought before. Often he had stood outside it shivering with fear and anger. Scarface knocked and opened the door.

"We have one here who claims he is summoned," Scarface said.

"Sirus Beck," said Morage, looking up from the paperwork on his desk. Beck stepped past scarface into the office and the door was closed behind him. He walked to the desk, pulled out a chair and sat.

"I did not give you leave to sit."

"I don't really care."

Morage glared at him. *He has not changed so much*, thought Beck. After ten years his beard was greyer and his red robes faded, but the man's eyes were still the malicious focus of his face. Morage enjoyed power—enjoyed meting out punishments.

"I could have you beaten and hung from the walls."

"You would do that to a Baptiser?"

Beck tried not to smile. He knew enough about Church structure and doctrine to know that, as a summoned Baptiser, he was the province of the Wife of Ovens only, not the Inquisition of the Church. Should Morage seek to exert authority over him he risked his own drowning jar. Thinking on this, Beck's gaze strayed to the corner of the room where a spherical glass jar a metre in diameter contained the remains of Morage's predecessor. The man was naked, his wrists tied to his ankles, his head lodged between his knees, his skin bluish and his eyes sunken away—the preservative he had been drowned in not being sufficient to prevent all decay. Baptiser or not, it wouldn't do to push Morage too far. Beck stood.

"I think it best I see the Wife," he said.

Morage sat back. "What proof do we have that you are summoned?"

He's starting to play, though Beck. *I should have been more circumspect.* "You know the proof as well as I."

"Yes, but perhaps before you are brought to the chamber I should hold you for a while. It would be easy for a potential assassin to claim to be summoned . . . "

Beck felt a sudden surge of anger and fear. Petty—that was Morage. Beck rested a hand on the butt of his holstered gun and leant across the desk.

"A lot of years have passed, Morage, but I haven't forgotten you," he said.

Morage glanced at the gun. He obviously had not seen it until then, and just as obviously the doorman would be in for a beating for not relieving Beck of this weapon. Morage tried to sneer as he waved his hand at Beck.

"Go to the Wife," he said. "I have no time for this."

Beck went, the anger and fear slewing away as he was once again on course, and being replaced by faint amusement in that the gun made it even more likely he was an assassin. Even then he could feel the presence of the Gurnard in his emotions.

In a moment he was on a main corridor leading into the centre of the church where the Wife of Ovens tended her fires. Already he could feel the increase in warmth and smell from flames of marsh gas. And as he walked the impetus took hold of him, drove him. He was vaguely aware that he was accompanied as the corridor he followed dropped down into the earth by sections of stairway, each marked by decorous drowning jars. At the end of the corridor he entered the huge central chamber, hot from the mouths of the ovens set in the walls. At the centre of this room, on a pedestal of heather wood decorated with sheep skulls, rested a wide glass pot, big enough to bathe in, and containing water the colour of bilge from an iron boat. Beck ran across the crumbling floor and thrust his hand into the pot. Something moved there. Spines entered his fingers and fire travelled up his arm. He vaguely noted two of the Clergy moving quickly forward to prevent him spilling the pot as he pulled away.

"He will have visions," somebody said.

"Of that I have no doubt. The chemistry is complex enough," said someone with an accent he did not know. He looked around as the fire hit his neck and branded the side of his face. The Wife of Ovens stood there in her robes and ceremonial apron. Next to her stood a creature with black skin, white hair, and blue eyes, and the strangest clothing. As he fell, Beck thought that the visions had already begun.

On Earth sheep eat grass and gurnards are the most unassuming of fish. In Nuremar, the day before a Baptiser's arrival at the church, a family was massacred by sheep, and in a hundred churches people prostrated themselves before pots of dirty water. Erlin considered these facts, recorded them, and made no comment. In a church of the Fish it was best to make no comments about anything—to remain the detached observer. When first she was shown to her room she thanked her escort and smiled, ignoring the threat of the empty drowning jar in the corner. She was here to observe and to study, not to judge.

"So anyone could be chosen to be a Baptiser?" she asked.

The Wife of Ovens, in her voluminous robes draped with a thousand amulets, and her thick hide ceremonial apron, nodded sagely and smiled her satisfaction. Erlin thought she looked precisely like a female Buddha; hugely fat, bald, and smug.

"Yes child, even you could be chosen."

Erlin turned away for a moment in an attempt to keep her expression serious. Here, the Wife was very old—seventy years solstan. Erlin, being a member of the human Polity and a citizen of Earth, had access to technology of a civilization that now spanned one tenth of the galaxy. She was two hundred and thirty years old and was determined to live forever, barring accidents.

"Yet it would seem," she said, "that no Northerners or island people are chosen."

The Wife showed a touch of annoyance. "That is so, but they could be chosen at any time."

Erlin nodded, her expression showing nothing but gratitude at having things so clearly explained to her. Of course she could have pushed it. She could have mentioned that in the entire history of this church no-one had been chosen who had not spent some time living in this building, eating the food, drinking the water. The same rule applied to every church of the Fish. Erlin irradiated her food and drink before ingesting it. She had no wish to get religion.

"So, please tell me again what now happens with this Sirus Beck."

"Sirus Beck will carry out the task charged to him by our Lord. He will carry the Holy Fish to the mountains of the Waters of Change. There he will baptise the Fish in each spring as in the birth. The Fish, meanwhile, will be reborn here in the new year, two days before the drinking of the Eucharist."

"Does anyone travel with him to the Waters of Change?"

"No, this is not allowed."

"What about the sheep?"

"The sheep will not attack a Baptiser."

There, thought Erlin, another dead giveaway. I'll have to get a sample of that new year's Eucharist. Loaded, sure to be. No coincidence either that the springs called the Waters of Change feed into every damned river on this continent. Erlin wondered how the Clergy got past the fact that each of the hundred or so churches had its own fish and its own new year.

Sirus Beck saw the grey shapes of Gurnards in deep pools and in rivers and streams blunt-nosed against the current. He felt their power—the power of God in them, and he hated it, hated that he could not resist it.

He saw sheep upon the hill feeding on bloody human flesh and the box moon opened and spilt writhing worms across the land. He saw his world and every part of it he saw was loaded with deep significance. The tangled branches of heather trees spelled out the glyphs of a secret language. A sugar dog defecating behind a rock was a sign from God, its every pant a holistic representation of the turning of the world. There was glory and there was terror. Beck, in some deeply buried and logical part of himself, thought it all too ridiculous. If this was holiness he wanted none of it. If there was a God then he should mind his own business. The resentment of that thought gave him pain, and the pain woke him.

This is the most comfortable bed I have ever slept in, thought Beck. The mattress was soft. He was between clean sheets and heavy scented blankets were layered above him. He was warm and dry and he did not want to move, until something prodded him to move and he felt a stinging in his fingers. This is how it will be, he realised. For the rest of his life this prodding would move him on as soon as he got comfortable. Like every Baptiser before him he would die an old man trying to get to that one last spring. It was one of the inconsistencies that had destroyed his faith—that the Gurnard was reborn even before it died.

"You are awake," said the Wife of Ovens.

Beck opened his eyes and gazed at the bulky shape standing at the foot of his bed. She smiled at him beatifically. He wanted to strangle her, but even a Baptiser would not get away with that. He glanced to one side of her, at the slim dark-skinned woman he had seen earlier. What was she? Some freak from the islands brought to entertain the Wife? Her clothes, he noted, were very clean and looked expensive. In fact he did not recognise the grey and orange material of her coverall. He sat up.

"Yes, I'm awake, and soon I have to be moving."

"Of course. That is how it must be," said the Wife.

"Yeah. Who's this?"

The Wife gestured with one pudgy beringed hand. "This, Baptiser, is Erlin Tazer Three Indomial."

"What kind of name is that?"

"It is the kind of name they give people from Earth."

"Funny."

"I must prepare the way for you. Dress yourself, Baptiser, then come at once to the tank room. The Gurnard awaits."

The Wife swept out of the room, gesturing for the purported Earther to go with her. To Beck it looked as if Erlin wanted to say or do something else, but she went with the Wife. That was always the safest move. Beck got out of bed and washed himself with the water and soap provided, before inspecting the well-made travelling clothes that had also been provided. It would not do for a Baptiser to be seen in the clothes of a common tramp. Beck was glad to see that his belongings, other than his clothes, had not been discarded. He still retained his pack and his gun. Opening the weapon to check it over, he saw that all three shells were in place in their chambers. He would be safe from sheep yet. As he dressed there came a sharp knock at the door and the woman, Erlin, quickly stepped into the room. She had some strange instrument in her hand. Holding a pair of sheep-hide trousers before his genitals he glared at her.

"I'm a doctor," she said quickly. "I need a blood sample."

Beck eyed the instrument.

"Then give one yourself," he said.

"Please, it's very important."

"Yeah, you're right, my blood is."

She stepped toward him and he quickly stepped back.

"I bet the Wife of Ovens doesn't know you're here," he said, and it was a threat. Erlin frowned at him then pocketed the instrument she had been holding. Beck peered with curiosity at the pocket she had put it in, at the cloth, the way it sealed, at the rest of her coverall. It was like nothing he had ever seen before. So was she.

"Are you really from Earth?"

"Yes."

"Turn round."

She looked askance at him. He nodded down at the trousers he was holding.

"I am a doctor you know."

"That gives you no rights to my body, now turn round or get out."

Erlin turned and Beck finished dressing himself.

"Now why should you want a blood sample?" he asked.

Erlin was indecisive. "They say you were an acolyte, but that you ran away, that you are a heretic and unbeliever."

"They say right," said Beck with some viciousness.

"How does it feel then to come back as a Baptiser?"

"It feels like Hell."

"How do you reconcile your—"

There came a rapping on the door before it was suddenly opened. Morage stepped into the room with a sneering grin on his face. Behind him came two priests obviously selected for their size rather than their piety.

"The Wife of Ovens awaits you, Sirus Beck. It would be better if you followed your calling willingly."

It was a mild dig. Morage's attention was on Erlin rather than Beck. Beck stooped and took up his pack. He caught Erlin by the arm. "The Wife awaits the both of us, as it happens." He led Erlin past Morage and his two thugs.

"Wait," said Morage, angry, but unsure.

Beck turned and addressed the two thugs. "I am a Baptiser. Do you seek to delay me?" When this elicited no response he hurried Erlin down the corridor.

"Damnit, stop. Stop them," Morage hissed, but the two thugs were too confused and scared to take any precipitate action.

"I never did like that one," said Erlin, once Morage was out of sight. "Something sneaky about him."

"Morage is a thief and a sadist. He strips the acolytes of their personal effects when they join the Church and he has been responsible for the deaths of many."

"The Wife allows this?"

"He would have taken you for religious counselling. You would have been stripped of your belongings and part of your skin before the Wife found out. She would have forgiven him his fervour. Why are you here, Earther?"

"I can look after myself," said Erlin, avoiding his question.

"Then do so!" he snapped, and left her as he took the most direct route to the tank room.

They sang hymns while Sirus took up the small carry-pot containing his unwelcome companion for the rest of his life. The tempo of the singing changed as he walked to the door and he knew, that once the door was closed, the rest of the day would be spent in sermonising, for most of the

Clergy anyway. There was one there, crouched coughing up blood in a corner, who would not make it through the day, let alone to the new year's Eucharist. Not that the foul water of the new Gurnard would have saved him. Something had died inside him, too deeply imbedded to be ejected as was usual, and the smell of death was on his breath.

As the outer iron-scaled doors of the church closed behind him, Beck lengthened his stride. It wasn't so bad really. The pot was not too heavy and wherever he went people would give him food and lodging for free. Some would resent it and others would make him welcome, but no one would dare refuse. He gazed at the hills, and at the mountains beyond, and strode on into his new life. Hanging at his left side, under his left arm, the Gurnard swirled in its opaque water reminding him that it was not his life. There were no more choices.

The church was out of sight and he was following a narrow path through a forest of heather trees sprung up through ground covered with blanket fungus, when a familiar voice called to him.

"May I join you for a little way, Sirus Beck?"

Erlin came toward him through the trees, her boots sinking into the blanket fungus. She had come prepared, carrying a large pack and wearing a rain cape. There also appeared to be some kind of weapon holstered at her hip. She was regarding the pot hanging at his side, not even trying to hide her fascination.

"You realise that if the Inquisition find out you are with me you'll end up in a drowning jar?" he asked.

"Yes, I realise that, but I don't know why."

Beck continued walking and Erlin fell in at his side.

"Neither do I," said Beck. "But then the Church has many rules that make no sense."

"Yet here you are, a Baptiser, carrying a Holy Gurnard to the Waters of Change."

"If I had a choice this pot would be smashed on the ground and I would be going my own way." And even as he said it he felt a stab of pain in his guts. It was dangerous even to think like that. There was a long silence between them, which Erlin eventually broke.

"You wanted to know why I wanted a blood sample?" she said.

"Yes, I did."

"I have an interest in parasites, and I have come here to study them."

Beck looked at her. The only parasites he knew anything about were sheep ticks.

Erlin went on, "There is a parasite here with a very strange life-cycle. Its eggs hatch out in the mountain springs."

"I don't see the relevance."

"Well, parasites have all sorts of strange strategies for survival, breed-ing . . . sometimes they use more than one host, though I don't think this one does. There's one on earth that actually gets into an ant, makes the ant climb to the top of a blade of grass and there cling on until a passing sheep eats it. The sheep is its next host you see—"

"On Earth sheep eat ants?"

"No, grass."

Beck snorted his disbelief. "If you're not going to tell me why you want a blood sample, just say so. I don't need this bullshit. I had enough of it in the Church."

"No really, I'm not lying."

Just then there came a coughing snort from the shade of the heather trees. This was followed by a low moan and a raspy panting. Erlin pulled her weapon from its holster and looked around carefully. Beck glanced with idle curiosity at little flashing red lights on the gun. After a moment he said, "No need to worry yet. That's only a sugar dog. Save your worrying for when we get beyond the trees. It's flockland there." To himself he muttered, "Grass indeed."

The sugar dog came out of the trees far to their right, paralleling their course. Erlin stared at it in fascination, took a device from one of her pock-ets and pointed it at the creature.

"What are you doing?"

"Recording images of it."

Beck studied the glinting little device she held. It was just the kind of thing Morage would like to steal. How it must burn him that she had es-caped him.

"Why?" he asked her.

"I've never seen one before. It looks like a cross between a bloodhound and a bull frog."

The words were familiar to Beck, but not in that combination. Bull he knew as a word for untruth, just as he knew of the little black frogs that lived in the southern swamps, that 'hound' was another word for dog, and that 'blood' was red in his veins and green in the translucent flesh of sugar dogs. So much was different about Earth. Perhaps if he had not been so wrapped up in his own concerns he would have been fascinated by this. Perhaps she hadn't been lying about the sheep.

The sugar dog huffed and wuffled through the leaves near them as they followed the trail, then it moved away to the West. In the distance, on the faces of the hills, flocks of sheep could be seen hunting, but they were no danger to sugar dogs. Sugar dogs were as poisonous as the plants they ate.

"Do you know why they are called sugar dogs?" Erlin asked.

"Because they like sweets," said Beck.

"Sugar kills them though."

"Yes, it also kills anyone caught feeding it to them."

Erlin waited for an explanation.

He told her, "They are protected by Church and civil law. Anyone caught feeding any form of sugar to a sugar dog is executed by posting."

"Posting?"

"Chained to a flockland post."

"Sorry, I don't understand."

"You will soon." He pointed ahead to a distant object jutting up out of the leaves. They walked in silence until they reached it. Here was a steel post cemented into the ground, from which hung a chain and a steel collar. All around it the leaves were trampled and scattered with chewed human bones. At the base of the post lay half a human skull that had been scraped empty. Erlin quickly grasped what it meant to be posted.

"The sheep don't attack Baptisers, so the Church tells us. I don't believe everything the Church says." With that Beck drew his gun and checked it, as he had done a number of times since leaving the church. He also made sure the shells in his belt were easily accessible, despite the Gurnard pot hanging at his side.

"Isn't that a bit awkward?" asked Erlin, indicating the pot.

"The discomfort would be greater if I did not carry it," said Beck. "Let's keep moving." He gestured with his gun and then kept it in his hand as they continued walking.

The sun was a blue-green ellipse on the horizon with the box moon in silhouette just beside it, when they saw their first sheep close to. A flock of twenty of them had trapped a ground skate and were levering up its wings with their claws and biting off chunks of fishy flesh.

"Sheep are nothing like this on Earth," said Erlin, then regretted speaking when two sheep turned their curled-horned heads towards her and exposed yellow fangs.

"Quiet. Keep walking," Beck whispered.

The sheep returned to their easy meal and did not pursue.

"Their heads are like the heads of Earth sheep and they have hooves on their feet, but on Earth, sheep are quadruped. They don't have claws." Erlin shivered. "They're like something out of Christian fable: Satan, or satyrs."

"You've never seen our sheep before?"

"No."

"Surely, when you came to the church?"

"I was dropped off there by air transport directly from the port."

Beck was vaguely aware that somewhere there was a spaceport, and he had often seen the transports flying overhead and the occasional flash of a star drive starting up out beyond the moon. It had been his intention to find out about these things. Then the impulse had taken away all his choices. It made him sad and it made him angry. *I am only just become a man*, he thought, *and my life is not to be used to my purpose*. He considered suicide and awoke pain in his guts.

"Tell me about parasites," he said.

"Will you listen?"

"I will there," he said, pointing at a low stone sheep sanctuary—a building that in another place might have used for protecting sheep from predators, but not here.

Within the sanctuary, coke was provided for a fire but there was no kindling to set it burning. Erlin started the fire with something that flared red and left burning bars of afterimages in Beck's eyes. He placed the Gurnard pot near the fire and removed the bung. A dead-fish smell filled the sanctuary, but movement in the pot showed that the Gurnard was not dead. Thankfully the smell of the burning coke soon displaced that smell. Beck and Erlin sat then before the fire and ate from their respective provisions.

"You know, any fish from Earth would have died in such a container."

"Why?"

"Earth fish require oxygenated water. Your Gurnards require no oxygen whatsoever. Oxygen is in fact deleterious to them, which is why they seek out still water at the end of their journey."

"Journey?"

"I was going to tell you about parasites."

"Do so, then."

"I am not entirely sure of some aspects. I don't know why there is only one Baptiser for each church. I can only presume messages are passed by pheromones or some such."

"This is about me," said Beck.

"Yes."

He nodded and Erlin continued. "I'll describe to you a life-cycle. You know what I mean when I say that?"

"I am not a complete idiot."

"Very well. As I said: The eggs hatch out in the mountain springs. After that males and females travel downstream, in water and on land, to the richer feeding grounds in the lowlands . . . where the churches are. After it has reached first maturity the female finds a pond—usually recently vacated by another female—and there starts laying unfertilized eggs out of which hatch the neuter parasites. These infect the water supply and end up being ingested by most life forms that drink from the pond. These neuters grow inside their hosts and can, to a certain extent, control them. The neuters are in turn controlled by the females, though I've yet to work out the mechanism of that . . . Second maturity for the female impels it to return to the hatching grounds to lay more eggs there. It is carried by a neuter-controlled host to do this. I believe that at one time the only hosts were sugar dogs, though I am relying on someone else's research for that information."

"I'm a sugar dog," said Beck. He wanted to explain to Erlin that it felt too dangerous to say outright that he understood.

She nodded and continued her narrative. "Sugar dogs vomit food into the ponds. The Clergy bring consecrated offerings to the tank room. All are infected."

Did that relieve them all of responsibility, Beck wondered, but he said nothing.

"All this while the males had been feeding in the same areas. The males have a higher resistivity to oxygen and feed mainly on land, on the various blanket funguses. When they reach maturity—they only have one kind—they head for the hatching grounds as well. Males and females from the same hatching do not return at the same time, which prevents interbreeding. Upon arriving at the hatching grounds, the females get their neuter carriers to place them in the waters. In those waters they lay eggs, usually attaching them to the bottom, to rocks, in the sand. The males, by the time they are mature, are usually averse to water and too big to get all the way to the hatching grounds. They release sperm packets which travel alone to the mountain springs to burst in the water in which eggs have been laid."

"Water worms," said Beck. "No one I know ever had a reasonable explanation for that. In some places they call them suicide worms. It never made any sense to me."

"Well, you have the sense now. They have one purpose in their brief lives and that is it."

"What are the males?"

"We saw one today."

Beck nodded. "Of course—ground skate." He felt slightly sick. So there was something inside him, jamming its spines into his guts. He realised some other things as well.

"The Eucharist, that's when we get infected."

"Quite likely." Erlin slipped into her sleeping bag and rested her head back against her pack. "I imagine that right about now the Wife of Ovens is having the ponds around the church netted in search of the Reborn Gurnard. Of course it won't be found until that one," she pointed at the pot, "is out of the area. Adolescent Gurnards don't encroach on a mature Gurnard's territory. Perhaps in the past they were killed, or perhaps it is because the hosts are all used up. I don't know."

Beck rolled himself in his blanket. He had the answer; the eighth moon netting of the ponds and the killing of the Gurnard Ghosts. That then was just the killing of immature Gurnards. He told Erlin about this.

"Yes, that makes sense," she replied. "Once established in its territory the new gurnard sends out the neuter-controlled hosts to kill off the competition, and keeps killing off the competition. I take it this netting and killing is continuous?"

"Every eighth moon," Beck confirmed. Then he asked, "What about the neuters left behind—from the old gurnard?"

"They die, their purpose served. Most of their hosts survive it, and survive to become hosts to the next Holy Gurnard."

Beck thought about the priest coughing up blood in the church and it took him a long time to get to sleep. He lay there listening to the sheep sharpening their claws on the stone walls and tried to come to terms with harsh truths.

There were no windows for morning light, but it did filter through cracks in the walls. Beck was beginning to feel discomfort as the impetus to move on grew in strength, when the door crashed open and figures crowded into the single room. For a moment he thought that sheep had learned to operate the locks and in panic groped for his gun. A heavy boot came down on his wrist and the butt of a heather wood staff pressed on the centre of his chest to hold him down.

"Do not struggle, Baptiser. I do not wish to strike you."

Beck recognised the two thugs from the church. One of them had Erlin pinned in her sleeping bag, the barrel of a gun, much like Beck's own, pressed against her forehead. After them, momentarily silhouetted in the doorway, came Morage, grinning unpleasantly. Morage was a master of unpleasant grins.

"Oh Baptiser, you have a travelling companion. Even the Wife will not berate me for my actions now. The Baptiser must seek loneliness and purity in prayer," he said.

"Sugar dog crap," said Beck. The thug holding him pinned was uncomfortable with such blasphemous profanity. Morage turned his attention to the thug who was holding Erlin.

"Let her up."

Erlin kicked out of her sleeping bag and stood up carefully, her gaze locked on the barrel of the gun.

"Now, Earther," said Morage. "I want you to undo your belt and drop your weapon to the floor." This Erlin did and Morage grinned his unpleasant grin again. "Now I want you to empty your pockets of all those wonderful gadgets." Erlin began to do this also, dropping device after device on her pack.

"This is not about religion. This is robbery," said Beck.

"Be silent, Sirus Beck, I will deal with you presently," said Morage without turning.

"You would delay me?" asked Beck, expecting some result of his query, perhaps some wince of pain from their captors.

Morage turned and grinned nastily at him. "I suppose she has told you all about the parasites?" Morage's grin got nastier when he saw Beck's surprise. "Do you think such knowledge would be lost to us? The Wives know, as do all members of the Inquisition. It is best that we are the only ones to know. You see, we keep ourselves pure, and we never truly take part in the Eucharist."

"You are free of neuter parasites," said Erlin.

Morage glanced at her.

"Yes, as are my friends here," he gestured at the two thugs, "which means there are things we can do that so many others in the Church cannot do."

Erlin shot a warning look at Beck, but he did not need it. He knew that Morage intended to kill the both of them. He noted that the thugs were uncomfortable with what was just beginning to occur to them. Well they might be; there probably had not been a Baptiser in their lifetimes, and now they might be told to kill one.

"Strip that garment from her," Morage instructed the one who held Erlin at gunpoint. "I don't want to have missed anything before she goes to the post."

Lying where he was Beck had a view of the door and realised that no-one else was looking in that direction. He swore at his captor to keep his attention. The thug became even more uncomfortable. The other thug was reaching for Erlin when Morage screamed.

The sheep had come in quickly and sunk its yellow teeth into Morage's upper arm. Beck knocked the staff from his chest, caught the foot of his captor and shoved him off-balance. There was a flash of red between Erlin and the other. A hand, severed and smoking at the wrist, thudded on the floor still clutching a gun. Beck came up onto his feet holding his own gun as he was grabbed. He sunk the barrel deep into a fat belly and pulled the trigger once. With a muffled boom and a horrible grunting sound, his attacker went up off his feet before thumping face down on the floor. Beck turned, saw the sheep fleeing from the sound of the weapon, saw Morage on his knees cradling an arm from which all the flesh had been stripped between shoulder and elbow. He was screaming. Beck pulled the trigger again and Morage flipped backwards out of the door, most of his head left on one of the door posts. One shot left. White shapes beyond the door baa-ing and snarling over Morage's corpse. Time. Beck turned. Erlin was back up against the wall, her face pale. The one left was trying to take his gun from his severed right hand with his left, while the stump of his right wrist squirted blood. He looked up, began to yell, the bullet went into his chest then out from his back, folding out one shoulder blade like an escape hatch. The impact threw him at Erlin's feet where he made bubbling sounds and died. Time. Beck cracked open his gun, pulled hot shell cases from their chambers, the skin of his finger-tips sizzling, put in three fresh rounds. He did not allow himself to think of anything else until he had done this. Then he stepped towards the door, shooting the first sheep as it came in, trapping the head of the second in the door as it tried to follow, shooting it through the eye then managing to get the door closed against the rest of the flock. Locking the door.

"Sirus . . . Sirus."

The thumping and battering against the door was short-lived. Beck rested there with his forehead against the wood, trying to get his breathing under control. Shit, that had been close. When sheep went into a feeding frenzy, God help anyone who got in the way.

"Sirus."

What the hell does she want now? Look after herself. Hah.

Beck turned and regarded Erlin. She stood in the middle of the room, distaste writ on her features. She pointed down by the fire. It hit him at once; the wrenching tearing in his gut. The pot was spilled, and the Gurnard lay on the stone, bulbous stalked eyes blinking, mouth gaping occa-sionally, spines fanned out round its head. Before he knew what he was do-ing Sirus scooped it up and put it in its pot, oblivious to the spines piercing his fingers. He then emptied his water canteen in it. It wasn't enough. He took up the pot and headed for the door.

"They'll kill you if you go out there. I'm sorry about this," said Erlin.

What is she talking about?

As he reached the door something hit him like a falling wall and a bright and painful light took him away.

Having filled the pot with water Beck corked it. As he did this he felt himself coming back to normality, gaining some control over his actions.

He put the pot aside and knelt there with his hands resting on the fronts of his thighs. He felt tired and his head ached.

"I'm back now. I'm in control," he said.

"Then you can carry your own pack," she said, and his pack thumped down next to him.

He'd woken still under the same powerful impetus. He'd picked up the pot, opened the door, and taken the Gurnard to the nearest source of water. He shivered at the thought of what would have happened had he gone out the door the first time, when the sheep were in feeding frenzy. He'd noted but had not been concerned about the blood, the few fragments of bone, clothing, and one chewed sandal which was all that remained of Morage. He turned to face Erlin, who was sitting wearily on the near-petrified stump of a tree that had fallen when this area had been forest, and when the sheep had walked on four hooves.

"You can have your blood sample," he said.

"I already took it," said she.

"What did you learn?"

"Not much, I merely confirmed."

"Can you free me?"

"Possibly. Are you sure you want to be free?"

"Yes," said Beck vehemently.

"Let's eat," said Erlin. "Then we can move on."

Beck agreed. They unpacked their supplies and ate their food. When it came to drink, Erlin filled a small container with water in which it boiled in moments.

"You drink boiled water from now on," she said.

"Why?"

"I don't know how long the neuter parasites encyst for."

"I don't understand."

"You could be rid of one only to be already carrying its successor inside you."

"I see."

After eating, drinking, and resting for a while they moved on. They reached the next sanctuary in darkness, watched by the night-glow of sheep eyes.

"Did you leave the door to the other sanctuary open?"

"Yes."

Erlin understood him perfectly. There would be nothing to incriminate by the time anyone else came to that place. She spoke with Beck for a little while about parasites and ways to get rid of them, then she watched him while he slept. It was her turn to find it difficult to sleep. What was she? Ten times older than him, yet she had never experienced such violence. She had frozen back there and it shamed her, shamed her so much she was now prepared to interfere, prepared to do something about the parasite he carried. She owed him at least that.

"Why are the sheep like they are here?" asked Beck when the mountains were in sight.

"I don't have all the answers. Don't make that mistake."

"Perhaps your guess would be better than mine though."

Erlin smiled before replying. "Livestock was brought to worlds like this, worlds with indigenous life, in what was called genetically plastic form. That means that they are able to adapt to environments very quickly. From what I have seen, grass did not take here and most of the other plants are highly toxic. The sheep adapted. They became carnivores rather than herbivores. As to the details . . . "

"I see . . . what did you hit me with?"

Erlin slapped her hand against the weapon she carried at her belt. Beck looked at it and rubbed the back of his head.

"I didn't physically hit you. This weapon has a stun setting."

Yes, Beck had read something about that, but he was so used to weapons that created huge holes in his enemies that it was a difficult concept to grasp. He chewed that one over as they set foot on one of the mountain trails and as stone and snow loomed above them. When they came to a defile jammed with ground skate and crawling with water worms he remembered her life-cycle lecture, and watched for a while until he saw one of the skate extrude a worm, and that sperm-carrying secondary life form wriggle away. With a bit of rock-scrambling they rounded the defile. On the other side, where some of the ground skate had got through and were flopping up the trail, Erlin squatted by a water worm and inspected it.

The worm was as long as an arm and twice as thick. It was green, translucent and segmented. It inched along like a maggot.

"I find these fascinating," said Erlin. "There is plenty of genetic justification for them but I've never come across anything like them before."

"Careful," said Beck.

Erlin shook her head in wonderment and prodded at the worm with the instrument she was holding. After a flaccid clapping sound, Erlin yelled and leapt back, with a sheet of creamy green sludge over the front of her coverall. Beck might have laughed then but something more urgent was calling him up the mountain. He walked on ahead, leaving her swearing and scraping the sludge from her body with a piece of slate.

The mountain was high, but Beck had the energy of that impetus and strode up the trail with the pot clutched close to his side. As he got higher he heard the sound of waterfalls to one side, and a damp mist gusted all about him, cooling his face. Soon he came to an area where thick bromeliads housed chirruping frogs, and ferny plants crawled across damp stone in search of soil-filled crevices. The spring gushed up in a wide pellucid pool where flat stones lurked like giant crabs. Beck knelt in the wet reddish shingle on a crescent of shore only just large enough for him. He uncorked the pot. He was here. At last he was here. He tipped the pot and the Gurnard slid into the water without a splash. The jolt of pleasure felled him and had him writhing in the shingle; stones in his mouth and in his boots, one arm in the water. He shit himself and he didn't care. The experience was too intense . . . religious.

"Sirus."

He wondered how many times she had said his name before he heard it.

"I hear you."

"What do you want, Sirus?"

"Get this fucking thing out of me."

"I can do that now. I think."

"Good," said Beck, and he slid into the water to wash himself.

They sat on slabs warmed by the sun and watched worms inching to the pool and dropping in. As soon as they hit the water they burst and turned it cloudy. Beck could see their remains being jerked about in the water as the Gurnard fed—taking on protein for its next session of egg-laying.

"Here, this is you," said Erlin.

They watched then as a sugar dog came to the shore, knelt as if to drink, then spewed a Gurnard and its water from one of its mouth pouches. As the dog fell and began to jerk about Beck turned away.

"This could kill you, you know."

Beck studied the boxlike affair with its glinting ruby lights, strange chrome things she had pressed against his flesh, and a screen across which marched an army of black ants. The pain in his guts had grown and grown and was now almost unbearable, almost.

"Now," she said, and held out the strange chrome gun-thing. He nodded. She pressed it against his arm and it spat fire into his biceps. For a moment the pain went away. She watched him. Then the pain came back so hard he screamed and set the sugar dog moaning. Later, he puked blood then something hard and chitinous. She shot something else into his arm and told him he was strong, that he would win. He kicked the pot then and it rolled off the edge and smashed down below.

"I will win," he said and he knew it to be true. So many people do.

The sugar dog howled.